Readers Love
B.G. Thomas

Anything Could Happen

"There is something so exquisitely inviting about the way in which B.G Thomas writes. From the first sentence to the last you are engaged, invested, and involved with all of his characters both major and minor alike."

—Top 2 Bottom Reviews

"This is a well-rounded and very well written story. I would highly recommend this book and the others that tie in with it. I am interested to see where Mr. Thomas will take us next."

—The Novel Approach

"This book explores being a gay man and what it can be like, for the first time, to enter a room where everybody understands who you are. It is coming of age, together with coming out. As such, it is a finely tuned and sweet story."

—My Fiction Nook

Grumble Monkey and the Department Store Elf

"A sweet holiday romance where one man's zest for life gives another man a new chance at happiness."

—The Romance Reviews

"I loved this story. I love the characters. I love the journey from dark to light. I love the relationship. And I love the warmth that the holiday season brings to this story."

—Joyfully Jay

"I loved this novella. A wonderful new take on the Scrooge story that had me smiling, chuckling and even getting a bit misty."

—Gay List Book Reviews

By B.G. THOMAS

NOVELS
All Alone in a Sea of Romance
Anything Could Happen
The Boy Who Came In From the Cold
Hound Dog and Bean
Spring Affair

NOVELLAS
All Snug
Bianca's Plan
Christmas Cole
Christmas Wish
Desert Crossing
Grumble Monkey and the Department Store Elf
How Could Love Be Wrong?
It Had to Be You
A Secret Valentine
Soul of the Mummy

Published by DREAMSPINNER PRESS
http://www.dreamspinnerpress.com

Spring
Affair

B.G. Thomas

Dreamspinner Press

Published by
Dreamspinner Press
5032 Capital Circle SW
Suite 2, PMB# 279
Tallahassee, FL 32305-7886
USA
http://www.dreamspinnerpress.com/

Spring Affair
© 2014 B.G. Thomas.

ISBN: 978-1-62798-871-1
Digital ISBN: 978-1-62798-872-8

Printed in the United States of America
First Edition
April 2014

This one's for Elizabeth North.

Oh yes!

Teacher, Confidante, Guide, Advisor, Guru, Publisher,

but most of all, *Friend*.

Thank you for helping me make my dreams come true.

Acknowledgments

Special thanks to Ariel for the French.

Merci beaucoup! Je t'aime!

Any mistakes made herein are entirely mine and not hers.

Thanks to Masau as well—I couldn't have done anything Samoan without her!

Ou te alofa ia te oe, my friend!

And I mustn't forget VJ Summers for her valuable input, and of course the wondrous Andi Byassee, who always makes me shine!

Spring passes and one remembers one's innocence.

~ Yoko Ono

If people did not love one another, I really don't see what use there would be in having any spring.

~ Victor Hugo, *Les Misérables*

To every thing there is a season, and a time to every purpose under the heaven.

~ Ecclesiastes 3:1, KJV

Chapter ONE

SO IT was the first Saturday of the month, and that meant it was Porch Night, the must-not-miss evening for the FF, aka the Fabulous Four. Sloan McKenna had wanted them to use another name for their crazy little foursome, but Wyatt had insisted that "fabulous" was much better. Far more indicative of their "fearsome fabulosity," and as Wyatt had pointed out, "Fantastic" was already taken, and copyrighted besides. Sloan hadn't seen what possible difference that could make—who would know?—but Wyatt was absolutely for certain that they would all be famous someday.

Famous for what? Sloan would wonder at Wyatt's constant assurances. He didn't know you could get famous from being a customer service rep in a call center.

Porch Night also meant the cocktails flowed freely—in this instance they were pomegranate ginger martinis—and Sloan thought they'd turned out pretty good, especially considering the circumstances.

"Now stop me if you've heard this one before…," that selfsame Wyatt—the bear of their quartet—said and then took a sip of his cocktail.

Orating really, thought Sloan—tonight's (somewhat) reluctant host. And like there really was any stopping Wyatt when he was on a roll.

"… but what do Winnie the Pooh and John the Baptist have in common?" He was practically bouncing in the high-backed wicker chair, which he had dubbed the "Morticia Addams Chair" and confiscated the instant he'd laid eyes on it. This evening he was wearing all black. Black jeans (so new Sloan was sure he had taken the tags off before driving over), a black sleeveless shirt (that was perhaps just a tad too tight), black cowboy boots (which looked suspiciously like cow*girl* boots) and a black fedora with thin gray pinstriping. He had a huge white-and-gold daffodil tucked in the hatband. It looked ridiculous, but this was Wyatt and Wyatt was… well… Wyatt.

Oh, my dear friend, thought Sloan with a bemused smile. *You really are a legend in your own mind.* At least he'd asked if he could pick the flower. Sloan was protective of the large garden that made up most of the front yard of the house in lieu of a lawn. His mother's garden. And what the hell was he going to do with it?

"Winnie the Pooh and John the Baptist?" asked Scott, the FF's curmudgeon (although a beloved curmudgeon). He scowled, shook his head, and gave his martini a taste. From his expression, Sloan couldn't tell whether Scott liked it or not.

Wyatt nodded enthusiastically. He seemed ready to explode with this one. Sadly, with Wyatt, that didn't mean it would be a *good* joke.

"What *do* they have in common?" asked Asher when the punch line did not come forthwith. Asher was their gorgeous godling, and he was sitting next to Sloan on the porch swing, arm slung over the backrest, absently playing with the nape of Sloan's neck. It was *very* distracting.

"Ready for it?" Wyatt all but squealed. "Ready for it?"

"We're ready," Scott grumbled. "We're ready…."

"Same middle name!" Wyatt fell back in his chair, giggling.

There was a pause as they digested the joke, and then Sloan and Asher burst into laughter as the meaning hit. Not Scott, of course. Sloan wasn't surprised. Scott had no sense of humor.

"I don't get it," Scott said.

Wyatt stopped laughing and looked at him agog. "What don't you get?"

"I didn't know John the Baptist *had* a middle name." Scott adjusted his expensive designer glasses. They weren't the only "designer" thing in his life. It was a compensation—some of them thought an overcompensation—for the fact that he hated what God had given him. He made no secret about the fact—had shared this opinion on many a Porch Night—that he hated his body, his life, his job. But he could buy things that he thought made him look cool. They all worried about this sometimes because they were sure he couldn't really afford such indulgences.

Asher stopped playing with Sloan's neck and leaned forward, his expression full of curiosity. "And you think Winnie the Pooh *does* have a middle name?"

"Well…." Scott paused, considered Asher's question. Sloan could see the wheels turning in his head. When he got it—and Scott's expression made it clear when he *had* finally gotten it—he let out a long groan. "Oh, dumb. That was really dumb."

"I thought it was *hil*-arious," Wyatt said.

"It was pretty funny," Sloan said. Not much had been funny lately, and it had been nice to laugh.

"It's stupid," Scott replied and sprawled back on the wicker love seat. It matched the Morticia Addams Chair beautifully and exaggerated the lanky look of his body. Sloan was sure Scott wouldn't be sitting like that if he knew, but opted not to say anything. Now if only Wyatt would do the same. It was that lanky body that had caused Wyatt to call Scott by a nickname that Scott hated. Spider Woman. If Wyatt used that name tonight, the shit would hit the fan!

"It's *not* stupid," Wyatt said defensively. "My jokes are not stupid."

Asher chortled. "Please, Wyatt. Most of your jokes are stupid. Not *that* one but—"

"Hey!"

"It's *stupid*," Scott continued. "Because A, 'the' is not a middle name…"

"It's a *joke*, dumbass," Wyatt snapped.

"… and B, comparing a character made up for kids with a mythological religious figure is dumb. The joke doesn't work."

"Which one is the character made up for kids," Asher asked, "and which one is the mythological religious figure?"

Sloan gritted his teeth and hoped this wouldn't launch into a conversation about religion. Asher had been acting a little… odd lately when it came to such matters. Sloan didn't know what was going on with his friend. Religion was one of those things Asher had never talked about one way or the other.

"Why, Winnie the Pooh is the one made up for kids," said Wyatt, not taking the bait.

Sloan breathed a sigh of relief and finished his martini.

"There is no historical proof that John the Baptist ever existed," Scott said with a superior air. "It is far more likely that he was made up by the early church." He finished his martini as well. "These are pretty good, Sloan."

Sloan jumped to his feet. "Refill? I'm getting one."

Scott nodded and held out his empty martini glass. "No more sugar on the rim, though, please. I'm watching my figure."

No pink sugar? thought Sloan. But wasn't presentation everything?

"Sugar on mine!" Wyatt offered his glass to Sloan.

Sloan took both glasses and looked at Asher, who downed his drink and handed his glass over as well. Empty, it was easy to take all four. He gave a nod and headed into the house.

"In fact," he heard Scott's voice through the screen door. "Did you know he didn't even invent baptism? It was no big thing. Everyone was doing…."

Mercifully, he couldn't hear Scott anymore by the time he got to the kitchen. He loved his friend—all of them, in fact—but when Scott got in one of his weird moods, it was easier to love him out of earshot.

Still. Sloan was lucky to have all of the dear friends who had gathered here with him tonight, especially after the last month. Month? Hell! Six months. His shoulders sagged, and he felt the tears *almost* prick at the corners of his eyes. Almost. But it wasn't happening. And that was a good thing. He didn't want his friends to see him crying. Not tonight. Even though he could. Even though it would be fine. He wanted to be brave tonight. Impress the hell out of them.

Were they talking about him now, or were they delving into a discussion of whether John the Baptist was real or not? At least Scott wasn't going on and on about one of his online romances—men he fell madly in love with and rarely met in real life. And when he did? Disaster every time. The last time Scott had actually flown to Chicago and checked into The Four Seasons, a very expensive hotel, so he could meet the man he just knew was Mr. Right. The two of them were supposed to share the costs of not only the room, but the plane tickets as well. That didn't happen. Scott and his romance *du jour* met, fucked, wound up having a huge ugly fight, and it was over. Scott had been devastated. For a couple of weeks. Maybe a month. Then Scott was right back online.

Scott, Wyatt, and Asher. They were the best friends a man could have, despite their eccentricities.

Scott was always there for him at an instant's notice, no matter what. He had actually been the first one Sloan had called on the worst day of his life, not more than a month ago. Scott had had a plan already set and instantly took over so Sloan could just throw himself on the couch and, well, not cry. That hadn't happened yet. He'd been too afraid to let the tears go until the funeral was over—he had wanted, *needed*, to maintain a sense of decorum until then. He could cry later.

Except he hadn't yet. Not really.

Wyatt was Sloan's clown. Wyatt was always ready to make him laugh and made it his mission to look on the positive side of life (succeeding almost always, unless the shit hit the fan over something with his lover). Wyatt had brought Sloan a ton of food over the days following the funeral, casserole dishes and Crock-pots full of it—all with the simplest directions.

(*"Put this in the oven at 350 degrees for forty-five minutes, remove and let set for five."*)

Of course it helped that Wyatt had a job he was in a position to leave now and again and a lover of over ten years, as well as a lovely home—

You have a lovely home now.

Sloan pushed the thought away. It was his *mother's* home.

Wyatt had arrived right after lunch that awful day, had only been able to take half the day off. He was the manager of Treasures of Terra, the local New Age store, and couldn't just leave. But he was still the first to arrive, and then somehow he had arranged to take the next day after that. Sloan loved the guy. He couldn't help it.

And Asher?

Oh dear God. Asher.

Asher was only one of the most gorgeous men Sloan had ever seen in his life. He had a crush on Asher, and he supposed he always would—to a degree anyway. He'd gotten over the worst of it—the love-sickness, the feeling he would die because Asher didn't love him back. At least not "in that way." But Asher still had a hold on his heart.

Sloan had fallen for Asher hook, line, and sinker (as his mom was wont—*had* been wont—to say). He had fallen for Asher before they'd even gotten back to his apartment the night they'd met at The Male Box. But for Asher, their evening (and the next day!) had been nothing but a hookup. At least as far as the sex was concerned. Sloan knew he was lucky he hadn't been tossed aside like most of Asher's other tricks.

At least Asher hadn't taken Sloan home because of the color of his hair. Sloan got a lot of that. Men who wanted him simply because he had red hair—and comments like "Wow! Are you as red down there as you are on top of your head?" Worse were those who said, "You know, I'm not usually into gingers, but with you…." As if they were doing him some great big frikkin' favor.

But of course that was better than being shot down simply because he *had* red hair. He got a lot of that too.

But Asher had not said any of those things. Never even mentioned its bright-copper new-penny color or his kazillion freckles or his blindingly pale white skin (that never tanned, only burned and then turned into another ten thousand freckles).

Asher *had* liked his eyes.

(*"So pretty. I can't tell just what color they are…. Wow. Brown? Not really? Something else. What? I could look into your eyes all night."*)

That and the fact that Sloan was actually going home with the tall, blond, blue-eyed, muscular stud had done Sloan in. Sloan had been in love. Quicker than a duck on a June bug.

As his mom used to say.

The sex had been amazing—possibly the best Sloan had ever known in his life. He'd been thrilled when Asher had told him to go ahead and spend the night. Sloan's imagination had gone crazy. When a man you picked up in a bar—or who picked you up—asked you to spend the night, didn't that mean something possibly special had happened?

The next day they'd gone out for breakfast at Chubby's, then hung out most of the rest of the day. They'd even gone to a movie at the Tivoli, an art house theater specializing in low budget independent films. Afterward they'd gone to Sloan's little apartment—that had been before he'd had to move back in with his mother, of course—and had more sex. Sloan was sure he had found Mr. Forever.

An hour or so later, he discovered he might have gotten ahead of himself. Asher left soon after round three and had dodged Sloan's good-bye kiss so that it hit his cheek instead of his mouth. Then he didn't call for over a week, or return Sloan's calls.

Sloan had been a ridiculous mess, moaning and sighing and constantly looking at his cell to see if he had any messages. Wyatt had tried to cheer him up, and of course, Scott had taken a more tough-love approach.

"When are you going to start separating love and sex? Mr. Gorgeous was a *trick*. Don't you know he goes home with more men than Paris Hilton?"

"Huh?" Sloan hadn't known what Scott was talking about.

"Asher is the guy everybody dreams of going home with. And if they're good-looking, sooner or later, they will. You're lucky. He must have been—"

"Been what?" Sloan had snapped. Slumming it? Jeez, Scott could be such an asshole.

Finally, after almost two weeks, when Sloan had finally given up, Asher had called. He wanted to know if Sloan wanted to see a movie at the Tivoli. "I mean, I can't believe I found somebody that likes my kind of movies," Asher had said.

So forewarned by Scott (of course) that the only reason Asher had called was that nobody else liked art films and Asher had been desperate, Sloan went, hoping for the best. The movie had been awesome—who knew a story about lesbians starring Annette Bening and Julianne Moore could be so good?—even though Asher had been acting a little aloof. He hadn't responded in any way when Sloan had kept pressing his knee against Asher's during the movie, nor even put his arm on the mutual rest between their seats so Sloan could try to take his hand.

Afterward, over a drink on the back patio of The Male Box, Asher had let him down.

"I'm just not looking for a lover," Asher had said. "I even avoid repeats for sex."

Sloan had been crushed. "But I thought we were really connecting."

"We did. We *are*. But I don't do the boyfriend thing. Not into that. Sex is sex. I get horny, I go looking."

I was nothing but a backscratcher for an itch that's hard to reach?

"If it makes you feel any better, I hardly have ever let somebody spend the night, let alone spent the next day with them. I liked you, Sloan. I *like* you. A lot. You're smart, and you like to talk about shit that most people give me the crazy-eye over. I mean, who else am I going to talk with about a movie where a lesbian has an affair with a man? Nobody, that's who. So if you want to be friends, I'm game. I'm just not wanting to date. Don't even hope for it, okay? I don't want to hurt you."

Trouble was Asher had already hurt Sloan. But Sloan took the offer of friendship anyway. Maybe hoping for a change of heart on Asher's part. But now, three years later, that change had never happened. Now Sloan was mostly over that (mostly), with only echoes of crushness now and again. Enough time had passed that he could sit with Asher on a porch swing and have the back of his neck played with and his heart would only skip a few beats. Even a year ago, it would have driven him mad with desire.

"He's a thoughtless son of a bitch," Scott had said more than once when Asher wasn't around. "He knows how you feel about him—"

"How I *felt* about him. I'm over that now."

"Sure you are." Scott had rolled his eyes. "Whatever makes you sleep at night. Or jerk off…."

Sloan had certainly done enough of that!

"Hey, need any help?"

Sloan jumped at the voice. He was so involved with his thoughts he hadn't heard the object of those thoughts come into the kitchen. Asher came up behind Sloan and slipped his arms around him, pulled up close. Sloan could feel the heat of his friend's body, feel that hard chest against his back, feel just where the tall man's groin was hitting him high up on his ass. He trembled.

"You okay, baby?"

Sloan didn't answer. *Baby.* God. It still could make his heart speed up when Asher said things like that.

"You shouldn't have done this tonight," Asher said. "You should have let me host. Or Scott or Wyatt. We all offered. It's too soon."

Sloan opened his mouth to respond, and his voice caught. He took a deep breath. Willed away the pain. "It'll never be the right time," he managed, "So why not tonight? At least I'm not in this house alone."

Asher pulled even closer to Sloan. Kissed the top of his head. Sloan let go and let himself relax against the big man. He couldn't help himself. It just felt so good to be in Asher's arms.

"Except that he doesn't want you that way, dear," his mother would have reminded him. "His loss. There are plenty of fish in the sea. One day he'll wake up and it'll be too late. You'll have found someone else."

Which had been part of the reason Sloan hadn't looked all that hard. Why, just a couple of months ago she had set him up on a blind date with the son of a friend of hers. A guy who had gone to his high school. He'd told the guy that he wasn't his type, which had been a lie. He'd been just the kind of guy Sloan went for.

Except for the fact that he wasn't Asher.

"No. You're not alone," Asher said and gave him a squeeze. "You know I know how you feel, right?"

But you don't, thought Sloan. *You don't!* The comment annoyed him as it always did. Enough that he suddenly couldn't enjoy the deliciousness of having Asher's arms around him. Sloan hated those words more than anything else these past weeks. All those people telling him they knew *just* how he felt. There was one time when it had been all he could do not to slap the woman who'd said it.

Sloan steeled himself for what was coming next. Asher's old stand-by: "I've lost someone close to me too. My grandfather. He died when I was in fifth grade, and I still miss him so much…."

Thankfully, that didn't happen. Asher was backing away. "Now about those martinis. Need some help? I'm ready for round two. How about you?"

More than ready.

Sloan nodded. "Sure," he said. "Round two coming up."

"Good," Asher replied. "A few more of these and maybe Scott will loosen up."

"Couldn't hurt," Sloan said.

"What couldn't hurt?" asked Scott, entering the kitchen as if on cue.

Wyatt was at his heels. "Who is that hot-*tie* who lives next door? Woof!"

"Who? Huh?" Sloan asked, not ready for such a question.

"Your neighbor! You been holding out on us, girl." The tipsier Wyatt got, the more queenie he got. It didn't take much. Thankfully, his lover—who didn't drink when he was driving and who had gone out to The Watering Hole to ogle go-go boys and slip dollars in their underwear—would be driving Wyatt home.

"I'm not holding out on you," Sloan said. "What are you talking about?" He was confused.

"Why Mister *Man*, of course. Bearded and hunky and *all* studly!"

"Wyatt's talking about the guy living in the house to your north," Scott explained. "He took one look at him and went all ga-ga. Started flirting right then and there. Yoo-hooing and everything."

Suddenly Sloan knew who Wyatt was talking about and looked at his friend in horror. "My God, you didn't!" The last thing he needed was to piss off the big man next door. Sloan had no doubt his neighbor could split him in half (although he seemed nice—hadn't he been at the funeral?).

"There he is!" Wyatt pointed out the window, and Sloan looked across the way and saw the bearded man framed in the window opposite, presumably doing something kitchen-y. Dishes? Getting a glass of water?

"Maybe he's peeing in the sink," Wyatt said in a lascivious tone. "God. Can't you just picture it? Him hauling out his big old—"

"I would rather *not*!" said Scott with disgust.

"Oh, like you never went pee-pee in the sink!" Wyatt waved his hands flamboyantly. "Why else even *have* a dick if you can't make the world your urinal?"

"Well, not in the *kitchen* sink for sure," Scott shot back, obviously disgusted. "You wash dishes in there! And it's so high! He doesn't look tall enough."

"Maybe he's standing on one of those little stepladder thingies…."

Sloan laughed. He couldn't help it. Leave it to Wyatt!

Kitchen filled with his loving friends, Sloan made the next round of martinis. Used the huge shaker Asher had given him as a gift earlier that evening. It made two rounds worth for the four of them instead of just the one.

It was a good thing too.

Because as it turned out, it was not an early night.

Chapter TWO

SLOAN SAT on the porch steps drinking his morning coffee, thanking his lucky stars he didn't have much of a hangover and staring at the beginnings of his mother's garden. Beginnings because it was March, and everything had just started to push up through the earth. The profusion of crocuses—purple, lavender, yellow, and white—that had been everywhere (even in strange places that Sloan couldn't figure out why his mother had planted them there) were done. They were making way for thick clusters of daffodils—all golden and orange, white and yellow, tiny and huge, and even triple petaled. He hadn't realized there were so many varieties. And there was the hyacinth too! Oh yes. Pink and purple, orange and white. Their amazingly cloying scent could be smelled five houses down if the breeze was right. He knew that because the neighbors had gleefully volunteered the information.

How could it be that just two weeks ago there had been six inches of snow on the ground?

The forsythia was about to explode as well. The huge bush—easily six foot tall with those long, thin branches—was already beginning to bud and would soon be covered in a riot of small yellow flowers. His mother had loved to take five or ten of the longest branches and put them in a large vase on the dining room table. He had to admit it had always been an arresting and impressive sight.

But what am I going to do with all of this?

The garden had never been Sloan's thing, but boy had it made his mother proud. Several times over the years she had won a "Best Yard" award for the neighborhood. She would positively glow when the sign was placed amid her flowers. People from up and down the street would congratulate her, and oh oh oh, how she would smile.

What it had gotten Sloan was some mighty teasing. Flower Boy had been the worst of the names they called him in grade school. What growing kid, trying to assert some sense of "macho," wanted to be known as Flower Boy? Like he was some kind of gay superhero or something. And then there had been the deep dread when he began to realize he *did* like boys.

No no no, he would cry. He would cry himself to sleep. *Can't be gay. Can't be gay can't be gay can't be gay. Can't!*

But he'd known. He'd known in fourth grade before he even knew what sex was. Known that he liked boys and how their bare chests would make his heart speed up. How when a friend came to spend the night and he saw him in his underwear—and why not? We're both boys, after all!— he would flush all over and be afraid to strip down. Afraid of what they would see. What they might call him or think of him. Flower Boy would be a good thing compared to words like "fruit loop" or "Tinker Bell" or "faggot." He remembered thinking that was why his father had gone away—that he hadn't wanted a faggot for a son. It wasn't until he was in high school that he found out it was because his father had had an affair and run off with a woman who was barely legal, and by the time Sloan learned all that, the man was dead.

It was the fact that his parents had never divorced that allowed him and his mother to move from Chicago to Terra's Gate—the town where she was born and raised. Before Sloan's father died, he foolishly (at least in his girlfriend's opinion) never bothered to have his life insurance policy and other legal documents changed. Between Sloan and his mother, they got everything, including the new house he had bought for said girlfriend.

"Best thing the louse ever did for me," Sloan's mother had said, although he couldn't help but notice how shell-shocked she looked for days, even weeks (maybe months), after his father's death. Between seeing her like that, and the ugly words she had used for the woman who had "stolen" his father (words she just didn't use—not his mother!), and the fact that Sloan's fantasy that his father would come back one day was shattered, it had been the worst time of his life.

Even worse, though, even more than realizing his dad was never coming back, was seeing that angry, resentful part of his mother. She had been Sloan's rock. She had been his shining example. It had taken him a while to see she was only being human and that all of it had hurt her deeply. It was the reason she'd been so different from who she had been his whole life, and it was the only time Sloan had ever seen an ugly side to his mother.

A meddlesome side, sure. More than once.

He'd seen her distraught and upset, especially when she had discovered he was gay—although how she could claim she didn't know was beyond Sloan. He knew she had found his collection of gay magazines and Colt calendars once upon a time, although she'd never let on. He knew because they were out of order, and he'd found the bookmark he'd placed inside one of the magazines lying on his bedroom floor, peeking out from under the edge of the bed. It had been a shock. A shock that had sent a cold shiver all through his body and made him throw his stash away.

Oh, to have those calendars now! They were collector's items, and he'd seen them go for quite a bit of money on eBay.

Sloan caught movement out of the corner of his eyes and looked up to see two—no, three—joggers run by. Two of them were quite good-looking, and all wore little more than tiny shorts and tank tops. They were sweaty too. He couldn't help but stare, and when one gave him a friendly little wave, he found himself blushing like a twelve-year-old. He made himself look back down at the golden faces of the daffodils.

What a shining reminder of his mother they were.

A sudden, overwhelming, and inexplicable desire to jump up and begin tearing the flowers—all of them—out of the ground swept over him. Flower Boy. They had called him Flower Boy!

It wasn't like he'd worn a big daffodil behind his ear or anything!

Oh, how Sloan had blamed those flowers for how much the kids had made fun of him in those way-back days. The flowers and his mother. But no. He knew the truth. He had started it himself. When he went into first grade, he'd gotten the bright idea to bring a big bouquet of everything that had been in bloom that August day to his teacher, and that had done it, for good and forever. Asters, chrysanthemums, and cosmos. Was it jealousy for the attention it had gotten him? The obvious step up from the apples other kids had given their teacher? Or how about the fact that the teacher, Mr. Kelso, was a man?

(Lord! In retrospect, how had he *not* known he was gay, because even then he'd been obsessed with that teacher and the hair that peeked out sometimes from the V of Mr. Kelso's shirt when he would loosen his tie and undo the top button....)

Another runner shot by, followed by two more, one of whom had removed his shirt. The muscles of his chest, smooth as marble, glistened with sweat.

Jeez! Stop perving!

Yet another man ran past, his shoes making popping noises as they hit the street.

Is it a runner's club or something?

Sloan unconsciously rubbed his stomach and felt his slight winter's paunch.

Maybe I should run?

He glanced down the street and saw two more men approaching. One had bright copper hair, almost more vivid than Sloan's own, and even from three houses down, Sloan could see the redhead's pale shoulders were already beginning to burn. The other man….

God!

The other could have been Mr. Kelso!

But of course, his first grade teacher would be, what? At least fifty today? Older? And the closer the two runners got, Sloan could see that the man—very well-muscled, with a tight, trim dark beard and a hairy chest—couldn't have been much older than Sloan himself.

Then to his surprise, Sloan saw the bearded man veer off and head in Sloan's direction. For some strange reason, it made his heart speed up. The guy was pretty hot, and it looked like he was heading right toward Sloan.

Oh hell. No he wasn't. The jogger was Sloan's neighbor.

(*"Mister Man!"*)

The guy was simply going home.

Their eyes locked, the neighbor's large and intense blue. He gave a single nod and changed course again.

Shit. He's coming over here!

Sloan stood quickly and, without realizing it, sucked in his gut.

His neighbor came to a stop a few feet in front of Sloan. "Morning," he said.

Sloan nodded back. "Morning."

The man lifted the front of his shirt and wiped his sweaty face, revealing a tight set of lightly hairy abs and a shallow belly button.

Sloan tore his gaze away from the sight and, when he looked up, saw the man had noticed. Saw it in the amused little smile. Sloan blushed. Busted.

"Look," said the man (what the hell was his name?). "I just want to say once again how sorry I am about your mom. She was amazing."

The remark caught Sloan by surprise, even though it had been the main thing everyone had been saying the last couple of weeks. He opened his mouth to respond, and his voice caught. Sloan took a deep breath and thanked him. Suddenly remembered that, yes, he had been at the funeral. In a suit, of course, and looking far different than he did at the moment.

God. He really almost could have been Mr. Kelso. He radiated masculinity.

Four more joggers ran past.

"What's going on this morning?" Sloan pointed at the men with his chin.

"Oh. A bunch of us get together and run on Sunday mornings. It's my church."

"Church group?" Sloan asked. How could a church group be running on Sunday morning?

"No. Not a church group. It's *my* church. Running. Makes me feel... I don't know. Alive. And there's no hellfire and brimstone."

"Sounds like my kind of church."

"You're free to join us anytime. We meet at Wagner Park around seven. Or I run most evenings if you want to join me."

Gosh. "Ah. Why. Thank you. That's nice of you."

"Sure, Sloan. No problem. It'll do you good."

Sloan touched his tummy again. *Do I look that bad?*

The man laughed. "No! Not for that. You look great. I mean, it'll occupy your mind. Get you out of the house."

"*Oh.*" Sloan nodded. "Yeah. It—" He glanced back at the house. "It feels so emp—" His voice caught again with a surprising hitch. *God. Don't let me tear up now! Please.* He blushed again, looked away, fought to regain composure. Looked back. Saw no judgment in those intense eyes. "I...." Sloan stopped. Took another breath. *Say something!* "Ah... look. I'm sorry. I am sure we've been introduced, but I don't remember your name. Forgive me for—"

"God, no! Don't worry about it. With all you've been going through? I'm Max Turner." Max held out his hand.

Sloan took it. "Sloan McKenna." He blushed again. *Dumb! Dumb thing to say. He knows my name.*

Max smiled and—*Bam!*—Sloan felt a rush in his chest as his heart skipped at least three beats.

God! What a smile.

"Nice to make it official," Max said. His grip was firm and strong without that forceful squeeze some men used—like they were proving their manhood or something.

They stood there in silence for a moment, neither saying a word. Sloan berated himself again for not speaking. Thing was he didn't know what to say. He hadn't been in a talking mood in the first place, and then this man—Max—had surprised him, and Sloan had been thrown back into Mom-thoughts and....

"I should probably get inside," Max said

No. Don't go. And that thought surprised Sloan. Hadn't he *just* been thinking that he hadn't been in a talking mood?

"I can get you some coffee," Sloan blurted.

Max shook his head. "No. I only have one cup a day, and I've had it already. Wish I didn't do that, but I'm addicted. What can I say?"

"I couldn't survive without it," Sloan said. "Especially lately."

"Maybe tomorrow? I don't have to be at work until ten."

"What do you do?" Sloan asked, trying to keep Max here with him.

"I teach at the university."

That was cool. "Really? Neat." *Neat? Did you just say "neat"?* "KU or our illustrious—"

Max nodded. Raked his fingers through his short, spiky, sweaty hair, revealing equally sweaty pits. The man was a walking (running) commercial for a gym. "Yup. WU." Wagner University. The town's college and main source of revenue. The students were the lifeblood of Terra's Gate. And one more thing named after the millionaire family who lived at the top of the hill that looked out over the whole of town.

"Do you like it?"

The smile was back, radiating tenfold. "I live for it," Max said. "It is my bliss."

Bliss. What an interesting word. *Do I even have bliss?* Sloan thought he probably didn't. It certainly wasn't working at Horrell & Howes as a call center customer rep. He'd liked it once—he liked helping people—but time had put tarnish on the job. Time and a supervisor named Shelia, spelled like She-lee-ah, but pronounced She-lah. Her supervisory style was rules rules rules—with Horrell & Howes's clients of utter and sacred importance and her employees nothing much more than peons and peasants, expendable one and all. She let them know that too—on a regular basis.

"I have two hundred applications in my desk from people who would love to have your job!"

She didn't, of course. *He* knew that if no one else did. Applications were the purview of human resources. All in all, as much pride as he took in helping the people who called in, the place he worked wouldn't or couldn't be his "bliss."

"So what do you say? Go running with me tomorrow morning?"

Oh God! Run? "Well, I can't tomorrow, Max. I have to be at work at—"

"What time?" Max asked before Sloan could finish his excuse.

Reason. It's not an excuse. "I have to be there by seven thirty."

"How long does it take you to get to work?"

Goodness. "Not long. Ten minutes."

Max smiled. It was a sexy smile. "Well, no problem, then. We could meet at six, run for a half hour—don't want to kill you the first day."

Six? Meet at six? Six in the morning?

"Then you should have plenty of time to get ready for work. Or we could meet at five thirty."

"Ummm...." *I don't know. Run? Really? Why did I even say anything?*

"Look," Max said. "I would love to talk more, but I need to get in and shower. Have to take my wife to the airport in just a little bit."

Wife? Crap. Of course there was a wife. Sloan suddenly flashed on a blonde with long hair. And why the hell was he even disappointed? It wasn't like he was looking for romance. That was the *last* thing he was looking for right now.

But Sloan's eyes still flashed up and down Max before he could stop them—*those legs!* Sloan might not be looking for romance, but he sure could lose himself in something else.

And as if on cue, "*Chéri!*"

They both jumped and turned to see the lovely blonde woman from Sloan's memories standing on the neighboring porch. "I was hoping you'd be back. We need to leave *dans une heure.*"

"Sure, Lauren. I'll be right in."

"What did she say?" *French? Was she speaking French?*

Max gave a slight shrug. "I think she said we have to leave in an hour, but it might have been a minute. I'm not sure."

"Yes, *lapin.* An hour. You *know* that." The woman took a step closer and crossed her arms. Sloan felt like he was being scrutinized; those staring eyes made him feel damned uncomfortable.

Well! You were ogling her husband. She must have seen that.

"I don't mean to rush you, *mon chou,* but we do have *une chose ou deux* to do before we leave."

Max nodded again. "Okay, honey." He turned back to Sloan. "I have been summoned. Tomorrow for coffee? Maybe a run?"

Sloan was surprised at the question. Apparently, Max wasn't just being polite. He'd meant both the invitation for coffee *and* a run.

"I…. Sure," Sloan said before he could stop himself. The guy might be straight, but that didn't mean Sloan couldn't stare. Wyatt would be proud. "How about just coffee, though? I haven't run in a long time. I'd just hold you up."

Max laughed. It was a deep laugh. Sloan felt a tingle run down his back.

"You won't hold me up. But coffee sounds good."

"It's really good coffee," Sloan said. "From a little place called The Shepherd's Bean. I try and go by every time I'm in the city—"

"*Minou!*"

Jeez, thought Sloan and looked over at the blonde woman. *Leash much?*

"Okay, then. I'll call you before I go on my run this evening." Max nodded and turned away. "You can join me then instead."

"Do you want my phone number?" Sloan asked before realizing he hadn't refused the offer.

"I have the house number," Max replied, looking back.

"You do? Ah. Okay." Why did Max have the num—

Because he's your neighbor and your mother gave it to him, dummy.

Max smiled again. "Later."

"Later," said Sloan and watched as the man walked away, marveling at the play of muscles in his legs and, yes, ass. God, what must that look like without shorts?

Then he noticed Lauren looking at him again. The look was clear. *Stay away.* She gave him a nod and was sure to kiss Max as he stepped up onto the porch. "Good morning," she said. And then the two of them disappeared into their house.

Now what an interesting turn of events.

Chapter THREE

MAX WAS a taken aback when Lauren practically tore his clothes off when they got inside. She was rarely sexually aggressive, waiting instead (or hinting) for him to make the first move. But what really surprised him was that she hadn't insisted he shower first.

"I want you all manly and sweaty, *chéri*."

And who was he to turn down a little sex? It was rare that she was in the mood these days. Not only had it been awhile—several weeks anyway—it would certainly be even longer before they would make love again, what with her being gone for two months this time.

Two months! Max had gotten used to her trips. It was part of her job, and she loved the traveling as much as he loved the staying put in the small town where they lived. As much as he loved teaching. But two months? He'd never been separated from his wife for that long. It was going to be weird. Scary, maybe. Not that he'd be alone. Logan, their son, would be there. Max would have plenty of company.

"That was nice, my dear," Lauren said—in French, of course. Oh, how she loved everything French. And how excited she was about this particular trip. Not her first to France, of course. But the longest since she'd lived in Paris for a year as a foreign exchange student.

"*Quel cadeau de départ magnifique!*" She propped herself up on one elbow and looked down at him. She was beautiful. Her long blonde hair was luxurious and soft as silk, shading from an almost white to a bright gold. Her eyes were so blue they reminded him of the Mediterranean Sea, where they'd taken their honeymoon. Her teeth were perfect and dazzlingly white—a product of regular dentistry starting in early childhood: braces to whiteners. And then there was her body. It was near perfect. For most of their relationship, she had been just as enthusiastic about her physical fitness as he was. Until a year ago, she'd run with him every day.

Max was often amazed that Lauren was his wife. Why him? A man who, in her eyes—and he knew this—had little to no ambition. He was happy with what he had. No real unfulfilled dreams. He had done what he wanted, gotten his professorship, found a job at a small college, bought a nice little three-bedroom house. As far as he was concerned, he lacked for nothing.

(Not really.)

Lauren, on the other hand, had high ambitions. She had big dreams. It was her growing success that kept her from running with him anymore. Her career carved away her time with a laser scalpel's precision and a starving man's appetite. He knew he should be happy for her; her dreams were coming true. But there was no doubt that a certain distance was growing between them. They had so little time together anymore. Running had been good bonding time for them, even though they rarely said a word. So it was surprising indeed that she'd wanted this loving with him before she left—that she had made time.

"Yes, baby. Thank you," he said in French, trying to please her. "*C'était méchant.*"

Lauren giggled. "I hope you didn't mean that…."

"Wha—" Had he massacred the language again? "I didn't say it was marvelous?"

She raised a hand and covered laughter. "No. You said it was 'mean.' What a relief that isn't what you meant. At least I hope not!"

Max blushed. "I meant… ah… *parfait.*"

She rewarded him with one of her brilliant smiles.

I guess I got it right that time.

"Better! *Que c'est gentil.* You are 'perfect' as well, *mon grand. Mon mari.*"

Max lost part of what she was saying. He'd caught that he'd been complimented, though. Told that he was sweet. And something about his masculinity. He used to be so much better with the language. For years, they'd always spoken French at dinner. It was important to Lauren that Logan be bilingual, and Max saw the sense in that. But as the years passed, they'd slacked off for some reason, and he'd lost so much of it. Logan hadn't, though. His French was nearly flawless. Of course, all those dinners since birth had something to do with that.

Lauren sat up, the sheet falling away and revealing a body that Max knew almost any man would consider perfect.

(Well, certainly not Sloan.)

Max bit back a smile at the thought of his neighbor as she swiveled around and climbed out of bed. "I'm going to have a quick shower. *Tu viens?*"

"No. I'll wait and jump through while you get dressed. It'll be quicker that way."

"All right, *chéri*," she said over her shoulder, and he was relieved that she'd so easily accepted his turning down her invitation. She loved it when they showered together. On the other hand, it had always made him feel uncomfortable. There was something almost aggressive in her insistence in helping him wash, her hands and fingers in places far too familiar. She'd only laugh at his objections. "We're married, darling. I only want to help. No reason to be shy. And you are *so* hairy."

Max had a feeling she'd use peroxide and rubbing alcohol if he'd let her. The way out had been for him to find excuses to skip the shared showers whenever he could. At least she'd given up on trying to get him to shave down there.

"Couldn't we at least shave your wonderful chest, Max? Don't you think a man's chest is far sexier without all that hair to hide his muscles?"

Max had put his foot down on that. A rare thing when he wouldn't compromise.

"Proud of you, Max," his lifelong friend, Cliff, had told him. "*Finally*! Max, believe me when I say you should *never* compromise with a woman."

"Cliff!"

"Give Lauren her way now and again, sure. Maybe even 45 percent of the time. Then make sure you get *your* way the rest of the time. But *never* compromise. When you compromise, *nobody* wins."

But don't you both win when you compromise? Maybe you did. Maybe you didn't. But when it came to the body-hair issue, Max *won*.

He'd been thrilled when, at puberty, hair had begun to sprout all over his body. It had made him feel like he was becoming a man. At fourteen he'd been fascinated with the dark hair spreading out across his chest and legs. And so soft!

Max had been embarrassed a time or two when he was caught absently stroking his own legs, marveling at how they felt, that his body was changing so much. Stick legs turning muscular and hard, his body responding to exercise in a way it never had before. And hadn't there been a time or two when he'd wanted to touch Cliff's legs too? To see if the hair felt like his own? It had looked coarser.

Max heard the shower shut off and was surprised at just how quick Lauren had been. She usually took long showers, was even more thorough washing herself—with what seemed like eighty-seven types of soaps, gels, shampoos, conditioners—as she was him.

He needed to shake a leg, and he snatched a pair of khaki shorts from his dresser and a T-shirt that was lying on the floor on his side of the bed (he sniffed it first to make sure it didn't stink) and headed into the bathroom. Max stepped into the tub just as Lauren was getting out.

Ah, she hadn't washed her hair. That was a big part of why she had finished so quickly. As they wiggled by each other, he marveled again at the differences between their bodies. Funny that he still did after fifteen years of marriage. Lauren's hips were wide while his were narrow, her legs so smooth and infinitely long, while his were thick and, yes, hairy. His wife's breasts were high and perfect, his own chest broad and hard. And then there was her hair, of course. Lauren's was so very blonde, those tresses falling down to her shoulder blades, while his was dark brown and short.

And that was just the external differences. He and Lauren were poles apart. Men and women. So unalike! Like cats and dogs, he thought, and not for the first time.

How do we do it? Live together? Make a home together? How do men and women do it?

Sometimes Max thought it must be so much easier for his brother, Dennis, despite the obstacles the world threw in his path. With Den and his lover Armel, it was two dogs—and surely men were dogs, right? With two dogs, there was less mystery. An understanding. There must be comfort in that kind of relationship, even with the whole "gay thing."

Dennis had come out while Max was a freshman in high school, surprising the whole family. Hell, it had shocked the shit out of Max, although he supposed he should have known. Everyone had taken it surprisingly well. Especially considering that was, what? Early nineties? Not really an excess of support in those days. No gay and straight student alliances. Not in their school anyway. Certainly no belief that there would be gay marriage in their lifetime. And now Den and Armel were legally married and everything.

"You better give me a grandson," their father had said, fixing Max with a steely expression the afternoon Den had come out. "God knows I won't get one from Den."

Max had frozen, like an animal in the middle of a highway—caught in the headlights of an oncoming car.

What? You've made kids my *responsibility?*

Well, Max had done that. Done his "duty." Given his father a grandson. Exactly one. But the job had been done, right? And Lauren had never pressed him for a second child. She'd even suggested he get a vasectomy, and he'd done it. No surprises after that. Max loved Logan with all his heart, but two kids would have driven him over the edge. And how crazy was it that he felt like that when he was a teacher?

But then it was the age of the students that made that work. The older Logan got, the closer Max felt his relationship with his son was getting. The last year had been pretty special. They'd gone on some camping trips, hiking, swimming, and more. They could talk about all kinds of things, although his son had been acting a little distant the last few weeks. Max suspected it had something to do with Lauren leaving. Logan didn't seem too happy about that.

"Max? Don't take too long in there."

Max started. Where had he gone? He'd been standing there, water spraying over him, lost in thought. He soaped up quickly, not too worried about nooks and crannies with Lauren leaving. Besides, he liked the way he smelled. Like a man, and what the hell was wrong with that?

He might even skip the deodorant. Wasn't it supposed to cause cancer anyway?

"SO HAS *le garçon* moved in?"

"Huh?" Max had his eyes on the road, looking for the KCI sign. "What boy?"

"The redhead," said Lauren. "Has he moved into his mother's house for good or will he be leaving soon?"

Sloan. God he had about the reddest hair ever. Shining red. Red like a new penny.

I wonder if his hair is that red down below?

Jeez. Did he *have* to go there? Could he help it?

Would Sloan be as smooth as most redheaded guys? Funny that Max had been happy he was getting hairy when he was a kid—that he refused to "manscape," as Lauren called it—but thought most men looked better without it. What was that about?

Max spared his wife a glance. "I don't have a clue what Sloan's doing. I didn't ask him."

"Hmmmm…." She looked away.

Max knew that "Hmmmm…." It was Lauren's way of saying her mind was on something—turning it over like a puzzle ring—and she wasn't done.

"You know he's *homo*, right?"

"I assumed it. So what?" Up ahead Max saw the blue sign he'd been looking for, signaled, and pulled over into the far right lane. He caught her shrug out of the corner of his eye.

"Do you suppose Den knows him? Perhaps you should ask."

"Den lives in Iowa, honey. Do you think gay people have some sort of network to keep in touch with each other?"

"You heard all the noise he and his… friends made last night." Ignoring his comment. "I hope that doesn't go on all the time."

"Lauren. It was a Saturday night. His mother just died. They were probably trying to cheer him up. Now what's this all about?"

"They went on until practically sunrise."

Her voice was stiff. The tone caught Max by surprise. It wasn't like her at all. She was usually so free spirited, always ready to laugh or try some new adventure. He decided to shrug it off. "I didn't hear them. Slept like a log. You don't care that Sloan's gay, do you?"

"No. It's just…."

"Just what?" Max turned the wheel to accommodate for the turnoff. A sign revealed that the airport was only two miles away. "We have gay friends. You love Den and Armel. Right?"

"*Oui, oui, bien sûr*. But Dennis and Armel don't drool over you."

"Drool?"

"You didn't see him drooling, darling? He was practically slobbering."

"He was not," Max objected. But then….

As Max thought about it, he couldn't deny Sloan had been checking him out. He'd caught his neighbor staring at his legs—

(maybe he wonders how they feel!)

—and then at his crotch. Oh yes. Max had caught him, and Sloan had known he'd been caught, and he'd blushed like one of Max's freshman female students.

"Oh, *toi*!" Lauren cried. "You do *too* know it. You're grinning!"

"I am not," Max said and realized he probably was.

"You and your ego. Your male ego! *Les hommes. Ils se promènent comme ça, aussi fiers que des paons.* Peacocks, thrilled to death when someone notices their big feathers."

Max burst into laughter. "What can I say? Maybe men *do* have an ego—"

"Maybe?" Lauren scoffed.

"—and maybe we *do* like it when someone notices us."

It's more than you do anymore.

"But the little *mec* is a *man*."

"So what? It's still a point for me." Max laughed again. He couldn't help it. The fact that Sloan had been checking him out *was* an ego stroke. What did it matter that Sloan was a man?

And the last thing Sloan could be called is little.

"Max! I just can't believe that you don't mind that—"

Max laughed. He knew he shouldn't, but it was out before he could stop it.

Lauren stared out the window for a moment, then said, "It's like our neighborhood is turning gay."

"Dear, just because Sloan is gay doesn't mean the neighborhood—"

"What about the Jeffries boy?"

"Honey, we've always known he was gay." Kit, the boy in question, had had a pink bicycle in high school. "Tell me again why you love Paris," Max said, deciding to change the subject.

She froze, her mouth half-open, and then she smiled. A big, perfect smile. "Oh, Max! *Parie*! The city of lights! The first time I saw it was at night! And I knew. I just knew!" She was almost trembling with delight.

Max smiled. "Tell me." He loved seeing her this way. So excited. He might not share her enthusiasm, he might be immune to the charms of Paris, but it didn't mean he wasn't happy for her. "What did you know?"

"Max, it was like I had come *home*! Like I'd been there before. Yes, I'd been waiting for months. Watched every movie. Pored through pictures. I had so many books! But the pictures don't—*can't*—prepare you. *C'est de la magie!*"

They came around a turn, and there was the beginning of the airport. They passed the signs that told them which terminal they needed. Max got into the correct lane.

"When I woke that first morning and saw the Eiffel Tower through my hotel window, I felt it even more. I'd seen it lit up the night before, of course. But during the day.... It... it was so much more... *vrai*! Powerful! Like a guardian watching over the city. Watching over *me*. Paris makes me wonder if there might really be such a thing as *réincarnation*. Who knows? Maybe I helped build it in a previous life!"

Max turned the car into their terminal, a giant, backward letter *C*, and followed around its inner circumference, watching for the correct airline.

"And now! Now I get to be there for two months. *Two months*! Oh, I hope my room looks out at the tower again. It's a glorious sight. You know, at first Parisians hated it. Now? Now they can say anything they want, but an outsider best not! *Aucune chance! Ce serait un désastre.* And now I think they love it. They are proud of their tower, Max."

Max pulled the car over into the loading zone and quickly got out. "You have your ticket, Lauren?" he asked for perhaps the tenth time.

"My husband, I have my ID and the printout and my passport. *Tu t'en doutes.*"

Yes, of course he knew that. Lauren? Ever in control? Ever ready? Certainly she did.

He opened the door for her, and she took his hand as he, ever her gentleman, helped her out. Then while she went to the man behind the counter at the curb—Max loved that they didn't even need to go inside the terminal—Max got her bags out of the trunk. Several, but not as many as might be expected for such a long stay. She would be fine. Of course she would.

It took only a few minutes to check the bags and get everything in order. She would of course still have to go through security and more, but she would handle all that with grace and style, charming everyone, and soon they would be waiting on her as if she were royalty. She had that ability.

Again he was amazed that she had chosen him. What might his life be like today had she not?

"You sure you don't want me to go in?" Max asked her when she had finished her business.

"*Non. Ce n'est pas nécessaire.* We discussed this. All is planned. No need for you to park the car when you can't sit at the gate with me. All is well, Max." She kissed him, just like a Parisian.

Max felt a little thrill. She was going to be so happy. She was ready for this adventure. More than ready. "Two months," he said and saw her eyes go wide and then her face light up with joy.

"*Deux mois,*" she repeated. "*Mon aventure!*"

Max pulled her close and hugged her. "Take care, Lauren."

"I will. Worry not!" She stepped back. He was surprised to see a flash of concern on her face. "Oh, Max. Should we have stopped and seen Logan one more time?"

Max laughed. Shook his head. "We discussed *this*. All is planned. We had dinner with Logan last night. And he's with his best friend."

For just a second, he saw a funny look on her face. As if she had gone away. Lost in thought. But no. It was only a second. Her eyes focused back on him. "Watch the ginger boy, *mon mari,*" she said. *My husband.*

He chuckled again. "Don't worry, my wife."

Her dazzling smile was back, and she stood taller, radiating her power. Venus or someone. Something mythical. "*Je t'aime.*"

"Love you too, sweetheart," Max replied.

And with that she turned and was gone.

Chapter FOUR

SLOAN OPENED the front door to find Wyatt standing there, arms crossed over a pink camo T-shirt. "Let's see that new *300* movie," his friend said. "It should be fun. No Gerard Butler, but *lots* of man flesh."

"What?" Sloan asked. He hadn't expected Wyatt. Sunday was Wyatt's day with his lover, Howard.

"A movie. Let's go see a *movie*. I thought lots of near-naked men running around would be good."

"Isn't that movie getting terrible reviews?"

"Who gives a shit. Near. Naked. *Menz*? Or if you want, we could see the new Muppet movie. I don't care. I just gotta do *some*thing."

"Muppets? Really? You?"

"What's wrong with Muppets?"

"Nothing. They just don't seem like you…."

Wyatt tossed back his head and placed his hand over his heart. "Moi *loves* the Muppets," he cried in a passable imitation of Miss Piggy.

"What about Howard? Aren't you two up to something today?"

Wyatt dropped his arms to his side and his shoulders slumped. "We had a fight." He plopped down dramatically in the "Morticia Addams" chair. Sloan opened the screen door and stepped out onto the porch.

"What in the world did you two fight about?"

Wyatt looked away.

What did you do this time? Sloan wondered. "Wyatt?"

"Howard says I'm getting too possessive."

"Possessive?" Sloan sat down on the love seat. "What does that mean?"

"He says he's tired of me getting jealous when he plays."

Plays. Sloan knew what that meant. It meant sex. It didn't have a damned thing to do with Monopoly or tag football or anything like that.

How had the word "playing" ever become a euphemism for sex? No. What Howard meant was that he thought Wyatt was too jealous when he had sex with someone. Without Wyatt.

Sloan started to say something like "I don't know how you can have an open relationship in the first place." He didn't say that, though. It wasn't what Wyatt needed right now.

The truth was he *didn't* know how Wyatt and Howard could do it. Sloan would be jealous too. He knew there was no way he could ever even consider anything but monogamy. As a matter of fact, he'd once broken off things with a co-worker just when the flirting was getting really interesting because he found out the guy was married. Sloan had really liked him too. And been incredibly attracted to him. But there was no way he was going to let anything progress after that, not only because there was no way they could ever have a monogamous relationship, but also because of his principles. Sloan was not an adulterer.

"But you wouldn't be committing adultery," the co-worker had told him. "*I'm* the one who's married. Not you. Let me worry about morals. You're a free man."

Sloan had been resolute in not allowing anything to develop between them. He wouldn't help the guy cheat.

"I'm gay," the co-worker had told him. "She can't fulfill me."

"Then come out and get a divorce," Sloan had said. "Don't you see you're cheating on her already? She thinks you're in love with her. She thinks she's your everything. End it now and give her a chance to find someone she can fulfill."

"She'll take the kids! I love my children."

"You should have thought of that possibility before you *had* kids in the first place."

After that, Sloan had gotten his supervisor to switch his lunch break. He didn't even want to eat in the same room with the man. Didn't want to take a chance they would sit at the same table. He'd felt weirdly cheated on, even though they'd never gone on a single date—not even out to lunch. Sloan knew he could never do that to someone else. Known it for sure when he'd spotted the co-worker with his wife one day at the grocery store. Saw the kids.

God! If he had he been willing to be a piece on the side, he would have helped hurt that family. How could he do that? The hurt would have been ten times worse than what he had felt. No. A hundred times. A thousand.

"Stop looking at me that way," Wyatt said.

"What way?" Sloan asked, genuinely surprised. He wasn't aware that he'd been "looking" at Wyatt in anyway at all.

"You're judging me."

Sloan shook his head. "I'm not judging you."

"Yes. You are. I can see it in your eyes. You've never approved of my open relationship."

"I don't approve of it for *me*," Sloan returned. "If you think it works for *you*—"

"See!" Wyatt jumped to his feet. "*If* I *think* it works for *me*. You're implying that it *doesn't* work for me, and that's judging!"

Was it? Was he judging Wyatt? No. No, he wasn't. "I don't judge my friends," he said aloud. *I'm judging your words. I don't believe that you believe what you're saying. I can see it in your eyes. I can see you're hurting. It's not working for you or you wouldn't be hurting like this.*

Sloan kept that to himself, though. Saying it aloud *would* be judging, wouldn't it?

Isn't it still judging? Aloud or just thinking it?

"Monogamy is not normal." Wyatt sat back down and crossed his arms again in a defensive posture.

"I know you say that," Sloan said, trying not to get defensive himself.

"Do you know the statistics of men cheating on their spouses?"

"High?" Sloan asked.

"Yeah. Like *really* high. I forget just what they are, but they're really, *really* high. I bet Scott would know for sure."

"I bet he would." Sloan was getting uncomfortable. He didn't want to hear the odds of his future lover cheating on him.

"And Howard has this book. Famous. The authors interviewed hundreds of gay couples and found that the couples that make it for years and years are the ones who eventually open—"

Sloan's stomach clenched. The idea made him cold and clammy. *No. Say what you want, but I am going to find a man who wants just me and nobody else.*

"I'll find somebody who wants what I want," Sloan said quickly, cutting Wyatt off. "There are seven billion people on this planet. One in ten is gay. Half of those are men. That leaves…." *What?*

"Don't ask me," Wyatt said. "I can't balance a checkbook. I can't add up numbers like that in my head."

"*Divide*," Sloan growled and regretted it. "It's…." He did the math in *his* head. "Three hundred and fifty million?"

"I don't have a frigging clue."

"It's a *lot*." Sloan crossed his arms in imitation of Wyatt. Two could play that game. "With odds like that, I have got to be able to find what I'm looking for!"

Wyatt gave a snort. "A *slave* is what you want."

"I want an equal."

"But you want to dictate what he can do! Who he can be with. How can one person fulfill every single need of another person? What are the odds of finding someone who is exactly sexually compatible? Jealousy is a sign of insecurity."

"Well, isn't that what Howard said about you?"

"But I'm not jealous! I'm happy that he can do things that I'm not into. There's no reason why he should have to do without. *Or* me. Hey! If I had to be monogamous, I would *never* get to top. He won't even let me rim him—"

Sloan tried not to flinch.

Somehow that is just more information than I needed to know.

"Then what was the fight about?" Sloan asked and immediately regretted it. What new intimate detail would Wyatt reveal? He already had an image of Wyatt and Howard having sex. Sloan had never found the big man the least bit appealing.

"The fight started because he's doing things that he *could* do with me and he won't! *I* need to get laid once in a while! And he wants to do it with Chuck Mueske. Chuck Mueske is a gnome! And Howard wants to do him today! Today is *our* day."

"Ah," Sloan said. Jealousy by any other name…. "Did you tell him no?" *I hope you did.*

"Darn tootin'." Wyatt nodded vigorously—then stopped. Frowned. "And that's when he called me a clingy, jealous little bitch."

Asshole, thought Sloan. He'd never liked Howard that much except for the fact that Wyatt loved him and said that Howard loved him back. Sloan had seen them through the years, and they did act like an old married couple. He really had no call to think that Howard didn't love Wyatt. But it wasn't very often that Howard *looked* like he was in love. None of that sparkle in his eyes when he looked at Wyatt, like what Sloan saw in Wyatt's eyes when he looked at Howard. Wyatt loved Howard.

Sloan didn't have to like the man, though. He only had to like the fact that Howard made Wyatt happy.

Well....

At least he thought he did.

"So now...." Wyatt's voice was almost a whisper. "Now he's at *Chuck's* place. I mean I *guess* he is. I stamped out like a big drama queen."

"Well, you *are* a big drama queen," Sloan said, hoping to lighten the mood.

Wyatt looked at him. "I suppose so."

"Suppose?"

"All right!" Wyatt threw his hands up in the air. "And I wear my crown proudly." He pretended to adjust just such a symbol of royalty on his head. "Now, let's go to a movie!" Wyatt jumped to his feet. "See if Howard enjoys *Up-Chuck* half as much as we enjoy a hoard of barely dressed warriors."

It was only then that Sloan was finally able to see there was writing on Wyatt's shirt. It was hard to notice pink lettering on the wild camo print of various shades of the same color. "Uppity Woman" it declared.

Sloan started laughing. "Okay, Uppity! Okay. Let's go!"

MAX'S PLAN was to pick Logan up from his buddy's house on the way home from the airport. Except that he was about five miles out when his cell rang. He rarely answered the phone while driving, but it was his son's ring tone—Lady Gaga's "Telephone"—and that was one Max always picked up. He figured he'd probably watched too many movies like "Taken."

"Hey, Chief," Max said. At least it was a Bluetooth, and he could make the call hands off. "You ready?"

That was when Logan begged to spend another night at Devin's house.

"You've got school in the morning, Son."

"*Duh*, Dad. So does Devin. Mrs. Simpson can take us."

"Hmmmm…." Max had been thinking they would do the whole father and son thing tonight. Pizza. A movie from Redbox. Maybe a video game?

"Please, Dad?"

Max sighed inwardly. Oh well. It was a little disappointing. He and Logan had gotten just a little distant since August, and he was hoping for some bonding time. But of course Logan wanted to spend time with his friend. Max could bachelor it. They had two months after all.

Hey! He could ask Sloan if he wanted to go for that run.

"Do you need anything? A change of clothes?"

"Nah. Mrs. Simpson said she'd wash what I wore yesterday."

What *had* Logan worn yesterday? Max couldn't remember. "Is it appropriate?"

"Jeez, Dad. Do you and Mom let me *own* anything that's not 'appropriate'?"

Max chuckled. "Okay, okay. Homework?"

"Dad. You know better."

And of course, Max did. Logan probably did his homework in study hall on Friday so he wouldn't have any for the weekend. Max tried not to be too much of the teacher to his son, but there were things he insisted on. Homework done and good grades were chief among them.

"Fine. Sorry. But do you want me to run anything by?"

"No. I'm good."

"All right, then. Have a good time. I *do* want you home tomorrow."

"Cool, Dad. No problem."

Logan signed off, no good-bye, no "I love you." Max supposed his son was getting too old for that, and it made him a little sad.

He'll be eighteen in four years. Wow. Soon he'd be bringing girls home, and before Max knew it, Logan would be married and have kids.

Max thought about going to his office at WU, but why? He'd graded homework, and he had his books for Monday classes at home. What would he do? No student was going to drop by on a Sunday afternoon.

So he was wifeless and sonless today. Should he just lie around at home and watch TV and drink a few glasses of wine?

That run. I can run with Sloan. His mom would like that.

Of course, it was early when Max got home.

He decided to do some laundry, both his and Logan's. Max certainly needed something for school tomorrow. The last two days had been focused on getting Lauren ready, naturally.

Max usually did the wash. He didn't mind. He'd set up his home office in the finished side of the basement, the washing machine and drier were in the other half. So it was easy to load both machines and then get lost in his studies or the piles of student papers and tests until buzzers let him know it was time to start the next load. Adding to the convenience was the fact that the chimney had long ago been converted into a laundry chute when the fireplace had been turned over to gas. All they had to do was drop their clothes through a little door in the hallway wall upstairs. The only problem was getting Logan to do it. Max's son was perfectly content to leave his dirty clothes (underwear included) all over his room.

Well....

That wasn't completely true. Logan had gotten better since he'd made friends with Devin. Thank God his son had some motivation, even if it wasn't from a personal desire to have a clean room.

The rest of the house was spotless. Lauren wouldn't have it any other way. And Max was all for it. As long as she left his desk alone. He was one of those people who could always find anything he was looking for, even on a desk that looked like pure chaos to anyone else.

In some ways Max even had fun doing the laundry. It didn't take much time, and Lauren did all the ironing. Of course, it was mostly her clothes that needed it, and she never forgot—or let him forget—the triangular burn his iron had left on one of her blouses when they were first dating.

"Do you have any idea how much this cost?" she had cried.

Max had simply shrugged back in those high school days. His parents bought his clothes at Walmart. And even today he rarely paid over ten dollars for a pair of jeans or a dress shirt. Jeans were jeans as far as he was concerned, and Walmart brand sufficed. Maybe it was a good thing. His thriftiness in the clothing department helped offset the cost of Lauren's clothes. That and the fact that she made good money. Unlike the average husband he talked to, it didn't bother him that she made more than he did. There wasn't much that bothered Max, in fact. He was the very definition of laid back and content. He'd accomplished his goals: finished school with high marks, married, gotten a job teaching, had a son—

(*"You better give me a grandson. God knows I won't get one from Dennis."*)

—and bought a house he would be happy to live in for the rest of his life. Could he have a more perfect life? Son? Wife?

Max briefly wondered if Lauren was in Washington DC yet. He looked at the clock. No, of course not. She wouldn't be there for another hour or so. And she wouldn't be in Paris until about three in the morning Missouri time—nine France time.

Max did just what he'd planned on doing—lost himself for a few hours doing laundry and preparing for tomorrow's classes—until he finally decided to call it quits. He folded the clothes from the last load from the drier, mostly Logan's stuff, and took it upstairs.

He was appalled when he opened Logan's dresser. His son may have stopped throwing his clothes hither and yon, but the contents of the drawers were a mess. Max supposed while Logan might be trying to impress Devin with a clean room, he wasn't so worried about what his friend *couldn't* see. Max decided he might as well be thorough, took the messy T-shirts out, and began to fold them.

That's when he saw the strip of pictures.

Max really didn't mean to be nosy when he pulled them out for a look. It was just that photos like these were always fun. He and Lauren had visited a photo booth or two when they were dating.

The first of the four pictures was typical of such strips. Logan and Devin with goofy grins, staring cross-eyed at the camera. The second had Devin sticking out his tongue far enough to make Gene Simmons jealous, and Logan was holding his hand in the devil-horns fashion behind his buddy's head.

The third wasn't as typical, though.

Sort of intimate for two boys. Their foreheads were pressed together, as well as their noses and they were looking into each other's eyes.

Huh.

But it was the fourth that caused Max's eyes to pop in shock.

The boys were kissing.

Chapter FIVE

WYATT PRACTICALLY shoved Sloan out of the still-moving car when they got back from the movie (where Wyatt had eaten a huge bag of popcorn as well as a chili dog and a large Coke). The bear was tickled as could be; Howard had called and left several messages on Wyatt's cell phone while they had watched "a hoard of barely dressed warriors," and he was apparently sorry. More importantly, he hadn't gone to "play" with "Up-Chuck" Mueske.

Sloan could hardly blame his friend for wanting to rush home. He'd want to do the same if there were a lover waiting for him. Even a man who wanted to "play" with others, he supposed.

No. Not that. That was where he drew the line.

What if Asher changed his mind? What if he wanted to be in a relationship as long as it was an open one?

Shit!

Maybe. Anything other than an empty house.

So empty.

Sloan heard the ringing as he was unlocking his front door and ran to catch it. "Hello?" he said, snatching up the phone.

"You ready for that run?" asked Max.

The phone call took Sloan by surprise. He actually pulled the phone away from his ear and looked at it. Holy shit. He hadn't really expected Max to call. His neighbor really did want to go for a run?

He put the phone back to his ear. "Now?"

"Why not?" came the quick response.

"You-you ran already today."

"I cut it short on account of my wife needing a ride to the airport."

Sloan shook his head. He couldn't believe Max had called. They didn't even know each other. Was this a feel sorry sort of thing going on? "Max. I—I'm not in that good a shape. I'd just hold you back."

"Bullshit, Sloan. You look great."

"Huh?" *Max thinks I look great?*

"I bet you work out."

Straight. He's straight. Straight guys compliment each other's bodies all the time.

At least that's what I've heard.

"Yeah," Sloan said. "Sorta."

"Sorta?"

"Not like I should. None of that five days a week stuff."

Max laughed. "Look. We'll go to the track at WU and take it as slow as you want."

You're not going to let me out of this, are you? "You're not going to let me out of this, are you?"

"Nope."

Why? "Why?"

"I think you need it."

"I thought you said I look great."

Max laughed. It was a nice laugh. Like Mr. Kelso's. Deep, but not too deep. "I meant you need to get out of the house."

And just like that Sloan felt tears biting at the corners of his eyes. He opened his mouth to say something but found he had no idea what to say. Because he knew what Max meant. Get out of that *empty* house.

"We can get a bite to eat if you'd rather do that."

"Why are you doing this?" It came out wrong. More of an accusation than a question, and Sloan immediately regretted it.

"I don't know. Do I need a reason?"

"I-I...." What the hell. "Okay."

"Good. I'll be there in five."

"Jeez. Give a guy a minute to get ready. I don't even know what I'm going to wear."

"It doesn't matter. You don't have to impress me. Wear what you wear to the gym."

Sloan sighed. *I'm gay. I* have *to try and impress you!* He didn't say that out loud, of course. "Okay. But give me twenty minutes."

"No way. Fifteen."

And before Sloan could answer, Max hung up.

MAX WAS already waiting in front of the house when Sloan opened his front door. *Jeez. This guy wants to go for a run!*

Sloan quickly locked the door, set the alarm with the transmitter on his key ring, scrambled down the steps, and walked briskly to Max's car— a little white Scion xB. *Funny looking thing*, Sloan thought, just exactly as he did every time he saw one.

Max not only seemed to be in a rush, but he wasn't very communicative either. He barely nodded when Sloan got in and took off with a little screech of tires. They drove in almost complete silence until they got to Wagner University. It was only five minutes, but it seemed weird after their phone conversation, and the more he watched Max, the more obvious it became that the man had something on his mind. He kept clenching the steering wheel until his knuckles went white and biting his lip, then running his left hand through his short brown hair.

Sloan almost asked him twice what was wrong, then decided to simply wait. If there was something wrong—and it somehow involved Sloan—surely Max would bring it up eventually.

Once they parked and headed over to the fenced-in track, Max finally seemed to relax. They did their stretches, and Sloan had a hard time not staring—especially when Max did something that caused his T-shirt to hike up high and expose that furry, flat tummy and the tantalizing trail that went from Max's navel (just the slightest indent in that mind-boggling flat plane) down into his low-riding running shorts. Or when Max bent over or stuck a leg out just so, and the slit up either side of those silky shorts afforded him a glimpse of the band of his jockstrap and the round butt cheek it framed.

Sloan forced himself to look away. He wasn't a letch. But hell, how did he not look? He hadn't been laid in he couldn't remember when.

Oh. No, he had. Though it could hardly be considered getting laid.

It was when that big burly guy—Robbie? Something like that—had burst in on him in the bathroom at a party. Before Sloan even knew what was happening, the guy had locked the door—

God! Why didn't I lock it in the first place?

—and dropped to his knees and started sucking Sloan's dick. It was a testament to how inebriated he'd been that Mr. Burly had been able to do that much before Sloan tried to stop him. It was a pretty feeble attempt, though, because—*shit!*—that man could suck cock! Oh, and he was so much Sloan's type. Hairy-chested (Sloan could tell that because Mr. Burly was wearing a V-neck shirt), muscular, bearded—

Why was I ever attracted to Asher in the first place? He is so not *my type.*

—and then he'd hauled a big, gorgeous hard cock out of his own jeans, and as if Sloan had had no control of himself—

You fell in love with Asher because you were so desperate for affection you mistook a one-night stand for something more than it was.

—he was having a powerful orgasm, and the stud greedily swallowed him down, and thank God, the guy jerked himself off while doing it. Once Sloan had cum, he regained his senses enough to be totally horrified at what he'd done—

And you were embarrassed when Scott started pounding on the door asking what the hell was going on.

—and there had been no way he could have reciprocated.

Oh, the look on Scott's face when Sloan had opened the bathroom door. Scott had stared at Sloan with open shock.

"You guys didn't even clean up your mess!" Scott had said in the car later on their way home. "There was spooge all over the floor!"

Sloan's horrification had only increased at his friend's diatribe. All he could do was assure Scott that the "spooge" hadn't been his own. And that he hadn't even realized that Robbie or Bobbie had left it there.

"Thank *God* for that much. I might be able to sleep tonight. The idea that I cleaned up my best friend's—"

"You cleaned it up?" Sloan had asked, mortified.

"Well what the fuck was I supposed to do? Leave it and let the next person to go in there think I jerked off and left it on the floor?"

And he never lets me forget about that night either, thought Sloan.

"You ready?"

Sloan jumped and turned his head to see Max giving a few running steps in place.

Am I blushing? God, I hope not. At least he didn't catch me staring at his ass.

"Sure," he answered.

To give Max credit, he kept it really slow.

"CAN I ask you a question?" Max asked somewhere during the fourth lap around the track.

Sloan was grateful he used the treadmill at the school gym. Thank God he wasn't gasping for breath and embarrassing himself. The fourth lap made it a mile, and treadmill or not, he was getting tired. "Sure," he said, trying not to gasp for breath.

"When did you know you were gay?"

"Huh?" The question took him completely by surprise.

Max didn't say anything for a good quarter of the way around the track before he repeated the question.

"Well…. Uh…." Sloan thought about it for a moment, trying to figure just how to respond. "That's not an easy question to answer," he said. "I mean…." He took a breath. Talking and running wasn't necessarily easy, especially when he was getting winded. And because he'd been asked something that, as far as he was concerned, was pretty personal. "Looking back I see I was always gay. (pant pant) But it was really important to my mom—all she ever talked about—was that I have a kid. (pant pant) She wanted me to carry on the name and all that crap."

Max grunted.

"Don't know why she cared. Dad left us when I was a kid." He shrugged. "So I tried to be straight. (pant pant) Found this sweet girl in college named Jennifer…. Got engaged."

"You were engaged to a woman?" Max said it like Sloan had told him he had discovered electricity or something.

"Yes," Sloan shot back. "Look, can we take it down to a walk?"

Max nodded. "Sure. A mile is good for your first time."

Sloan found the comment pleased him. It soothed the sting he was feeling.

They slowed down, and Sloan took a moment to catch his breath. Max didn't say anything. Then: "Like I said, I was trying to be straight."

"Trying?"

"Yeah, trying. Sleeping with her was starting to nail the coffin lid shut. I couldn't believe how different sex was with her than with a guy, and all I'd ever really done was…. Well, never mind. Anyway, that was when Jennifer made this little mistake…."

"What mistake?"

"She asked me to be friends with her brother. Her *sexy* brother. Her sexy *gay* brother."

Another grunt.

Sloan glanced over at Max, who was staring directly ahead as they walked.

"She caught us in bed together."

Max stumbled. Not badly. By the time Sloan could react, the man was fine. "You…. You had… with…. Her brother?"

"Coop started in on me the minute we met."

"Kewp?"

"Short for Cooper. That was her brother." Sloan flashed back on Coop's face. So clear. Other faces from his past were beginning to go out of focus, just like his mother had told him they would. He had only the vaguest image of his father anymore. But not Cooper. He could see those flashing eyes, that mischievous smile, the dark blond hair. In fact, he'd looked something like Asher. *Hmmmm….*

"I resisted for a while." Tried to. Coop had known he was gay the second they met. Known that Sloan had wanted Cooper as much as Cooper had wanted him. But God! He was Jennifer's brother. There was something so… creepy?… about it.

"I knew if he got me alone I wouldn't be able to resist." Sloan had made sure Jennifer was always around whenever her brother was there. He hadn't allowed himself to be alone with Coop at any time. When Jennifer pushed him to have some one-on-one time with her brother, Sloan would have them meet somewhere very public. Never his apartment or Coop's place. "I don't know how she didn't see what was going on. He was so obvious sometimes."

Max gave another… well, the only word was "grunt." "Sometimes we can be blind."

Sloan sighed. "Then one night when Jennifer was supposed to be out of town, Coop stopped by with beer and pizza, and about the time we were done with the six-pack, he had me in bed. And my God! It was everything Jennifer never was!" Sloan hugged himself. He could see Coop, sprawled out on that bed, his head on the pillow, his eyes heavy lidded, his mouth pouting sensuously, and his cock hard with sexual need and excitement.

"Wait. You were sleeping with the girl?" Max stopped walking, put his hands on his hips.

"I told you that."

"You did?"

Max looked dazed. What was going on with the man? "We were doing it," Sloan said. "But I wasn't liking it, really. I didn't even like cuddling after."

Max looked at Sloan as if he were crazy. "I don't get it."

"Get what? I had sex with Coop and it was different than with Jennifer. *So* much better. I finally realized I *was* gay. It wasn't something I was going to grow out of."

"But if you *could* have sex with a woman, wouldn't that make you bi?"

Sloan shrugged. "If I am, I'm not *very* bi. A Kinsey 5.5 or something. Maybe even .75."

Max shook his head. Didn't ask what Kinsey was. Of course he *was* a teacher after all. He had to know about the Kinsey Report.

"But even that little bit," Max said. "You could have had a normal life. Married that girl. Had a family. Fit in."

"Oh, Max. I could have 'fit in' maybe. Had a 'normal' life. But I wouldn't have been happy. Being gay is more than liking dicks over vaginas. It's here." He laid a hand on his chest.

Max stared at where Sloan's fingers were spread. Seemed to study them, and didn't look up.

"In my bones. My heart. I wasn't *in* love with Jennifer. Never was." He started to walk again, not looking to see if he was being followed. With just those words, he felt the old guilt settling over him like a heavy blanket. He knew he had hurt her badly. She had been caught in the fallout of *his* mistakes. If only he could take it back. But of course, he couldn't.

Sloan sensed, rather than saw, that Max was walking with him. He didn't look. He felt too smothered by the shame. God, he wanted to take it back. "If only I had met Cooper first. I think that's all it would have taken."

"So he was the first.... He was your first guy?"

"The first I ever had *sex* with. You know"—Sloan felt his face heat up—"fucked with. But I still should have known. I'd played with my best friend all through high school. From the time I was fourteen."

"Oh fuck!"

Sloan turned just in time to see Max practically fall back onto a bench that was conveniently located right there. Otherwise the man might have fallen right on the ground.

"Max! You okay?"

"Fuck me," Max muttered.

I'd love to, Sloan thought.

"My son."

Son? "What about him?"

"I—I think he might be gay."

Chapter SIX

MAX HADN'T said a word for a few minutes after that, and hell, Sloan hadn't known what to say. He'd just stood there, looking down at his neighbor, trying to think of how to respond.

The first thing, of course, would be *Why do you think that?* But somehow, he knew not to say anything. Not yet.

So Sloan had waited.

And finally Max had stood and suggested that they get the hell out of there.

Sloan had followed him back to the car, and after they pulled out of the university parking lot and down University Blvd. to Green Street, Max finally said, "Want to get something to eat? I could eat a horse."

Sloan gave a shrug. "If you want."

"Is vegan all right?"

"Vegan?" He'd never eaten vegan. What did vegans eat? Well, vegetables of course. But—

"There's this place I like a lot called Café Namasté. Lauren doesn't like it much, so I usually have to go by myself."

"Sure," Sloan said. "Wherever. We're kinda stinky, though, aren't we?"

It was Max's turn to shrug. He lifted his arm and sniffed. Looked over at Sloan. "I think we're okay, but we can go back to the school and shower if you want."

Uhn-uh. No way. There was no way he was going to let himself be nude around Max. He'd spring a boner in one half less than no time.

"I don't have anything to change into. 'Sides, wouldn't it be faster to just go back home? I could be in and out fast."

Max gave a nod that seemed more distracted than anything else. "Sure." He nodded again. "Okay."

A few moments later they were home, and Sloan assured him he'd only be a minute. He dashed in, stared longingly at the shower, and wondered if he could take a quick minute.

Fuck it.

He splashed water on his face and through his hair, ran a wet washcloth under his pits and around his balls, and changed into some jeans and a polo shirt. He'd almost made it a T-shirt, but the dark blue looked so good with his hair and....

This is not a date, idiot. He won't even notice what you're wearing.

Sloan actually made it outside before Max, and he had enough time to wonder if he could have showered after all when Max came out onto his porch. "Sorry," his neighbor called over. "But Lauren phoned just as I walked in. She was boarding for Paris and only had a minute."

Sloan nodded. "Sure."

Max locked the door as Sloan did the same, and they met at the Scion, which was parked exactly between their two houses on the street.

Mom's house.

Would he ever think of the place as *his* house? Despite the fact that he'd spent most of his school years there, once he'd moved out it had always seemed like his mom's house rather than *their* house. Maybe it was the damned flowers.

Max walked up and surveyed the garden even as Sloan cursed it.

"The daffodils are looking amazing. See those?"

Sloan looked to wear Max was pointing. "Those are daffodils?" he asked. They were pink and multipetaled, and he didn't see a trumpet.

"Yup. They're called a Replete. Your mom was pretty excited about them too. I'm sorry she didn't make it long enough to see them."

Sloan's breath caught. He managed a nod. "Me too."

"They're beautiful, aren't they? Better than I hoped."

Sloan looked at them. They were lovely. "How do you know about them?" he asked.

"I planted them for her. She tried, but she was really sick that week. The chemo, you know."

Sloan did know. In fact it was the chemotherapy that made him give up his apartment and move in. "Where was I?"

"You were at work," Max said.

Sloan nodded. Felt his heart catch. Work. He'd felt so guilty he couldn't quit. Still did. But his mother had insisted. Said she could get to the doctor's herself. That the neighbor was always there to help.

Sloan snapped his head in Max's direction. This neighbor?

How could he have not known that? Known the fucking neighbor who took his mom to the goddamned hospital?

You were a little occupied.

Yes. Yes, he was. Occupied watching his mother die.

It had been horrible.

"You okay, Sloan? Hell. Of course you're not. I shouldn't have brought up the stupid flowers."

"They're not stupid," Sloan managed. "They're beautiful."

THE RESTAURANT was nice. Sloan wasn't sure how he hadn't seen it before, especially considering how many times he'd been down Green Street. Wyatt worked at the New Age store on this street, for goodness sake. It was mostly dorms and university housing and some weird little shops and cafes that appealed more to the college kids than anyone else. A comic book store, a sports clothing store, a coffee shop called The Radiant Cup 2, Wyatt's New Age & pagan store Treasures of Terra, and the vegan restaurant Café Namasté.

It was pretty nondescript from the outside. All natural wood, boards lined up vertically almost like paneling, and tinted windows, with its only bid for attention the gold painted letters of the sign.

The inside wasn't all that unlike the out. "Understated" is what Sloan would have said. Lots of blond, natural wood, plants, and paintings on the walls. The latter seemed mostly spiritual in some way. Not religious, really, although one large one was of a Buddha eye. Mostly the images were like a silhouette of a human figure glowing in rainbows of light— chakras maybe, Sloan thought—plants with Kirlian fields surrounding them, a shimmering pyramid, a brightly painted head of an elephant with a broken tusk. One wall had a gigantic mural of a woman made of flowers and leaves, rising up from a colorful field. Mother Nature perhaps? It made sense.

A young woman—simply dressed in jeans, a T-shirt with a miniature of that mural across the front, and a woven fabric belt—greeted them with a "Namasté" (as well as a blush and a "Hello, Mr. Turner.") and led them to a small table near a back corner.

"You are blessed," she said and left only long enough to bring back a carafe filled with water and two glasses. She filled them and told them she would be back after they'd had time to look over their menus.

Sloan glanced down at his and was lost.

C1: Muladhara: Curried lentils and golden potatoes with Indian spices over quinoa with fresh spinach, sprinkled with tamarind, and spicy mint chutney on the side. Enjoy brown rice as an alternative to quinoa.

Qwin-oh-ah? What the hell was that? What did tamarind taste like? And Sloan didn't have a clue how to pronounce "muladhara."

C2: Svadhisthana: A big bowl of our famous chili—you chose if you want it plain or spicy—with all the fixings, including black beans, diced tomatoes & onions over brown rice with avocado and sprinkled with cashew ricotta cheese.

Cashew ricotta cheese? Sloan couldn't even imagine what that meant. And if mu-lad-haray was weird, how in the world did one even begin to pronounce svadhisthana?

C3: Manipura: A unique version of pizza with a marinara sauce, tomato, fresh basil, red onions, nut Parmesan & cashew ricotta cheese served on a live sunflower crust.

Live crust? The idea almost gave him the creeps. Live? What the hell did that even mean?

Thankfully, Max rescued him. "If you have any questions, just ask. I can make some recommendations, though."

"What in the world does 'live' mean?" He pronounced it "liv."

"Well, it's 'lhyve,' not 'liv'—"

"Oh!"

"—and what 'live' basically means is that the vegetables are totally raw. Cooking vegetables can destroy their nutritional value and even chemically alter them into types of toxins and even poisons, free radicals, and well… other stuff. I don't always keep it all straight. But when you can have veggies raw, or barely heated, then they're better for you. Like their soups here? They make them in a blender and instead of heating them on an oven, they just blend them a little longer than you might at home, and the friction raises the temperature."

"Wow," said Sloan. He looked down at the menu again, then up at Max. It sounded a little kooky. New Agey. He would have to ask Wyatt if he'd been here. It sounded right up his alley. Well, except that Wyatt loved steak so rare it moved out of the way when you tried to cut it. "Poison?"

Max laughed. "Not like curare-poison, or arsenic or something like that. But something doesn't have to be cyanide to be poison to us."

"I don't think I understand," Sloan said.

Max smiled. "Don't worry about it. No lectures or sage advice. Let's just enjoy. By the way, the sage burger is delicious."

"Sage burger?" Sage was good in dressing on Thanksgiving, but in a burger? He found it on the menu. It didn't really say a whole lot. *Served either on a bed of lettuce or in a Kamut or flax bread and with optional pine nut cheese.* What was with all the nut cheese? *How do you even make cheese out of nuts?* "I don't know…."

"Or the vees-shoo-dah. That's one of my favorites and I think you might really like it."

Once more Sloan looked down. Part of him was just wishing Max would order. He found it.

C4: Vishuddha: Pesto polenta and a puttanesca sauce served over sautéed spinach & spaghetti squash and topped with our Brazil nut parmesan & fresh basil.

Well, there was yet another nut cheese. "What's with the cheeses made out of nuts? I mean how could nuts possibly taste like cheese? Why not just use—"

"Because they're vegan, not just vegetarian. So no dairy. Plus dairy is horrible for you. I mean, do you realize we are the only animal on earth that drinks milk *past* infancy?"

Sloan sat up straight in his chair. *Well, I'll be*, he thought. He'd never thought about that. But it was true. "But I thought we *needed* milk to get calcium."

"So a billion-dollar dairy industry would have us believe. When in actuality, not only is it not true, but daaare…. Oops! There I go again!" Max sat back and gave a roll of his eyes. "Sorry."

"No." This was interesting. "Tell me more."

"Not tonight. Tonight we just enjoy the food."

"Are you ready, Mr. Turner?" said the waitress, as if on cue.

Max looked at Sloan (with those intense and gorgeous blue eyes) and raised his thick brows. "Trust me?"

"Oh please," said Sloan. And thank God. *Yes, please order!*

So Max did.

THE VISHUDDHA was absolutely and amazingly delicious. From the first bite, Sloan's eyes rolled up in their sockets it was so good. The top was something that at first looked like a thin yellow kitchen sponge—he assumed it must be the pesto polenta—but was decidedly not anything used to wash the dishes! It dazzled the tongue, and God, the spaghetti squash tasted so close to pasta it was easy to forget it came from a vegetable. The sauce was very flavorful, and the Brazil nut parmesan really *did* taste like cheese. It was remarkable.

"My God," he said with a gasp after swallowing that first bite (and knowing even before he said it that he would be back for more). "I can't *believe* how good this is!

Max grinned like a kid, his blue eyes flashing. "I'm glad you like it." It was obvious he was pleased.

Sloan lost count how many times he said it. Over and over again he told Max how good the food was. And every time Max told Sloan how happy he was that Sloan liked it.

"I just can't believe vegetarian—*vegan*—food can be so good!" He grinned. "And so good *for* you!"

"I know. But I can't get Lauren here. She nibbles on my leftovers, though, and admits it's good, but she won't come with me. Hell, we hardly ever go out for dinner anymore. We hardly ever go to a movie!"

"How come?" Sloan asked, taking a drink of the lukewarm water they'd been served and reminding himself to ask again why there was no ice.

"It's her career," Max said. "It doesn't leave her much time. So it's mostly just me and Logan."

"Logan is your son?"

Max nodded.

"And you think he's gay?"

Max looked down at his nearly empty plate, gave another nod.

"How come?"

"He has this… friend. Named Devin. I'm pretty sure they're fooling around."

"Oh. Well." Sloan sighed. How to explain? "That's kind of normal. It doesn't mean he's necessarily gay. I mean, didn't you and a buddy ever jerk off together?" Sloan felt his face redden. He was doing that a lot around Max.

Sloan spared a quick glance up when Max didn't answer. He was digging in his shirt pocket instead. Then he pulled out a strip of paper. He opened it; it had been bent in half.

It was a photo strip, the kind you could get taken in one of those little booths with the curtains. Max laid it on the table in front of him. Looked normal. Two kids carrying on.

And then he saw the fourth picture.

"Oh," he said.

Sloan looked up. Bit his lip.

"Ah." He cleared his throat. "I think you might be right."

Chapter SEVEN

I THINK you might be right.

The words kept echoing around in Max's head.

I think you might be right. I think you might be right. I think you might be right.

God! Is this my fault?

Did I do this to you, Logan?

Max looked up at Sloan. He was sitting back in his chair, his brown eyes filled with…. What was it? Pity?

"Is it my fault?" Max asked.

"Of course not," Sloan replied.

Had he asked that question out loud?

"It's no more your fault than it's my mother's that I have red hair."

Sloan leaned forward, that red hair shining like copper under the little lamp that hung from the ceiling and over their table. Against the blue of Sloan's shirt it was… *gorgeous.* For one second Sloan took Max's breath away.

"It's genetics," Sloan continued. "And it might have come from your wife."

He doesn't have a clue what I'm talking about.

"Look," said Sloan. "You want to get out of here? Have a beer or something? Oh. You probably don't drink beer, do you?"

Max gave a bark of laughter. "What makes you think that?"

"The whole one-cup-of-coffee thing. Cheese made out of nuts. Running eighty times a week."

Max smiled. Tried to. "Not that many times. And a beer sounds great."

Sloan waved the waitress over and asked for the bill, began to dig in his back pocket.

"Nope," said Max. "I forced my vegetables on you. I can pay."

"I liked them," Sloan said.

"Nevertheless."

"Let me get the beer, then."

"As long as it's not PBR." Which wasn't true. Max knew he'd drink fermented moose pee right now.

Sloan grimaced. "Definitely *not* PBR."

THEY PICKED up a six-pack of Boulevard Irish Ale—were happy to find it since it was a seasonal for the brewery and its time was about done—and headed straight back to Max's house (which looked like it could be featured in *House Beautiful*, rather than the homey, almost kitschy, house that Sloan's mother had created) and out through the kitchen to his deck overlooking the backyard. It was more a wooden patio, really. There was a small "porch," for lack of a better word, right off the kitchen door, but there wasn't room on it for two grown men to sit comfortably. Not unless they wanted to fold up their chairs every time someone wanted to open the door to go into the house.

But the porch led down a flight of eight or so steps to a very nice deck indeed. It was surrounded by hedges and even had a railing. "Something to lean against," Max explained.

Max had turned off the deck light, but they were hardly sitting in the dark. The neighbor two houses to the north had a porch light you could see from orbit.

"What do they need such a bright light for?" Max wondered aloud when they sat down with their cold brewskies. "Do they want to bring in the mother ship from *Close Encounters of the Third Kind*?"

"It's probably a security thing," Sloan opined.

"In Terra's Gate? What are they worried about? The Bloods? The Crips?"

"We *do* live in a college town. Kids will perform pranks." Sloan took a drink of his beer. It went down cold with a rich, toasty finish.

Max cleared his throat and gave Sloan a long stare. He couldn't see Max's face very well—the light was behind him and made it look like his head was surrounded by a silver halo. "Don't you think *I* know it's a college town?" Max asked.

Sloan laughed. College teacher. Of course he'd know.

"I believe most kids are pretty good by nature. At least from what I've seen through the years in my classes."

Speaking of kids, does Max still want to talk about his son? Sloan wondered.

Oh God, Logan. Did I do this to you? Max wondered.

The two men were on the same chapter, just on different pages.

Then, at exactly the same time…

"Do you want to talk about Logan?"

"Could I have made my kid gay, Sloan?"

… and…

"Is it my fault?"

"No, Max. You didn't make him gay."

… and…

"No?"

"No."

"Are you sure?" Max asked

"I'm sure," Sloan replied.

"How can you be? You don't know."

"I *do* know."

And thinking…

Sloan: *Surely you know that. You're a teacher. They must have taught you that, since you might—would—have gay students.*

Max: *He doesn't know. How could he know? But don't gay men always know? They can sense it, can't they? Isn't that why he—*

"Max. My mom used to be worried about the same thing. Parents can't *make* their kids gay."

"But what about that whole gene thing they're talking about now?"

Sloan shook his head. "It's a game of chance. A parent has no more choice in their child's sexuality than they do the color of their eyes or their hair or if they'll be a boy or a girl."

Max dragged his fingers through his short dark hair. "Poor Logan."

Poor Logan? Sloan thought. *No. Poor Max.* He didn't seem like the kind of man to have problems with other people's sexual preferences. *But then his son isn't "other people."*

"Would it be that bad, Max? If Logan is gay? Would you still love him?"

"Of course I would," Max snapped. "But if he is, it's going to be so hard for him. I mean, Sloan. Wouldn't you rather be straight if you could be? Wouldn't life be easier?"

The comment jolted Sloan.

Easier?

For a long time Sloan had thought just that. Four years of high school denying he was gay, that he was playing with guys because he hadn't found the right girl yet. Or one interested in him. Until Coop, that is. He'd finally stopped fighting it then.

Sloan reached out and placed a hand on Max's thigh. "Max. It's not like when we were in high school. Nothing like when our *parents* were in high school. Being gay. Being lesbian. Bisexual…."

"Bisexual?" Max sat up.

"Gay people can get married now," Sloan continued. "DOMA is gone. I read somewhere that the most popular couple on television is Kurt and Blaine from *Glee*. Gay kids have role models. For the first time, maybe in history, gay people are growing up *knowing* they're okay. That they're normal. My God, think about it! What is their generation going to be like when they're our age? A generation who didn't have to hide who they are."

"Do-do you think?"

"I *know*."

Liar, thought Sloan.

Liar, thought Max.

You don't know that at all, they both thought.

Sloan and Max were quiet for a moment, then Max leaned back in his chair with a sigh. Muscles flexed in his thigh, and Sloan was suddenly conscious of where his hand was. He let go quickly—as if he had laid his hand on the surface of his—

(*his mother's*)

—electric stove. Instead of being burned, his hand tingled where it had been touching Max's leg. The muscles moving under that skin. God.

Sloan thought: *The hair is so soft.*

Max thought: *His hand is so warm.*

Sloan: *It's been too long.*

Too long since he'd touched someone. Too long since he'd been touched *by* someone—other than his friends.

Sloan: *Stupid. I'm being stupid. Max is straight. He's married. And I'm being selfish. I'm supposed to be here to help Max deal with his son, not get a hard-on. God. He can't see it can he?*

Max: *God. He's pretty. I can't believe how pretty he is.*

How had he not seen it before? Sloan wasn't masculine. Not macho at all. Decidedly not a girl, but still so pretty. His skin was like ivory. Even now he could see how red Sloan's hair was. Was it that color everywhere? Max had seen through the years that it wasn't uncommon for a redhead to have body hair that was more brown. Would Sloan's pubic hair be brown or bright red? How would that look with his creamy white skin? How would Sloan look right now without that damned porch light from two doors down?

In the light of the moon?

And how crazy was it that he was having such thoughts about Sloan?

Max: *I'm straight—*

Liar—

I need to be thinking about Logan!

And that brought Max back—like a snapping rubber band.

Gay. My son.... He might be—no. He is gay.

Two and two had met up and made four.

Was it "normal" for a fourteen-year-old boy to keep his room clean for another boy? He wouldn't want a girl to see his underwear on the floor, but he wouldn't care about another boy, would he?

Hadn't Logan started showering every night lately? No begging, threatening, pleading, or bribery had been necessary. Did boys Logan's age care if they smelled bad or not?

(*"Let me spend the night at Devin's. Please, Dad?"*)

Had Logan so much as mentioned a girl lately? Didn't most fourteen-year-old boys talk about girls all the time?

Cliff's son sure did, and both boys were the same age, although not classmates, of course. Cliff and his family lived in Kansas City.

(*"Oh my God, Dad! Katie's got this huge rack! And how!"*)

Did Logan even like any girls—women—from television? In the movies? There were no posters of sexy women on his bedroom walls. Hadn't he himself had a poster of Madonna when he was about that age?

Because Cliff did. You got one just like his—the poster where she was in the water with her hands over her head and you could almost see her tits. It was all Cliff ever talked about. Did I even give a shit about Madonna?

Try as he might, Max couldn't answer the question.

Did boys put up posters of women nowadays?

Wait. Logan had a poster of Tebow, didn't he? In profile with a sleeveless shirt. It was a fairly sexy poster too.

Crap!

Wait! He liked Lady Gaga! He had begged for her concert at Madison Square Garden on Blu-ray just this past Christmas. He even had a rather sexy T-shirt with her on it. Had begged to get it, too, for Christmas.

Wait… it also had "Born This Way" on it, didn't it?

Max actually felt his face grow numb.

"Sometimes we're blind," Max muttered.

"What?" Sloan asked.

Logan had been so distant lately. Max had been so close with his son the last several years. Except lately. Since about August. When school started.

When Logan met Devin.

(*"He's the coolest! His parents bought him this weight set. He's teaching me to work out! Look!"*—and Logan pulling up his shirtsleeve and making a bicep for Lauren to properly "oooh" over.)

And dammit, how often had Max offered to take Logan to the gym with him?

The sleepovers!

(*"Let me spend the night at Devin's. Please, Dad?"*)

He wants to spend the night at Devin's because they're lovers.

Max knew it. Except he didn't think of the word as "lovers." He thought of it as *LOVERS*—in big huge capital letters the size of the Hollywood sign. He thought it, and the word bounced around inside his skull like it might if he'd shouted it inside Mammoth Cave.

"Christ on a crutch! What do I do, Sloan?"

"Max, there isn't anything you *can* do. I hope you can accept him."

"Accept the fact that they're having *sex*? Would I let him sleep with a *girl* at his age? Should it make a difference that it's a boy?"

That made Sloan think. "No. I don't suppose so."

"Don't *suppose*?"

Sloan: *I was having a grand old time with Kenneth at that age. What the hell would I have done if Mom had found out? Made us stop?*

Max thought, *Me and Cliff fooled around that one time, didn't we?*

Once. Only once.

(*"You better give me a grandson. God knows I won't get one from Dennis."*)

And he had finally touched Cliff's—

(sexy)

—legs, and no, that hair hadn't been as soft as his own.

Max stood up very abruptly. "I guess I need to call Devin's parents. Make sure they get in there and stop—"

"Oh God—no, Max. No!" *He could scar Logan for life!* For one horrible second Sloan could *see* his mother walking in on him and Kenneth—cocks in hand. They'd never done much more than that. The image of his mother catching them was so real the hair on the back of Sloan's neck stood on end.

"Huh?"

"Max, you can't!"

"But—"

"If they're doing it, they're doing it. Leave it."

"But—"

"If you have Devin's parents interrupt them"—and he voiced his thought out loud—"you could scar him for life."

Max had a blazing vision where he pictured his father walking in on him and Cliff that one and only time. *Oh crap oh crap*—"Oh crap!"

Sloan nodded. "Oh crap is right."

"Then what do I do?" Max's question was almost a shout, and he cringed at his own voice.

"Right now you finish that beer," Sloan said. "Then you drink two more. And if you need it, take one of mine. I'm good for the cause. Then tomorrow you get up and maybe go for your run. Maybe cancel your classes. You think this through. Calmly. Step by step."

"But—"

"But nothing. If they're doing it, it's done. Deal with the aftermath. In the meantime, try not to think about it. I know it's not exactly an image that appeals to straight guys, especially when it involves their sons—"

But that wasn't what Max was thinking about. Not exactly. Different images were filling his mind. Images he'd built a wall against all his adult life.

The two men were reading the same book. Perhaps even the same chapter.

But they were on very different pages.

Chapter EIGHT

THE RINGING woke Max from a foggy sleep, and he had to fumble for the bedside phone. His head felt like it was stuffed with about a bale of cotton, and his tongue was so dry it was stuck to the roof of his mouth. What time was it? He grabbed the phone as his bleary vision took in the glowing red numbers on his alarm clock. Seven thirty. Jeez. He was usually up long before now.

"Hello?" He sat up and immediately regretted it. It felt like someone had hit him in the forehead with a rubber hammer. A big one.

"*Bonjour, chéri. Tu étais sous la douche?*"

"W-what?" *French. Lauren? God! I'm dying.* "I didn't catch that, Lauren."

She laughed. "I didn't wake you, did I? I waited until I knew you'd be up. I am *si* exhausted. I never sleep well on the plane."

"Oh. Sorry. I…." God! Would that hammer stop? Please.

"*Qu'est-ce que tu as*, Max?"

"Uggh. English, baby. Please?"

"Max? What's wrong?"

"I…. Nothing. I…."

"What, darling? Is everything okay with Logan?"

Slam! The memory was back. Logan. The pictures. Kissing a boy. Devin. Gay. Logan is gay.

And right now he's probably spooned up tight with—

"Max!"

Don't tell. Not yet.

"Logan's fine."

"Then what is it? Should I be worried?"

"No. No reason to be worried." *Tell her something!* "I had some beers last night, honey. Too many."

"Max? *You?* We drink *wine*. Not beer."

"I do, Lauren. Sometimes. *Good* beer."

Her voice grew stern. "Was it 'good' beer, Maximilian?"

Maximilian? "Yes. But I should have stopped at three." Which was true. He should have stopped at one. Beer was so much more fattening than wine. Not good for him at all. He couldn't even pretend it was good for his heart.

You wanted to forget.

No. Not forget. Not exactly.

Put off. Yes. That's it. Put off.

"Max? Are you there?"

"I'm here, baby," he said and slipped back down into the bed, his head sinking into the memory-foam pillow. Not feathers. One of the few things he'd insisted on, despite Lauren's protests. "You just woke me up is all."

"Well, maybe it's a good thing. You're always up by now. And here I was worried I'd interrupt your meditation."

Somehow Max thought he'd skip the meditating today. Jeez. He'd only had four beers. But considering he rarely drank more than a few glasses of wine with Lauren over dinner, perhaps one out on the deck in the evening, was it really surprising he was feeling like shit?

"What did you *do* last night, Max?"

"Nothing much," he replied. *Found out our son is gay.* "Went to Café Namasté."

"You got Logan to go there? I'm surprised."

"He likes it there."

"Oh please. A boy likes his pizza."

"Logan spent the night at Devin's."

In his bed?

"Again?" Lauren's tone surprised Max. Almost.... What? Alarmed? There was a long pause, and just as Max was about to ask if they'd been cut off, she said, "Max. I think maybe Logan is spending too much time with Devin."

Max sat up fast—and paid for it. Hammers on anvils. Stars before his eyes. "Argh," he moaned and fell back again.

"What?" came Lauren's voice from thousands of miles away.

"Why-why do you think he's—Logan's spending too much time with—

Gay!

"—Devin? He seems like a nice boy."

"*Chéri*, don't you think he's a little… *feminin?*"

"Devin?" No. Actually the boy had seemed a little, well, rough was the word Max had thought of when he'd met Logan's new friend. He hadn't really known what his son saw in the kid. They had seemed as if they didn't have anything in common.

Except they're both—

Max couldn't even use the word. It is all that he *had* thought of for about the last twenty-four hours, more or less.

Get used to it.

(*"Would it be that bad, Max? If Logan is gay? Would you still love him?"*

"*Of course I would."*)

"Max?"

"You're tired, honey," he said, trying to change the subject in a different direction. "And this hardly seems like a conversation that either of us should be having right now."

"I know. I should have brought it up before I left…."

No fucking kidding!

There was another long pause.

Then: "Max? Were you drinking alone last night?"

"Yes," he said and was surprised at how fast the lie came to his lips. *Now why did I do that?*

Be impeccable with your word. It was one of the mottos he lived by.

So why did he lie?

Because you were with Sloan.

So what? I don't have anything to lie about. All I did was have a few beers. Tell her.

No.

An image of Sloan flashed into his mind—the rash of freckles across his pug nose and cheeks. Those eyes.

Stop! Don't do this!

"Are you sure?"

"Of course I am," he shot back and cursed himself for the second lie. What was he doing? And now that there were two untruths, how could he take them back? He didn't lie to Lauren. He didn't *lie*.

Really? You don't lie?

You haven't lied to yourself for years?

"Fuck!" he cried.

"Max!"

"I'm sorry, Lauren," he said in a rush. "I'm so sorry."

"*This* is why you shouldn't drink, my husband."

"Y-yes," he returned. "You're right."

"And… so are you. This isn't the time to be talking about Devin. Let's Skype this in a day or so, *non*? We need to see each other's faces when we talk about this."

Don't want to do that!

"I have some things I need to do," Lauren continued. "I'm worn out and want to go to bed but I have to reset my inner clock. It's only after two thirty in the afternoon here." She yawned as if it were timed. Who knew? With Lauren it could have been. "Maybe you need another hour or two of sleep yourself?"

"Maybe I do. And I'm sorry for snapping at you."

"*C'est pardonné*," she said softly. "Forgotten."

"I love you, Lauren," he replied. And he did.

"And I love you, darling."

"What would I do without you?" he asked.

Be gay?

"I'm sure I have no idea. It would be no good, I'm sure."

"Yes," he said and thought of Sloan.

Why am I doing this?

"Good night," she said.

"Good night, Lauren."

There was a gentle click, and she was gone.

And suddenly Max had never felt more alone.

Chapter NINE

MONDAY MEANT the boys of the FF worked out at the gym. It was not a must-not-miss event like Porch Night, but they seldom missed it. Wednesday, maybe. Friday was a certain possibility. But Monday? No. It was a not-*want*-to-miss event. Because that was when all the college boys—trying to make up for a weekend of partying?—filled the place and the man candy was on display.

But today was even better than normal. The gym was packed. They couldn't figure out why.

"Spring break is next week," opined Sloan. "Maybe they know they're going to eat a lot of crap they shouldn't and are trying to get some kind of man booster."

"Next week?" asked Scott. "This is only mid-March."

"It's early this year," Sloan answered.

"But Easter isn't until April."

Sloan shrugged.

"Who cares why?" Wyatt grinned. "Let's just enjoy." Today he was wearing very small black shorts and a flesh colored T-shirt with a bare muscular chest on the front. From the right angle it almost looked good. From the side his paunch ruined the effect. Wyatt didn't care. He thought it was *hil*-arious. Especially the back, which had the word "SKINS" written on it.

"My *gawd*," hissed Scott. "Will you look at that guy in the blue one-piece? You can see the head of his dick!" The object of Scott's attention had his arms over his head and was doing what appeared to be an infinite number of chin-ups. How he was doing it with his hands gripped at the far ends of the bar was beyond Sloan. Regular chin-ups were a bitch!

"Ssshhhh," Wyatt hushed. "Do you want him to hear you?"

"Like he can't see you staring?" Asher pointed at the piece of equipment Scott *wasn't* using. "Are you going to use that, or can I?"

Scott glared at Asher and finished his set at the weight machine with grunts and groans. Then he climbed off the stool and relinquished the station to the muscle god among them. All four of them were working out today, and while none of them could hope to accomplish what Asher could, he was able to give them pointers when they were using a machine incorrectly. Scott desperately wanted a more muscular body and had a vested interest in using the machines properly. When he wasn't staring at men.

"Do you think he'll shower?" Scott wondered aloud to his friends while Asher added weight for his set. "I hope he showers."

"Probably not," said Sloan sadly. "The really hot ones shower at home."

"Or don't shower at all," said Wyatt with a groan. "They go home and fuck their girlfriends with all that work-out sweat."

"That's disgusting," said Scott.

"No it's *not!*" Wyatt rubbed at his arms. "Give me a man all covered in sweat *any* day!"

"Give me a man smelling of clean, fresh soap any day," Scott countered. "What do you think, Sloan?"

Sloan wasn't paying attention to the conversation or the young man in the more-than-skin-tight blue unitard. He was too busy watching Asher. The man was lifting nearly twice the weight Sloan had lifted and seemed to be doing it effortlessly. There was indeed sweat. It crossed Asher's forehead and wet the underarms of his shirt even though it was sleeveless. Asher thought that sleeves confined his workout. In fact the words printed across Asher's shirt said, "Abolish Sleevery." He'd gotten it from Wyatt, of course.

"Earth to Sloan," said Scott. "Come in, Sloan."

"Huh?" Sloan looked up at Wyatt and Scott.

Wyatt rolled his eyes. "He's busy, Scott. Leave him alone."

Asher stood and stepped away from the lat pulldown. "Why are we standing around?" he asked. "Someone could have been on the next machine."

"I am," Sloan said, embarrassed that Wyatt had caught him staring at Asher once again. Sloan scrambled onto the chest press and hoped he was doing it right. Half the time he couldn't remember if he faced the thing or had his back to it. When Asher didn't correct him, he breathed a silent breath of relief. The machine looked like a giant upside-down horseshoe with grips on either end. Unlike a bench, where the weight was pushed upward, on this machine the weight was pressed forward. The same muscles were used, but this was far safer.

He pushed. His eyeballs almost popped out.

"You want maybe I should lessen the weight just a tad?" Asher asked, leaning past him and not waiting for a reply. "This thing is set higher than I would try."

"Ah, thanks," Sloan replied and breathed in the scent of his friend, who was half-leaning on him as he adjusted the weights.

"I'm gonna see if blue-tights needs a spotter," Wyatt declared with a flip of his hair, which of course hardly moved with the amount of product he was using.

"You most certainly are *not*," Scott said.

"Don't do it," Asher advised. "He's free weighting a big load there, and I don't think you could help him if he got in trouble."

Wyatt sighed dramatically. He took Asher's place on the lat pulldown and fixed the weight level to the least among the four of them. "Maybe if I build up a little more mus-kells, I can help one of these hot menz in the future."

"Well, you better start pushing yourself a lot harder than that," Asher told him. "At this rate you won't be able to spot a third-grader."

"I don't want to strain myself," Wyatt said, and gave a huff. "What good will it do if I tear something?"

"Good job," Asher told Sloan, who had been trying his best on the weight Asher had set for him. He had been using more energy to appear as if he weren't about to have an aneurysm than lifting the weight. "Seriously, Sloan. I upped it another ten pounds from last week. You're looking good, man." He reached out with his big hands and grabbed Sloan's chest. "Looking real good."

A jolt went straight to Sloan's cock and he prayed he wouldn't bone up right here in front of everyone. God! The way Asher was touching him!

"Hey!" Wyatt gave a little yip. "Isn't that Mister Man?"

Asher let go and leaned back, and Sloan had to shake himself. He glanced in the direction Wyatt was drooling and to his surprise saw it was indeed Max. He had taken over blue-tights's position on the bench. There was quite a bit of weight on the bar.

"Oh fuck me," Wyatt said with a long sigh.

"Adam Levine is gonna fuck you before *he* does," Scott sneered.

Wyatt gave him a withering look. "Sooner *me* than *you*, string bean." He turned back to his object of lust.

In fact, all of them, even Asher, stood and watched. Max was wearing a tank top, and they could all see his muscles bulging as he pressed the bar at what had to be two hundred fifty pounds at least.

"Lord and Lady," Wyatt said.

"Damn," said Scott.

"I wonder if he'd get a look like that on his face while I fucked him," Asher said.

"He's straight!" Sloan all but shouted and blushed when his friends turned as one to stare at him.

One of Asher's brows rose. "Never stopped me before."

"No!" Sloan stood up. "He's my *neighbor*," he said with an intensity that surprised even Sloan. "He's *off*-limits."

"I think Sloanie boy has a new crush!" Wyatt grinned.

"I do not!" Sloan bit the insides of his cheeks. Why was he acting like this?

Asher's second brow raised. He smiled. "Is that true?"

Sloan shook his head. "No. I just don't want you guys making fools of yourselves *or* embarrassing me. I have to live next door to the guy."

"Does that mean you're staying in the house?" Asher asked.

Sloan froze. Did it? Is that what it meant? "I still don't know."

"Don't look now," Scott said. "But here comes neighbor man now."

They turned in unison to see Max approaching, towel over his shoulders. "Hey, Sloan." He gave a dazzling smile. "Good to see you. I *knew* you worked out with your build."

Sloan's vocal cords seized up. *My build? Max thinks I have a build?* He nodded, unable to respond.

"We've never seen *you* here before," Wyatt drawled.

"I usually work out early. I slept in this morning. Your buddy here got me drunk last night."

"Is that all he did?" Wyatt said with a swivel of his hips.

"Wyatt!" growled Sloan and felt his face catch on fire.

Max nodded. "Sure. What else?"

Wyatt looked at Sloan over his shoulder with a pout. He opened his mouth, and Sloan gave Wyatt a look that made his mouth snap shut.

"Sorry," Sloan managed. "Hope you didn't have a hangover."

Max shrugged. "A little bit, but that's the price you pay. Next time I'll stop one earlier. Or stick with wine. Wine never does that to me."

"Does what?" Asher asked.

"Gives me a hangover. Although it can just about kill Lauren if she's not careful."

"Who's Lauren?" Scott asked.

"His wife," Sloan said.

"So you guys are good friends of Sloan's?" Max asked.

"We're the *best* friends," Scott said.

"Sorry," Sloan apologized. He made introductions.

"I remember you from the other night," Max said as he shook Wyatt's hand.

Wyatt winced and wagged his hand when Max let go. "Strong grip," he moaned.

"Really?" Asher asked and took Max's hand. There was a long pause as the two of them obviously played that who-can-squeeze-harder game. It seemed to confuse Max, though. He gave Asher a funny look when he finally let go of Max's hand. Then with a little shake of his head, he focused his attention back on Sloan and gave a nod. "Getting a good workout?"

"Yeah," Sloan said.

"How much you lifting?" he asked and looked over Sloan's shoulder. "Wow. That's great!"

Sloan looked back and was surprised at the weight. It was thirty pounds more than he'd lifted. How the hell...? He glanced up and saw Wyatt wink at him. Apparently Wyatt had increased the weight.

"Ah...." What did he say? Should he tell his neighbor the truth?

"He just added an extra ten pounds today," Asher said before Sloan could decide what to do.

"Well, I said he looked good," Max told Asher. "Didn't I?" He looked back at Sloan.

Sloan gulped and gave a single nod.

"Well, I gotta hit the shower. Logan will be home soon, and I haven't seen him in a few days. I want to be there when he gets there."

"Who's Logan?" Scott asked, then whispering to Sloan, "The down-low boyfriend?"

"My son," Max said. He turned to Sloan. "Maybe we'll run tomorrow?"

Sloan gulped. "Maybe. Call me."

Max grinned. "I will." He nodded at the group and left them there, staring after him.

"God, look at that butt," Asher said.

"Did you see his basket?" cried Scott.

"Stop it!" Sloan's friends were pissing him off more by the second, and he wasn't sure why.

"I'm gonna go take my shower right *now*!" cried Wyatt.

Sloan reached out and grabbed Wyatt's arm in a viselike grip. "No, you're not!"

"Hey! That hurts."

Sloan didn't let go. "You're not going anywhere."

"I just want to see his dick. For fantasy material later." He made a rude jacking gesture.

"No!" The idea appalled Sloan. "You're *not*."

"Why?" Scott said. "Who amongst us hasn't done a shower run to see some hottie naked?"

"He'll know," Sloan said. "He's not stupid."

Wyatt rolled his eyes dramatically. "He doesn't even know I'm gay."

They all burst into laughter.

"What?" Wyatt put his hands on his hips.

"Wyatt," said Asher. "There isn't anybody who doesn't know you're a big old fag."

"What's that supposed to mean?" Wyatt asked indignantly.

"You're not exactly macho," Scott answered.

"Oh! And *you* are, with your thirty-dollar haircuts and your Versace glasses?"

"Having some class does not make me a fag!" Scott's brows came together and he gritted his teeth. He pointed at Wyatt's shirt. "At least I don't wear such ridiculous clothes!"

"Me? *Me?* At least I have my own style and don't let fashion magazines tell me what to wear."

"Enough!" commanded Sloan. "You all are embarrassing me!" And with that he stood up and walked to the next machine.

"Well, what's gotten into *her?*" Wyatt whispered, though not so softly Sloan couldn't hear him.

Asher bit his lip. "I wonder," he replied.

"Well, I don't care what our holier-than-thou friend says," Scott replied. "I'm going to go get a look—"

Asher's hand and considerable strength shot out and grabbed Scott by the shoulder in a sure grip.

"Hey!" cried Scott.

"You heard Sloan. You aren't going."

Scott opened his mouth to protest, but Asher glared at him.

"You *aren't* going!"

"Look. I haven't seen a man naked outside of porn and locker rooms in a long time. You gotta give me something."

"You can scope out all the dick you want," Asher said. "Just not the neighbor's dick."

Sloan could have kissed Asher. *Thank you,* he thought and began his set on the weights. And to his relief, Sloan's friends didn't run into the locker room to get a look at Max—at least that day. Sloan could only hope his neighbor would go back to his morning workout ritual (and that Wyatt wouldn't change his).

And yes, Sloan liked to check out the naked "menz," just like his friends. He wasn't about to eschew one of the benefits of being gay: the occasional ability to see a hot guy without his clothes at the gym. Fuck all that 'don't you think it's hotter to leave some things to the imagination?' shit. You had to use your imagination every day; why not take advantage of those times when you didn't have to? He was definitely curious what Max looked like without those few scraps of clothes he apparently chose as his usual attire (did he teach like that? If so, Sloan needed to consider going back to school!).

What red-blooded gay man wouldn't be interested? Was Max cut? Uncut? (Sloan liked both, but....) How hung was he? The bulge in his shorts promised something over average, even if it was mostly potatoes and not meat. (Sloan liked both, period, no buts.) Was Max as big as Asher (who was almost ridiculously large)? Smooth butt? Hairy butt? (Which would be nice, since Sloan always liked body hair. Sadly, God had chosen to give Sloan only a little red patch over his cock and in his pits and a light covering over his lower legs that was almost invisible unless the sunlight hit it just right or if it was wet.)

But no. Sloan had to live next door to the guy—

(*"Does that mean you're staying in the house?"*)

—and what if Max caught him looking?

So the FF waited until Max had left and Sloan waited until his buddies had showered and wasn't even in the mood (for once) to get his thousandth look at Asher's perfect nakedness.

Sloan waited and showered alone, with nary any man candy in sight.

Chapter TEN

MAX WAS back in the locker room thirty minutes after he'd left—just enough time for Sloan's friends to be done and on their way. He was in a panic. He didn't have his wallet, and was there any feeling worse than that?

The whole day had been agony. The hangover had only been a part of it. The extra hour or so of sleep had helped, but in the end he'd resorted to a Bloody Mary—at least he'd used Van Gogh vodka ("If you're going to drink vodka, then don't waste your time with shitty vodka." That's what Lauren always said, and he couldn't agree more). Alcohol wasn't his usual way of dealing with problems or difficult situations—the opposite in fact. But then he didn't usually wake up with a pounding headache, a product of drinking more than he usually did in the first place. Karma he supposed. Didn't the Buddha teach that alcohol was a poison that clouded the clarity of the mind? To make matters worse, hadn't he skipped his meditation today?

And how absurd was it that he'd gotten so messed up over four beers? He must be getting old.

But it was the issue with Logan—

(the gay issue)

—that he was so troubled over. Troubled wasn't the right word, though. It was worse than that.

Gay. My son is gay.

It wasn't even that Max had a problem with homosexuality. He loved his brother dearly. He loved Dennis's partner (but boy hadn't their father all but had a heart attack—not only was his oldest son a "fag," but he'd chosen an African-American as a partner. Of course, he hadn't used the words "African-American" or "partner").

Max had gay students. He had gay neighbors. Kit Jeffries from two doors down had been around long, long before Sloan, and that didn't bother him in the least. But try as he might, Max just couldn't shake the idea that life would be hard for Logan if he were, in fact, homosexual. Sloan's assurances hadn't done anything to alleviate Max's fears.

(*"For the first time, maybe in history, gay people are growing up knowing they're okay. That they're normal."*)

The fact that Logan's school had a gay-straight alliance group did squat. The world just wasn't made for gay people. Sure the times were a changin' (as Bob Dylan used to sing), but they wouldn't change enough in Max's lifetime and probably not in Logan's either!

There would be no children.

(*"You better give me a grandson...."*)

Hell! What *was* his father going to say?

But Max knew. It would be something like:

"Jesus F'in' Christ, son! One job! That's all I gave you. One job. Your fairy brother ain't doing it. And you? One kid. One. What did I say? At least two. Two boys. And now the one you shot out is a pansy just like his uncle. Hell! I failed with both of you. The best part of me ran down the inside of your mother's thigh."

Max's gut clenched at the thought.

He's going to blame me.

(*"A parent has no more choice in their child's sexuality than they do the color of their eyes or their hair or if they'll be a boy or a girl."*)

The sudden memory of Sloan's words did nothing to help either.

"But what *about* heredity?" he'd asked Sloan. "Generations of dark-haired people aren't likely to have—well—a redheaded kid."

"True," Sloan had been willing to admit as he'd handed over that hangover-inducing fourth beer.

"Families can pass on diabetes," Max said. "There's a lot of that on Lauren's side of the family. She could have passed on the dis—"

"Hey!" Sloan had snarled. "You aren't comparing being gay to having a disease, are you?"

"Why not?" Max had almost returned. He stopped himself. But he *had* said, "If everyone were gay, we'd die out as a species."

"But everyone *isn't* gay, Max. Just like everyone doesn't have red hair. Besides, plenty of gay people have kids. Gay men and women who got married because they thought they *had* to—"

God!

"—and there's adoption. Even surrogates. God knows my mom kept reminding me of that. All 'cause she saw it on that show awhile back called *The New Normal*."

The worst of it was that Max had no idea what to do. Did he tell Lauren? He was going to have to at some point. Did he talk to Logan? Hell! He was going to *have* to! There was no choice there. And when he did, what did he say? Did he tell Logan he found the pictures? Logan would think he was snooping.

"Yeah," Sloan had agreed. "He probably will. So don't lie about it. You tell him exactly what happened. How you found them. Be *honest*. Hell, if his drawer hadn't been a mess, you wouldn't have found them in the first place."

Okay. So he let Logan know he'd seen the photographs and let the cards fall where they may. Then what?

Well, for one thing, Max knew he was going to have to stop the sex. Logan was too young, boy or girl. He knew kids did it—Max wasn't so naïve to think otherwise—but that was not only how teenage pregnancy happened, it was a cause of the rise in HIV transmission in teens as well. But it was beyond that. A kid just wasn't mature enough for sex at fourteen.

Again Max's stomach clenched.

"You don't even *know* that they're doing anything, Max."

"They're kissing!" Max had cried. "You think they aren't fu—" He hadn't been able to finish the word.

"Max, an awful lot of fourteen-year-olds kiss or hold hands and don't do anything else."

"That's because an awful lot of fourteen-year-olds don't have a perfect opportunity to do more than that. Parents don't let boys and girls sleep over. But what parent stopped two boys from spending the night at each other's house? Boys! All those hormones? Behind closed doors? Hell! When I was his age—" Again, Max's mouth had shut with a snap.

The hair on Cliff's leg had been coarser than his own. His erection had been shorter too. But thicker.

Then to Max's surprise, he felt his cock shifting in his shorts at the memory of that day twenty-some years ago.

"Fuck!"

"You don't know that they're doing that. I mean. Well. I didn't. My buddy and I didn't. Pretty much all we did was jerk each other off a lot. Even straight boys jerk off together."

Max's jaw clenched.

My fault. Is this my fault?

"Max!"

"What do I *do*, Sloan?"

"You drink that beer. Then tomorrow you get on Google. You see what the experts have to say. I'm sure Dan Savage has something to say about the subject. You tell Logan you know and you're concerned, but that you still love him. You let him know you always will. You will, right?"

"Of-of course."

So Max had googled it. And Sloan was right. It seemed everyone from Anne Landers to Pat Robertson and his so-called "Focus on the Family" had something to say on the subject—some of it horrifyingly ugly.

The problem was, how did he know who was telling the truth and who was just promoting their own agenda? Making up statistics rather than reporting something real. And what was real? What to believe? It was Benjamin Disraeli who said that there are three types of lies—lies, damn lies, and statistics (although some people credited it wrongly to Mark Twain).

The diametrically opposed articles and essays only confused Max more. He'd get promising information from one only to have it possibly squashed by another. The advice was as wide and far apart as the sides of the Grand Canyon. Everything from sending Logan to antigay camp to having a smiling meeting with the boys and both sets of parents. The former swore homosexuality was an abomination and that Logan's immortal soul was in danger, and the latter promised they were at the beginnings of a new and enlightened age.

Max did indeed cancel his classes for the day, or turned them into study halls—uncharacteristically letting his students have extra time to finish essays that were due at the beginning of class that day.

When Max finally realized it was only a couple hours to when Logan would be home, he headed for the gym. A hard workout always helped him. It was part of his religion, like running. The energy he exerted, the endorphins released, made him feel closer to—well, maybe not God, exactly. But something that was powerful and all-encompassing and very ancient. Something bigger than himself.

The steam room was magic too.

Then the beating of the hot shower.

Max had left the gym after the coincidence of seeing Sloan again and headed for the grocery store. He supposed he shouldn't have been all that surprised to run into his neighbor since Sloan *had* mentioned that he worked out. There were only two gyms in Terra's Gate, and one of them was the college facility that for a nominal charge anyone could join. And it had been an unexpectedly nice surprise, hadn't it?

He'd been smiling, thinking about the situation when he'd gotten to the Thriftway to pick up a few items for dinner. That was when he'd realized his wallet was missing. He'd flown back to the gym and hadn't even stopped at the front desk to see if it had been turned in—had run for his locker in the futile hope it would be there—

(and how could it be? Who would give up the opportunity to take it, even though there were only a couple of twenties in it? But his ID. His cards. Pictures of Logan as a baby!)

—and he'd flung open the metal door—BANG!—and of course the wallet wasn't there….

But it was.

It was up on its end, looking like a tiny pup tent, and the dark color had prevented him from seeing it right away in the shadows of the locker. Maybe it had prevented someone else from seeing it as well?

Relief washed through him as he took a great inward breath—losing the wallet would have been the capper for the day—closed his eyes, pressed the wallet against his chest, and leaned back against the lockers, feeling a rush of gratitude.

Thank you, God. Thank you.

And when Max opened his eyes, it was to the sight of a man taking a shower.

Through the steam, it was just a glimpse: wide shoulders tapered down to a narrow waist and high buttocks. Max looked away before he was caught, put a foot up on the bench and busied himself with his shoelaces so he could more discreetly look up without appearing to. He'd gotten quite adept at that through the years. There was a flash of red through the billowing white. The figure was all but disappearing in the steam. As pale as the man was, Max realized it was that bright hair that must have caught his eye.

Like Sloan, he thought.

Then the man turned, arms raised, muscles flexing as he began to scrub at that red hair, and when the fog parted for a moment, Max quite suddenly saw it *was* Sloan. Max almost gasped at the beauty of his neighbor. That skin. Flawless. The grove down his back, riveting. That butt, high and round and deeply dimpled and perfect. Sloan continued to turn, tilting his head back, ready to rinse off the soap that filled his hair.

Max forced himself to look away—as much as he wanted to see all of Sloan—feeling his cock filling as he strode from the locker room. What if Sloan had seen him looking? *Looking? Hell. Staring. God! Am I showing?*

Max glanced down, saw he wasn't noticeable through his soft gray shorts yet (thank God for jockstraps), and dashed from the gym—ignoring the greetings from a couple of his students—and out to his Scion.

Shit, he thought, sitting in his car, hands tight on the wheel.

Proves it!

Fucking proves it!

My fault. Logan. I'm sorry. I passed it on. Like fucking diabetes.

Because Max had always known he liked men.

Knew he was feeling more excitement than his friend Cliff that one and only time a million years ago (or so it seemed) when they were both high school freshmen. The same month his brother had told the family he was gay, and his father had commanded Max to be straight.

Luckily—*thank you, God!*—Max liked girls too. He always had. Had always loved to be around them, hang out with them. Holding hands was fun and made him feel grown up. They were so pretty—especially when they had long blonde hair. He loved the way it swayed around their shoulders when they walked. He never found girls annoying like many of his friends did. He could even go to malls with girls and wait while they tried on clothes. In fact, Lauren had said that was when she knew she wanted to marry him, that she realized she had already met the right man while still in high school.

The right man?

He was the *right* man.

He loved Lauren.

And so what if her body—the bodies of women—had always seemed… what? Alien to him? No. That word sounded awful. Mysterious? That was a little better.

The planes and angles were so different from those of a man—wider where a man was narrow and narrow where a man was wide—but women were still lovely. Who didn't love the Venus de Milo? Who could deny its beauty?

What difference did bodies make anyway? Bodies were *just* skin and muscle. "Bags of mostly water" as some science fiction show or other had once said. Water and a few pounds of chemicals. It was the person *contained* in the body that was important. Breasts or vaginas or cocks? Nothing!

Nothing.

Max let go of the steering wheel and stuck it with his fists.

Not important.

Not important.

Not important!

Max closed his eyes again, trying to relax, but instead Sloan's body—creamy pale skin, muscles playing beneath it, those impossibly high and round buttocks—filled his mind.

It would be so much easier if Lauren were here. She was his shield. She had been since high school. Whenever the desires would start to get too overwhelming, he would lose himself in her. Buy her flowers, take her to dinner, *make* her dinner. Take her away on a romantic weekend trip to a place where they were sure to be surrounded by heterosexual couples, and he would wrap that world around him like a blanket.

But now? With Lauren gone? For *two* months?

"Fuck!" he shouted.

Two kids who had been walking by froze and stared at him through the windshield with wide, startled eyes. Max felt his face burn, and he couldn't meet their gaze.

He had to get out of here. Go home. Logan would be there soon, if he wasn't already.

Max's stomach filled with lead.

God.

With a sense of dread, Max started the car and pulled out of the parking space.

Chapter ELEVEN

THE HOUSE seemed especially empty. Sloan felt it the minute he unlocked the front door—hands full of mail and some package addressed to his mother, and what the hell could it *be*?—and pushed it open. It swung open at his unintentional hard push and hit the wall with a bang. It echoed as it would only in a house devoid of furniture or even rugs.

Sloan found he didn't want to take another step. For a long moment, he just stood there on the rag rug—one his mother had made—and looked into the living room. It was all in shadow; he hadn't flipped the light switch yet, hands still full. Even with the golden-yellow walls it suddenly seemed… unwelcoming?

Or did he just *want* to feel unwelcome?

Suddenly, he felt like a stranger in the house, which was ridiculous because he'd lived here for years before moving out on his own.

But it didn't *feel* like his home anymore.

It was his *mother's* house.

There was a chill then, gooseflesh skimmed up his arms and….

God.

He felt something else. Like… a presence?

"Mom?" he asked before he even knew he'd done it.

The moment passed, and he laughed at himself and the laugh didn't echo. He shook his head and rubbed his arms and was glad no one was there to see him act like such a fool.

Except he wasn't glad he was alone. The house was too *damned* empty without his mother, and he didn't know what to do.

Sell it.

The thought came to his mind like a bubble floating to the surface of a pond. Pop!

It wasn't the first time he'd had the thought either.

Please don't, came his mother's voice. It wasn't a ghost. Just what he knew she would say. *At least not yet. Wait*....

Sloan stepped into the room, closed the door, and put his keys in the little basket that hung from the doorknob.

I never, ever *lose them that way*, said the memory of his mother once again.

Echoes.

Empty. Too damned empty without her there. She had always *been* there. His mother had been larger than life, and when she set her mind to it, she was a force to be reckoned with. Naïve and opinionated, she changed her mind only slowly, like the Colorado River grinding away at the stone to form the Grand Canyon. Centuries had to pass.

"You're what?"

In that moment, Sloan could see her blinking eyes. *See* her set the can of Endust on the end table and plop down abruptly on the couch with the pattern of huge roses that looked painted on the fabric. The memory was so real Sloan could feel himself sitting down next to her, and he sat now—same place, same cushion. He looked at the empty space next to him as if she were still there.

"Gay, Mom," he said.

"Gay?"

More blinking, her hands clenching and releasing, clenching and releasing the small pillow with a needlepoint rose that she had pulled into her ample lap. Her work, of course.

"Yes, Mom."

"But you're getting married."

"No, Mom. It's over."

"But it *can't* be!" She leapt to her feet. "You've talked to Pastor Swindoll. Jennifer has picked out her colors! We chose the bridesmaids' dresses."

They had. Sloan's mother and Jennifer together since Jennifer's own mother had passed when she was only twelve.

His mother began to pat at her bright red football helmet of hair, all but shellacked with spray (and how many times had Sloan teased her about how she was one of the primary agents of the hole in the ozone layer). "This is all just a big misunderstanding. Jennifer has gotten the wrong idea. I'll call her."

She'd started for the phone.

"*Mom*. There's no misunderstanding. I'm *gay*." He had to make it clear. To make sure she didn't have any "hope." How else would she get to a point where she could accept him? No need to tell her that Jennifer had caught him in bed with her brother. No. None at all.

She turned, eyes wide now and overly bright. "But honey…. What about grandchildren?" And that's when she burst into tears.

It broke Sloan's heart. It broke it again now. He'd held her for a while, all the time her saying over and over that she didn't understand and could it be her fault? Was it something she had done wrong? Was it because she hadn't remarried and given Sloan a strong male role model, and was she too masculine? Imagine! *His* mother, masculine!

Then she'd gone to her room, and he'd left, feeling as if his heart had been torn in two.

But a week later she'd shown up at his apartment—in Terra's Gate the college didn't require he live in the dorm—with a dish of lasagna. And a platter of his favorite cookies: peanut butter with a Hershey's Kiss. She usually only made them for him for Christmas, so he knew this was something unspoken for her—and he didn't make her speak it.

Sloan would give ten years of his life for some of those cookies right now.

He was a terrible baker—he'd tried to make some. Not from scratch, but he'd bought one of those tubes of the frozen stuff from the grocery store, and he'd burned the first batch and the second? They'd been okay. Nothing like his mother's. They were too small, and the Kisses were absurdly large for their size, and in the end he threw them away. They were like Always Save ground pepper after experiencing fresh ground peppercorns served over food at a fine restaurant. No comparison.

Sloan's heart grew heavy. He could feel a dull cloud sweeping over him, felt as if a crying storm was on its way. But no. Once again, it wasn't happening. Wet eyes, yes. But no tears.

What the hell was wrong with him? Why couldn't he let it out?

He looked around the room. It suddenly seemed cavernous without her. She had always been the star of this show. Hell, she had *been* the one-woman show.

And now she was gone, and Sloan didn't know what to do.

"I failed you, Mom. No grandkids. Sorry."

Chapter TWELVE

LOGAN WASN'T home when Max got there. He checked his watch. Shouldn't he be? Well… maybe not. Logan frequently did stuff after school. Helped decorate for the dances, worked with the theater team to design and build sets, even helped the costume department. And he'd been in more than one play. He was actually quite good. Max and Lauren had been very proud of his performance in *You Can't Take It With You.*

Had Logan mentioned rehearsals coming up? It seemed to Max that he had. It was so hard to keep it all straight. The older Max got, the faster time passed. Programs that his son said he was going to get involved with came and happened and then went with an almost alarming speed these days.

Theater.

Didn't a lot of gay people get involved in theater? Oh God. Had Logan *ever* even once gone out for sports? A shop class? Shown any interest in ROTC? No. He hadn't. He ran, but never tried out for the track team. No, the most he'd ever been interested in was being an assistant to the coach, helping before and after games, passing out towels in the locker room—

Max groaned.

My God. Sometimes we're blind. So damned *blind.*

He glanced down at his watch again. Hell, Logan wasn't really late at all, was he? Ten minutes. Anything could account for that. Talking to a teacher about a grade. Bullshitting with some buddies. A fascinating car accident he'd stopped to gape at.

Kissing Devin.

"Oh God oh God oh God," he said. "What am I going to do?"

He still didn't have a clue. Any minute—Max checked his watch again—Logan was going to walk through the front door.

Max began to pace.

Stop Logan and his friend from having sex: that was number one. Everything he'd read agreed on that point. Fourteen was too young to have a sexual relationship, boy or girl, gay or straight. Maybe there were times or places where a boy was considered a man by fourteen, but not today and not in *this* world. And what about physical injury by not knowing what they were doing? Health? Safety?

Max froze. Shit. Logan had access to the Internet and worshipped his computer. He'd probably watched a step-by-step how to have gay sex video. He probably knew more than Max did—which wasn't a hell of a lot.

That disturbed Max. A lot. He'd watched gay porn a few times so he could see what two men really did. It had taken him years to build up the nerve to watch any. He'd been way too afraid to rent it. What if someone found out? He didn't want to buy it. What if Lauren found it? Then came porn on the Internet, and it had still taken him forever to build up the nerve to download it. He'd heard way too many stories of viruses and such. What if he did something horrible to his computer? Finally he'd found a site he was willing to trust, and it had still taken him another forever to do so.

It had disgusted him.

Max remembered from college that porn had no plot. He didn't know why it surprised him that gay pornography didn't have any either. But at least the straight stuff he had watched had the pretense of a story, no matter how silly. But when a guy goes in to get a physical, and in what couldn't have been much more than about fifteen seconds, the doctor was sucking his cock and then fucking him without a condom? Who was supposed to believe such a thing? And a doctor? Not using a condom? What message, subtle or not, had that given impressionable young men?

In desperation, Max had watched a few more, but they were all the same.

Two men approach each other in ridiculous circumstances: a man is getting his car repaired at a garage, and suddenly a dangerous looking mechanic is forcing him to his knees and hauling out his cock. A man wakes up on a beach and is told the plane he was on has *just* crashed, and even though he's injured and bleeding, in the same fifteen seconds or so, he and another man are sucking each other off.

Is that what it was like? Did gay men really fantasize about such quick encounters? If he had caved in to his desires, would the sex have been random and indiscriminate and anonymous?

Experience made him believe that might be the case. Two years ago he'd been out of town at a convention. The teacher that he'd been paired up with to share a room had hit on him the first night. A married man too. He hadn't been subtle either. Bastard claimed he'd spotted Max as a "fairy" the minute they'd met.

Max had requested another roommate. No. Demanded.

Max looked at Dennis and his lover, and they seemed to be in love. But were they? Or did their kind of love mean one-night stands with any other gay man they met? One more reason not to bend to the temptation to have sex with another man. As a married man, what could he have with another man? He could have anonymous sex. He could cheat on his wife. That was something he didn't want to do. Couldn't do. Would never do. Trust was a rare thing. He wouldn't betray the trust Lauren had given him.

Although there was a part of him that thought he'd betrayed her the moment he asked her to marry him. Certainly the day he'd given her his vows. In a way, wasn't he cheating all along?

Max shook himself, began pacing again.

Anonymous sex. Was Logan involved with that? He knew what went on in the library bathroom at the college. Did things like that happen at the high school?

Getting ahead of myself, aren't I?

What's going to happen when I tell Logan they have to stop? I mean, I can't make *them stop. I can ask. I can insist. But he's going to do what he's going to do! Where there's a will, there's a way.*

And how would he like it if he were making love with someone, the deed was done, and he loved it—and he was told he had to stop?

I would hate it!

He could run away! Fourteen-year-olds have done that since time immemorial.

And how would he survive?

Max suddenly pictured his son and Devin standing on some street corner selling themselves, turning tricks to be able to live. Like Keanu Reeves and one of those Phoenix boys, he couldn't remember which, in that Idaho movie. My Own Idaho? No. *My Own Private Idaho.* That was it. He had only seen part of it, and it had made him way too uncomfortable to keep watching. But they were hustlers, weren't they?

And what horrible things could happen to Logan? He could be murdered, that's what! Some serial killer could kill him and Max would never know. Or he could get AIDS. Didn't hustlers learn they could make a lot more money if they didn't make their customers wear condoms?

No! No no no no!

Max stopped pacing, sat down on the arm of the couch.

Getting ahead of myself. Logan isn't going to fucking run away and become a hustler! Letting my imagination get away from me. Max shook his head, glanced down at his watch.

I hate this. I hate it. Being a parent is the worst thing on the planet. You think it is going to be fun and wonderful. You're going to dress them up in cute costumes for Halloween and root them on when they join Little League. People are going to look at your son and tell you what a chip off the old block he is.

But nobody prepares you for all the other shit.

From colic to biting their best friend in preschool to bad grades and setting off the fire alarm. Of course, Max was the one that had done that. Set off a fire alarm at school about a trillion years ago when he was in second grade. It had been an accident, but no one had ever believed that, even his father. *Especially* his father.

So Max had decided then and there he would *never* doubt *his* child.

But he had, hadn't he? Because sometimes kids lie. They aren't perfect, no matter how you raise them. Logan had never given Max too many reasons to distrust him. Not too many.

And then there were all the childhood traumas! Like when Logan broke his arm in the fourth grade. How had *that* been? It had been horrible. Max had cried as much as Logan had. He'd just done it locked in the stall in the restroom at the hospital. He'd had to be brave for Logan, and that had been one of the hardest things he'd ever done.

Until now.

Until he found out his son was just like him.

He liked his own sex.

Maybe he's bisexual too. Maybe he likes women. Maybe I can make him see the wisdom of putting the part of him that likes boys aside. Show him that as a bisexual he can choose *to ignore that part of him. To take the path of heterosexuality.*

Quite unbidden, the memory of Sloan standing nude in that shower—turning slowly, more and more of him becoming visible—sprang to Max's mind. Max had fled before he saw everything. But now he wondered. Couldn't help but wonder. Would his penis have been as pale and creamy and lovely as the rest of him? Would Sloan's pubic hair have been as bright red as the hair on his head? Max wanted to know. He *wanted* to see Sloan naked. Of course that wasn't going to happen now, was it?

I should have waited just another few seconds.

But what if he saw me? Saw me standing there, practically drooling.

To Max's surprise, he very abruptly wanted to cry. It was all too much. The years of *not*. The years and years of not even once—

(well, sort of once, and hadn't holding Cliff's cock in his hand been about the most exciting thing that had ever happened to him in his whole life?)

—allowing himself to be with a man the way he wanted. Never touching. Not just a cock, but skin. *Anything.* Never getting to feel another man's chest. To see how the muscles felt in comparison to breasts. Never kissing—

(kissing! The thought almost made him dizzy)

—another man, seeing what the stubble on a man's upper lip might feel like against his own. Or a beard!

Or just the strength of another man.

Or taking a cock into his mouth.

What must that be like?

Max trembled at the idea.

Which only proved it was his fault Logan was gay.

Of all the things I could have passed on to him, I passed on a curse.

Max turned at the sound of a key in the door. It opened and there he was. Logan. His son grinned. "Hey, Dad," he said and slung his backpack onto the couch.

Chapter THIRTEEN

AFTER A while, Sloan stood up and went to the kitchen, opened the refrigerator, and reached for a beer. That's when he realized he still had the package addressed to his mother under his arm.

He let the door shut and looked at it. There were holes in the side. Weird. Max reached into the first drawer next to the dishwasher and got a knife. He didn't know what Harvest of Beauty was—that was the name above the return address—but he'd find out. He cut the box in short order, opened it, pulled out some plastic packing and saw….

What did he see? Some plastic bags, more holes in their sides, and round things and…

Bulbs.

Yes. Of course.

His mom would have ordered them months ago. But she didn't live long enough to plant them, let alone see them bloom.

The heavy feeling came over him again. Like there were tears just waiting to be cried. Tears he had always reeled in before they could get going. Because he was afraid that if he ever let them go—*really* go—they might never stop.

Sloan forced his attention back to the contents of the package. He saw then that there was writing on the sides of the bags.

The first said "Gladiolus Bulbs Black Beauty." He knew what gladiolus were. But black? Really? He didn't know a lot about plants, but he'd never seen a black flower, let alone a black gladiolus.

The second bag said "Gladiolus Bulbs Peter Pears." Pears? Did that mean green? Yellow? Tan?

He sighed.

The third bag revealed the bulbs inside were "Peacock Orchid Bulbs" or "Gladiolus acidanthera." Sloan didn't have a clue what that could mean, because orchids and gladiolus were not, nor ever had been, the same thing. Orchids were parasites, weren't they?

He looked into the box and saw there was a catalog inside. Maybe there would be pictures.

Sloan put the bags back in the box and headed into the living room, then changed his mind and went out onto the front porch. He started to sit down in Wyatt's big chair—

(his *mother's* chair)

—and at the last moment—his butt had been halfway to the cushion—he changed his mind and sat on the love seat instead.

Sloan closed his eyes. Used his imagination. Opened them again.

He could almost see her sitting there.

She was smiling. She would be because there was a slight breeze and the wind chimes—and there were a dozen of them—were making music. "I love that sound. I never get tired of it." She looked at him. Smiled wider, brown eyes glowing. He'd always loved her eyes. They were warm, as if they absorbed the sun. Not brown exactly, but what color were they?

"My favorite set, though, are the new ones," she said and pointed.

Sloan looked but there was no need. He knew which ones she meant. It was the same every time. Whatever newest gift he gave her was her favorite.

Sure enough, she was pointing at the wind chimes he'd given her for Christmas. The base was a good eight inches long, narrow, with rounded corners. Two rows of small and slim solid silver rods, instead of the usual hollow tubes, hung beneath it. They weren't loud, not the huge ones she fantasized about that reminded her of an Asian monastery, but they were musical. The problem with the big sets was they were shockingly expensive, and even after seven years at the call center, he barely made twelve dollars an hour.

I didn't buy them because I didn't think she would live long enough to enjoy them. The truth was she didn't even make it through February.

Why doesn't that make me feel better?

"What do you think of the Repletes?"

It took him a second and then he remembered. Max had told him. The pink and multipetaled daffodils. "They're nice," he said. "I would never have known they were daffodils if the neighbor hadn't told me."

She raised her brows and gave him a big smile. "Max? What do you think of him? If only he were older or I were younger!"

No wait. Back up. Erase. She wouldn't say that. Not his mom. Rewind.

"Mr. Turner, you mean?" she asked, her voice now innocent of anything but motherly intent. "He is such a nice man. Such a gentleman. He helped me in with the groceries the other day."

Max *would* do that.

Sloan closed his eyes again, tried to imagine how the conversation would continue, but before he could open his eyes, a memory came back instead.

"I ordered some bulbs today. It was stupid. I was seduced."

Sloan smiled, and remembered smiling. "Seduced?"

"You should never have bought me that laptop. I spend all day doodling on it."

"You mean googling, Mom?"

She waved her hand, fanning his words away. "Doodling. Goog-a-ling. I get e-mails, and I click on the little linky thing, and I go to these places that show me beautiful flowers, and before I know it, I've bought them. I won't live long enough to plant them."

"Mom, you know I hate it when you say that. You have to *believe*. The doctors say the people who make it are the ones who believe they will. You're going to live."

She looked at him then, a weak smile on her face. She winced and he knew from experience that the pain was back (not that it ever went away) and he jumped up. "Let me get your medicine, Mom."

She nodded and he knew it was bad. She usually refused the first time.

He dashed upstairs—he *remembered* doing so—to the medicine cabinet. He found the bottle of pills fast; he had marked it with a big X so he would never have to worry about taking long to find the right ones, or worse, grab the wrong thing.

Sloan was back down in less than a minute with the pills and the plastic cup next to the sink filled with water, and when he got there, he groaned. She had that look on her face. Dull. Faraway. How had it happened so fast? Usually she started acting… well, like a child first.

This could last minutes. It could last days.

For Sloan, this was pretty much the worst of it. Physically, he *saw* his mother, the loving woman he had known all his life. But mentally? This wasn't his mother. There had been some Mormons who had come to the door one day who thought she was mentally challenged.

Sloan supposed they were right.

He clenched his teeth and felt the anger sweep over him. How could this happen? How could anything so evil exist?

The tumors were deep, one as small as a pea, the second a grape, and the third almost as big as a golf ball. When it had all begun, she'd complained of headaches, and the doctors had given her pills and then advised her it might all be in her head.

It almost made Sloan laugh. In her head. They were in her head all right!

His mother blinked and he gasped, caught his breath. *Please. Please God.*

She looked up at him, and at first her eyes weren't focused. Her brows came together and he felt a burst of hope. She was *trying* to look at him. *Please please please.*

"Sloan? What are you doing here? You should have told me you were coming. I would have made us something to eat."

God. Here and not here. She didn't remember that he lived here.

"It's okay, Mom. Here. Take your pills."

She turned her gaze to the little pills in his open palm, and then to the glass of water. "Oh yes. Thank you, baby. My head is really hurting today." She fumbled for only a moment, then managed to get them, popped them in her mouth, and took the glass and drank. She closed her eyes. "That water is so nice and cold."

Sloan nodded, felt tears that he knew wouldn't come.

She opened her eyes and suddenly smiled. It transformed her whole face, and for just a second, he could pretend there was nothing wrong. She looked beatific. "Thanks, Son. That was fast."

Fast?

"You must have run upstairs to get them."

She remembered now? Was she back? *Please have her be back.*

He nodded.

"You should be careful. The way you run around? What if you tripped and fell? Then we would both be bicycle."

Bicycle? He sighed. She was back and not back. He took a deep breath, smiled, and sat down next to her. "I'll keep some of your pills downstairs. That way I won't have to run."

"You don't have to anyway, baby. They're pain pills. They take a while to work if I get them in one minute or five minutes."

He nodded. "Indulge me, Mom."

She laughed—winced again. Smiled. "Okay, Sloan. Now what do you want me to make for dinner."

"Already taken care of," he told the memory. "I'm picking up your favorite from P.F. Chang's." She loved the place, but he worried about taking her there. Anything might happen. So he called in the orders and picked them up instead, and sometimes she actually ate it.

And that was a good thing.

Chapter FOURTEEN

LOGAN STARTED up the stairs without a second look, and Max took a deep breath and took the plunge. "Wait, Logan. I need to talk to you about something."

Logan stopped and looking over his shoulder, gave Max a wary look.

Of course he did. *He's a teenager*, thought Max. And his father just told him that he needs to "talk to you about something." Should he be the least bit surprised he was getting such a look?

"What's going on, Dad?"

Max sighed, and swallowed hard.

"Just sit down, okay, Logan?" and Max sat first. He knew that standing while the person you need to talk to is sitting can make them very uncomfortable. There were times, as a teacher, he'd used that very technique to his advantage. But today it was the last thing he wanted. What he wanted was honesty. What he wanted was for Logan to be able to talk.

"I… ah. I've got some homework, Dad."

"Won't you need your backpack for that?" Max asked and pointed to the couch.

"Ah! Yeah." Logan gave an unconvincing laugh. "Forgot." He came down the stairs and leaned over the back of the couch, reaching for the backpack. It was only then that Max noticed the rainbow patch on the front of the pack.

Sometimes we're blind. Completely blind.

"Son. Please." Max patted the cushion. "Sit."

Logan's eyes widened slightly, and then he nodded. "Okay, Dad." He came around the couch, but sat at the opposite end instead of sitting next to Max.

I hate this, thought Max. And then as he looked at his son—short for his age with large deep brown eyes and a mop of unruly dark brown hair—he saw the unreadable expression on Logan's face.

(*Unreadable? It was fear!*)

Max was very suddenly filled with a wave of deep love for his son.

I won't hate this. I won't let myself. We are going to work this out.

"Son. I was washing clothes yesterday like I always do, but since your mom is out of town, I put them away instead. And when I went to put your shirts in where they go, well, they were an awful mess—"

A look of relief spread across his son's face. "Aw, sorry about that, Dad. Won't happen again. I was in a rush to grab stuff for Devin's. I was going to fix it."

That look is going to go away in a minute, thought Max. He held up his hand to stop the boy's excuses. "I don't care about that right now, Logan. But something happened, and I have to let you know about it."

"Something happened?" A weird look came over Logan's face. "Is Mom okay?"

"Yeah, sure, Son. Mom is just fine. I talked to her this morning."

Relief again.

"This is about your drawer," Max said. "I decided to refold your shirts and, well." Max swallowed again. *Just spit it out.* "I found something, Son. I didn't mean to."

He saw Logan's Adam's apple bob and his eyes widen slightly again. "Found something?"

Max sighed. "Yes, Logan."

"What?" There was a desperate sound in Logan's voice.

"I... I...." Max paused, and then went for it. "I found this," he said and picked up a book on the coffee table, opened it, and took the photo strip he'd placed inside it. He handed it to Logan.

Time stopped. Logan's hand was halfway to the strip and then froze in place. His eyes had gone to the pictures, and Max had held it in a way where his son could see just what it was. Logan's lids came halfway down. He bit his lower lip. Then he looked up and laughed. It wasn't real. Max knew Logan's laugh. This wasn't it.

"Ah, Dad! We were just foolin'.'"

Max simply looked at him for a minute, hoping Logan would change his story. *Tell me, Son. Just tell me.*

"What?" cried Logan.

"Logan, I know what you were doing. I can see with my own eyes what you and Devin were doing. Now just tell me, okay?"

"Tell you what?" Logan shot back.

"Are you gay, Son?" Max was surprised at how fast and easy the words came out.

Logan looked away. A little jolt passed through him, as if he had burped or something. Then he looked back. Max could see a sheen had come over his boy's eyes. "Dad, why were you messing with my stuff? Just because you saw something in my drawer doesn't mean you should have looked."

"Maybe you're right. Maybe I shouldn't have. I'm sorry. I was just curious. I didn't think it was going to be something like this."

"Like me kissing my boyfriend?" Logan said, his voice strong but catching at the last second and rising into a squeak.

Max took a deep breath. *Boyfriend. So it's true.* "Yeah," Max said. "I wasn't expecting to see you kissing your... boyfriend."

Logan looked away again.

"So you're gay?"

Logan looked back, his eyes gaining defiance. "Yes," he said. "I'm gay."

"I see." It was Max's turn to look away. "Are you...." He stopped himself. *Look at him when you talk to him.* "Are you sure, Logan?"

Logan's mouth turned into a lopsided but tiny smile. "Yeah, Dad. I'm pretty sure."

"I mean, it's pretty normal to fool around with your buddies at your age. I did once."

Logan's eyes went their widest yet. "No, Dad. I don't want to hear about that!"

Of course he didn't. Who wants to think about their parent, mother or father, having sex? It did make Max feel old, however, even though he was only thirty-five. *But I must seem ancient to him.* "I only meant that just because you.... Well, you and Devin.... That doesn't make you gay."

Logan gave him an are-you-shitting-me expression.

"I mean, you're young, son. Boys… do stuff together. You have all those hormones raging wild and no way to relieve…." He felt his face heat up even as he saw Logan blushing as well.

"*Dad.*"

Max plunged on. "In a few years, after you start dating girls—"

Logan's expression grew even are-you-shitting-me-er. "Dating girls? I'm not going to be dating any girls."

"How can you be sure?" Max cried in a tone that was way too loud, and he immediately wished he could take it back.

"Because girls are *yuck*!" Logan came back, his voice just as loud.

"Logan! Lots of boys think girls are 'yuck.'"

Logan rolled his eyes. "I like *boys*, Dad. *A lot*. And I like Devin *a lot*. I *think* I might even love him."

Max was glad he was sitting down. Love. *Love?* "You're pretty young to be in love, Logan. I'm sure it *feels* that way."

Logan jumped to his feet. "Dad¸ I *knew* you'd be like this. I *knew* it. Uncle Dennis said I should trust you but I just *knew*—"

Uncle Dennis? My brother? "You've been talking to my brother?"

"Yes!"

Max couldn't believe it. "You talked to your uncle and not me?"

Logan looked at him, eyes agog.

"Why would you talk to him and not me?"

Logan rolled his eyes again. "Duh! He's *gay*!"

Max opened his mouth to respond, and then it slowly closed. He didn't know what to say. Duh, indeed.

"And before you get mad at him, *I'm* the one that chose not to tell you. Because I *knew* you would start all this 'how do you know you're gay?' shit!"

Shit? Logan says shit?

And that's what I'm worried about?

Before Max could help it, he was smiling.

"What's so funny!" Logan snarled.

"Never mind." He didn't want Logan to think he was laughing at him. "Logan." He reached out. Touched his son's knee. "Logan. How do you know I'm gay?"

Logan gave him a funny look. "Wha-what did you say?"

"I asked you how you knew you were gay."

"That's not what you said, Dad."

"Yes it is," Max insisted. What else could he have said? "How do you *know* you're gay? How do you *know* you won't feel different in a couple years? Maybe you're bisexual. Maybe you'll—"

"Dad." Logan put his hand on his father's. "That's not how it works. I know. I like girls. But not that way. My friends? They *like* girls, Dad. They sneak their dad's *Penthouse* magazines. They try and look down girl's shirts. All they talk about is girls. They like boobs. God, that's all Casey talks about all the time! Boobs. Boobs boobs boobs."

It took Max a second to realize who Casey was. Then it hit him. Cliff's son. This time he really did smile. Casey did love to talk about breasts. "And you don't like them? Ah… boobs?"

Logan made a face.

"But-but you like—"

Logan blushed again. "Yeah, Dad. *A lot.*"

And that meant…. "So you and Devin…?"

Logan locked eyes with him. "Devin and I *what*, Dad?"

Max took his deepest breath yet. "You're… lovers?"

Logan gave him an incredulous look. "*Dad*! I'm fourteen for God's sake. We haven't even done *it* yet!"

Max's mouth fell open. *What?* "Logan, you don't really expect me to believe that, do you?"

"You don't trust me now?"

"You went behind my back with Dennis."

Logan slumped in his seat. "I was afraid to tell you, Dad."

Afraid? Is that what he'd done? Made it so his son was afraid to talk to him? To be honest with him? He thought he had to hide himself?

"Son. That's what I'm afraid of."

Logan shook his head. "What do you mean?"

"That you're going to have to hide yourself. From me. From friends. From—"

"Dad. All my friends know."

Now it was Max's turn to look at his son agog. *What?*

Logan nodded. "Dad, the whole school knows."

"Logan! My God! How did they find out? Has anyone threatened you?" Max sat up straight. He very abruptly remembered a black eye a few months ago. "You've been beat up, haven't you?" He leaned forward. "Logan. You've been bashed—"

Logan laughed. "No, Dad. I haven't been bashed."

"But that black eye you had—"

"I got punched because I wouldn't let Tony the Goon cheat off my math test."

Of course, that is what Logan had told them. "Was that really it, Logan?"

"What? You don't trust me, Dad?"

Max sat back.

"I punched the shit out of him too. Why do you think he didn't try anything when Devin and I came out?"

Max just shook his head. What did he say to that?

"Besides, if he had tried anything, I would just tell everybody what happened at Devin's birthday party."

"What happened?" Max asked before asking himself if he really wanted to know.

"Do you really want to know?" Logan asked.

The look on Logan's face made him wonder. Did he?

But wasn't trust what they were working on right now? And boy, this whole thing wasn't going at all the way he'd imagined, was it? And he'd imagined quite a few things.

He nodded.

"We all jerked off, Dad. You know. Boys *do* that."

Inside he was screaming. Outside Max kept his face passive. Lose it and everything would be over.

"We all did it several times. But then Devin and I…. We realized we weren't like the other boys. You're right, Dad. They were doing it because they can't get with a girl and they're horny. But me and Devin? We were doing it because that is what we *wanted* to do. If I didn't know I was gay before, I knew it the first time we all did it. And so me and Devin finally talked." He blushed. "Well, we did a little more than that. We kissed. And Dad—if the rest didn't tell me I was gay, the first time Devin kissed me, I *knew*. I've kissed a girl. In junior high. Jack Rojas had a pool party last summer and we played spin the bottle—"

Max nodded. He remembered parties with spin the bottle. He'd done the same damned thing.

"Dad. When I kissed Jenny I... I...." Suddenly tears were in Logan's eyes. "It felt... *wrong*, Dad! It was... gross. And I *hated* myself!"

"Logan!" Max's heart broke. He *felt* it crack open. *Hated himself?*

"I was *supposed* to like it. All the other boys said *they* liked it! I thought there was something wrong with me."

How many times had he, Max, felt the very same thing?

"And then Devin kissed me, Dad." Logan sighed, and then the sun rose on his face. One tear slipped down his cheek, and it was as if all the rest had vanished. "Oh, Dad! One kiss!" Logan stood up and rubbed his arms and smiled. For a moment it looked as if he might dance. "Dad. One kiss. *Just one.* That was it! I couldn't believe it. So different than kissing Jenny and those other girls. Suddenly, I was so happy I could die."

What did he say? Happy?

"Oh, Dad! *Then* I understood! There wasn't anything wrong with me at all. This is what most boys feel when they kiss girls!"

Max swallowed hard.

He didn't have one clue what Logan was talking about.

Kissing had never been a big deal for him. He'd never really understood what the big deal was. They were kind of messy, really. He'd never had the passion for it that Lauren had. He had no idea what to say. He didn't know what his son was talking about. But he could see Logan was waiting for something. So he pretended. He smiled. He nodded.

Logan's smile got even bigger. "I don't know why I was chosen to be gay—"

"Chosen?" Logan felt *chosen?* Did he mean to use that word?

"—but Dad! I am so glad I was." He threw himself back down on the couch. Tears were welling back up in his son's eyes, and with a rush of wonder Max saw they were tears of joy.

"I've been reading about it, Dad. Do you realize how many famous people in history were gay? Oh my God! Alexander the Great, Dad. Did you see that movie? Colin Farrell kissing a guy? I got the *biggest* boner watching that!" Logan giggled.

Boner? Did his son just tell him Colin Farrell gave him a boner? Max wanted to scream again, but he remembered what a mistake that would be. If he lost it, he would lose a lot more. His son might never talk to him about such important things again. Logan was *talking* to him. He was sharing his soul.

Max fought back the tears. A shudder passed through him, and he forced a smile. He nodded. And he didn't even know what he was crying about.

Logan sighed a big and obviously happy smile. "Richard the Lionhearted, Dad. And Michelangelo. He's the one that painted the ceiling of that famous church. And Leonardo Da Vinci. And the guy who wrote *Moby Dick*. And Tchaikovsky." Logan did a little spin. He laughed. "I didn't even know who Tchaikovsky *was* until I looked him up. Dad! He was this composer. You should listen to his music. I thought Lady Gaga was amazing, but then I listen to his stuff and I see that there wouldn't be a Lady Gaga or a Katy Perry or anybody without people like him!"

Was this his son? His *fourteen*-year-old son? Was this boy ranting about Tchaikovsky? And had Max known Tchaikovsky was gay?

"And Elton John. Do you know who he is, Dad? He's great! I didn't know who he was and when I found out that Lady Gaga was the godmother to his sons, I looked him up too. Oh my God! He is fripping *awesome*."

Did he know who Elton John was? Max wanted to laugh. Of course he knew who Elton John was. He and Lauren had seen him in concert and it had been amazing.

"Hans Christian Andersen too. He wrote *The Little Mermaid*. And the guy who plays Mr. Spock in the new *Star Trek* movies. He came out. And *boy* is he *hot*!"

Hot. Logan thought the actor who played the new Mr. Spock was hot.

"All these actors are coming out. Dad, it's a cool thing. I was just reading online about these gay couples becoming prom kings and queens."

Logan stopped and spread his arms over his head. "Daddy—"

Daddy?

"I was *chosen*!"

Chapter FIFTEEN

SLOAN DECIDED to go ahead and make something to eat; a bagged, frozen, supposedly Italian concoction, and only after he'd made it—

("Ready in only fifteen minutes!")

—did he realize it was freezer burned. The first bite made him gag. He'd spit it out onto the plate, scraped it all down the garbage disposal, and then worried that he should have thrown it away in the trash instead. His mother would have known. Now his stomach was queasy, and even the idea of ordering delivery made him a little nauseous. Not even P.F. Chang's. He'd have to go pick that up himself since they didn't deliver, and he just didn't have the motivation. Plus, he was pretty sure if he ate even one more of their lettuce wraps, he'd turn into one. It was his mother's number one choice—he had *no* idea how many times they'd gotten them there at the end—but she often didn't eat much, and he would be forced to eat her portion as well as his.

Sloan decided that maybe he should just lie down and take a nap.

And for no reason he could fathom, Max sprang to his mind. It was probably the fact that he had seen him at the gym, looking all sexy as hell, and dammit, the man got under his skin. Maybe it was because Max reminded him so much of Mr. Kelso, and maybe it was because he hadn't been laid in about nine thousand years. Maybe it was because his heart went out to the guy and how he was going to handle things with his son. Maybe he should call and offer to be there when Logan got home?

But no. Sloan had hinted about that last night, and there hadn't been so much as a nibble.

So he climbed the steps to the second floor instead, knowing it was way too early to go to bed but not wanting to face the emptiness and not having the desire to see his friends. He loved them, and they were the only thing keeping him sane, but no. Not tonight.

Sloan threw off his clothes on the way, shoes at the bottom of the steps, shirt over the balustrade, pants unbuttoned in the hall…. And then he saw the room where… where….

He stood in the doorway of the room that had been his mother's for as long as he could remember. The hospice bed was gone. They'd taken that away, and he'd set up her old bed in its place—made it up with the chenille bedspread, the kind with those weird little bumps in the pretty pattern. And the quilt she had made too. It had taken her so long, and he remembered helping her cut out the squares of fabric when he was about nine or ten. He'd been so proud of that. His mom had acted like he made the whole quilt himself, when of course she'd done the part that took so much time and energy.

Now Sloan looked at the bed—*so* his mother—and wondered if he'd made a mistake. Maybe he should have put it in the attic and gotten something new instead. Looking at the bed now, all he could do was see was where she *wasn't*. There was even a slight dent in the mattress where she had lain for so many years—always on the right, never taking up the whole bed as she could have, as if she were waiting for his father to come home.

It was the logical side to sleep on. The side closest to the bed stand and the bathroom. That's all there was to it.

And somehow the idea of making the room look like it wasn't hers seemed a crime. Wrong. Pretending she didn't exist. As a matter of fact, he hadn't gotten rid of anything, although Asher had tried to talk him into having a big garage sale.

"If you're going to stay here, you have to make it your house."

Except it wasn't *his* house. It was his mother's house. And it always would be, forever and ever, amen.

He stepped into the room, sat in the rocker next to her bed.

And she was there.

"Baby?" She reached out with a hand so weak she could barely hold it up.

He took it, that ghost hand—or pretended to. "Yes, Mom?"

She'd been losing her hair at the end, and oh, that had seemed to hurt her most of all. She had been so proud of her hair. She hadn't even begun to go gray until she was in her fifties.

The radiation took her pride and joy. Not that there was a hope of it saving her. There wasn't. The tumors were too deep in her brain, inoperable. No, the radiation was to help control it, slow it down. There were side effects, of course: memory loss, a lot like Alzheimer's. Some days were worse than others.

"Promise me something?"

"What, Mom?" Heart pounding. What would she ask him? Would she ask about his grades or how Little League was going? Would she ask him to go get his father, he was down at the bar on the corner hanging out with that tramp Elvira? Ask him to let Myrtle, the dog who had died ten years ago, out?

But she'd been completely lucid at the end. He just hadn't known it was the end.

"Promise me you'll stop holding a torch for Asher? That you'll move on?"

"Mom?"

It was the first time she'd ever talked of Asher. In that way.

"I didn't," she said. "You know? Move on? I could have. Mr. Beauchamp at work has hinted for years—"

"Your boss?" he asked, incredulous. The heavy, balding…. "He's so old!"

"I'm old, baby."

"No you're not, Ma. And when you get better, we're going to go to Cancun and find you a hot young cabana boy—"

Her hand had gripped his with surprising strength then, and there was an amazing awareness showing on her face—which had been dull so often these past days, another product of the radiation (and the morphine of course, the bag hung from the stand beside the bed. The home health nurse had just left half an hour or so before).

"Sloan, I'm not going to Mexico. And cabana boys are more your style these days, don't you think? Even Mr. Beauchamp hasn't been around in a long time…."

The motherfucker!

"Mom…."

"Sssshhhh," she hushed. For a moment she looked like she did when he was a boy. Something about the orange glow of the bedside lamp; it hid the dark shadows under her eyes, made her hair look full and red. And her eyes! Glowing and alert. "Now promise me."

"Mom!"

"I know that you love him, but he's not for you. He's a gigolo, and you need to see that. He's never going to settle down, not with you or *any* man."

Sloan swallowed hard. He didn't even tease her about the word "gigolo." He was just too surprised that she was giving him advice like that. She had accepted it finally, truly. That he was gay. She had even begun setting him up on dates, blind ones, some with disastrous endings. The last guy had been nice but hadn't been Sloan's type.

Type? What type? You mean he wasn't Asher is what you mean. Because that guy was much more your type than Asher ever was.

He focused his attention back on his mother, nodded. It was what she wanted.

"And he's an actor. You need someone with a *real* job. Someone like that boy Dean you went to school with. Such a nice young man. He owns a coffee shop. He's going somewhere. He can provide for you...."

"Mom," Sloan protested, even though he knew he shouldn't. He should just let her talk. Who knew when she would suddenly revert and ask him to grab that hoe and help her with the weeds? "Mom. Asher is going to be big time one day. Tonys and Oscars and—"

She waved his words away with her free hand and he felt her hard grip with the other begin to weaken.

"Mom?"

She nodded, smiled, squeezed his hand again. "And you can't look for a man in a bar. That's the wrong crowd, no matter what kind of bar it is. I met your father in a bar, and look where it got me." She'd been working part-time as a server, and the legendary Mr. McKenna had always made sure he was in her section and teased her and told her how pretty her hair was—his was red as well. Big surprise, what with his last name. He'd asked her out and asked her out until she'd finally given in, and he'd taken her to see *The Man Who Shot Liberty Valance*.

"So after he left, I waited. I waited and I waited. And he never came back. Even after he died, I waited. Promise me you'll stop waiting."

"Mom!" Again Sloan felt the cloud, creeping up over him, surrounding him. The memory so real.

"Promise!"

"Okay...." Anything to calm her down. "I promise."

"I'm sorry about that day."

Day? Was she fading away again?

"When you told me you were gay. I behaved a fool. I knew. I *always* knew you were gay."

"You—you what?"

"Mothers know. Sometimes we pretend. So stupid. We have plans, you know, Sloan? My first plan was to get out of my father's house—that horrid, horrid man—and find true love. To get married and live happily ever after. That didn't happen, although it was good at first. And in my world, you marry for life, if he turns out to be a louse or not. Then he went away. So then I looked to *you* to live my dreams instead, and that was so unfair."

Sloan got up and sat on the edge of the bed and looked down into his mother's face. "It's okay. I understand."

"You have to get out there. I don't know how gay men do it, but they do. Look at your friend Wyatt. His boyfriend is a little strange, but they're happy."

Were they? Sloan almost looked away, almost said something, but made himself keep looking down into her face. He nodded. Smiled.

"Join one of those online groups. Or join a club. There are gay clubs, aren't there? My friend Karen told me that. Her nephew met a boy in a bowling club. I think it was bowling...."

"Okay, Mom. I will."

"I don't want you to die alone. Not like me...."

"You're *not* going to die, Mom. You're going to outlive me."

She smiled. It was beautiful. She was twelve.

And then she wasn't. One side of her mouth slid down—just a bit. Then more. "No I'm not, Carl."

Carl? "Mom?" Carl. His father. *No. No no no no....* Carl was his father.

"Can we go to *The Man Who Shot Liberty Valance*? I know you wanted to see *The Manchurian Candidate*, but I just love Vera Miles."

"Mom?" The tears threatened. They stung the corners of his eyes. Would he *finally* be able to cry?

"And James Stewart. Ever since he was in *It's a Wonderful Life*. And it has John Wayne! You like John Wayne, right?"

"Yes, Muriel," he said, using her name. He'd never called her that before. But then he wasn't talking, was he? In her mind, it was his father—her husband.

"*Liberty Valance* sounds fine," he said. "We'll go. But why don't you take a nap first?"

She closed her eyes and gave a single nod. "Thanks, Carl." Went to sleep just like that.

And never woke up.

Of course Sloan didn't know that at the time.

He sat there for a long time looking at the empty bed. Remembering.

He didn't cry.

Chapter SIXTEEN

MAX ORDERED pizza. Not healthy, perhaps, but it was the universal comfort food. Besides, hadn't he planned on ordering pizza last night? At least it was whole-wheat crust with vegetables. Logan had only rolled his eyes in that way that he, and every teenager, could and said not one word about it. He'd simply gone up to his room to do his homework. At least this time he remembered his backpack.

(*"I'm chosen!"*)

Max sat on the couch staring at the blank television screen. He couldn't believe the direction this evening had taken, and he'd imagined quite a few scenarios.

I was worried he might run away and become a street hustler. It was enough to make him laugh.

Max didn't laugh, though.

He had been so worried about Logan. He'd agonized. And Logan felt chosen? Here Max had thought it was a curse.

"Dad, I wouldn't *want* to be straight."

Boy, had that comment surprised Max.

"Not sayin' there's anything wrong with being straight—"

Wrong. With being straight!

"—and *if* that's what you're into, then I'm happy for you. But me? I just don't get it, and I never have. Even when I was little. *Really* little. To me it's like cats and dogs—they just don't play well together."

Max had to work to keep his mouth from falling open this time. *Cats and dogs. Cats and dogs?*

"Cats don't get dogs and dogs don't get cats," Logan continued. "Sometimes they get along okay, but mostly cats just want dogs to act like cats and dogs just want cats to act like dogs."

For a moment they locked eyes and Max forced himself to look away. Who knew what he might give away without meaning to?

"I'm a dog, Dad. And I *like* dogs. Cats are okay. I really like *other* people's cats. But give me a dog any day."

It was all Max could do to keep this brain from locking up. *Cats and dogs.* How many times had he thought the same thing?

"Speaking of dogs…," Logan began.

"Logan!"

Logan put his hands on his hips. "Dad!"

How in the world had they gone from sex to dogs? "You know your mother isn't going to allow us to have a dog—"

"Allow?" cried Logan. "Don't *you* get some say? Why does she always get what *she* wants? This is just what I'm talking about. It's the battle of the sexes!"

Battle of the sexes? How had Logan ever heard of such a thing? Did people even say "battle of the sexes" anymore?

"Now, Son," Max replied. "Don't go trying to pit your mom and I against each other."

"I'm not! I just don't understand why the girl should *always* get *her* way."

"That's not how it works, Logan. I get my way—"

(like when he'd refused to shave his chest!)

"—but I just want to keep the peace. You know what they say. When Mama ain't happy, ain't *no*body happy."

"See what I mean? Thank *God* I'll never have to worry about that!"

Max bit the insides of his cheeks to keep from laughing. "Logan, I daresay it won't make any difference. People are people, men *or* women. Maybe you should have asked your uncle about that—"

(when you were talking to him behind my back!)

"—because I can tell you that he and Armel have had some fights that were real doozies. Do you remember the week your uncle came and stayed with us a year or so back?"

"Yeah."

"That's because he and Armel had a fight."

And that reminded Max he was going to have to talk to Den. His brother should have *told* him!

"People in love fight, no matter who they are," Max said. "They say it's the couples that don't ever fight that don't really care about each other."

Logan sat back down and pursed his lips. "Devin and *I* don't fight."

Max looked at him disbelievingly. "Never?"

Logan pouted. "Well…. Maybe once in a while."

Max nodded. "And that's perfectly normal." It wasn't until the words were out of his mouth that he realized what he'd said. *Perfectly normal. Perfectly normal for my son to fight with his boyfriend.*

"Yeah. My friend Susan and her boyfriend Oz fight at school all the time."

"Oz?" What the hell kind of name was that?

"Yeah. He looks just like that guy from *Buffy the Vampire Slayer*. The werewolf? So we call him Oz."

Max just looked at him in confusion. Was it always this way talking to a teenager? Hadn't they been talking about fighting with your other half, and now they were talking about *Buffy the Vampire Slayer*?

"You know, Dad. Oz. The cute kid with the red hair…."

(Red hair!)

Sloan flashed to his mind.

"Dad? Hello? You zoning out on me?"

Max shook himself. Changed the subject. "Look, Son. My biggest concern for you is that you'll have to live in secret. Gay people have to hide who they are. At least your friend… Susan? At least she *can* fight with Oz at school. You're going to have to keep your relationship with Devin hush-hush—"

Logan laughed. "Dad! I told you. *Everybody* at school knows."

Max's mouth fell to his chest. It felt like it hit the floor. "What?" he said once he could.

"Yeah. Everybody knows. We walk around at school holding hands."

"What?"

Logan rolled his eyes (of course). "Dad! This isn't the caveman times like when you were a kid."

Max's eyes popped. "Caveman times! Why, you little shit!"

Logan laughed more. "It's the twenty-first century, Dad! Get with it! All is well. All is cool."

All is well.

Well I'll be damned.

Chapter SEVENTEEN

IN THE end Sloan called Asher. To hell with being alone. Because really, he wasn't alone, was he? His mother was haunting him this evening. With her memories, and worse, with her so *not* being there. Haunting him with the emptiness.

Sloan thought first of calling Wyatt. Wyatt was his clown after all. Always ready with a joke—

("*Did you hear about the gay butcher that accidentally backed into the grinder? He got a little behind in his work!*")

—or some other outrageous behavior. Sometimes he'd show up with some new flavored vodka, like dragon fruit (and what the hell was that anyway?) or pink cotton candy. Anything that would fit Wyatt's cosmopolitan-themed cocktail because for Wyatt there was nothing *but* a cosmo.

And of course it was always delicious.

Or maybe he would bring a movie, usually *hil*-arious (*Bear City 2*, much better than the first, which had been pretty damned good considering its budget) or the *wonderful* online series ("Now Available on DVD!") *Where the Bears Are* (and Sloan *had* laughed his ass off). Or sometimes an erotic and over-the-top movie (*Short Bus*, and could anything have prepared Sloan for the scene where one of actors lay down and flipped his legs over his head so he could ejaculate into his own mouth?).

Maybe Wyatt would show up and grab Sloan by the hand and drag him off to one of his "witchy rituals" (as Scott called them) and talk him out of his clothes—

(*"I've seen you naked!"*)

—so the celebration could be performed "skyclad."

(*"Come on, are you going to be the* only *guy there with clothes on?"*

"Not sure I can do this, Wyatt...."

"Of course you can. Besides you have an a-may-zing butt! And baby if you've got it, you have got to flaunt it."

"Wyatt, I'm not even... whatever it is that you are. Witch? Pagan?"

"So what? You're not a lesbian either, but you went to the Sappho poetry reading thing last month. Live a little! Expand your horizons!")

And of course as weird as it had been standing in a circle with a group of naked men who were smearing red mud on their faces and chests and... other parts, and singing some song about the return of spring, he had to admit the experience had been... horizon expanding. And dare he say it? Fun?

The problem was that sometimes being with Wyatt could mean dealing with depression or anger because of the latest Howard incident. Listening to that today was not something Sloan could deal with.

Scott was plain out of the question. Sloan loved Scott, even though he could be whiny and cantankerous and a know-it-all. He was always quoting some little known fact that could ruin the good mood of a party—

("Did you know that pubic lice can not only be found in your pubic hair, but chest hair and even beards, eyebrows, and eyelashes?")

—or making sure they *all* knew how *stupid* they were for believing in God or things paranormal or even Buddhist philosophy—

("There is no proof that Jesus Christ ever existed—and his name certainly wouldn't have been either Jesus or Christ. The first Gospel wasn't written until at least seventy years after He supposedly lived and rose again—"

"Scott!"

"And the Buddha? None of his teachings were recorded until five hundred years after his death. All of his words were passed down by word of mouth for five centuries! Who knows how many Eastern gurus teachings got lumped together? And there is no proof he even existed."

"Oh, Scott...."

"And don't even get me started on ghosts and all that crap. I won't believe in phantoms if one shows up in my bedroom rattling chains, moaning, and telling me I'll get visited by the spirits of Christmas past, present, and yet-to-come. I will know it for what it is: an undigested bit of beef, a blot of mustard, a crumb of cheese, a fragment of underdone potato!")

—or possibly the worst of all, bitching about his body—

(*"Look!* Look *at me!" he'd shout, nude, in the middle of the locker* room. *"I work out harder than* any *of you except for maybe Asher—"*

There was no maybe about it.

"—and I'm skinny! Emaciated! My chest makes the Salt Water Flats look like the Grand Tetons. My ribs are showing. I look like a survivor of a concentration camp."

"No, Scott. You don't. You're slim. Wyatt would kill to be as slim as you—"

"Wyatt eats anything *that can't run faster than he can—which I admit isn't all that fast. Wyatt will* never *be slim* unless *he* goes *to a concentration camp!"*)

The comment had pissed Asher off royally. In fact, Scott didn't know how close he'd come to getting cold-cocked.

(*"And I'm not even going to mention my* dick. *If there* was *a God, I would* hate *Him, because it's a joke. He made me seventeen feet tall and gave me a three inch pecker!"*)

Scott, of course, was not seventeen feet tall—he wasn't as tall as Asher—and while Sloan had never seen his friend with a full-on erection, he had seen Scott chubbing up when he'd been ogling a man in the shower at the gym. Sloan *knew* that Scott *did* get bigger.

(*"So you're a grower and not a show-er, Scott. So what?"*

"That's easy for you to say, Sloan. If I had meat like yours or Asher's—"

And *who* had meat like Asher?

"—swinging between my legs, maybe I would believe in God.")

But even though Scott *could* be whiny and cantankerous and a know-it-all, and despite the fact that his crazy behavior had made it so that the members of Fabulous Four were pretty much Scott's only friends— despite all of that, Sloan loved Scott.

Sloan had seen something in Scott few saw.

Once they'd gone into the city to see the Kinsey Sicks—"America's Favorite Dragapella Beautyshop Quartet"—and they'd had to park a few blocks away from the church where they'd been performing that night.

Imagine. A church that allowed a gay group to perform on their stage!

What he'd told Max was right. The world *was* changing. It really was getting better.

After the concert was over—and it had been amazing fun—he and Scott got to party a bit with the "girls." Scott knew one of the singers, Daisy Buckët, who was local, and so they were invited to hang out. But that meant when it was time to leave, it was not only well after dark, but the streets were seemingly deserted. So they'd been quite surprised—hell, shocked—when they were very abruptly surrounded by a street gang. The circle of African-American youths seemed to have just magically appeared out of the night, and their apparent leader had a knife. A big one.

"You two a couple of faggots?" the young man had snarled. He was tall, and as dark as Sloan was pale, and terrifyingly intimidating. Sloan's blood had turned to ice.

Then, just like that, Scott had thrown himself in front of Sloan. "Yeah! We *are*," he had growled. "And this is my boyfriend! Gonna make something out of it?"

Sloan hadn't known who was the more shocked. Himself or the gang leader. The young man's eyes had gone wide—two incredibly white orbs in his obsidian face—and he'd even taken a step back. Time seemed to stand completely still, and then the leader spoke.

"You know it ain't smart for two white boys to go walking in this neighborhood at night. Not too smart at all."

"We were at a concert at Saint Sebastian's Episcopal, and we just got out," Scott said. He'd dropped his tone of voice down a bit, but not much. "We're just walking to our car."

"What'd you park so damned far away for?"

Scott shrugged. "It was the only place we could park. We got here late. All the good parking was taken."

The leader looked at his buddies for another long moment and then turned back to Scott. "We'll walk with you," he said and motioned for them to start moving. The ring of young men—some not more than boys really—stayed around them until they got to the car and then waited around until they got in and started it up.

"Next time you two get here early, okay man? We might not be around to watch out for you."

"Thanks," Scott said, and they were on their way.

Sloan hadn't known whether to burst into tears or collapse into maniacal laughter. He'd been terrified.

And Scott had stepped right in the way of a knife. He'd been willing to take a blade for Sloan!

Sloan didn't allow himself to cry or laugh. He'd been afraid that if he did either he wouldn't be able to stop. Instead he just sat in the passenger seat and tried not to shake.

"Fuck," Scott said, breaking the silence. "I *think* I peed myself."

Then they had both broken into hysterical laughter.

It was a moment Sloan would never forget.

He also didn't forget that Scott had been the first to arrive when his mother died.

While Wyatt did practical things (almost unheard of for him) like making sure Sloan had food, it was Scott who made sure he ate it. Wyatt brought the booze, Scott made sure Sloan didn't drink too much. Wyatt made calls and added personal touches to the funeral, like helping Sloan pick out pictures of his mother for the slide show. Luckily, his mother had long ago made a lot of the decisions, but it was Scott who made sure all the legal details were taken care of. He got Sloan where he needed to be, helped him know what to sign and what to nix, and far more. Scott wasn't a lawyer, but he worked for the law firm of Baily, Cranston, and Watch and was friendly with the partners. Scott's OCD behavior was well appreciated there. Scott made sure everything legal ran smoothly and helped Sloan navigate around the pitfalls a lot of grieving people fell into. He was the master of organization that Sloan so needed—one who made Sheldon from *The Big Bang Theory* look like an incompetent slob.

Scott even moved in for a few weeks, almost a month, and didn't whine or get the slightest bit cantankerous, and any of his know-it-all behavior was aimed in the right directions (like those pesky legal issues or making sure the funeral home didn't dupe Sloan into buying something ridiculous that the FF could handle for next to nothing).

And Sloan loved him for all of it.

But still….

Tonight wasn't the night to call Scott.

And so Sloan called Asher.

Against his better judgment.

Chapter EIGHTEEN

MAX AND Logan were sitting, eating pizza, and watching DVRed *Glee* (Kurt was singing a wonderful song) on TV when Max found he just had to ask a question. "You really expect me to believe you and Devin aren't having sex?"

Logan turned to him and took a bite of pizza. He rolled his eyes, which surely was nothing new. "We aren't, Dad. And it isn't because he doesn't want to. I *want* to. But…."

Max waited for it.

"But I want it to be special, Dad." Logan looked down, looked at the half-eaten piece of pizza in his hand, and then back to Max. "In some ways it's already…. Well…. Not *ruined* exactly. But there's no…." He sighed. "You know Mom has stopped hiding my Christmas presents. She wraps them but she doesn't hide them away anymore. Half the time she *tells* me what you guys got me."

Max nodded. Lauren had decided that now that Logan was a teen and didn't believe in Santa any longer, there was no need. "He's practically a man," she'd said.

"But you know what? I miss it, Dad. The anticipation. The surprise. I miss wondering what's in the box. I miss them all magically appearing under the tree on Christmas and running down to the tree before you guys get up and shaking a box and trying to figure out what could be in there."

"Sure," Max said. He missed it too. Lauren rarely wrapped any of his presents anymore. They bought each other's gifts together while shopping for Logan. Lauren was a businesswoman to the marrow, and deciding on how much they would spend on each other, when they only had one account anyway, seemed silly to her.

Although she did like the occasional surprise gift he gave her, didn't she? He would never really understand her.

Cat and dog. That was just what it was.

"So it's like that, Dad. I've seen the present unwrapped already. I mean we've seen each other naked already." At those words, Logan finally had the good grace to blush. "And we've already…. Well, I told you what."

Jerked off together, thought Max. He didn't even know what to think about that. He'd jerked off with Cliff at the very same age, even if it was a million years ago. And he'd wanted it. It was more than just being horny, and it was surely more than the fact that he had no opportunity to do anything with a girl. He knew that. Had *come* to know that.

As the years went by, he had to admit he would have done it again if it hadn't been for what happened with his brother. His brother had pretty much fucked up everything.

(*"You better give me a grandson!"*)

"You listening to me, Dad?"

Max jumped and looked at his son. "Sorry. I was just…. Never mind."

Thinking about being naked with Cliff. How exciting it had been to hold another boy's cock. Why, his heart was starting to speed up now!

I loved it, thought Max. *My God I loved it. I would do it today if I could.*

If I wasn't married.

But I am.

He looked at Logan again. His son wanted to talk about this. He was opening up. And as much as it was… as it was strange to hear—it wasn't a conversation Max ever thought he would be having with his child—there was another part of him that recognized how significant this was. In some ways it was the reverse of Logan not wanting to hear about what Max had done sexually. You didn't want to think about your kid having sex. But as much as it made him uncomfortable, he knew he had to *get* comfortable. If he messed this up, Logan might never talk to him again.

"Devin and I can't exactly be virgins for each other. Not totally. But we *can* save one or two things. Besides, what if he's not 'the one'?"

"The one?" Max asked.

"You know, my forever and ever. Like you and Mom."

Max's stomach clenched.

"If Devin and I do everything, then I won't have something special to give the guy I *do* spend the rest of my life with. And let's be real. I'm fourteen. I'm probably not going to spend the rest of my life with Devin, as much as I like the idea."

Once more Logan was surprising Max. His son was so mature. How had he not known that? He was a man in a boy's body. Max shook his head. He was stunned, really. Max realized he had spent that last twenty-four hours or so acting like a big drama queen, worried to death about all of this. How to confront Logan. How to tell him he'd found the pictures. Worried about what Logan would do when he forbade him to be sexual with Devin.

(Like he could really do that. Boys would do what boys were going to do. Where there was a will, there was a way.)

Yet, here was his son, fourteen years old, acting like the adult.

"You amaze me, Son." It was then that Max realized something else. He was proud of his son as well. So he decided to tell him so. "I'm proud of you. Really proud."

Logan beamed. "Thanks, Dad," he said and went back to eating his pizza.

What kid falling in love for the first time doesn't think it's happily ever after? They think they're going to marry their first boyfriend or girlfriend and it's going to last forever.

Of course in Max's case, he had married that first girlfriend, hadn't he? And here they were, going on twenty years. Forever, right?

Happily ever after?

He looked at his son, saw a wisdom beyond his years. Logan knew all kinds of things that he didn't. What's more, Max trusted Logan completely. *Knew* his son wasn't lying. "I am just so amazed that you are so cool with all this."

Logan turned back, mouth still full of pizza. "Cool with what?"

"That you're gay."

"It's better than being one of those one in three teens that kills himself because he's gay, isn't it?"

"Christ, yes!"

"I read that every two hours a gay teen commits suicide. Can you believe that? A kid named Jamey Rodemeyer killed himself because of bullies and Lady Gaga made a big deal about it. She dedicated her performance of 'Hair' to him during a big show in Las Vegas! That's when I think I fell for her, Dad. Zachary Quinto came out because Jamey killed himself. And that was just one teen. Every two hours. I can't even think of how many that is. I read that and I thought, 'screw that!' Kill myself, hide myself, or choose to be proud of myself? No contest."

He turned back to *Glee*.

And all Max could do was sit in wonder.

Chapter NINETEEN

ASHER TOOK over an hour and a half to arrive. And even though it was only seven, he was drunk. Halfway there anyway.

"Sorry, Sloan," he said with only the softest slur to his voice. "I was kind of… ah, in the middle of something."

Of getting cocktailed, Sloan wondered, smelling the alcohol on Asher's breath. "That's okay," he said, trying to mean it. "Guess it's pretty stupid that I called and bothered you anyway. I just didn't want to be alone tonight."

With all the ghosts.

"No problem," Asher said. He held up a brown paper bag that obviously had a bottle in it. "I come bearing scotch."

Scotch? Really?

Sloan took the bag when it was handed to him and put it down on the end table.

"Don't you want to take that to the kitchen? We can open that fucker up and pour us a couple."

I don't want any, Sloan said and then realized he hadn't said it. "Sure," he replied instead. How could he refuse Asher anything?

They went to the kitchen, and Sloan grabbed two juice glasses— liquor had never touched them, not in *his* mother's house. Meanwhile Asher unbagged the bottle and opened it. He raised it to his face. Sniffed. Sighed happily. "Oh yes. This is going to be good."

No it's not. It's scotch. *I hate scotch. And he knows that too.*

"I know you're not crazy about scotch, but this is pretty good stuff, Sloan. Johnny Walker Black. It's not cheap shit."

Sloan shrugged and Asher poured. "You want this on the rocks?"

Sloan gave another shrug.

"Well, then, never mind," Asher replied casually. "Over the lips." He raised the glass and drank. He gave only the slightest wince, scrunched his eyes, and let out a long, happy, "Aaaahhhh.... Good stuff!" Asher clinked his glass against Sloan's and gave a nod of encouragement. "Over the gums, my friend."

Sloan sighed and sipped.

Look out stomach, here it comes.

He couldn't say whether it was good stuff or not, but it was certainly smooth and went down easy, and when it hit bottom, it was with a warmth that spread through Sloan's stomach instead of an explosion. He smiled and pretended to enjoy it. How could he help it when Asher was looking at him that way?

Is there anyone on earth with eyes like that?

And God, the way Asher was looking at him!

Asher chose that moment to shift his weight onto one leg and lean on the counter. It brought his face dangerously close to Sloan's. Asher raised an eyebrow ever so slightly and gave him an equally slight smile.

Oh my God! thought Sloan. *He's going to kiss me!* He closed his eyes, heart racing, and raised his chin....

"Do you mind if I take a quick shower?"

"Huh?" It took Sloan a moment to catch what Asher had said.

"I wanted to rush over here as fast as I could—"

Rush. As fast as you could? You call that fast?

"—so I didn't take time to... ah... clean up. You know... after."

"After what?" Sloan asked stupidly.

Asher grinned mischievously and wagged his eyebrows.

It hit Sloan like a punch to the gut.

Asher hadn't been in the middle of "something."

"I'm a little, well, sticky-icky."

Asher had been in the middle of some*one*!

Probably balls deep.

Hell, knowing Asher, he might have taken Sloan's call while he was at it!

The clench in Sloan's belly traveled upward and twisted his heart in a taloned grip. *Asher. You fuck. You complete fuck.* He curled his hands into fists to fight off the very real and sudden urge to cry.

Fuck me! I can't cry about my mother dying, but I'm about to over Asher's dicking some nameless stranger?

"Sure," he heard himself say. "Go ahead. Towels are in the upper cabinet next to the tub."

"Thanks, buddy," Asher said, gave him lightning quick "buddy" hug, and dashed out of the room like a big galumphing blond Labrador puppy.

This isn't happening. Were you trying *to make me feel worse?* More *alone?*

The answer, of course, was no. Asher would never do anything to hurt Sloan intentionally. But in pure ignorance he could and did. He did it all the time.

My fault, Sloan thought as he listened to Asher bounding up the stairs to the bathroom. *I keep hoping. Stupid. I am so stupid!*

There was a whine as water began to flow through the ancient pipes running inside the kitchen wall and up to the shower upstairs.

He's naked.

Without even meaning to, Sloan called the image of Asher's amazing naked body to mind. In his imagination he *saw* that body, covered in soap suds, water running down his powerfully built frame—over his wide shoulders, his finely muscled chest and back, his narrow waist, his long thick cock, those stallion-like legs, and finally his perfect feet.

Stop! This is stupid! Why do I do this to myself?

I might as well be in love with a straight man.

And for some reason, Max flashed through the movie screen in his head.

Oh no! Oh no you don't!

Sloan grabbed the glass of scotch and tossed it back. He coughed. Smooth or not, it was a lot of booze to down all at once.

Piss on it.

Sloan poured again and drank it all in two, three, quick swallows. Smooth and then…

… warmth—as if some small internal furnace had kicked on deep in his tummy.

Sloan heard the water shut off. Too quickly, there was that clomping sound over his head as Asher came back down the stairs and then—

—he was back in the kitchen, a tiny towel around his waist and a bigger one over his shoulders. Asher put his jeans and polo shirt and even his socks (!) right there on Sloan's kitchen counter and began to fiercely dry his hair.

"Much better," Asher said, and Sloan turned to him, could hardly control the *wanting* of him, barely help watching the muscles in his friend's arms and shoulders and chest as they danced with an erotic rhythm. When he forced himself to look up into Asher's face, he saw the playful look in his eyes, that slight knowing smirk.

For some reason, this time—

(finally!)

—he wasn't embarrassed.

He was hurt.

He's doing this on purpose. Playing with me.

You're supposed to be my friend, he almost—almost by a fraction of a fraction—said aloud. He shut his mouth tight instead.

"What?" Asher asked.

"Nothing," answered Sloan.

There was that arching brow again (a challenge?) and then Asher whipped off the tiny towel from around his impossibly trim hips (*what's he wear, a size 32 waist?*) and Sloan quickly turned away, denied his desire, and did *not* look.

Asher came up behind Sloan, put thick, strong arms around him, and pulled him close. Sloan could feel the hard muscular chest against his back, feel Asher's penis pressed up against his ass.

God! He's so big I can feel him through my sweat shorts.

Why are you doing this? he wondered.

"Why are you doing this?" he asked.

You know how I feel about you. How much I want you.

But did he?

The thought brought him up short.

Did he really want Asher?

He had. Had wanted Asher like a man dying in the desert wanted water. But now?

Very suddenly, Sloan wasn't sure.

"Why am I doing what?" Asker asked him.

Perhaps his desire for Asher was nothing but a habit?

He pulled away from Asher. "You know, I think I've changed my mind, Asher. I think you should go."

"Ah, Sloan." Asher grinned foolishly. "I'm just funnin' with you."

"Well I guess I don't feel like being 'funned' with tonight." Sloan said, surprised at how calm he felt. Surprised, too, at the words tumbling from his lips.

Did I just say that?

Neither said a word and then Asher said, "I'm sorry, Sloan."

Are you?

To his relief he heard the rustle that told him Asher was getting dressed.

Good.

Asher stepped around in front of him, dressed again, clothes blocking Sloan from seeing—

(thankfully)

—all that glorious flesh.

Glorious?

Really?

Glorious?

Hadn't Sloan seen a hundred, *five* hundred, or even more, men who were just as hot, just as built, naked in the locker room at the gym? Wasn't that a perk of having the membership at the college gym? College *studs*? Athletes?

And not one of them has hurt me. Or strung me along. Or made me think I have any *chance of being with them. Not like I want to be with Asher.*

But did he? Did he really want to be with Asher?

He looked at his friend and realized he was no longer so sure.

How many gay men had he told Wyatt were probably on this planet? Three hundred and fifty million? *And I'm sitting around waiting for Asher? Asher is never going to settle down. He's a slut. He's always going to be a slut.*

And who was Sloan to say there was anything wrong with that?

He moved past Asher, through the dining room and into the living room.

"Sloan?" Asher called after him. "What did I do?"

Sloan stopped.

You don't know. You really don't, do you?

Sloan faced his friend. "You know I love you, right?"

Asher bobbed his head once. "Sure. I love you too."

Now it was Sloan's turn to challenge Asher with a look. He stared into his friend's face, locked eyes with him, and didn't look away.

It seemed to last forever, but in reality it was probably no more than twenty seconds, and then he saw a flicker in his friend's eyes. Asher broke contact. Looked off over Sloan's shoulder.

Again, neither said a word. Again, it seemed to go on forever.

"We need more Johnny."

"Take it," Sloan said. "I don't like scotch. You know I don't drink—" *scotch, but you brought it anyway. Not for me. For you. God. I've been so damned blind.*

Sloan grabbed the phone and walked to the front door and opened it, turned and looked pointedly at Asher.

"You're throwing me out?" Asher asked, clearly shaken.

No one's ever done that to you before, have they, dear? He began to dial Scott's number. His friend wouldn't be happy, but he couldn't let Asher drive like this. Sure, Asher would think nothing of it. He came here that drunk. But Sloan wouldn't be responsible for something terrible happening to him.

"I'm asking to be left alone," he said. "I *need* to be alone. I should never have called you in the first place. You should never have had to rush—"

(he had to fight to keep the word "rush" from sounding sarcastic)

"—over here. It was a mistake."

Asher only stood there, hands half raised at his side, obviously incredulous, a what-the-hell-is-happening-to-me? expression on his face. Sloan almost felt sorry for him. *Almost.*

Sloan turned and stepped out onto the porch. "Scott?" he said, when his friend answered the phone. "I need you to come get Asher. He's too drunk to drive." He looked out across the street and then up toward the sky. It was almost full dark and would be very soon. *Another day done. The sun still rises and sets.* Without his mother. It seemed wrong somehow.

"No. He can't stay here. Please, Scott. … Okay, thanks." He jumped at a bang as Asher came out of the house and let the screen door slam behind him.

"Sloan?" Asher's hand came down on his shoulder, turned him around. Asher's face was mostly in shadow but Sloan could still see those eyes of his.

Pleading? Really?

"You know I *do* love you, right?"

Sloan didn't respond although he could feel those damned tears building again. All for the goddamned wrong reasons. *Don't cry over Asher!* It was a waste of tears.

"I can try to be more if you want. If that's what I have to do."

Sloan narrowed his eyes. More? What was Asher up to now?

Asher pulled Sloan into his arms and he stiffened. *Asher. What the hell are you doing?*

Not…?

Asher moved his hands up Sloan's back, then ran his fingers into his hair and cupped the back of his head. Their faces were mere inches apart, and Asher looked deep into his eyes.

"Is this what you want from me?" Asher asked and pulled him into a kiss.

For an instant—one thrilling second—Sloan's heart raced like a rocket reaching for the sky.

Kissing me! He's kissing me! My God, he's really, really—

And then….

He remembered that those cherished lips had been kissing someone else not two hours ago. Surely those selfsame lips had been sliding up and down some nameless trick's cock. And when Sloan let Asher take him upstairs to bed—

(God, how long had he wanted that? To be held by Asher again? Kissed again? *Fucked* again?)

—and let Asher fuck him—

(and that's what it would be, *him* getting fucked because Asher never *got* fucked)

—it would be with cock that had been *inside* some other man—

(*"I wanted to rush over here as fast as I could—"*)

—and the rocket

just

stopped.

Gone.

There was nothing.

No anger. No regret.

And no desire.

How can this be?

(*"Promise me you'll stop holding a torch for Asher? That you'll move on?"*)

With a gasp, he pulled back, had to struggle, had to almost fight to back out of Asher's arms and away from that mouth and tongue that had been trying to gain entrance into his own. Finally, he had to *push* Asher away from him.

Asher made a grunt that sounded almost angry, then grabbed at Sloan and tried to force him close again.

"No. Asher, stop!"

Asher's eyes flashed and his brows turned into on solid line. "What?"

Sloan shook his head. Stepped back another step.

"What? So now you *don't* want it?"

It? So now I don't want "it"?

"You moon over me all this time like a bitch in heat and now that I'll give it to you, you change your mind?"

Sloan reeled back another step. The words were like a slap. Like stabs with a long thin blade. *Asher! Why are you saying that?*

Alcohol. He's drunk. That's it.

Asher reached out and grabbed Sloan's wrist and yanked him forward again, slammed him against his chest, and when Sloan tried to push away, it might as well have been against concrete and steel. "Asher," he cried. "Please. Let me go—"

"Hey!" came a shout that made them both jump, and before Sloan knew what was happening, Asher was spun about and shoved back against the door.

Standing before them was Max, his hands curled at his sides, eyes blazing. "I think the gentleman asked you to stop!"

Sloan was stunned speechless.

Chapter TWENTY

MAX POURED himself a glass of wine and went out to sit on the porch. The days were growing long again, and even though it was just after seven thirty, the sky to the west was still touched by just the faintest pinks of sunset. And it was a nice day. They whole week and been nice. He'd been in shorts all day. It was just now that he was getting cool enough that he was tempted to get an afghan and cover his legs.

My son is gay. And he's totally cool with it. Proud of it!

I was worried about nothing.

In fact, Max realized something else.

He was jealous.

He was jealous that Logan had his whole life ahead of him, knowing who he was and happy about it. No guilt. No fear. No obligation to be anything but himself.

What would I be today if I had done the same thing? The same thing as my son. The same thing as Den.

Why didn't I tell my dad to eat shit and tell him I was gay as well?

The thought made Max freeze, glass of wine halfway to his mouth. Gooseflesh ran up his arms. He felt like crying. He couldn't believe the thought that had gone through his head.

What if I had told Dad that I'm gay?

But you're not gay.

You're bisexual.

Bisexual.

Is that what he was?

He let his mind drift to that day with Cliff, staying up late, half-bombed on whiskey stolen from Cliff's father's bar. They had gone to see the movie *Jurassic Park* and had loved it, and the velociraptors had scared the shit out of them. They'd come home and gone out in Cliff's backyard and the central air had kicked on and they'd both screamed like girls. The big condensing unit for the house's central air made a noise just like a velociraptor! And sitting on Cliff's bed, they were laughing about it. And somewhere along the way they talked about sex and what it might be like, and that led to them admitting they masturbated. The whiskey, of course. And then Cliff asked him if he wanted "to do it." Max had been mad with excitement and nodded before he'd even realized it.

"I wanted it," Max said aloud. "I wanted it so bad I could die."

And they had done it. Leaning back against the wall, legs tangled together, first playing with their own erections, and then Cliff daring Max to lend him a hand.

He had.

And when Cliff grabbed *his* cock, he'd lasted only minutes before he was shooting everywhere. Cliff had been in awe.

Max knew he couldn't wait to do it again.

But that was before Den came out and ruined everything.

But it wasn't Den's fault.

It was your own.

You knew what you were!

I was bisexual!

Really? Bisexual? Really?

Yes! Bisexual.

Surprisingly, it was Maurice who came to his mind then. When the image of the student swam to the surface of Max's mind, he almost gasped.

Five years ago? It was before 2010, when he and Lauren had gone on the cruise.

Maurice had been an excellent student, but Max would be lying if he said that was what first made him notice the young man.

He was a ginger, of course. What was it about guys with red hair?

(Sloan)

Max didn't know, but it was true. They always caught his attention. He wasn't attracted to redheaded women. No, with women it was blondes almost every time.

(Lauren—how could he help but be attracted to her?)

But a guy?

For one thing it always made him want to see them naked. So many gingers had smooth bodies with little to no body hair. Not true of them all, naturally, and he'd made a study of it of sorts. A ginger could draw him into the locker room every time, like steel to a magnet, no matter how much he resisted.

Hadn't Maurice done that?

But that had been a few months later. The first time had been in his Asian philosophies course. The young man had walked in late. It was a smaller class, taught in a large classroom but not one of the auditoriums. That's why Maurice hadn't been able to sneak in. That and it was less than a minute after Max had called roll, something he liked to do. He wanted to *know* who attended and who didn't, and the huge classes made that all but impossible. It made it difficult to think of his students as people as well, and he wanted to *know* them. He especially wanted to know who was interested in a subject that Wagner University wasn't known for.

So when he had looked out over the mostly eager faces of his students, he couldn't miss the fact that one young man had just slipped in and tried to quietly take a seat. It didn't make any difference how quiet he had been. Who could miss someone with hair so red?

It wasn't the new-penny color of Sloan's. No, it was darker, more like a deep candy-apple in the way it caught the light. He also had a sparse beard that was valiantly trying to grow on his cheeks. Did that mean he had hair on his chest, Max had immediately wondered, all thoughts of the Buddha or Confucius temporarily whisked from his mind. Would the hair around his penis and balls be bright or the almost brown of other redheads?

Then they locked eyes, and the young man smiled, and it was like he'd looked right in Max's head and read his mind. He had found himself blushing and trying to look anywhere except at those green eyes—eyes he could see clearly even from the front of the room. He had opened his notebook, the paper kind and not electronic (for which some of his fellow teachers teased him) and picked out the one male name he hadn't checked off? "Maurice Sinclair?" he asked.

"Here," said the young man, maybe twenty-one. Maybe. He was half covering his smile when Max dared looked up, but he could swear from the look on the boy's face that he had indeed been caught staring. The student was surely smiling back.

Max dashed out after class was over. He all but ran. What if the young man had tried to talk to him?

Max knew he had to be careful. Not that he had done anything wrong. So what if an occasional student suspected the truth? Suspect is all they would ever be able to do. Not only because he would never risk anything unprofessional with a student, but he was married. And cheating was nothing he would ever consider. So he never put himself in a position where he might be tempted. He knew that was possible. *Knew* that he could very well be tempted. Especially with someone who had a brain as well as looks. Max had been able to resist that colleague he'd had to share a room with. The man had wanted nothing but sex in the most disgusting of ways. But a meeting of the minds as well as desire of the flesh? That could do Max in. And he wouldn't be done in. No.

Luckily, Maurice hadn't approached him. Not directly.

He had reached Max through his papers though. The kid was brilliant. His papers were insightful and well-paced, interesting, and it was obvious he was interested in the course and not one of those unfortunates who thought they were taking a class they could skate through. Not that Max ever let any student do that.

It was three weeks into the course when Maurice had done a paper comparing the teachings of the Buddha with those of Don Miguel Ruiz that had particularly grabbed Max's heart. The New Age spiritualist and neoshaman writer of *The Four Agreements* was a hero of Max's, and he'd been lucky enough to meet the man and had found him to be as intellectual and clever as his writings. It wasn't as if the subject of Maurice's paper was that unique. There were many obvious comparisons. It was that Maurice so clearly understood, on a deep level, what he was writing about.

It had made Max feel safe. How could anything develop between him and a student who so clearly understood Ruiz's teachings on "Always do your best," and the Buddha's on "Right action"?

So he'd asked Maurice to stay after class. He had done so, and soon they were deeply launched into a long conversation, which they had taken to the cafeteria over coffee and then lunch.

So it had surprised Max when Maurice had, what felt like from nowhere, asked Max what he thought the Buddha's stance on homosexuality had been.

The question had completely thrown Max for a loop. One moment he had been speaking freely and openly, his heart singing in the ways that he and Maurice were connecting and sharing. He dared say that both of them had been speaking eloquently, and Max couldn't remember the last time he had so enjoyed a conversation.

The next moment Max was stumbling over his own words. "Home… ah… homosexuality?" He had felt his face go red and didn't fully understand how he had so quickly become inarticulate. The expression on Maurice's face had gone completely unreadable. He didn't know if his student was being genuine or just trying to get to him. "I… ah…. Maurice…."

"I'm asking because I'm gay, Mr. Turner. It worries me a bit, although I try not to go there. I've already had to turn my back on my mom's religion. I don't want to have to turn my back on this one too."

Max had actually trembled and felt sweat begin to run down his left side. "Well… ah…."

"If it makes you uncomfortable, Mr.—"

"No! Ah, *no*. You just caught me by surprise is all."

"You knew I was gay, right?"

Again Max's face had gone red. It had felt like it was burning in fact. "I…. Well." He took a deep breath. Heard the first of the Four Agreements in his mind as surely as if someone were whispering in his ear. *Be impeccable with your word.*

"Yes. I assumed so."

Maurice nodded but didn't say what Max found he was terrified his student would ask. "You are too, right?"

"Well…." He took a deep breath, then a drink of his now-cool coffee.

"Want me to freshen that," Maurice asked. "Let you gather your thoughts?"

"Yes," Max managed. One word. Simple.

And the few minutes Maurice was gone did give him the ability to somewhat compose himself. "There are several schools of thought on the subject," Max said almost immediately. *Keep this as teacher to student*, he thought, and almost instantly *felt* the loss of their confidence. He plunged ahead anyway. "In one it is felt to be pretty forbidden."

He saw sadness strike Maurice's fascinating eyes. All afternoon those green eyes had been beaming with excitement, blazing with light and life. Now? It hurt to see it.

"Once the Dalai Lama said that homosexuality is not allowed in Buddhism—but he didn't say why, and I've heard he's changed his stance. I don't know." The truth was Max was afraid to look. It had bothered him when one of his heroes had made such a statement, and he didn't want to find out that the Dalai Lama hadn't changed his mind. "I have read those who say as a Buddhist, one should give up all pleasures of the senses. Homosexual sex can be argued to be sex simply for pleasure with no other goal in mind. Gay men are pretty promiscuous. I've read how even gays who are in committed relationships aren't monogamous."

"You've *read* that?" Maurice snapped.

"I…. Well, I don't *know* it." He thought about the teacher who had practically thrown himself on Max when they were out of town. But for all he had seen, if Dennis and his lover were in an open relationship, they hadn't told Max about it. "I am just saying that there is a school of thought that gay sex could be seen as an ultimate pleasure of the senses, and that could be interpreted to mean it is wrong."

"But didn't the Buddha teach the Middle Path?" Maurice asked. "That rather than going to one extreme or another—for instance no sex or wild crazy sex—one should take a more balanced approach? Instead of giving up all sex, or instead of spending all your free time going to orgies, that sex when it expresses love is a good thing?"

Max found his mouth moving like that of a fish out of water. He was frozen.

"Gay sex doesn't have to be about *just* getting off, just like straight sex. What about love?"

Max gulped. "I'm sorry, Maurice. I was just trying to tell you what I've read. I'm not gay."

Maurice looked startled, then worse—suspicious. It broke Max's heart. Should he just stop talking? Against his better judgment, he went on. "Buddhism is also against unlawful sexual behavior."

There was a flash of anger on Maurice's face. "And gay sexual behavior is unlawful?"

Max still didn't know how the conversation had so quickly soured. It made him feel sick. Could he fix this? "Maurice, I don't remember ever seeing anywhere in the Buddha's teachings a place where he fully defined what 'unlawful sexual behavior' is. But one of the biggest problems is that the Buddha did forbid any behavior that harms others. And you can't deny that gay men spread all kinds of disease."

Maurice jerked back as if he'd been slapped. "Jesus, do you really think that?"

"I read all the time about how gays who fully know they are HIV positive go ahead and have sex and don't tell their partners that they have it—"

Maurice stood up. "*I* don't," he said. "First of all I'm not HIV positive. Second, I always use a condom. Not only am I protecting myself, but just in case I *have* caught something and don't know it, I don't want to pass it on. I got gonorrhea once when I was seventeen. I don't plan on getting it again. And I am not promiscuous either, Mr. Turner. I'm a one-man kind of guy. Did a three-way once—"

Max flinched in surprise.

"—and I didn't care for it. Jealous. And I don't think the Buddha was too happy about jealousy either."

"I… I'm sorry Maurice." God! Why had they had to have this conversation? He had completely messed everything up! Why had he said the things he said? About spreading disease? Did he really think that?

"And I saw that look on your face. Three-way. Guess that just confirmed what you think of fags, huh? You're disgusted with me now?"

"Maurice, I never said—"

"You didn't have to, Mr. Turner. Look. I'm going to be late for a class. And I know what you think of students being late for class." He turned and took a step, then came back. He leaned down over the table. "What does Buddhism say about dishonesty?"

"What do you mean by that?"

"You know *exactly* what I'm talking about. We spotted each other the second I walked into your class."

Max went pale. *God. Oh God oh God.*

"No. No, Maurice. There's been a misunderstanding."

There was a long pause, and then a new expression came over Maurice's face. "Oh." He nodded. "I get it."

"Get what?" Max asked.

"I guess being dishonest with yourself doesn't count, does it?"

He didn't see Maurice in class after that. He had dropped the course. Max had been ashamed of himself when he realized he was relieved.

But what would he say today? To his son? Logan, who felt chosen? Who not only was at peace with being gay, but exuberant about it? Logan certainly didn't feel that gay sex was "unlawful." Not only that, but he had decided to wait. He wanted to make sure the first time he had sex with a man that he was in love.

Such a fool! I am such a fool!

There was a bang of a slamming door, and Max jumped, nearly spilling his wine. He turned to his right and saw two men on the porch next door. Even in the darkening night, he saw one of them was Sloan.

Max's breath caught, and his heart instantaneously sped up. *He's so… pretty!*

Max was surprised at the thought, and then wondered why he was surprised. *I thought he was pretty the first time I saw him.* But Sloan's mother was dying and Max was buried with work, and it had been easy to forget about him. But now he saw it was just like Maurice.

Sloan had me the first time I saw him.

Just then he saw the bigger man take Sloan into his arms and kiss him. Straightaway Max felt a rush of envy. No. Not envy. Jealousy. He wanted to be on that porch with Sloan right now. Kissing him. Finally seeing what kissing a man was like.

Max was surprised at how fast he felt his cock stir. Once more and again his body acknowledged what he suppressed. *I can trick myself now and again. But not my body.*

But thoughts of his cock and of kissing Sloan were whisked away in the next second.

"No. Asher, stop!"

Wait. The guy…. He was hurting Sloan!

And before he knew what he was doing, he was dashing down his steps and rushing to Sloan's side.

"Hey!" he shouted and bounded up the three or four steps of his neighbor's porch just as Sloan was crying out:

"Asher! Please. Let me go—"

Max reached out, grabbed the bigger guy's arm, and spun him around with all his might and slammed him against the front door.

Max snarled, baring his teeth. It was one of the guys that Sloan had introduced him to at the gym. He was big. About an inch or two taller than

Max. And he was built too. But Max didn't think he outweighed him. Not by much. Those arms were big, but not bigger than Max's own. He had a pretty big chest too, but Max thought maybe they were pretty close. He thought he could take the guy if he had to. But most of the time, a fight was all about attitude. Come on strong and tough, and you could usually avoid fists. He took two steps toward the guy, clenched his hands. "I suggest maybe it's time for you to go."

The guy stood up. What was his name? Andy? No. Asher. Like the book.

"Well, if it isn't Mister Man," Asher growled. Would it be a fight after all? "Who the hell do you think you are telling *me* that *I* should leave? I've known Sloan for years. You met him the other day? Maybe *you* should be the one to leave."

"Asher!" Sloan stepped in between them. "I think Max is right. I did ask you to leave."

Even as the shadows grew darker, Max could see that there was an anger that had not yet begun to be released in Asher. It could come out swinging any minute. And it could go for Sloan. He had to redirect it back to himself. "You heard the man. Go."

Asher stood up taller. *Just like a cat puffing up its fur.* Max almost laughed, but knew how bad that would be.

"Please, Asher. I want you to go. I want to be alone."

"But *he* can stay?" Asher said, and it was the cry of a child. His shoulders slumped.

It might be over, Max saw. Hoped.

"Don't worry," said Max. "I'll leave as soon as you do."

"Sloan. I didn't mean any—"

"Asher," Sloan said. "You've been drinking. Call me tomorrow when you're sober, okay?"

Asher shuddered. "Fine." Pouted. "I'll go."

He pushed past Max, and Max took his arm. It could mean a fight. He was tempted to let Asher have his one last bit of bravado. Max didn't need to prove himself. Let Asher have some sense of masculinity. But it was also obvious that the man was too drunk to drive.

Then, magically, a car pulled up front. The inside light came on and Max saw it was one of Sloan's friends. The guy got out of the car. "Someone call a taxi?"

Asher pulled away from Max's grip and started down the walkway that led from the house to the sidewalk, stopped halfway and looked back at Max. "You can go now," Asher said.

"I will just as soon as I know you're gone. I promise."

Asher stood there for another minute, and Max wondered if this wasn't over after all. Then he heard the "Fuck you," and Asher headed toward a truck parked at the curb. Luckily, Max didn't have to do anything. Just as Asher opened the door, Sloan's friend took him by the arm. There was some hushed conversation, and then Asher let himself be led to the other car. A nice car. Much nicer than Asher's truck, which was not a new vehicle. Not by any stretch.

"Th-thank you," Sloan called out, his voice hitching.

Sloan's friend gave a half wave and then climbed into his car, and seconds later, they were gone.

Max turned to Sloan.

"Th-thanks," his neighbor said again. And then Sloan burst into tears.

What the hell was he supposed to do?

He did the only thing he could think of. He stepped forward and pulled Sloan into his arms.

Chapter TWENTY-ONE

THE DAM had broken. Finally. At last.

And why did it have to be Asher who did it?

You fuck you fuck you fuck!

Sloan needed to stop crying. What the hell did Max think of him? He started to pull away, but Max only pulled him closer. And unlike Asher's arms—arms that were taking him as if he was Asher's possession—

(and really, isn't that what he'd been for the past three years or so?)

—Max's arms felt different. It was a strength without force, safety instead of exposure, relinquishing without being controlled.

Oh stop. You're being silly. You're imagining things. He's being a nice guy. What's he supposed to do?

Sloan started to pull away again, but Max shushed him and wrapped those arms around him more firmly.

Sloan surrendered. He let himself be held. The arms were so strong, and it felt so good to be in a man's arms and God…. Sloan let it go and cried, *finally* cried, all the harder.

He cried for being such a fool. He cried because he had seen something in Asher that he hadn't wanted to see, and God, it had hurt. Was the man he'd fallen in love with nothing more than a selfish ass? He cried for the loss of love, and that was surely what had happened tonight. The feeling had been blown out of him. It felt like a rug had been pulled from beneath his feet, and he'd fallen from love into something deep and empty.

Mostly, though, at last—

(*at last at last at last!*)

—he cried for his mother. Cried for the loss. Cried that she was gone. Cried because he would never, ever see her again. He wouldn't hear her silly little sayings or eat her food or listen to her concerns for his future or be embarrassed when she tried to set him up with the son of one of her friends from a book club or PFLAG or the Red Hats Society. He cried for all those days and nights of watching her die—become something other than the strong and loving woman he had known all his life.

He cried until he body ached and his muscles spasmed—

(but Max's arms seemed to press all the right places and ease the pain in his body)

—and even his face hurt.

Max just held him, and he melted against that chest.

(It was so hard!)

Sloan had never felt such strength and comfort in another person's arms. Maybe this was how a father or big brother's arms were supposed to feel?

Then to Sloan's surprise, he felt his body responding to Max—

(definitely *not* a father!)

—and knew he *needed* to pull away before Max felt him. He shifted, trying to signal that he wanted Max to let go, but….

That shift made him feel something else.

There was a hardness pressing against his own.

Sloan blushed in confusion. What was happening? One minute he was crying—

(*wait. I'm not crying anymore.*)

—and now he was feeling a hard-on pressed up against his and…

… well….

(*Well, what?*)

Sloan pulled back slightly, only enough so that their erections were no longer pressed alongside each other quite as tightly and enough that he could look up into Max's face. His own was burning, but in the dark he couldn't really see Max's face. Max was looking at him. He could see that much but…

… but what?

Sloan didn't know what to do. Should he pull away?

But the arms felt so good. He didn't ever want Max to let go.

What are you doing?

What is going on?

His cock throbbed, and he marveled that it had happened so fast. One minute he'd been disgusted by Asher's sexual advances—disgusted by Asher period—and now here he was, standing with this man he barely knew, and they both had erections, and what was going to happen next? Was Max going to make a move on him? Would he let him?

Another throb told him that he would.

But Max didn't make a move. Not any move at all.

If only Sloan could see! How had it gotten so dark so damned fast? It had been twilight and now he could barely see. But the more he looked up into Max's face, the more he *didn't* see *anything*.

Why, it was almost as if Max didn't know what was happening.

Did he even know he was hard?

How could he *not* know?

"Do-do you want me to leave?" Max asked then.

"Do you want to leave?" Sloan asked.

"N-no. I don't. But you said you wanted to be alone."

"I don't anymore," Sloan said quickly. *What I want is for you to take me upstairs and fuck me.*

What are you doing?

Sloan stumbled back. What the hell was he doing?

He had just made one man leave. Now he wanted another man to stay? Hadn't lust already turned his life upside down? Now he was standing here wanting to succumb to lust again? Lust for a straight man?

Had he finally gotten away from a gay man who didn't want him only to try to jump into bed with a man who couldn't want him? At least not the way Sloan needed to be wanted. More than sex? More than lust?

"What do you, do you want me to do?"

I want you to fuck the bejesus out of me is what I want.

No. Not this man. Max was married. Max was no more available than Asher. Or the married co-worker who wanted Sloan to have an affair with him!

I am not going to get rid of one hopeless situation for another!

"I'm sorry, Max. I... I think I do need to be alone."

"Are you sure? Are you okay? Will you *be* okay?"

And then....

Why, suddenly Sloan knew he *would* be okay. Something had happened. The dam had broken. He had finally let himself grieve, and—

"What if you start crying again?"

"Then I'll cry. Maybe I need to do the next show all on my own. I'm sorry. I feel like an idio—"

"No. Don't even go there. We all need to let it all go every now and again. I am so sorry for what he did to you. I hope it was okay for me to come running over here—"

"Oh, Max. No. I mean, yes. Thank you. I don't know what would have happened if you hadn't have been there." Surely Asher wouldn't have raped him. Surely not. "And it wasn't just Asher. It was all kinds of stuff. It was—" His words stopped. He didn't want to say the word "Mom" out loud in fear that he *would* start crying again. And since Max was obviously the kind of man who wouldn't judge him for crying, he might hold him again. Sloan thought that might be a bad idea. Because what if he folded to this lust and they did have sex? Then what? Max *wasn't* available.

And what if he doesn't even know what's going on? What if he doesn't realize what happened?

How could he *not* know?

"I really need to be alone," Sloan said.

"I…. Okay." Max gave a nod. Sloan could see that much. Then his neighbor adjusted himself, and surely he knew *now* what was going on.

But maybe not.

Max gave another nod and then started down the porch steps. "Call if you need to," he said.

"I will," Sloan replied.

Max crossed over to his yard, climbed his own steps, and with a wave, went into his house.

Chapter TWENTY-TWO

MAX WENT home, his senses buzzing. He felt high. He felt even more confused. He didn't know what to do.

He could still feel Sloan. Feel his hard, but yielding body against his. It felt nothing like a woman's. There was no cushioning. Sloan was all muscle, despite the fact that he seemed to think he wasn't fit. When Max had taken Sloan into his arms, it had only been to comfort him. That was all.

He'd had no idea the impact it would have.

It was like his body remembered Sloan. That was preposterous, of course.

But God! Could he deny how glorious it had been?

Was his body responding to Sloan because he was male? Once more was his body telling him what he hadn't allowed himself to see? That he fit with another man? That it didn't matter that the two of them couldn't come together the way a man and woman could—that he felt a joining he had never felt with Lauren. He felt it even though they had both been clothed.

He remembered the way Sloan's erection had felt against his own, and God, hadn't that been a shock and a surprise?

No, he'd never held a man before. His father had never been very demonstrative. In fact, he couldn't really remember a hug. For years Max had wondered if all that Freudian stuff was right. Did he desire men because he'd never had a proper relationship with his father? Were his sexual desires just misdirected need for the affection his father had never given him?

But to him that just sounded sick. He had no desire to be touched, hugged, or anything else by his old man. His father was an asshole.

Then why have you spent your whole adult life and more trying to be who he wants you to be?

Told me to be! I wasn't given any choice.

Of course you had a choice. You weren't commanded to be straight; you were commanded to have a kid. And you didn't have to do even that! Den did what he wanted to do. You could have done the same.

Logan seems to like it. He feels chosen!

Chosen. Had Max been chosen?

Chosen by what?

God? The Universe? Thor?

Was there any "choosing," or was it all just genetic accident? Like Sloan said, was being homosexual just a roll of the dice, sexuality being no different from how you got brown or blue eyes, brown or black—

(or red)

—hair?

So what might have happened if he had chosen to reject his father's wishes? What would he have done? Found a boyfriend? Stand out? *Have everyone notice you?*

It doesn't seem to have hurt Dennis.

And Logan feels chosen.

And if his son was "standing out" because he was gay, he didn't care. Apparently, no one else did either.

(*"Dad! Everybody at school knows."*)

It was more than Max could take in.

Here he'd been fighting who he was all these years…

… and he didn't have to?

Max plopped down on the couch.

Why was he surprised? He'd watched it all around him. Gay people slowly coming out all around him. Slowly? Hah! Hardly! Not anymore. Why, it had turned into a geometrical rocket. Just last year something like eight states had passed gay marriage. Or was it nine?

Was he a caveman?

My God.

He closed his eyes, let his head fall back. Let out a long shudder. *Oh God. Oh God oh God oh God!*

"What the fuck do I do?" he cried.

"Dad?"

Max jumped and turned around. Logan was halfway down the steps, his face filled with concern. "You okay?"

"I... I...."

Logan took another few steps down. "It's me, isn't it? Dad. I'm sorry, but—"

"No," Max said quickly. "It's not you." *It's me. I just needed a fourteen-year-old to show me!*

"Is it because I'm gay?"

Yes. I am fucked up because you're gay.

But only because you are making me see....

No. No no no.

What about Lauren? What's this going to do to Lauren and me?

And how had he jumped there?

Getting ahead of myself again.

"Son, it's not you. It's me." *See, I'm gay—*

Bisexual!

Bullshit. You're gay and you know it.

The idea terrified him.

And thrilled him.

"It's okay, Son. Finish your homework." *Please. I have to think!*

"You sure?"

"I'm sure." He gave his son the best smile he could. It must not have been a good one because he could see the indecisiveness on Logan's face. "I promise it's not you. Go on. Finish your homework."

"Okay. I'm almost done. Can I call Devin when I'm done?"

Max took a deep breath. Let it out. "Yes."

Logan smiled, happy again. "Cool! I can't wait to tell him what happened!" He turned and pounded up the steps.

Max shook his head.

God. What do I do?

He felt like he was going insane. Too much had happened in the last twenty-four hours. And wasn't that the way life was? You could be going along, minding your own business, and then—*Wham!*—your whole world was different. Like those people in the Philippines last year. Or the people hit by the tsunami in Thailand. One minute clear skies and sunshine. The next their entire lives were upside-down. He felt like he was going insane.

Meditate.

That's what he needed to do. Meditation was his bedrock. He'd skipped it today.

Max got up and went down to his basement. He locked the door on the way down so he wouldn't be disturbed. He went right to his CD player and switched it on, pressed the play button, the music he wanted already in the machine. As the sound of wind chimes filled the air, he pulled his meditation mat and pillow out from under its accustomed place in his special cabinet and then opened the doors.

The Buddha greeted him.

The statue was about two feet high, made of what looked like brass (but was in fact resin) and painted to look antiqued. It was an Enlightenment Buddha. He had one hand in his lap, the second reaching down to touch the ground, calling the Earth to witness his subjugation of Mara, the demon of desire.

Max took a few thin sticks of incense, poked them down in a small bowl of sand, and lit them. It was Nag Champa, his favorite—sweet and earthy without being overpowering. It reminded him of churches and monasteries. For some reason it made him feel closer to… to what? To something sacred.

He stripped off his shirt and shorts, kicked off his shoes, and danced on one foot at a time as he pulled off his socks and then went to his pillow and mat. He always meditated naked—threw off any barriers that separated him in any way from the level he was trying to reach. He sat down, crossed his legs, placed his hands in his lap, and closed his eyes.

Clear your mind.

He took a breath, let it out slowly.

Enlightenment Buddha…. The Buddha that had set aside worldly desires.

Like sex with a man? Isn't that what he'd said to Maurice?

Maurice? Why was he thinking of Maurice?

Clear your mind.

Breathe.

In.

Out.

In....

Had he picked that particular Buddha statue on purpose? God. When he had decided to set aside his desires for men—sex with no function but pleasure—had he picked this one out of the other possible statues on purpose? He could have picked the Meditation Buddha. Wouldn't that have made more sense? Or the Happy Buddha? Had he, without thinking, picked this particular Buddha out of the over one hundred versions? Had he set aside his...?

Aaarrgghh!

Stop. Start again. Clear your mind.

Breathe. In. Out. Slow. Clean. In, out, in, out....

Maurice had taken great exception to the idea that gay sex was only for pleasure, hadn't he? It had pissed him off! And Max hadn't even told him about the major reason the Dalai Lama had said homosexual sex was wrong, which was because it used the mouth and rectum for sex instead of the natural connection of the two types of genitals that created new life.

Of course, straight people gave blowjobs or performed cunnilingus. He and Lauren rarely did as neither of them had any great love for doing it.

And wasn't that a big thing for gay men? They loved sucking dick. He'd seen the holes in the bathroom stalls in the basement floor of the college library. He'd even seen a guy jerking off through one of those holes. The guy had even asked him to stick his dick through.

He'd fled that bathroom and had rarely used it since.

Rarely.

But sometimes when he really wanted to see a man's penis he would....

Dammit!

Stop! Stop stop stop!

His eyes popped open. "Dammit," he said with a groan.

No. Don't get angry.

Return to breath.

He closed his eyes again.

And instantly saw Maurice in the shower.

Max had been there first. He'd had a particularly good workout, and he was feeling the body electric. He felt so alive it was like his heart was dancing. The steam in the steam room had been invigorating, and then the hot water of the shower had made him want to spin and whirl under the pounding spray. He had been undulating under that flow, letting the water hit him everywhere. He realized he was feeling sexually excited and wondered if he could get Lauren in the mood for sex.

Or if maybe, if he timed it right—could he get away with a quick jerkoff?

That was when he saw Maurice.

He was standing under another showerhead across the room. He was covered in soap, and he was moving in a slow dance, letting his hand slide slowly down his chest and into the curls of dark red hair above his penis. Max had gasped at the young man's body.

Maurice was looking at him through heavy-lidded eyes, biting at his lower lip, and letting his hands move so that they framed his penis, thumbs in his pubic hair, fingers cupping his balls.

Max's mouth fell open, and he felt the blood rush to his face, and his cock.

Maurice took one hand, wrapped it around his penis, and slowly began to fondle it and bring it to erection. He turned, just as it was reaching full length and arched his back, pushing out his ass, and Max's own cock leapt to its full hardness.

Maurice ran a hand down his buttocks, then into his crack. He pushed his ass out more, spread the cheeks with his fingers, and Max was startled to see the pink of his hole. Maurice stuck one finger inside, in and out, in and out, deeper, until it was almost completely buried.

Max didn't even know when he had begun to stroke himself.

Slowly, Maurice turned back around. He was openly masturbating, licking his lips lasciviously, opening and closing his eyes—but never looking away.

He began to moan, thrusting his groin out, making little cries, thrusting faster.

He was going to cum. Maurice was going to cum.

It was only then that Max realized what he was doing. Matching the gorgeous man stroke for stroke. And as the boiling feeling began in Max's balls, rushing outward and upward—Maurice did cum. It was in great, arcing spurts, shooting farther than Max would have thought a man could shoot—and then he was cumming too, and his legs were buckling, and it was only by falling back against the tiled wall that he kept from falling on the floor.

He almost blacked out.

Then Maurice was walking toward him. Max's heart, which was already pounding from his powerful orgasm, began to race all the higher. He swore he could almost hear it, like an engine being pumped with gas.

Maurice got within inches of him and opened his mouth and the world was put on hold while Max waited to hear what he was going to say.

"I guess I was right, Mr. Turner. Being dishonest with yourself doesn't count, does it?"

He turned and left, and the shame washed over Max in a tidal wave. It was all he could do not to cry right there in the shower room.

What had he done?

What did I do? Max wondered and saw that once more, he had fallen from his mediation. Hell. He'd never gone into it.

Max felt shame for that day—the shame of what he had done, the shame for the fact that he had cheated on Lauren. He could pretend all he wanted that he hadn't. That all he'd done was jerk off. That he and Maurice had never touched.

It didn't matter.

He'd cheated in his mind and heart. And hadn't Jesus said that mattered just as much as the real thing?

But despite all of that, Max realized he had an erection even now.

There was no way he was going to be able to meditate. It wasn't happening.

Tears came to his eyes.

What do I do?

His cock throbbed, and he knew there was no way he would sleep until he masturbated. His dick was hurting, it was so hard.

So he lay down, placing his head on the pillow on which he usually sat, closed his eyes, and took his cock in hand. He knew it wouldn't take long.

It wasn't Maurice who came to his mind.

It was Sloan.

He lasted all of a minute.

Chapter TWENTY-THREE

WHEN SLOAN went to bed, it became obvious very quickly that he wasn't going to be able to sleep. He couldn't stop thinking about Max. Couldn't stop thinking about how it had felt to be held by the man.

Couldn't stop thinking about their erections pressed up alongside each other.

Laid. You need to get laid.

How long had it been since he'd had sex? Sex besides that blowjob in the bathroom at that party? Sex where he could hold and be held? Kiss, touch, hold, feel, lick, suck…?

Fuck?

Too long. Way too long.

Sloan thought of jerking off, but the idea only made him want to scream.

He needed sex.

He *had* to have sex.

He needed a man.

Sloan thought of going to one of the bars. He could get lucky. He wasn't bad looking. He was a little boyish for his own taste. He so wished he were hairy. How had he ever loved Asher's body like he had? The man was nearly as fur free as Sloan. Hairy meant *man* to Sloan. Girls were smooth. Boys were furry!

He had even bought a bottle of Rogaine when he was a kid in hopes that if he used it as body wash, he would grow body hair. Of course, it hadn't worked. Thank goodness there were men who liked smooth bodies as much as he liked the opposite.

Not that it had done him any good lately.

"You don't get out there," Wyatt would tell him. "How can you get your sweet spot taken care of unless you go where the gay men are in the first place? Gods. You could get on Craig's List at least. It works. Howard and I have found some really hot sex there."

Craig's List?

Could he do it?

His balls were aching. God, he wanted to be held. He wanted to touch a man. He needed to be touched.

Wouldn't it make him just as bad as Asher?

Hell to the no. No one could be as bad as Asher.

Heart in hand, Sloan went to his computer and fired it up.

Now what?

He sighed.

Open the Internet obviously. Then google Craig's List?

Google let him know two things. First, as far as computer land was concerned, it was "Craigslist" and not "Craig's List."

(Who the hell was Craig anyway? Was he gay?)

Second, he had to specify which city he needed. Craig's List—no wait, *Craigslist*—was everywhere. It was like Pizza Hut and McDonald's. He would have said Blockbuster not long ago, but it was true—nothing remained the same. Blockbuster was gone. He bet Sylvia Browne didn't see that one coming!

Okay, so since there was no Craigslist for Terra's Gate—

(*big surprise!*)

—he brought up Kansas City instead. Maybe someone in K.C. was willing to take on someone about an hour away?

The main page brought up all kinds of things, of course. Housing and jobs, discussion forums, and all kinds of items for sale: from antiques to motorcycles to beauty and health and oh! Look. Pets. He'd been thinking about looking for a dog. It could help with how empty the house felt.

Sloan's cock gave a cry for help, and he remembered why he was there. He was so nervous. His stomach cramped at the thought of what he was about to do. Under the category "personals" was a list:

strictly platonic

women seeking women

women seeking men

men seeking women

men seeking men

misc romance

casual encounters

missed connections

rants and raves

With a deep breath he took a leap and clicked on "men seeking men."

The next page informed him that by going any further he was confirming that he was at least eighteen years old—

(and of course no one underage *ever* lied and went further!)

—that he understood that "men seeking men" just might possibly include adult content—

(he laughed at that one—really? *Really?*)

—that he would flag any ads that violated the law or Craigslist's "terms of use"—

(he didn't bother to check what those were—did anyone?)

—and finally, that he would release Craigslist from any liability related to his use of the site.

Sloan laughed over that one as well. What was he going to do? Sue over a bad lay?

He almost missed the line that said "Choosing safer sex greatly reduces the risk of contracting STDs, including HIV." Sloan wondered if that caveat made "Craig" feel better.

Sloan shrugged and clicked away.

Another list popped up.

Totally different kinds of choices now, though. He was there. The area was open. Sloan began to read the titles.

Masculine Guy for Relaxed Fun [39] (Leawood/SKC)

Do you need it? [45] (Joco)

late night or now, BJ? - 69? - m4m [45] (midtown/north hyde park area) pic

Hairy married masc dad is horny in office - m4m (Overland Park) pic

mwm for hanging out (and more?) tonight [41] (independence)

"mwm?" Oh. Married. God. Cheaters, cheaters everywhere. And like there was any question that the guy placing the ad *didn't* want to do "more." *Right.*

Sloan kept reading.

want a black top - m,bi,thug,discrete bi dl thugs etc [42] (kc)

cum get me - m4m [22] (liberty)

Sissy slut wants to sext lingerie pics and vids!! [18] (KC) pic

Gay couple seeking other couples or singles to get to know (NKC)

Don't click on that one! thought Sloan. Jeez! Wouldn't it be great if he responded to an ad and it turned out to be Wyatt and Howard? Of course, Sloan wasn't looking for a three-way anyway. He wanted to at least pretend this was more than sex. Maybe he would meet someone nice.

Yeah. Right. And maybe he would meet Hugh Jackman on the down-low.

His cock jumped and Sloan smiled. Little Sloan liked the idea!

Home alone [38] (South Olathe) pic

looking to drink/smoke and fuck [21] (grain valley) pic

WBIBTTM FOR BLKTOP [41] (kc)

buscando a un amigo mayor [21] (oakpark mall) pic

What the hell did that mean? Was it Spanish? And at Oakpark Mall? Did that mean the guy wanted to meet at a mall? Sloan shuddered.

use and abuse! - m4m [41] (Kcmo)

Are you into DILFs? [40] (Plaza) pic

DILF? What the hell was *that*? English, yes. But what did it mean? Don't Include Little Fingers? Damned Illegal Laotian Fundamentals? Do Insects Love Farmers?

He had to know. Clicking on it didn't tell him much.

> *"Daddy looking for a younger guy (18—25) who wants to play with dad (masage/meantoring/fun). Im happy to teach you about other things as well. Curious guys are especially welcome. I especially like masculine guys, frate boys, and athletes. I am completely discreet. Nice guy here—discreet, DDF, negative. Like football, outdoors and normal guy stuff. I'm 40, six four, 230#. Can be one time or on-going meantoring."*

The guy couldn't spell for shit. Did the "D" mean "Daddy?" Maybe. There were guys who liked men older than them. Howard was a good ten years older than Wyatt. His friend rarely noticed anyone he didn't call "Daddy" or—

(worse)

—"Mister Man."

Why can't Max be on here?

But that would mean he would be on the down-low, wouldn't it? Sloan didn't want that. He not only wanted to pretend he might find the love of his life here, but there was *no* way he was going to help someone cheat!

He googled DILF.

The answer started a snickering fit.

Dad I'd Like to Fuck!

Silliness incarnate.

Couldn't a guy just say he was into older men? So what? But "Dad I'd Like to Fuck?" Sloan giggled enough he had to wipe his eyes. His erection went down a bit. Laughter wasn't often an instigator of hard cocks.

WHO HOSTING NOWWW - m4m [28] (kc to joco) pic

Looking for someone who enjoys male fun [44] (south kcmo)

Seeking Masculine Hairy Guy under 35 For FWB or more [35] (Cameron, MO) pic

Cameron? That gave Sloan some hope. Cameron was a good hour drive north from Kansas City. If the traffic was good. So this *is* where you posted when there wasn't a page for Terra's Gate. With hope, Sloan looked on.

Horny [28] (Joco) pic

Chub guy looking for fun - m4m [35] (KC metro) pic

Seeking a MD, RN or other Health Professional [38] (Kansas City)

MD or RN? Shouldn't the guy be calling Ask A Nurse or—

Oh.

Naïve Sloan figured it out. He grimaced. Every doctor he'd ever had was at least two million years old with very cold hands. Were there people into that?

He grimaced again and then reminded himself that he should judge not, lest he be judged.

Cub looking for oral buddy [35] (SKC)

wanting to suck cock, get your nut on my face [28] (Brookside) pic

You Want a Blowjob? [58] (N Joco)

Why, yes. A blowjob sounded good. It sounded damned fine indeed. But fifty-eight? Sloan had nothing against older men, but that was over twenty years' difference. A bit too much for him. Of course, the ad right above that said he could "nut" on the guy's face. Somehow the thought both repulsed Sloan and turned him on at the same time. But there was a "pic." It made him curious.

He clicked.

The picture was hot indeed. A stunningly gorgeous man stood over another equally gorgeous man with his mouth hanging open. The shot was taken over the ejaculator's shoulder and the man was cumming like a fire hose. Could anyone ejaculate like that? Photoshopped! So obviously *not* a real picture. And it couldn't be the *poster's* picture. Sloan felt misled— and wasn't that silly? Was anyone on here real?

He scrolled back to the top and clicked randomly on other ads that mentioned they had a pic. Some were obviously real, others weren't. The ones that were real were either so good-looking Sloan thought the guy would never be interested in him, or they were plain disgusting. Had they *looked* at the picture they used before posting it? Guys with dicks smaller than a pencil eraser or with ribs sticking out or assholes that looked like they were covered in purple rashes.

Sloan turned green.

Mistake.

This is a big fucking mistake.

He was reaching to turn off the computer when he saw it.

Hairy Guy Looking for Smooth, Gingers a Plus [35] (Terra's Gate)

Sloan's jaw dropped open. As much as it sometimes annoyed him that someone would want him simply because he had red hair, this looked promising. And there was a picture.

Shit! Did he dare?

Big Sloan decided to dare it, because Little Sloan was waking up again. Memories of old doctors and "Dads I'd Like to Fuck" slipped away with a strange little hope. He clicked.

Hey. I'm 35 years young, hairy chested and bearded. I don't like that I'm so hairy but I guess other guys are into it. Are you? Please be smooth but DON'T shave your cock. I like men and not little boys. I will suck you until you pass out. That's what I'm wanting bad tonight. But I might like a little bit more. Looking for love in all the wrong places? This is the wrong place but take a chance.

Sloan swallowed hard. He couldn't believe it. Was it real? And the picture? Not a cock or asshole. It wasn't a face, and he understood why it was the rare man that did that. It was a chest, nice, muscled—but not over the top, with just the right amount of dark hair. The guy who posted this ad didn't like his chest? Jeez. And it was a lot like what Sloan imagined Max might look like without his shirt.

Sloan's cock jumped and a sheen of sweat broke out across his forehead.

Should he?

He did.

Chapter TWENTY-FOUR

IN THE end, Max called Dennis. His big brother picked up the phone on the fourth ring. "Hello?"

"Did I wake you?"

"Max? No. Armel and I were in the hot tub. I almost didn't answer—"

Oh God. Had he caught them having sex?

"—but then I got one of my premonitions, you know? Is everything all right?"

No, thought Max. *I just finally figured out that I'm probably gay, and I don't fucking know what the hell to do about it.* He didn't say that, of course. Instead he said, "Den. I need to talk to you."

Dennis sighed. "Yeah. Logan said you'd probably be calling. I thought you might wait until tomorrow, though. You mad at me, bro?"

You're not even close, Max thought. *Not even.* "No, Dennis. I'm not mad. How can I be mad? Logan is what he is."

"Well, I thought you might be mad at me…."

"You mean for talking to him behind my back?" Max said.

"Well, yeah."

How *not* important was that now? It almost made Max laugh. Boy, could a perspective change fast. "No, Den. I'm not mad. I mean, I wish he hadn't *had* to talk to you. I wish I hadn't been the kind of dad that made him think he couldn't talk to me—"

"I don't think that was necessarily it," Dennis said.

"—but…. Look. I am glad you could be there for him. Next time I hope you'll ask him to talk to me…."

"I did, Max. I—"

"I told you. Don't worry about it. This is something else." He opened his mouth to say more and found he couldn't find the words. Well, he could. They were, *Dennis. I'm gay. Pretty sure anyway. And I have no idea what the fuck to do about it!*

And I am hot for my next-door neighbor—

"Well. Okay. What is it, Max?"

—who is this steaming hot redhead who gave me a boner tonight and—

Wait. Dennis had asked him something.

"What did you say, Den?"

"I asked you what was going on. How can I help, Bro?"

Bro? White guys still used that word? Dennis was so macho-macho man, wasn't he? He's the straightest gay man on Earth. *He's straighter than I am. How can he suck cock?*

And the very words made Max hard again.

My God. I want to suck cock!

Wow. Like this is news? You've wanted to suck cock since that day a million years ago with Cliff.

God. He did. He wanted to suck cock!

Max laughed. Yes, Of course he did. He wanted it so bad he was getting hard sitting here talking to his brother.

"Max? What's going on, man? You're weirding me out. Tell me what's wrong."

The desire to laugh went away. *Whoosh!* Instead Max wanted to cry.

What am I going to do?

"Dennis…. So much…. I… I don't know how to say it. I *can't* say it on the phone. I…. Can I see you this weekend?" He bit his lip hard. *Whatever you do, don't cry!*

"Come see me? Why, of course you can."

"I don't want to wait that long but I can't cancel any more classes…."

"Cancel classes? You?"

"Well, I didn't exactly cancel them. But I might as well have. And I would have to cancel some if I came to you before Friday night and—"

"Look, Max. Why don't I come to you?"

Max stopped midsentence. What? What did Dennis just say? "What?"

"I've been meaning to come into Kansas City anyway. You're so close. And I've been wanting to spend some time with you. It's been too long. Why don't I come.... Hold on...." There was a rustle and Max thought he heard his brother saying something, probably to Armel. Something like *will you be okay for a few days if—*

"Dennis!" he said in a voice loud enough that he hoped his brother would hear.

"Did you say something, Max?"

"Bring him. I want Logan to see you together. Not that he hasn't before. But I want him to see that—"

That what?

For some reason tears gathered again.

"I want him to see two men in love. You've always been... casual around Logan."

"At your wife's request."

Guilt bit at him. "Yes."

"Did she think we were going to make out in front of him?"

"Make out away, Den."

"Huh?"

Maybe I need to see it too.

Interesting that jealousy hit him then. He couldn't deny it. No. It wasn't jealousy. It was envy. He was envious that Dennis had been brave enough to be who he really was. *How different would my life be today if I had only been as brave?*

"Be yourself. Both of you. I don't care."

There was a laugh at the other end. "You know Armel and I aren't going to make out in front of you. Sorry man. Don't want to get you too hot and bothered."

Max froze. "Wh—" What had Dennis said? "What?"

"Just shitting with you, Max."

"I...." Of course. There was no way Dennis could have a clue. "I just want you to be yourself."

"And Lauren?"

"She's in Paris, Den. How's she going to know?"

There was another pause. Then: "I can be there tomorrow night."

Tomorrow night? Max almost panicked. "Wow. I wasn't expecting…."

"And Armel just said he thinks he can make it too. Is tomorrow night too soon? You want maybe—"

No! Tomorrow wasn't too soon. In fact, it was about a thousand years too long! "Tomorrow will be fine, Den. Please." He let out a long sigh and fought back a wave of emotion that threatened to overwhelm him. "*Please.*"

"Max. You're starting to freak me out. You're not going to tell me you have cancer or something?"

Max almost laughed. Might not cancer be easier?

(*"You aren't comparing being gay to having a disease, are you?"*)

Sloan wouldn't think it was easier, would he? The thought made him feel even guiltier. Fuck. More guilt? "No, Den. Not cancer."

"You and Lauren okay?"

I don't know, Dennis. I don't have a fricking clue! "Fine," he said instead.

"O—okay Max. I will see you tomorrow night."

"Thanks, Den."

"What are brothers for, Max?"

Indeed. What were they for?

"Tomorrow."

"Tomorrow, Max. Love you, Bro."

"Love you too, Bro," Max said. And meant it.

They hung up, and Max went up to Logan's room. The door was open, and he was at his computer, fingers flying at the speed only a kid raised in the age of computers could type.

Chatting with Devin?

"Logan?"

Logan stopped and turned to him. "Yeah, Dad?"

"How would you feel if I told you Uncle Dennis and Armel were coming to visit?"

Logan grinned and jumped up from his chair! "All right! That would be great!" A wary look came over his face. "Is this about the gay thing, Dad?"

If you only knew, thought Max. *If you only knew.*

That's not what he said, of course. Instead he assured his son that all was right in the world.

Chapter TWENTY-FIVE

EVERYTHING HAPPENED surprisingly quickly after Sloan sent out that e-mail. He'd sent it, gone to the bathroom to pee—his bladder had gone crazy when he sent that e-mail and then realized fully what he had done—and by the time he came back, he already had a reply in his mailbox.

> *WOW! You're in Terra's Gate? That sounds too good to be true. Do you have a pic?*
>
> *Nude not necessary!*

Thank God for that. The last thing Sloan had was a nude of himself, although Wyatt had advised him to get those kind of pictures on about two or three million occasions. A face "pic," though? That he had.

He found a picture of himself he didn't hate too much and attached it to his response.

> *Here it is. It's from gay pride last year. My friend took it. A real friend and not a "friend-friend." I hope it doesn't scare you.*

Sloan's heart was pounding so hard he thought it might be a heart attack. He finished the e-mail with, "Will you send me a picture too?"

Quickly, before he could change his mind, he pressed the "send" button.

Then he leaned back and chewed his fingers. His balls started moaning. "Oh, fucking calm down, you two," he said and gave them a gentle massage. They thanked him.

God. What if the guy didn't answer? What if it was someone he knew? What if the guy thought he was ugly? Sloan thought he was ugly. Well, not ugly. But not hot.

There was a "plunk" noise and Sloan knew he had an answer.

Oh God! Do I do this?

Jeez! In for a penny, in for a pound! Isn't what his mother always said?

He checked his e-mail, and sure enough, there was a message from Craigslist. He opened it....

> *Sure! You can have a pic. Hope I don't scare you. You sure don't scare me. I am sitting here leaking looking at your pic. Let me cum see you? LOL! Let me make you feel better? It will make ME feel better for sure. Lay back and let me treat you how you should be treated! I want you, baby. I can be there in minutes. Is there anyplace in this town that isn't five minutes away? What's your address?*

God. How wild was that?

Now his picture will be horrible. He will look like one of those guys from Duck Dynasty, *I just know it.*

Except the picture wasn't horrible. The guy was pretty hot as a matter of fact. Little Sloan and the twins begged, just *begged,* him to send the man his address.

God! What if he's a serial killer?

Little Sloan didn't care.

Finally, neither did Big Sloan.

IN LESS than half an hour there was a knock on the front door. And the bell rang too.

It had taken Asher three times longer than that to get here.

Scared to death, Sloan answered the door.

The guy was shockingly sexy.

He smiled. "Hey," he said in a rugged voice that sent a shock right down to Sloan's cock.

"Hey," Sloan said.

Sloan didn't know what to do after that. It wasn't like he was a virgin. But easy sex had never really been his thing. Not that he hadn't had it a time or two. You couldn't hang out with the *Fab*-ulous Four and not get pushed into something. And of course, he couldn't even lie to himself and say he hadn't had some one-night stands before. He was a man. He had a dick. Damn if his little head didn't sometimes do the thinking for his big head.

I'm just like Asher. I'm a slut.

Ha! No *one can be as big a slut as Asher!*

"You gonna let me in, or are we going to get it on out here on the porch?"

Sloan gulped and stood aside. "Come in."

The man—whatever his name was—came in.

His beard was a little thicker, a little longer than Sloan might have liked, but who was he to complain? This wasn't about forever, right? Wasn't the biggest mistake of his life not knowing the difference between a one-night stand and forever?

And from what the e-mails they had exchanged said, this was probably not even supposed to be a one-hour stand.

I can't believe I am doing this! I'm better than this. Am I really going to let this stranger—a man whose name I don't even know—suck my cock?

The nameless man pushed him back against the door and kissed him.

He was a good kisser too.

And the beard, a little long or not—

(at least it wasn't *Duck Dynasty* thick)

—felt good against his face. The kiss felt good. How could *anyone* like kissing someone without facial hair?

Asher doesn't have a beard.

He probably couldn't grow one if he tried.

Max has a beard.

Max is straight. He's married. You going to exchange a man who doesn't want you for a man who can't *want you?*

The man who was kissing him wanted him.

Sloan felt his cock turn to steel. He decided to stop worrying about it.

He managed it. Barely.

Wyatt would have been proud.

SLOAN SAT on the toilet. Lee was gone. That was his name.

Remember his name. Do that at least.

It was Lee, right? That or Leigh. Sloan wasn't entirely sure, and Craigslist etiquette seemed to imply he shouldn't ask more than once.

He felt sick to his stomach.

I can't believe it. What did I do? In my mom's house!

In no time, Lee—

(or Leigh)

—had walked in, sort of crab walked him back to and around and down onto the couch.

(*Mom's couch!*)

Lee had then dropped to his knees and kissed Sloan in a way that made the kissing he'd experienced in his life so far seem like nothing. How could that be? This man was a stranger. How could the kissing be that good?

(*Don't think about it! Let go. Enjoy it. Stop worrying. Regret later.*)

Then Lee/Leigh was kissing down his neck and unbuttoning the few buttons on his polo shirt, and when he couldn't kiss any lower, he roughly—

(God, it had been sexy. Could he deny it?)

—yanked it over Sloan's head and started sucking his nipples so hard that had he been any less horny, it would have hurt.

(*Do it! Hurt me!*)

But the lights. They were so bright. Why hadn't he turned them off? Lit a candle or maybe the dining room overhead instead.

(*No, the kitchen light—just enough to see without* seeing.)

"The lights," he said with a grunt.

"Huh?" the guy said—said like he was high.

(*Not high. He just didn't understand what you said.*)

"I want to turn off the lights."

Lee grunted and pushed him back deep into the couch—

(*please. pleasepleaseplease close your eyes, Mom*)

—and got up and went to the front door and flicked off the light switch. "That okay?" he asked.

"The dining room," Sloan said. If you're going to be an ass, in for a penny, in for a pound.

He came here a half hour after you first contacted him on fucking Craigslist. He's not Jesus. He's a trick. A trick... tricktricktrick

Keep telling yourself that.

Lee/Leigh mumbled something, spun about, and all but ran to the dining room and turned off the light.

Perfect. Just enough light coming from the kitchen, but not too much light.

"Is that okay, or do you need me to turn all the lights off?"

Sloan couldn't help but hear the annoyance in the man's voice.

"It's great," Sloan said.

"Thank God."

"I'm sorry. I don't usually—"

"No fucking duh," said Lee/Leigh.

(*It's Leigh.*)

He was pretty sure it was Leigh.

Leigh strode back into the room and dropped back onto his knees and looked at Sloan like he was food set before a starving man. He growled. "Hot. You are *so* fucking *hot!*"

Me? thought Sloan. *Me? Hot?*

(*Go for it. Let go. For once in your miserable life. Go for it!*)

Then Leigh was tearing open his jeans and Sloan's erection jumped out of his fly like Jack from his box.

At least my cock knows what it wants.

Leigh didn't waste much time after that. He took Sloan into his mouth—

(it was wet and hot and magnificent)

—and sucked him like he really did need Sloan as much as Sloan needed just a little bit of human contact.

Sloan knew very quickly this would be over way too soon. So—if you can't beat 'em, join 'em—he reached down and took Leigh's face in his hands and pushed him back, "Let me see your cock." Because when was he going to do this ever, *ever* again?

(*Go for it! Let go!*)

Another grunt. But this time Sloan knew it was a good one. Leigh stood up and fast as lightning popped open his 501 jeans, and out leapt a quite impressive cock.

(*Do it! Suck it! Stop thinking. Don't think. Suck. Suck it!*)

Sloan sat up and wrapped his fist around Leigh's cock.

Is that his name?—Fuck!—Don't worry about it. He *isn't worrying about it. Has he asked your name even once?*

But his ad said that he might be looking for more!

Yeah. Right!

Fuck it! Sloan took Leigh's cock into his mouth.

It was thick and warm, and it was human. It was man. Jesus, Mary, and Joseph, how had he *ever* thought he could marry Jennifer? He was so gay he made Cameron Tucker from *Modern Family* look like a Terminator.

The cock was uncut—

(*why hadn't Leigh mentioned that in the ad, or their exchanges? Wyatt said that uncut cocks were a major plus.*)

—and that was okay, and he took the really thick thing deeper into his mouth and let himself go. He ignored and vanquished *any* voice that told him he was doing something wrong.

Sloan lost himself. He forgot right and wrong. He let himself fall into his most base nature. He made those grunting noises that Leigh had made when he was sucking on Sloan, and boy, that seemed to turn the man on! In no time Leigh was pulling his cock out of Sloan's mouth—

"I want you to cum first!"

—and then he was sucking Sloan again. And before he knew what was happening, he was ejaculating so hard it felt like the marrow of his bones was pumping out of him. Leigh swallowed like Sloan was giving water to that man who had crawled through the desert for days.

(*Jesus, he's just as desperate for some human contact as I am*)

Before Sloan could begin to recover, before he could think about returning the favor, Leigh let out a cry, leaned back, and jerked himself off. He shot all over his chest and body and then collapsed against the coffee table, gasping for breath.

"My God," Leigh finally said. "That was mind-blowing!"

Sloan had to agree. Dammit, how could something so fucking base be so good?

Is this why Asher is such a fucking slut? Is it orgasms like this?

Because if it was, Sloan understood.

Until Leigh left, that was. He left about two seconds later. Gone. What happened to those last words in Leigh's ad? "But I might like a little bit more. Looking for love in all the wrong places? This is the wrong place, but take a chance."

Sloan sat on the toilet and somehow kept himself from crying. How could something have been hot one second and now make him feel so alone? It made no sense. Or did it? He had let all of his values go. He'd let them go for an orgasm.

I could have jerked off.

But would jerking off have been as exciting as Lee?

(Leigh!)

Maybe not as exciting. But for some damn reason, even a man as hot as Leigh turned out to be nothing in the end.

And right then Sloan made a vow. He would never have sex again unless he found the man with whom he wanted to spend the rest of his life. No matter what.

He would rather be alone the rest of his life than feel like he did right now. Sloan felt like the man on the moon. He had never felt more alone.

Chapter TWENTY-SIX

SLOAN THOUGHT lunchtime would never arrive and was relieved as shit when it did. He wanted to get the hell out of Dodge. Thankfully, he was going to get to do just that.

He'd gotten to work about twenty minutes early, the same way he did every day, just like clockwork. He liked it that way. It gave him plenty of time to settle, sit down, drink his coffee, take a deep breath, and be ready for the deluge of calls he would be taking. And a deluge it had been. The fact that the new script for the diabetic monitor client was for shit hadn't made the day any easier. And it was only half over!

Sloan had considered calling in sick. He'd wanted to simply lie in bed all day. But the more he thought about it, the more he knew he needed the distraction of work. The customer calls would keep him busy, keep his mind occupied.

Last night had turned his world upside down. So much had happened. Asher. Finally crying over his mother's death. The crazy thing between him and Max. The crazier sex he'd had with a complete stranger.

The crying had been a good thing at least. But any freedom he'd gained by that had been overshadowed by the mouth and cock of anonymous sex.

How did Asher do it? How did he jump from man to man with such ease?

"You know that's slut shaming," Wyatt would say. "Just because you're a prude doesn't mean we all have to be. Some of us are free. As long as no one is hurt, no one used—that didn't want to be used, that is—then what's the problem? Sex is exciting!"

Yes, it had been exciting. Sloan had needed the human contact. He'd needed sex.

But afterward he felt even emptier and lonelier than before. It wasn't about being a slut or not being a slut, or being free or not free. He had just come to see that in the end, he simply wasn't wired that way.

He wanted love.

Asher's fault. That son of a bitch. Why in the world did I ever let him in my life? How did I ever fall for the asshole?

And to misquote *Brokeback Mountain*, he wished he could quit the man.

But the more Sloan had lain there on his bed in the dark last night, the more he realized that maybe, just maybe, he *had* finally "quit" Asher. He wasn't sure he ever wanted to see him again.

He was going to have sex with me!

He'd waited for three years for a damned encore, and as he thought about the sex with Leigh, he couldn't help but connect it with Asher. He had to be honest with himself. If he had let Asher take him upstairs, fuck him, it would have meant nothing more than the sex he'd had with a guy off of Craigslist. It would have made things worse. With Leigh, at least, sex was pretty much all he'd expected. That bit about possibly something more? Please. It was sex from beginning to end. They hadn't talked about anything except turning out the lights.

Why did I do it?

It had been so damned hot *while* he was doing it. While his balls were screaming for release. Leigh was hot, and he had a hot cock and he knew how to kiss and boy oh boy did he know how to suck dick. But it was all over and done within minutes. There was nothing more. It was just gratification with no heart. That is what Sloan had really wanted, *needed*, so badly. Instead, he'd settled for sex.

What's wrong with me?

He'd looked at himself in the mirror and studied the reflection that looked back at him. Not his type, but he wasn't ugly. Sloan certainly couldn't say, "I'd do him," as Wyatt liked to do now and again when passing a mirror. But he wasn't *ugly*. Lots of people said they liked his eyes. He had his mother's eyes, and he'd always loved those. He had a nice enough smile. People liked his dimples.

He didn't like his freckles. He had more of them than there were stars in the sky, it seemed. About a ton of them across his cheeks and nose. They covered his arms, especially from about the elbows down, and there were at least a zillion on his upper chest. Why so many there and so few lower down?

His mom had said that their freckles were like the average man's tan. Where the sun touched the most often, there were freckles instead of a tan. They had an Irish farmer's tan, she would say, laughing every time.

It never made Sloan laugh. He hated them. He wanted a *tan*. He wanted to lie out in the sun and soak it up and not have to worry about getting fried like bacon on a griddle. Most guys could lie out and turn a lovely brown color. Wouldn't that be nice? Why, he might even dare to go to that "witchy" camp that Wyatt liked and lie naked out on the raft on the lake. But the one time Wyatt had dragged him out there, he'd been too chicken to take off his trunks.

Why?

"You've got such a nice dick, buddy!" Wyatt would say. "Why not show it off? God, if I had something like that swinging between my legs, I'd never wear clothes! I'd want everybody to see it. Instead, I got Little Guy down there."

So while Sloan didn't like his looks so much, he knew he wasn't hideous. Hey, his mother had said so, and she wouldn't lie, right? Right!

He wasn't unattractive, and he was a nice guy. He had a job. He was intelligent. He could carry on a good conversation. And according to Wyatt, he had a nice dick. So why was he single? And why did he obsess about unavailable men? What the hell had happened to his life?

He'd had it all planned. Everything. Once he'd finally realized he *was* gay and wasn't going to grow out of it. After Coop, he found out all about the married guys on the down low; thinking they *had* to get married and being ashamed of who and what they were and occasionally—when they couldn't *stand* it anymore—slipping out and getting a little dick on the side. Well, that was something he knew he wouldn't, couldn't, do. The idea had appalled him.

Sloan decided he was going to be out and proud like Coop!

And the first step on his new path would be to tell his mother. It had taken him about ten (a hundred, two hundred!) times more courage than it had taken him to ride the RipCord with its 189-foot tethered free-fall at Worlds of Fun (him screaming like a banshee the whole time). But he'd done both. That meant he had the freedom (especially after the cookies his mother had brought him a week later) to find a husband.

Oh yeah.

He would meet a nice man, maybe at school (although it turned out he dropped out before graduating) or at some job or maybe the park sitting in the shade of one of the sycamores. The man would be tall and muscular with a hairy chest (a beard would be nice too), and he would walk up and ask if he could sit on Sloan's picnic blanket, and they'd fall in love that afternoon. They'd date, and then one day the guy would get down on one knee in the middle of dinner at a very public restaurant and ask Sloan to marry him in front of everybody (there would be much applause, of course). They would have to go to Massachusetts—that was the only state where two men could get married when Sloan was first making all these plans (fantasies). But hell. Maybe they wouldn't get legally married. A marriage license was just a piece of paper, right? Yeah. They'd have a big ceremony, and his mom would sit in the front row and sob happy tears. *Then* they'd live happily ever after, growing old together and dying within weeks of each other—the survivor unable to go on with the other. Very dramatic. *Very* Nicholas Sparks.

But that hadn't happened.

Now he was thirty years old, and he'd never even had a real boyfriend. Never one longer than about six months.

Coop had hit the road the day after Jennifer had caught them— "Sorry, Sloan! My sister hates me, and I just can't deal with the guilt!" (*Although Coop had been able to set his guilt aside long enough to seduce him!*)

After that it had been a series of mostly first dates with long dry spells in between—and the occasional trick from one of the bars in the city.

Like Asher. God. Asher.

Why? What the hell had happened? All his plans had gone to hell. Why couldn't he find a man? Find one that wanted him for more than his red hair and a one-night—

(or ten-minute)

—stand?

"What the hell is wrong with me?" he cried, now, looking in another mirror—the one in the bathroom at work.

"Nothing," said his friend Peni, coming out of one of the stalls.

Sloan blushed. God. He hadn't known there was anyone in the bathroom with him. "*Talofa*, Peni," he said. It was Samoan for "hello." Peni had taught him the word and a few others.

"Hello, my friend," Peni replied.

"*O a mai oe?*" Sloan asked automatically. It was one of the only other things he knew how to say in Peni's native language. Or more accurately—Peni would remind him—it was his family's language. He had been born in the States, and the one time he'd been to Samoa, he'd been a little kid. He couldn't remember much of anything except beaches and the ocean.

Sloan liked using the little Samoan he had learned from his friend. "*O a mai oe*," meant "How are you?" And it always put a smile on Peni's face when Sloan stumbled through the phrases he could remember.

"Samoans like it when you try to use our language," Peni had explained once. "It's a sign of respect."

But then Sloan looked at Peni's dark and exotic face in the mirror and saw that the answer to his query couldn't be a good one. He turned to look at his co-worker directly. Had Peni been crying? "Peni? Are you okay?"

Peni turned away and wiped at his face. "*Manuia, fa'afetai, ae a oe?*" he mumbled—their usual response. (I'm fine. How about you?)

"To tell you the truth, I feel like I've been wrung through a wringer," Sloan said. "My mom died, you know." Of course Peni knew. Everyone at work knew. The words had just tumbled out of his lips. He didn't stop there either. "And I think I'm finally over the ridiculous crush I have on my friend Asher."

Peni turned back around, red eyes showing surprise. "I—I...."

Sloan waved his own words away. "I've been carrying a torch for that guy for three years. I'm an ass."

"You're not an ass," Peni said. "You're just human."

Sloan shrugged. "Whatever."

"I mean it," Peni said. "And—and—I just broke up with my boyfriend."

Peni's words caught Sloan completely by surprise. Not because Peni was gay. He'd always known Peni was gay. But he'd denied it. Even gotten a little huffy when Sloan had assumed it.

Peni's broad shoulders slumped. "Yeah. I know. I'm gay. There. I said it. So sue me."

"But—"

"What can I say?" Peni replied. "I'm Mormon. The LDS Church pretty much calls homosexuality a grievous sin." He shrugged. "I could be excommunicated if they find out."

"Mums the word."

"Thanks," he said, then bit his lower lip. "Shit. I am going to start crying again." He turned and made a dash for the toilet stall.

Sloan walked to the door but didn't open it. He knew he should leave—or should he? He wanted to help. "I'm just so surprised, Peni—"

"No, you're not," Peni said, his voice hitching. "You knew the minute we met."

True. Sloan had known. "I can't say a damned thing, Peni. I denied I was gay until my ex-fiancée's brother fucked the hell out of me back in college. I always told myself I'd grow out of liking guys."

"Me too," said Peni. There was a single sob. "Piss!" The door swung inward and Sloan almost fell into the muscular man's arms. "This sucks! I *hate* feeling this way!"

Sloan nodded. "I know. It sucks shit."

Peni wiped at this eyes. "It sucks whale dick."

"Did your boyfriend have a whale dick?" Sloan asked, hoping to make Peni laugh.

It worked. "Not really. But it was nice."

"Look, you want to get out of here? Gary already told me I can take an hour lunch." Gary was their manager.

"Is that going to piss Shelia off?" Peni asked. "She doesn't like it when we go over her head." It was the truth. It was their supervisor's number one pet peeve. The thing was Sloan hadn't done that.

"I didn't. Gary was in her office when I asked. I told her my mom's death was really getting to me today, and he told me I could go. Gave me his blessing even. If we asked, I bet you could get an hour too."

"You think Shelia would let me? It's been awfully busy today."

"Can't hurt to ask."

Peni let out a long, deep sigh. "I would love to get out of here," he said, and Sloan saw the tears welling up again.

"Then let's blow this Popsicle stand."

Chapter TWENTY-SEVEN

To THEIR mutual surprise, Shelia let them both have an hour. She did raise an eyebrow. "Did your mama die too?" she asked Peni, her tone suggesting she didn't believe any such thing.

"I—I—" Peni started.

"I need someone to talk to," Sloan cut it. "I'll stay an extra hour today. Help with the shift change." What had he done? He wasn't sure he could survive three more minutes, and he'd just volunteered to be here for five more hours?

"Deal," she said and turned back to her computer.

They both had stood there, surprised at how easily it had gone.

"Go! Get out of here before I change my mind."

They wound up at Café Namasté of all places. Sloan had told Peni about it the day before, and it had made him curious enough to give it a try. He'd even suggested it when Sloan asked him where he wanted to go.

There was a special on portabella mushroom tacos. They went for it.

"So tell me about this boyfriend. I can't believe you kept him a secret. How long did you two go out?"

Peni grimaced and dropped his face into his palms. "Six days."

"Excuse me?" Days? *Had he said—*

Peni looked at him through spread fingers. "I know, *I know*. How can I think I'm in love when it was only a week? I know!"

Sloan couldn't help but roll his eyes. "I got you beat. For me it was one night. Asher picked me up in a bar, fucked the freckles off my ass, and I thought we were in love. Turns out I was just a trick. But then we became friends, and I've spent the last forever hoping he'd change his mind and ask me to marry him. Trouble is Asher's a slut."

"Bobby too. I got over there last night for dinner, and he had this guy there. Pulled me aside and said he'd 'accidentally' made two dates for the same time and would I be interested in a little 'man on man on man action.'"

Sloan gasped. "He *didn't.*"

"Oh, he most assuredly *did.*"

"What did you do?"

Peni sighed. "Well, according to Bobby, I threw a big sissy hissy fit."

Sloan covered his mouth to hide a grin.

"Maybe I did." Peni leaned forward on one elbow and rested his chin on his fist. "Is this what it means to be gay? Are we a bunch of sissies? The Church says gay relationships are contrary to the will of God."

Sloan shook his head. "I don't think that. Not anymore."

Peni look up. "But you used to?"

"No. I didn't think it was a sickness or anything like that. And I can't believe God gives two cents who I have sex with. He's got more important shit to deal with. Planets to keep in their orbits, you know? Keeping protons and neutrons together in an atom instead of them blowing to the four winds."

"That's kind of what I've been thinking."

The waitress came and brought their food. Sloan had told her they didn't have a lot of time, and he was happy to see how fast she'd brought their meals. She'd get a good tip for sure.

They bit into their tacos. The shells were soft and obviously not the white-flour type Sloan was used to. They were some kind of corn instead. He'd never had soft corn shells. Turned out they were delicious. The insides too.

"Oh my God," Peni said. "These are to die for!"

"Live for!" the waitress said, refreshing their waters.

That made Sloan remember to ask why Café Namasté served room-temperature water. But before he could ask, she said, "Remember! Our words have power. They manifest!" She turned and sped off, tossing, "Never say 'die for!' Say 'live for!'"

Sloan and Peni just goggled after her and then burst into laughter.

"So you're a bottom, then?" Peni asked.

Sloan almost spit out his drink of water. He coughed. "Wh-where did that come from?" he asked and coughed again.

"Sorry! I didn't mean to make you choke."

"W-where—" *Cough cough.* "—did that come from?"

Peni gave him an innocent look. Then a tiny little smile. "Well you *did* say that your friend topped you. And your fiancée's brother. Did you really have sex with your fiancée's brother?"

"Peni! Not so loud." He looked around the room, but if anyone had heard Peni, they either weren't letting on or they could care less.

Peni was resting his chin in his hand again, eyebrows raised in curiosity. "You didn't answer my question."

Sloan gulped. "Well… I don't know. I just seem to keep winding up with tops…. And I do like to bottom." He said the last at barely above a whisper.

"*Tell* me about it," Peni said. "Bobby wouldn't let me near his butt with my penis for love nor money."

Bobby. He knew a Bobby. Kind of wished he didn't, but he did. Wouldn't it be funny if Peni's boyfriend was the same guy who had blown him in the bathroom at that party?

"Oh, Sloan. What do I do?" Peni cried. "I'm so darned in love with him. And yes, I know it's stupid to be in love with a man I met a week ago—"

"No more stupid than me falling in love with Asher in one night!" Sloan admitted.

"—but what am I going to do? For the first time in my life, I allowed myself to *be* gay. My God, Sloan. Just his kiss! Now I know why I didn't like kissing all those girls in high school. I'd go to these parties and make out with some girl, and it was like kissing a doll. Nothing. I couldn't figure out what all the fuss was about. I thought there was something wrong with me. But then in the shower in the locker room, I kept getting hard-ons, and I would have to run and hide before someone saw. You know?"

Sloan nodded. He knew.

"I mean, how could I know that just a kiss would be so different?"

"Yup." Sloan smiled. "I know what you mean, Peni. I loved Jennifer—my fiancée. She was good-looking. Sexy! Sweet as can be. But when it came to sex…." He shrugged.

"I never got to sex with a girl. Too much guilt. Besides, a good Mormon girl, especially a good *Samoan* Mormon girl, isn't supposed to let a boy go to second base, let alone go all the way. Not until she's married. And then I met Bobby, and oh, Sloan."

Peni sighed, and it looked like he might cry again.

"Man. All man. A big, hairy, muscular, *he*-man. He couldn't have been more *not* a woman. One night with him and I was done for. I was so enthralled with him—darn it, I still am—that I didn't even feel guilty. I just wanted him to hold me again. Touch me again—"

"Kiss you again," Sloan said. "Touch *him* again."

"Suck him again," Peni whispered. "Have him inside me again. I never felt so…. So…."

"Alive," Sloan finished.

"Yes. Alive."

And that's why it had been so hard to let go of Asher, wasn't it? Because even though Asher only thought of him as a friend, he was intoxicating. He had made Sloan feel alive.

"And now," Peni continued, "I feel so dead."

"It will get better," Sloan said. "One day you will just… *know* you are better."

"Thanks, Sloan."

"For what?"

"For not making fun of me or telling me I'm acting stupid. I can't help how I feel."

"No one can, my friend. No one can."

Yes. That was it, wasn't it? Sometimes you had to take life as it came.

And look at all that had come in the last twenty-four hours!

He'd finally cried over his mother. A terrible weight had lifted with those tears. He could breathe again. Not that he was ready to go skipping merrily down the street! No, she was gone. He would *never* see her again. It was going to take a long time to get used to that, if he ever did.

And he was done with Asher. He didn't care if he *ever* saw that son of a bitch again. He was free.

But…. But what did he *live* for now?

They fell into silence.

Then after a moment, Sloan said, "We better eat. Shelia is going to be mad if we don't get back in time."

Chapter TWENTY-EIGHT

MAX WAS a big man—six foot one, broad shouldered, and thick in the chest—but he still *looked* like a little brother next to Dennis. His brother hugged him, and Max was struck once again, for about the billionth time, by his size. Six four, with a chest and arms that dwarfed Max's build.

I'll always be second best, he thought.

Even Dennis's head looked big, although it probably was no bigger than anyone else's. He had a beard, like Max, and like Max he kept it trimmed. His hair was short as well—in fact, nothing much more than a buzz with a pair of hair clippers. He was starting to lose it and had decided he might as well be done with it. "Not gonna be one of those dudes who lets it grow long on the sides and then combs it over the top," Dennis had told him the day he did it. "Doesn't fool *any*one. How come Mom passed this on to me and not you?"

"It's a game of chance," Max had replied, and couldn't help but think of other things that were nothing but a game of chance: eye color, the color of someone's hair—

(red)

—or if they were a boy or a girl.

Or if we're straight or gay.

Dennis held Max out at arm's length. "It's good to see you, Bro! Been too long. How's it going?"

I'm completely lost, Max thought. "I'm doing okay," he said.

Dennis gave his a skeptical look and Max shrugged.

Logan, meanwhile, who had been the first out the front door and had already greeted Dennis, was now down the steps and hugging Armel.

"Looking good, Uncle Armel!" he was saying, and Dennis' lover had responded with a, "You too, Logan! You've grown two inches since I saw you last."

"Aw, it's only been since Christmas."

Max turned to them. "It's true," he said. "Thank God his new Levis were a little long because now they're almost right." He pointed to the hem of Logan's jeans. "He'll need new ones in no time. He's growing fast."

"Becoming a man," Armel said and smiled. It was a dazzling smile. He wasn't nearly as big as Dennis, nor Max, but he was well built. A gymnast's build. And he was stunning—truly—with skin the color of hazelnuts.

Not as beautiful as Sloan.

Max took a deep breath.

Beautiful? Really? A man? Beautiful?

And then for just one second he could sense the weight of Sloan against him, smell his hair—clean and fragrant—feel the softness of it against his face.

"You look happy," Armel said.

Max blinked. "I do?"

"You were smiling."

"I was?"

"I'd thought you'd be more—'

"More what?"

Armel stepped closer. "Dennis is pretty worried."

"Yeah, well." Max forced a grin, hugged his brother-in-law. "Maybe he overreacted."

Armel looked at him doubtfully.

"Let's get your stuff inside," Max said.

There wasn't much to carry—two duffel bags and a shaving kit. "We may be fags," Dennis said. "But we're not the kind to pack six suitcases and a steamer trunk for a weekend. Although I'll tell you, I had to train Armel out of that—"

Armel laughed. "Fuck you."

"No time for that right now, baby."

Max blushed and Logan hooted, and then Max sent them on in and upstairs. They knew which one was the guest bedroom.

"You mind if I take a quick shower?" Armel asked.

"No problem. Whatever. I put towels on the end of your bed. You two settle in. I'll be getting the grill ready. Hope you're hungry. I bought steaks."

Max went out to the back porch cum patio and pulled the cover off the grill, then opened it. Looked good. He'd cleaned it well last time, so he didn't need to do anything on that front. By the time he got back inside, Dennis was coming back downstairs.

"Got any brews?"

Max couldn't help but think of the beers that had led to his hangover and groaned. "No. Sorry, Den. But I've got some really good wine."

"You've got wine for days," Dennis commented. "But at least you've got some *good* wine. I think it's Armel's favorite thing about coming here."

"You know where it is," Max said with a smile.

"But *you* know what I'll like," Dennis shot back.

"Okay, okay." Without another word, Max went down to the basement and his climate controlled wine cabinet, looked over the thirty or more bottles there, and found a red—not too dry and not too sweet—that he thought his beer-preferring brother would enjoy. He found Dennis standing at the open refrigerator, scrutinizing the platter of food.

Dennis pointed at the two patties at one end. "Are those what I think they are?"

Max put the bottle down on the kitchen counter. "What do you think they are?"

"Is that veggie burgers?"

"Why yes, Den. That's exactly what they are."

Dennis screwed up his face, "I just don't get it," he scoffed. "Why try and make something taste like meat? Just *have* meat!"

"Actually, I don't think they taste much like meat at all. They're made from black beans—"

"God!"

"—and I made them myself. They're organic, no preservatives, no egg even. I got the recipe from the local vegan restaurant."

"That place is still open?" Dennis asked, amazement in his voice.

"It's thriving, in fact," Max said smugly.

"You know, I could understand it if it was in San Francisco or Venice Beach. The Village or someplace like that—maybe even Kansas City. But Terra's Gate?"

"College town, Bro.'"

"Ah!" Max almost saw the light bulb go off over Dennis's head. "Of course…."

"And what's wrong with black beans? You always liked Mom's black-bean soup."

Dennis shrugged. "Huh. Maybe I'll try one."

"No! That's okay." Max held his hands up. "I wouldn't dare push any of my tree-hugger food at you. Besides, I only have two patties left. It's bleeding steak for you."

Dennis grinned. "I'll live."

"I'm going to open the wine."

"Sounds good to me."

Max did just that and poured them both a glass. Dennis sipped, then smiled. "I like it."

"I thought you might. Want to take this out on the deck and wait for your hubby to come down?"

Max got some glasses, Dennis grabbed the bottle, and they made their way down the steps and got comfortable.

Chapter TWENTY-NINE

SHORTLY AFTER lunch the calls had slowed down, finally. A bit. Instead of being instantaneously connected to the next caller when Sloan hung up the phone with the last, there might be a thirty-second delay. If he was lucky, a minute. Even two!

In fact, he thought he might go to the bathroom.

He clicked on the "Log Out" button on his computer, took off his headphones, stood up, and almost walked right into Shelia.

"Bathroom," he said before she could ask him why he was up. It was what she lived for. Watching people like a hawk. Swooping down the minute she saw something she didn't like.

Why oh why, had Neil had to take that job on the dude ranch? He hadn't been their supervisor for long, but he had been amazing. Now they had Cerberus, the guardian of Hell.

"I need you to take a call…."

"I was going to use the bathroom."

"Sure. I understand. But Sloan…. Unless you just can't wait, well… I would really appreciate it if you could wait and take this call. We've got this lady on the phone. Charleen couldn't help her. And…. Well. I can't seem to help her. She's crying."

Crying? And you want me to take the call? "Crying?" he said.

"She called about her new monitor. She can't figure out how to use it. We're going through the script step by step, and it's not working—"

That's because the script is for shit.

"—and she won't cooperate. She's getting hysterical."

Great. Just great.

Shelia looked around the room, gazed daggers at the few operators that were looking their way, then leaned into him said something he hadn't heard her say before.

"Please."

He had to fight to keep his mouth from falling open.

He nodded and sat back down.

"I'll connect you," she replied.

"Sure," he said. He swiveled his chair around, put on his headphones, and stared at his monitor. He brought up the main page for the New Life Blood Glucose Monitors script. A few seconds, and then with no notice, he heard the crying.

God.

"Ma'am?"

For a second, the tears stopped—then began again.

"Ma'am?" He looked at this screen. Read the first page. "My name is Sloan. Whom am I speaking to?"

No answer.

"Ma'am? May I help you?" He used his mouse to click on the "Next" button.

"I can't do this," the woman wailed.

Choice #3 seemed to best apply to her response, as stupid as #3 was. "You're having problems with your New Life Blood Glucose Monitor?" He clicked the "Next" button.

"*Yes!*" It was the only thing she said. She was sobbing too hard.

Choice #1. *God. Did he really have to say that?* He didn't want to. But he knew Shelia was listening. So-called "auditing" the call. "Have you read the instructions, Ma'am?"

"They don't make any sense! I was a teacher for forty years, and I can't figure these instructions out!"

God.

He looked at his screen. Clicked on "Offer to Help Caller Step-by-Step."

"Do you want me to read them to you? If I take you through it, will that help?"

"I want someone to come here and help me!"

Of course, there was nothing like that on the list of choices in the script. Nothing but the advisement that he ask her the same basic question again. The only reason he did was because he could almost hear Shelia breathing in his headphones. He knew that wasn't true. She would be on mute. But it felt that way.

"I can help you walk through it if you want me to, Ma'am." He was paraphrasing the words, but Shelia couldn't complain too much, could she?

"No!" She all but screamed her response, and then if she hadn't been hysterical before, she was now.

"Did you just get diagnosed with diabetes recently?" he asked. Choice #5 on this page.

"N-no. I... I've had it for years."

Hmmmm....

"Have you never used a blood glucose monitor before?"

"No. Yes. No. My h-husband. He's always done it."

"Is he there, Ma'am?"

"He's dead."

It felt like a punch to the gut.

"I'm so sorry, Ma'am."

"He died last month. I don't know what to do!"

Fuck!

"I can't even figure out the thermostat! The house is a furnace, and I'm sweating up a storm. I can't figure out how to change the settings!"

Fuck it. Fuck the script.

"Ma'am? My mother just died a couple months ago. Cancer."

Pause. "She did?" Another pause. "My Freddie died of cancer. Bone cancer."

"God. That's terrible, Ma'am." *Ma'am. He couldn't call her that one more second.* "I've always liked the name Freddie," he said. "What's your name?"

"L-Lois."

He smiled. It was said a person could hear a smile over the phone. "That's a pretty name."

"T-thank you. I like it."

She wasn't crying.

"And Lois? Let's just forget that damned monitor, okay?"

There was a little gasp, and then she laughed. "Okay." Then: "What was your mother's name?" she asked.

"Muriel," he said, and suddenly, for the first time, he didn't feel like crying. There was no dark cloud. Had he really cried it all out last night? Could it be?

"Really?" Lois asked. "I had a friend in college named Muriel. I always thought it was such a pretty name. She was pretty too. Was your mamma pretty?"

"Yes, Ma'am. Lois. She was beautiful."

"It-it's hard, isn't it?"

"Yes, Lois. It's really hard." And no. He wasn't cried out. The tears were coming back. But.... But this time it didn't feel like a dark cloud about to come down on top of him. It didn't feel like an abyss ready to swallow him up. "Sometimes I don't know how I'm going to make it."

"Me too," she said. "Freddie and I were married for sixty-three years."

"Wow," he said. "I would never have guessed. Your voice sounds so young." It didn't really. But why not say that? If a woman liked to be guessed younger face-to-face, he was sure she would like it over the phone.

"You're silly," she said.

And then he asked her how she and Freddie met. It seemed it was at Coney Island. He'd bought her and Muriel, her friend, a hotdog. And then they had ridden the Cyclone, a roller coaster. Not too long after that, Freddie was taking her everywhere. He didn't have much money, and they'd had to run away to get married because her father had forbidden her to marry him. Lois told him how it nearly killed her when Freddie went off to war. "Double-u double-u two," she said. Told him how she was terrified he'd die over there in some foxhole. But he'd come back. And by then she'd had a baby he'd never seen, and he promised to never leave her again.

He hadn't until recently.

Sloan asked her to tell him a funny story about Freddie. She did. She told him how he'd climbed the trellis on her father's house so he could sneak in her bedroom window to give her a kiss, and how her father had burst in and Freddie had jumped out the window and sprained his ankle. "He could have killed himself!" she said and giggled like a schoolgirl.

It was only when his bladder started to hurt that he realized he'd been on the phone with her for fifteen minutes. If Shelia wasn't ready to fire him for going so far off script, she would be ready for his head by now. They weren't supposed to have people on the phone for more than ten minutes, tops.

"Lois?" he asked.

"Yes?" she answered.

"I've really enjoyed talking to you, but I should probably go now."

"Oh yes!" she exclaimed. "I'm sorry! Making you listen to a crazy old lady."

"You're not crazy," he replied. "You're a sweetie."

"Oh, you!" She giggled again. "And you are a very nice man."

"You know," he said. "Before I hang up, what do you say we try that monitor one more time."

"But…."

"I think that any woman who could wait for her husband through months of not hearing a word during World War II, and *any* woman who could teach school for forty years, can handle this like a pro. Can we try? Please?"

"I—I… I'll do it for you, Sloan."

He grinned. Five minutes later they were done, and she was signing off with an overabundance of thank-yous—even a laugh or two. "Bless you, young man," she said. "I can do this! On my own. It's not easy to be on your own."

Sloan thought of his mother. "No, Lois. It's not."

"Thank you. I hope that company knows what it has with you."

"Thank you, Lois."

Sloan ended that call feeling the best he had in longer than he could remember. Shelia was probably going to be pissed. He was surely going to hear about it. But right then, in that moment, he didn't care.

Chapter THIRTY

THE WINE was good, and sitting out here on a fine spring evening, Max could almost forget why his brother was here in the first place.

"I do like it out here, Max," Dennis was saying. "You should let these hedges grow taller. Then you could sit out here in the nude. Get a hot tub."

"I'll think about it," Max said.

They sat in silence for a bit, drinking their wine.

Dennis was the one to break the silence. "So you going to tell me what's up?"

Max froze, then let out a long sigh. "Later, okay?"

"You just have me a little worried is all. You don't usually call me for help."

Max gave a nod. "Later. I promise?" If he could do it. He knew he shouldn't be worried; Dennis wasn't going to freak out on him. But he'd never said the kinds of things that were running around in his brain out loud, not even when he was alone.

And he wasn't ready to talk yet. He didn't have the words. One thing teaching had taught him was that he should never talk about anything really important until he had the words. And with what he needed to talk about, he didn't have them yet.

Thank goodness he'd been able to meditate this morning. His mind wasn't quite as chaotic as it had been yesterday. The meditation had probably been aided by the fact he'd masturbated again that morning, first thing. He'd woken with an erection so hard it was almost painful and a memory of how Sloan had felt in his arms—

(what a remarkable feeling it was to hold another man like that!)

—with Sloan's hard cock pressed alongside his own.

Why had that been so exciting? It made *no* sense. As a teacher, he always needed to make sense of things. How could he teach a student something *he* didn't understand?

When a man and woman came together sexually, excitement rested in a genetically deep imperative to reproduce. A male dog was driven to a bitch in heat. When a female cat came into season, every male cat in the neighborhood was howling and crying outside the house of the hapless owner of that cat.

Of course, sex for humans was about far more than making children. Hell. Otherwise he and Lauren would either have about fourteen kids or they would have stopped having sex the day he got a vasectomy.

So what Max couldn't figure out was if gays and Lady Gaga were right, that they were "born that way," then what was the reason for two people of the same sex to be driven to each other? Wasn't sex ultimately, *really*, to keep the species—whatever that species might be—from going extinct?

What sense did homosexuality make? It was *illogical* for two men to want each other!

And why oh *why* would it be hot for two penises to rub against each other? Or was it not so much hot as it was the frustration of that male dog that can't quite find the entrance to his mate? Two penises could not join!

Max wanted to scream at how irrational it was.

Before Max even knew it, the words were tumbling out of him. "Dennis, when you and Armel—well, ah, make love...."

Dennis's eyebrows shot up. "You're not going to ask me which one of us is the boy and which one is the girl, are you?"

"No!" Max's face went red—he could feel the heat of it. Although he did sometimes wonder which one of them—

"Because if you're asking me about fucking—"

Max cut him off. "I'm not!"

"—then I like pitching *and* catching."

"Dennis!" If Max's face was red before, it was blazing now.

"TMI, Bro?" Dennis looked terribly amused.

"Ah...."

"Did you suddenly get an image of your big brother taking it up the ass?"

"Don't flatter yourself!" Max looked away, willed the blush to calm. "That's not what I was going to ask you."

"Then shoot it to me, Max. Right from the hip."

"I—ah…."

"Spit it out."

"Do you like to rub your dick against Armel's?" And dammit if his blush didn't rage all the more—

"Hell, yes!"

—but Dennis's reply made his curiosity throw his embarrassment to the side. He looked Dennis in the eyes. "Really?"

Dennis growled. "Love it."

"But why?"

"Ah, because I'm *gay!*"

"But what's so thrilling about something like that?"

Dennis shrugged. "I like dick, Max. What can I say? The only thing hotter than a dick is two dicks. Armel's is hot. And I like mine quite a bit." He grinned lewdly. "Don't you like yours?"

God! Was his face ever going to look normal, or would it just stay red forever? "I don't know. I suppose."

Dennis snorted. "You '*suppose.*' What man doesn't like his dick, Max? I don't care if you're straight, bi, gay. What man *doesn't* like his dick?"

"I guess I do." Max forced himself not to look away. He did take a swig of his wine, though. And when he thought about it, he knew Dennis was right. He did like it. He knew by looking around in the locker room he had nothing to be ashamed of. He didn't have a porn-star penis, but it was of average length, at least from what he had seen to compare himself to. And when he masturbated, he did like to look at it. Maybe wonder what it would be like to have one in his face. What he would do….

"I *love* having a dick," Dennis continued. "Aren't dicks great? My best friend—right here!" He gripped his crotch. "I love feeling it flop around in my shorts. I like the feeling of the bubbles in a hot tub jiggling my nuts. Love skinny dipping and feeling the water all around him…."

Him? Had Dennis just called his genitals "him?" Of course, he wouldn't call them "her," now, would he?

"I like it when I sit down naked and my balls hit first, how the chair or the blanket feels on them. And I like having sex with it. I would have sex with me if I could. Clone myself and get it on!"

Dennis burst into laughter, and despite himself, Max joined him. He had to admit that it had occurred to him now and again (especially lately) that he had thought about some of the things Dennis was saying—and that he did like them. Did like having a… dick.

"Men like having a dick! I don't know if chicks like having vaginas as much as men like having a pork sword between their legs, but I hope they do."

Max started laughing again. "Pork sword?"

"Yeah! A pork sword! A love muscle! A *love* stick. A meat Popsicle, a kielbasa, tube steak, a bologna pony…"

"God!" Max fell back in his chair, laughing all the harder.

"… a middle leg, third leg, tonsil tickler." Dennis growled again. "An anal *impaler*!"

"Stop! Please!" Max wiped tears from his eyes.

"A cornholer, main vein, a heat-seeking *love* missile. A beef bayonet. Power drill. Jackhammer."

"Den." Max gasped, guffawed. "You gotta stop!"

Dennis grinned so wide it was a wonder the top half of his head didn't fall open like a Pez dispenser. "Joystick, Jack-in-the-box, little solider, tallywhacker. My *Divine Rod*!"

Max was cackling now and then—*shit!*—he started to cough. Hard.

Dennis jumped up and whacked him on the back. "Somethin' go down the wrong pipe, there, Maxie?"

Max nodded, coughed harder, tried to get a breath.

Dennis smacked his back several more times. "Breathe! Breathe!"

Finally Max sucked in a huge breath, coughed some more, and began to get himself under control. He wiped at his face with his sleeve. "*Main vein*, Den? Your Divine Rod?"

Dennis was positively beaming. "So what do you call it? A pee-pee? A weenie?"

"A cock, I suppose," Max said and had to fight to keep from laughing again. God, it had felt good to laugh!

"Technically, a cock is a hard-on. You know that, right, Mr. Teacher?"

"Oh? Really? Please elucidate."

"Yeah. Cock. Like a rooster. All pumped up and struttin' around. Soft, it'd be your dick."

"Fine!" Max took another big drink of wine and saw it was time to pour again.

"So what were we talking about again?" Dennis asked and held out his glass for more. "Oh yeah. You wanted to know if me and Armel liked rubbing our sticks and stones together, and the answer is yes. It makes the sparks ignite, Maximilian. Don't you remember the song?"

Max wasn't sure what song Dennis was talking about, but nothing Dennis had said had even begun to alleviate his confusion. "I just don't know why you would think it was hot. Two dicks can't do anything together. Isn't it just frustrating? I mean…."

"Max. Sometimes you gotta stop being the teacher. Some things just *are*. I don't know why. Sometimes things don't *make* sense."

"But they *have* to!" Max cried and almost leapt from his seat.

Dennis rocked back in his. "Max?"

"Why would I—why are people gay? It doesn't make sense!" He couldn't stop thinking about how Sloan had felt in his arms. About how that hard cock felt pressed up against his. They hadn't done anything, and yet it had been one of the most exciting things that had happened to him in as long as he could remember. "Give me that bottle."

"You've downed two glasses already, Max. Is it going to be like that?"

Max shrugged. "Maybe."

"What do we have there?" Armel said, coming down the porch steps and joining them.

"See," replied Dennis. "The wine. His number one joy in life."

"Number two," Armel replied and walked up and gave Dennis a little kiss.

Max turned away and poured Armel a glass.

"Can I have some?" Logan had just joined them.

"Hah!" That was Max's only response. "But you can make a salad."

"Dad. Mom would let me."

"No she wouldn't."

"If we were in France with her she would. Everyone drinks wine in France."

"We're not in France, are we?"

"Max," Dennis said. "Give him a sip."

"Dennis!"

Dennis winked at Max.

What the hell, Max thought. "Fine."

"Here," said Armel, who had already poured his glass.

With a huge smile and big eyes Logan took the glass. He took a drink. It wasn't a sip. He had no sooner swallowed than his whole face screwed up. "Oh my God! That's *horrible.*"

They all laughed, and Armel took his glass back, took a sip. "No it's not, little man. It's marvelous."

"I'll stick to Coke," Logan said.

"That sounds good to me," Max said. He couldn't help but smile. It was nice to know that Logan wasn't quite as grown up as he'd seemed the last few days. Maybe they could still be Dad and Son a little while longer.

Chapter THIRTY-ONE

SHELIA CALLED Sloan into her office at the end of the day.

I'm screwed, he thought. Would she fire him? Hopefully, all she would do was write him up.

When he went into her office, he found that he and Shelia weren't alone. Gary, the manager, was there. And—holy shit! It was Peter Wagner, the man who owned the company. The very man who's family founded Wagner University—the lifeblood of the whole town.

Crap. This did not look good.

"Why don't you sit down, Sloan?" Gary asked. He was sitting on the edge of Shelia's desk. She didn't look happy.

Sloan sat. What was this about?

"You took a call today from a Lois Bennett?" Gary asked.

Sloan nodded. "Yes, sir. I didn't know her last name was Bennett—"

"But you sure know her husband's name, don't you?"

"Ah. Yes, I do." Sloan glanced over at Mr. Wagner, whose expression was unreadable, then at Shelia, whose face was twisted in anger.

"I've looked over the script for New Life Blood Glucose Monitors," Gary continued. "And I didn't see anything about asking for a husband's name."

Crap. "I'm sorry, Gary. I know I broke from script—"

"Broke?" It was the famous Peter Wagner interrupting. "I think you threw it in the trash is what you did!" And then to Sloan's surprise, he smiled.

Gary nodded. "You also called the client's product a 'damned monitor.'"

Crap crap crap! "I'm sorry, Mr. Wagner. It just slipped right out and...."

Mr. Wagner chuckled. "Yes. Well. I can't say I approve of that one too much, but I have to tell you, I was pretty impressed with how you calmed Mrs. Bennett down. Not only that, but you got her through her first time of ever using a blood monitor all by herself. You not only helped her, but you gave her a little self-respect too. You gave her some dignity."

"Well, I...." He wasn't sure what to say. He was too amazed.

"You know, son," Mr. Wagner said. "Sometimes in the customer service industry, the true meaning of service is forgotten." He glanced pointedly at Shelia, and Sloan felt his stomach do a few flips and spins. "Sometimes it is also forgotten that 'customer' doesn't mean only our clients. It means the customers *of* our clients."

"Yes, sir."

"Sometimes the needs of our clients aren't met by making sure we don't talk to a caller for more than eight point four minutes, ten minutes max. Now and again, we have to take longer than that. We might take fewer calls, but I will tell you one thing. Lois Bennett is going to be a lifelong customer to New Life Blood Glucose Monitors from this day forward. The few dollars we might have lost because you served one caller instead of two is going to be made up by the money that will be made by your actions. The next time one of her Red Hat Lady friends—"

(and once more Sloan couldn't help but think of his mother)

"—mentions she might be needing a new monitor for her diabetes, who do you think Lois Bennett is going to recommend?"

Sloan felt a grin spreading over his face. If the call with Lois had made him feel good before, now it was making him feel infinitely better. This was *the* Peter Wagner praising his actions!

"Yes, sir, Mr. Wagner."

"Peter, please. Mr. Wagner was my father, and he was a bastard."

Sloan laughed. He couldn't help it.

"May I ask what made you deviate so 'damned' far from your script?"

Sloan spoke before he could think about it. "The script sucks," he said. "The options suck. The words we're supposed to say are stupid. No one talks that way. People don't appreciate being spoken to that way. They want to be treated like a human being." He didn't dare look Shelia's way. He could feel the heat of her gaze. "You ever phone a call center where you feel like you're a nuisance?"

"I dare say it has been some time since I have done so. But yes, I know just what you mean. How long have you been with us at Horrell & Howes, my boy?"

Boy? He hadn't felt like a boy in some time. He'd been feeling pretty old lately. But he supposed that to a man Mr. Wagner's age—*Peter's age*—

(*imagine, being told to call a man whose family was one of the founders of Terra's Gate, one of the wealthiest men in the country—imagine being told to call him "Peter!"*)

—he probably was a boy.

"Seven years," Sloan said.

"Hmmmm…. Have you always felt this way?"

"Well…. Yes. Except when Neil Baxter was here. He was letting us go off script whenever we wanted."

"He probably didn't want you to use the word 'damned,' though," Gary interjected.

"Why, let's hope not," Peter said with a gasp. "The world would come to an end, wouldst it not?"

"I miss Neil," Gary said. "He's the best damned supervisor I ever had in this department."

Sloan was extra sure not to look at Shelia right then. "And now he's off in Arkansas wrangling horses," he said.

"Horses," cried Peter. "Wasn't it Churchill who said that 'There is something about the outside of a horse that is good for the inside of a man?'"

"I don't know," Sloan said.

"I envy Neil sometimes," Gary said. "Sometimes."

Sloan nodded. "Me too."

"Sloan," replied Peter, the tone of his voice turning serious. "How would you change the scripts?"

"I—why, I would change them *completely*," he said. "I would role-play with my co-workers and come up with things that customers might really say. And I would come up with the kinds of replies that wouldn't make them feel like I care more about my product than them."

"Interesting." Peter looked at Gary and nodded.

"I tell you what, Sloan. Peter and I have been talking about you. Actually, even before today."

"And wasn't it fortuitous," Peter added, "that happenstance allowed me to be in-house while your manager was auditing Shelia auditing your call?"

Sloan's mouth dropped open. "What?"

"Tomorrow when you come in," Gary continued, "I want you to take the small conference room. I want you to pick out who you think are our eight best operators and then take them off the phones for one hour each. Do that all day. Then after that, I want you to use the next day to come up with something. Friday, you bring what you've got to my office. How does that sound?"

Sloan's mouth would have fallen open had it not already been that way. He couldn't believe his ears. "Really?" he said, incredulous.

"Yes. Really."

"Why, that sounds *great*! It sounds *wonderful*!"

"Okay, then. Get out of here. Get a good night's sleep. It seems like you've got quite a few days ahead of you."

"Yes, sir!" He leapt to his feet and this time he did spare Shelia a glance.

Wow.

If she had been the Medusa, he would have turned to stone.

Fortunately, she wasn't.

"Mr. Wag—*Peter!* Gary. Thank you!" he shook both their hands and dashed out without looking back. He did hear Peter's last comment.

"Oh, relax your face before it sticks that way, Shelia. You had your chance. Now move over while someone else takes theirs."

Chapter THIRTY-TWO

THE STEAKS and veggie burgers weren't going to take long—the patties were basically cooked already, and the grilling was just to heat them up and give the outsides a good searing, which made them delicious. As far as the steaks went, the meat eaters—one and all—liked their cow all but mooing.

It was only sheer coincidence that Max was standing in just the right place and facing the right angle to see Sloan through his kitchen window. Sloan raised a hand and smiled at him. Max waved back.

Dennis turned and looked in the same direction. "Who's that?"

"Neighbor's son," Max explained. "Well, I guess he's the neighbor now. His mom passed a month ago. He had moved in to help her. He doesn't seem to be in a rush to leave."

"He's cute," Armel observed.

"Is he?" Max replied, refusing to look either of them in the eyes.

Dennis raised an eyebrow—and luckily said nothing.

Sloan's back door opened and he stuck his head out. "Evening, Max. Company?"

Max looked up and looked into that face and dammit if he didn't blush. All he could think of was how not twenty-four hours ago, he'd been standing on Sloan's porch and—

Played dueling boners with him. That's what you did! You felt his and he felt yours. You know *he did.*

Of course he did. How could Sloan have helped it?

Max gulped. "Yes, Sloan. This is my brother Dennis. I told you about him. And this is his partner, Armel." He waved a hand to indicate them both.

"*Husband,*" Dennis corrected him.

"Husband," Max echoed, standing corrected. "And this *not* company here"—he cocked a thumb over his shoulder—"is my son Logan."

"Well hey, everybody!" Sloan smiled that smile of his that made those little dimples show (especially the right one) and turned his eyes all squinty.

"Everybody—this is Sloan."

There was a chorus of "helloes" and such.

Sloan came out onto the top of his back steps. "Where are you guys from?"

"Iowa," Armel chimed in.

"You just getting home, Sloan?" Max asked, his mouth suddenly going dry. *Dammit!*

"Yeah. I stayed a little late and—"

He grinned such a huge smile it was as if his whole being were smiling. Max's heart began to pound. *What's happening to me?* Max couldn't move. Boners were forgotten. This wasn't about last night. Sloan had quite simply—out of the blue—taken his breath away.

Not out of the blue, an inner part of him whispered.

He's beautiful. He really is!

Max felt almost high looking up over the fence at his neighbor.

"—well, something really exciting happened at work today!"

"Have you eaten yet?" Dennis asked.

"No."

"Well, we have plenty." He looked at Max. "Right?"

In a panic Max tore his gaze away from Sloan and stared at Dennis. He had to fight to keep from reacting. Sloan coming over here? But…. He hadn't even spoken to Dennis yet. And Sloan was a center for all of his confusion.

(Dicks rubbing together and God it had been exciting and….)

Dennis was looking at him in a most amused way. "Right, Max?"

"I—ah—plenty," he mumbled.

Dennis turned back to his neighbor. "Hear that? There's plenty. Come on over and tell us all about your day."

"Okay! I'll be right over!" And while it should have been impossible, Sloan's smile grew brighter yet.

Chapter THIRTY-THREE

SLOAN'S HEART was trip-hammering. He knew it was stupid, but he couldn't help it. He couldn't believe how excited he was.

It was a mistake to go over to Max's house, but he was bursting at the seams to tell someone what had happened at work, and for some reason, he didn't want to tell his friends. Scott would just give him a lecture on how he needed to quit his job and get a real one that paid more than twelve dollars an hour. He would say that Horrell & Howes was just going to use him again and spit him out. But Sloan didn't think so. He had met with Peter Wagner! *The* Peter Wagner! And why he didn't want to tell Wyatt yet, he didn't know. He certainly didn't want to talk to *Asher*!

Hadn't his mother asked him to move on? That Asher was never going to feel for him what he felt for Asher? Well, that had been proven dramatically last night, hadn't it?

No. He would go next door. Meet new people. Gay people! There were gay people next door: a whole passel of them, it seemed. New gay people he could talk to besides his motley crew of freaky friends—sluts, pessimists, and New Age crazies all. Not that he didn't love them, of course—

(except for that fuck Asher)

—but oh, the idea of new people was too much to miss.

He could talk about real things. Things besides movies with hot actors in them, how stupid it was to believe in God, how hot that stud over there by the free weights was. Something besides Wyatt's jokes, if *People* magazine should have picked Adam Levine as sexiest man of the year or if it should have been Channing Tatum (or Bradley Cooper or Jake Gyllenhaal), and other such world-shatteringly silly stuff. Not that he didn't like to be silly.

But Sloan needed something different tonight.

And dinner at Max's….

His heart sped up even more.

He still couldn't believe what had happened last night, and the more he thought about it, the more he wondered if Max hadn't even realized what was going on. Straight men could be pretty frigging dense.

Oh come on! You were rubbing dicks with each other. How could anyone do that and not *feel it?* Sloan had certainly felt it. Max couldn't be *that* dense!

True. Max had to have known. But it had been rather intimate—the way Max had held him—and bodies and dicks could have minds of their own, and Max's could have simply reacted to being pressed up against another body. How could his dick know it was a man's body instead of a woman's? Maybe he hadn't realized he was getting hard until they started rubbing together.

I shouldn't go over there. I shouldn't!

But of course he did.

"THAT IS amazing," Max was saying, and Sloan found himself staring at the man's mouth. It was sexy. In fact, there wasn't a damned thing about Max that wasn't sexy.

"Who is this Peter Wagons again?" Dennis asked.

"Oh come on, baby," said Armel. "Peter Wagner. Stop playing dumb hick boy. We all know how smart you are."

"I'm just not sure who he is *supposed* to be. You all are saying his name like he's Jesus or something."

"Besides his ancestors helping found this town, they also started the college," Sloan said.

"Or might as well have," Max added. "It wouldn't have happened without them."

"And then Peter Wagner took the family fortune," Armel said, "and by the time he was done, he became one of the richest men in the country. He's on the *Forbes* billionaire list."

"He's *high* on the list," said Sloan. "And he's gay. It's never been a secret, but in the last decade or so, he's made a point not to hide it."

"Okay—I can dig this," Dennis said. "And you met him. Cool."

"And he wants me to work on the script for New Life Blood Glucose Monitors. I mean…. Wow."

"Why wow?" Max asked. He couldn't keep his eyes off Sloan. He'd been thinking about how beautiful Sloan was—and he'd never really used that word to describe a man—but his neighbor wasn't effeminate by any means. He had a broad face and a rounded chin and his mouth was decidedly male. What would it be like to kiss that mouth?

(To kiss a man!)

And of course, there was that red hair, a weakness of Max's forever.

An image of Sloan standing nude in the shower flashed through his mind and sent a jolt right to his crotch. It startled Max. It was like a mini lightning bolt.

But it was more than how Sloan looked. It was an energy…. No, not exactly that, but he was certainly glowing tonight. Which was nice considering all that the kid—

(*not a kid. He can't be* that *much younger than me.*)

—had been through lately. Max couldn't put his finger on what it was about Sloan that was absorbing his attention more with every day, every hour. But there was no denying it.

"It's wow because…. Because… it's just this job of mine. I used to like it, and then I came to hate it. *Hate it.* I mean, a bunch of us have started calling it Horror House instead of Horrell & Howes. But when I was helping that lady today, it reminded me of why I liked the job. Helping people. And I might finally get to. I'm so excited thinking about it. Peter Wagner is giving me this incredible opportunity to really *do* something and not just take a thousand customers and rush the people through their calls like… like… I don't know what."

Max smiled. He felt something in his chest lift, felt something in his heart stir. "It's like when I teach, Sloan. And when I see this light go on in a student's face. I'm helping someone."

"Yes," Sloan cried excitedly.

"And teaching at a college like Wagner University, I get the chance to try all kinds of things that I might not get to do at other colleges."

"Wow," Sloan said with a big smile—

(And oh, his smiles were so sweet.)

—"Just think! It's Peter Wagner for both of us. Isn't that cool?"

Max smiled as well. He couldn't help it. "It is pretty cool."

Max looked at Sloan, and suddenly, there was no one else there. And Sloan looked back. For a second it was like there were these little doors in front of his eyes—like it was okay to look at him but not *into* him—but then the doors were simply gone, and Max *was* looking in. He couldn't look away. Couldn't. Could not.

"Ah-hum," said Dennis, breaking the spell.

Max jerked, found himself blushing for about the billionth time in the last few days, and looked at the others. They were all looking at him. Logan was looking back and forth between him and Sloan.

Shit.

Shit shit shit.

"How about a little more wine, Bro?"

Max gulped. "Just a little." It was their second bottle, and it seemed like it was about done—yes. Dennis poured the last few drops in his glass. "Should I get another?"

"I say yes," Armel replied.

"Of course you do," Dennis said.

"Dad, mind if I go inside? Got a little bit more homework."

"Go ahead," Max said. "You going to call Devin?"

It was Logan's turn to pinken. "You don't mind, do you?"

Max shook his head. "I don't mind."

Logan grinned and took the steps two at a time and flew into the house.

"How's that going?" Sloan asked.

Max turned to him.

"The whole gay thing."

"The whole gay thing?" Max asked, his voice cracking at the last word.

"With your son. He *is* gay, right?"

"Oh." Max faked a laugh. "Yes. He's gay. And proud of it."

"And how are you with that?"

"I'm—I'm okay with it."

And damn if he wasn't. He thought of Logan and Devin, and he saw he wasn't picturing them rolling around on a bed making out—

(and who wanted to picture their child doing such a thing?)

—but this sweet image of them cuddled together playing a video game or something. He smiled. "I'm okay with it," he said in amazement.

"I'm glad to hear it," Sloan said.

"I mean…." Max chuckled. This time it was real. "I mean, I just suddenly find I can't be anything *but* okay with it. I don't understand it—"

"That's 'cause you're straight, Max," Sloan said and then glanced away for an instant.

"It's just that *he* is so damned okay with it. He's not worried in the least. He's not worried about the things I've worried about." Max froze for about a tenth of one second and then shot out, "With *him*, I mean. I mean *I* would be worried in his place. How life was going to be. How I was going to fit into a straight world…."

"You know, Max. It's getting less 'straight' every day. Especially with celebrities coming out left and right. Wanda Sykes, Jason Collins, Jodie Foster, John Barrowman…."

"Yeah! Fuckin' *hot*!" Dennis interjected.

"David Ogden Stiers," Sloan continued. "Denis O'Hare…. Barney Frank, Matthew Mitcham…. Michelle Rodriguez, Victor Garber…."

"Yum," said Armel.

"George Takei…."

"And that new Spock guy," added Dennis.

"And David Hyde Pierce…."

"Well, who *didn't* know *he* was gay?" Armel asked. "He was about as big a surprise as Ricky Martin or Sean Hayes!"

"And Tom Daley came out recently," Armel said. "The adorable little Olympic swimmer who was denying it."

"And, Max," Sloan said. "Not only are people getting over the whole gay thing, but it's more than that."

"What do you mean?" Max asked.

"The world is changing for all kinds of people. I mean, look at what Facebook did recently! It added like fifty different terms people can use to identify their gender. I mean, I remember when I knew *one* transgendered person, and that was it. I wasn't sure at first; she was just a little… manly. Real big hands and tall as could be. But I didn't think much of it. Then one day my mom told me that she used to be a he, and I was so shocked." He rolled his eyes. "Now every time I turn around I am either meeting someone who is trans or reading about someone or seeing a show about it or a movie. One of the best movies I've ever seen is *Transamerica*—"

"Do… do you want to be a, a woman?" Max asked, not even realizing he'd cut Sloan off.

Sloan's eyes went wide, and then he laughed. "Me?" He spread a hand over his chest. "No. Not me. I like—"

"Having a dick?" Dennis asked, his turn to interrupt.

This made Sloan giggle. "That's not what I was going to say, but yeah. I do."

For some reason Max felt a great rush of relief. Then wondered if that made him an asshole. "Not that there would be anything wrong with that," he said with a rush. "If you wanted to…."

"That's just the point," Sloan said. "There *isn't* anything wrong with it. I look around and see more and more that being trans is becoming acceptable. There are high school kids deciding to change their sex. A few decades ago, none of this could have happened. If Christine Jorgensen hadn't been the first, who knows when it might have happened? She became a role model. Then a couple years ago, Chastity Bono became Chaz in front of the whole world. He's a hero to the transgendered. Made it a household conversation again. The world is changing, for the better, faster and faster. I think a big part of it is the Internet. The world is an open book now. All this information readily available."

"Yes!" Max agreed excitedly. "I've been saying that. Suddenly women who thought they had to cover up their whole bodies except for a little slit to see through have access to information that says that they are not property or second best to a man, and they're starting to say 'screw this!' and taking a chance at a better life."

"Some of them are dying for it," Armel interjected.

"Yes," Sloan said. "Gay men in the Middle East can take their lives in their hands by coming out. Russia, for God's sake, making antigay laws! But step by step by step the *world* is waking up. People are seeing that you can be whoever and whatever you want to be."

It was all Max could do not to jump to his feet. He was catching Sloan's fire, and he was liking it.

"I want to cry I am so happy for your son. He knows who he is *now*," Sloan said. "I wonder what my life would be like today if I would have accepted I was gay when I was his age. I wouldn't have gotten engaged. Not to a woman. I wouldn't have wound up hurting her so bad."

Max was rocked by a jolt.

(*I wouldn't have gotten engaged. Not to a woman.*)

Jeez.

"I'm glad I came out in high school," Dennis said. "I never played that pretending-to-like-girls thing."

"Really?" asked Sloan. "I did. Mom wanted me to get married and give her grandchildren *so* much. I don't know how I fooled myself." He shook his head. "I didn't even like to *kiss* a girl, and the sex? It wasn't bad. But I had to think about guys to get hard. Shouldn't that have been a clue?"

"We've all got our issues to deal with." Dennis draped an arm behind Max's chair, let his hand rest on Max's shoulder.

Normally, Max wouldn't have minded. But now—and he didn't know why—the gesture made him uncomfortable.

"Me?" Dennis said. "Never kissed a girl. Not in a sexual way or anything like that. You know—kiss! kiss!—maybe." Dennis made little kissing motions at the air. "That kind of thing, sure. But never a *kiss*. Never felt a girl up or even wanted to. I just always, always *knew* in my bones. I would see a guy in a bathing suit when I was little, and I wanted to see what he looked like without it. I would get all hot and bothered over the packaging on the underwear at Walmart!"

Everybody laughed.

"And when was this?" Max asked.

Dennis thought about it for a second. "Third, fourth grade? I know I sure wanted to see my buddy Foster naked when I would go to his house for sleepovers in fourth grade."

Max's mouth fell open. Dennis had wanted to see one of his buddies naked when he was in the *fourth* grade?

And I was worried about Logan, and he's a freshman in high school?

"I finally just decided to let it all hang out when I was a freshman. Had fisticuffs once or twice, but that was it. I mean, I wasn't a whole lot smaller than I am right now." He cocked his thumbs back at himself. "Who was going to mess with *this* shit?"

Sloan nodded. "It freed you, right?"

"Hell yes!"

"Now think of Logan up there." Sloan bobbed his head in the direction of the house. "He's free already. He will never have to go through all that bullshit. Never have to hide. Never have to be something he's not."

Each word was like a gentle slap to Max. He knew this was supposed to be about Logan. The things Sloan was saying were good. He was seeing that. It was as if a huge crack in the Universe was opening a little bit at a time and shining this pure white light down on him. But still—for some reason—Sloan's words were a twisting inside of him.

Free. Logan is free.

"He is never going to marry a woman and wind up hurting her."

Lauren! God!

"I don't know what Lauren is going to say," Max blurted. "I'm going to have to tell her!"

(*"Max. I think maybe Logan is spending too much time with Devin."*)

Too much time with Devin! Max wanted to laugh. What was she going to think now?

(*"Chéri*, don't you think he's a little… *feminin?"*)

What was she going to think of *Devin* now? Feminine?

Max sat up in his seat. *God. Is that what she had meant?* "Shit. I think Lauren already knows!"

"Mothers tend to," Armel said. "When I came out to mine, she said she'd known since I was in grade school.

Grade school. Damn.

Max's mood crashed. He wasn't sure just why, but it was like a pit had opened up beneath his feet.

So much. So much was happening. It was happening so fast!

"You okay, Bro?" Dennis asked.

Max opened his mouth to answer, but nothing came out.

"Lauren will deal with it, Maxie. She's smart. She'll deal."

Smart. Oh God.

(*"You know he's* homo, *right?"*)

She had gotten so damned weird about Sloan.

(*"You didn't see him drooling, darling? He was practically slobbering."*)

Drooling? He looked over at Sloan, only to see him looking back. His face was so open. Once more he fell into Sloan's eyes and instantly felt totally naked to him.

Max jerked back, jumped to his feet. Alarmed.

"Bro. What's going on?" Dennis asked him again.

"I need to go for a walk," Max said. "Sorry. I'll…." He started to look at Sloan, and found he couldn't. "I'll be back." And he headed toward the gate.

"Wait up, Max," Dennis called after him. "I'll come with."

"Only if you can keep up," Max said. And as soon as he was through the gate, he took off running.

Chapter THIRTY-FOUR

MAX FOUND himself running full tilt, arms pumping at his sides, legs pounding the sidewalk and blacktop, air rushing in and out of his lungs. He had no idea where he was running. He just felt he had to get away.

Get away from what?

You know *fucking what!*

He fought back tears.

God, you fucking fairy! Don't fucking cry!

"Max! Christ. Let me catch up."

He ignored Dennis. The thing was he *was* running fast, and he was starting to get tired.

Fuck it.

He slowed down to a jog, sucking in air with long, deep breaths.

"Thank Christ! Are you trying to kill me?" Dennis arrived at Max's side.

"You slipping, Mr. Athlete?" Max asked.

"Running was never my sport. That was yours, Maxie."

"You know I hate that."

"Maximilian, then."

"And that. Can't you just call me Max?"

"Fine. Max!"

Max slowed to a walk.

"You know I hate it when you call me Den, right?"

Max stopped and looked at his brother in surprise. "You do?"

"I know I've told you that."

Max shook his head. "No. Or I wouldn't have done it."

Dennis shrugged. "Oh. *Hmmmm….*"

Max began to walk again, neither talking for at least a block. They came out at the far end of Wagner Park, and on a whim, Max took an abrupt diversion down into the grass.

"You gonna tell me what this is all about? I mean, I did drop everything and drive three hours to see you."

"I think I'm gay, Dennis." It was out of his mouth before he could think about it. Before he knew what he was going to say. Before he had said "it" out loud even to himself.

"Well, it's about frigging time you admitted it."

Max froze, almost fell forward from his momentum. He turned to Dennis in complete shock, mouth opening and closing like a fish. "W-what?"

"I've known it for years."

"*What*?" Max staggered and Dennis directed him a few feet over to a conveniently located park bench. He plopped down—thankfully before he fell down. "You…. You knew no such thing."

"Of course I did. Jesus, Mary, and Joseph Clifford Montana, Jr.! Why do you think I came out when I was in high school? Outed myself to family and every-frigging-body?"

Max had no clue what Dennis was talking about and told him so.

"It was so *you* could come out too."

Max looked at his brother, eyes goggling.

"I knew you were gay. I'd been figuring it out while I was figuring myself out. Finally realized that was the score. So I figured if *I* came out, you would know that *you* could."

Max dropped his head in his hands. "I don't believe this is happening."

"I was wondering if that was what this little trip was all about. You wanting to come out."

"I—I'm so confused." He shook his head. Suddenly felt like crying. "You *knew*?"

"Sure. I watched you watching boys. Saw you gettin' a boner staring at the guys at the pool. Watch you drop your hand in your lap when some hottie was on TV."

Max sat bolt upright. "I most assuredly did *not*!"

"You did. Oh yeah. All the time. You did it tonight staring at the cutie that lives next door."

"What?" asked Max, stunned.

"We all saw it. Me. Armel. Even Logan. And I'm sure Sloan saw it."

Max looked at his brother in complete horror. "Logan? No!"

Dennis shrugged. "Dropped your hand right in your lap and then started to rub your dick with your thumb."

Tears broke out in Max's eyes. "God, no!"

"Ah, fuck." Dennis put an around Max's shoulders. Pulled him closer. "Don't cry."

"What must he think of me?"

"Who? Logan or Sloan? I mean Armel was smiling. Your son is probably relieved. And Sloan? I think he'd do you in a New York second."

Max did the fishmouth thing again.

"Are you really telling me you're just figuring all this out now? You had to know guys turned you on!"

Max sighed. Fought the tears. "I guess."

"You *guess*?"

"Okay. I knew. I *know*. But I'm bi, Dennis. And Dad said I had to give him a grandson so…."

"No, he didn't. His *highness* told you to give him a grandson!"

God! Hadn't that occurred to him just the other day?

"So that's why you got frickin' married? Jeez, Max. You didn't have to get *married* to do that! Gays have kids all the time."

Max just stared at his brother in wonder. "I can't believe this is happening."

"*You* can't? I can't figure out how it took you so damned long. Was it Sloan? Did you two rub your sticks and stones together?"

"Goddammit, Dennis—"

"Did it make the sparks ignite?"

"—do you have to make a joke out of everything? I'm losing my mind here!"

"How did it happen? Did you do him? Is that why you were asking me about it?"

"I…. It was an accident!" Max dropped his face back into his upturned palms.

Dennis let out a puff of air. "How do you have sex with someone by accident?"

"We didn't have sex. He was crying!" *Like I'm trying not to do right now.* "He sorta fell into my arms. And I was standing there holding him when I realized I was getting an erection. Jeez, Dennis! I started to pull away, and then I felt his. It was pressed up against mine."

"And it got you going?"

"God, Dennis. I almost came in my pants."

Dennis didn't say anything for a while. Just sat there next to Max, arm around him. "It's going to be okay, Maxie. I mean, Max."

"How is it possibly going to be okay? What do I do? I'm so confused."

"I've been confused for fifteen years. I couldn't believe it when you married Lauren. I thought you were just seeing guys quiet-like, on the side."

Max half sat up. "No. When I saw I *could* have sex with her, I was relieved. And I so didn't want to be gay, Dennis."

"Why?"

"Because it wasn't accepted. It still isn't. You and Sloan and Logan can preach about how much better it is all you want. But there are terrible things happening to gay men every day. Women too. Getting beat up. Killed. Fired. Do you honestly think that just because there are states you can get married in now that people are doing hand flips of joy over it? How the hell do you think Dad is going to react when he finds out about Logan?"

"Who gives a blue fuck?" Dennis said. "Do you think I care what that son of a bitch thinks? I haven't seen him in a year, since the last time you made us all come here for Thanksgiving year before last."

Max groaned. That had been a disaster. Dad making faces at Armel and telling gay jokes—and not the funny kind. It was only by great effort that they managed to keep Armel from overhearing any of the black jokes. Of course "black" isn't the word their father had used.

"I hate that old fuck," Dennis said. "I wish I didn't. Armel's dad…. Max, he's amazing. He calls me 'son.' I figured out one day that I don't need our father as a dad. I had Armel's."

"See what I mean? So Armel's father is great. But there are so many people out there like Dad."

"Max." Dennis reached out with his free hand, put it on Max's opposite shoulder, and swiveled him around on the bench so he was facing him. "Do you really care what other people think about you? Aren't you like a Buddhist or something like that?"

"Not exactly. But what's that got to do with anything?"

"You've been quoting that stuff at me for years, Bro. Stuff about holding things with your hand open or something like that...."

Max sighed. Felt something come into focus just a little bit. "Holding things with an open hand" came the familiar words.

"Takin' it day by day?"

"Not sure the Buddha ever said that exactly. But yes. But, oh, believing something and following it aren't always the same thing."

"Max. You are what you are. And from what I understand from what you've told me about that stuff you believe in, the suffering comes from how you handle what comes your way. Isn't that what you said?"

Max nodded. "Yeah. The suffering is not caused by what happens, but our reaction to it. By our identification with it as something we don't want in our lives." He sighed. "We try to push away or deny the things that hurt, and that only makes it hurt all the more."

"Or we try to hold on to something that isn't ours any longer," Dennis said. "And that's the hurting part. Right?"

Max looked at his brother, rather amazed. "Have you been replaced by a pod person?"

Dennis snickered. "Yes! And I have placed a pod just for you under your bed, and tonight when you fall asleep—"

"Fuck you, Dennis."

"That, my brother, would be incest. And while I am a bit of a perv—and you do have a swell ass—I am just not *that* perverted."

Max cracked up. "I don't believe the shit that comes out of your mouth."

"What can I say? I love to be shocking."

And then it all hit him again. Holding with an open hand or not, the enormity of it all loomed before him like a canyon. "What am I going to do?"

Dennis relaxed back against the bench. "I don't know, Maxie. How do you feel about this guy?"

Feel about him? "I don't know that I feel anything for him, Dennis."

"Well you were looking at him the way a dog looks at a piece of bacon…."

"Max, I don't even know if I *am* gay or not. I've never done anything with a man."

"What does that have to do with the price of tea in China?"

"What if I do something and I don't like it?"

"Max, you almost shot your wad rubbing up against him through your clothes. What do you think would have happened if those dicks had been skin on skin? You tellin' me you don't *know* that would be hot?"

Max felt his penis stir. *God.*

"Max… if I were you, I'd see if that pretty little ginger next door will give you some of that mighty purty little ass of his and then you'll know—"

"Dennis! Goddammit, I'm married!"

"And I don't think it's cool to cheat, Max. But if you think there is any possibility that you're *not* gay, you need to find out one way or another. What are you going to do? Be married and celibate for dudes the whole rest of your life and be miserable? Or get divorced and find out you don't like it?"

"I sure am disgusted by the gay stuff I've seen online."

"Maybe you were just watching the wrong stuff," Dennis said. "There's all kinds of porn out there. What have you been lookin' at?"

Max told him all about the scenes he'd seen online, with quick pickups and men dropping into bed at the drop of a hat.

"Sounds like you need the softer stuff."

"I don't know, Dennis. Somehow strokin' off to online porn sounds a little gross."

"Suit yourself. I like it. Armel's got a pretty good sex drive, but it ain't enough for the tiger down here." Dennis groped himself.

Max burst into laughter. "Are you trying to be gross?"

Dennis looked hurt. "My dick isn't gross," he whined.

Max slumped back.

"Think maybe you could tell your old lady? Maybe Lauren would let you give it a try? Or maybe you could find a bi dude and the two of you do him together? I know guys who do that. They like it a lot."

Max looked at Dennis like he was insane. "*Lauren*?"

Dennis shrugged. "Just offerin' you some options."

Max shook his head. "That isn't one. I can tell you that." He closed his eyes. Rubbed them. "Oh, Dennis. I am right and truly fucked."

"Not yet you aren't," Dennis said, and oh, they laughed again.

Max was going to need all the laughs he could get.

Chapter THIRTY-FIVE

WHEN MAX got home, he went straight up to his son's room. The door was closed, but there was light coming from underneath. Heart in hand, he knocked.

"Hold on!" came the call from the other side, and Max waited. He didn't wonder why he had to wait. It was none of his business.

But it was only a few seconds later when the door opened and he saw Logan standing there, looking up at him. Up, but not by much.

He really is growing fast. He could remember the day Logan was born. He was there after all. Was the first to hold him, a little purple ball, arms moving slightly at his sides. He hadn't cried a tear. Max helped the nurse stamp his tiny little foot against the ink pad and then the hard piece of paper—counted those toes, five and, yes, five, and ten fingers. He brought Logan to his wife, laid him on her chest and she held him. Rocked him. It was the most beautiful thing he'd ever seen. He and Lauren had been so close in those days. Loved each other so much. And on that day, they became three. It was one of the happiest days of Max's life.

"He needs to cry," said the nurse.

"Why?" Max had asked. He was pleased that Logan hadn't felt the need to cry.

"Because he's not getting a deep breath. See? His color? He needs to cry to draw in oxygen."

Against his better judgment, Max had pinched his son's tiny butt until after twice, baby Logan finally let out a small cry. It had hurt Max to hurt his son. It had been his first moments in the world. Wasn't he going to hurt enough in life?

He's not hurting right now, Max thought.

"I was just telling Devin goodnight."

"That's nice," Max said. "Um. May I talk to you?"

"Sure." Logan stood aside and Max walked in. The room was clean as it had been lately. Hey. Devin was having a good influence on Logan.

(*"Chéri, don't you think he's a little… feminin?"*)

"Effeminate" or not. And of course, he wasn't. There was nothing nonmasculine about Devin. If anyone was feminine, it was Logan.

Jeez, what was Lauren going to say?

About Logan? Or about…?

"Logan? I have something I need to tell you."

Can I do this? Should I do this?

He knows, according to Dennis. So be the man you want Logan to be when he grows up and tell him.

"Uh-oh." Logan sat down on the corner of his bed.

Max chose the chair at Logan's desk. He took a deep breath. *God!* "I'm not sure how to say this…."

"Dad, take it from me. It's usually best just to spit it out."

Spit it out. Has everybody gotten smarter than me recently?

Logan looked at him expectantly.

Shit.

Just spit it out.

"Logan…"

Spit it out!

"… I'm gay."

Time stopped. He was sure of it. There was no sound. No movement. Nothing.

Then: "I think I kinda knew that, Dad."

"You…. You what?" *Dennis was right?*

"I don't think I knew for *sure* until tonight."

Max was able to do little more than just breathe. Words started to form, and then he lost them.

"You like Sloan, don't you, Dad?"

Dennis was right. Damn him.

"It's cool. I like Sloan a lot." Logan looked away.

It's cool?

"Does Mom know?"

He's so calm about this.

"God," Logan said, eyes going wide. "I just thought of something. You're not blaming yourself 'cause I'm gay, are you?"

Is this happening? It was like something out of *The Twilight Zone.* Max could almost hear the theme song in his head.

"You are, aren't you? Well stop it. And if you *did* make me gay, then thank you."

Twilight Zone. Dah, dah, dah-dah. Dah, dah, dah-dah….

"You knew?"

Logan nodded. "Thought so, anyway. Then the way you were looking at Sloan tonight…. Are you in love with him?"

"No, I'm not in love with Sloan."

Logan looked doubtful. "You think he's cute, though, right?"

Fucking Twilight Zone! "Logan, I can't believe you knew about me. I didn't know!"

Logan's eyebrows rose. "Really? As smart as you are? You teach *college*, Dad…."

"Yeah, well. What can I say?"

Sometimes we're blind.

"How did you not know, Dad?"

"How did *you* know?"

"That I was gay? Or you? Both are pretty much the same thing."

"What?"

"Well, I like dudes, Dad. Always have. Since long before I realized just how *much* I liked them. I don't even look at girls. Not that way. And you? It's the same. I didn't see it at first, but once I realized *I* was gay, I like, started noticing the same thing about you…. Like when we watch *Hawaii Five-O.* Every time Steve McGarrett takes his shirt off you are, like, glued to the screen."

I am?

He thought of the actor who played McGarrett—that muscular body—and God yes, he was hot, and maybe he had stared and….

Yes. He did stare, didn't he?

"I like Danno. He's hairy." Logan smiled. "Hot."

And Alex O'Loughlin was all smooth.

Like Sloan.

Max felt a blush coming on again. Coming on? It had happened already.

"Maybe it was blinders, Dad."

"What?"

"You know. Like they put on horses so they can only see one direction? You had blinders on, I guess."

Damn. "When did you get so smart, Logan?"

Logan shrugged.

"I thought maybe you'd be mad or something," Max said.

"Why? I think it's kinda cool."

"You do?"

"You're gonna have to tell Mom. Although she's kinda gotta know already. I mean if *I* know, she has to have figured it out. She's a smart one, Dad. I can't pull anything over on her."

"I guess I will have to."

And won't that be fun?

"I'm here for you, old man."

"Old man?" Max asked, indignant. Since when was thirty-five an old man?

"What do you think is going to happen, Dad?"

"I don't have a clue, Logan. Not a clue."

Chapter THIRTY-SIX

SLOAN COULDN'T stop thinking of what had happened next door. The way Max had been looking at him. His eyes had been blazing! And when he'd jumped to his feet? Why, for a second he'd thought Max was going to kiss him, right there in front of his whole family. His son.

Crazy!

Sloan was brushing his teeth when the doorbell rang. *Now who the heck could that be?*

He spit and rinsed, and there was a knocking.

Hold on, hold on! Must be Wyatt. He was so impatient.

But when Sloan opened the door, it wasn't his bear buddy standing there. It was Max.

"Max," he said, surprised.

"Hey, Sloan."

They stood there looking at each other. Then Sloan said, "Ah. Did you want to come in?"

Max nodded. "Yeah. Or we could talk on the porch."

"Talk?" *What did he want to talk about?* Was it about tonight? The way Max had been undressing him with his eyes. Or it had felt like it anyway. He wasn't sure at first. Straight guys stared sometimes, especially when they'd been drinking. Sloan had had more than one het guy make a pass at a straight friend's party. But when he took them up on it, they panicked and ran. Why, he'd even gotten a guy as far as his bedroom once. The married guy who lived above his old apartment. One night in a huge dramatic fight fit for the Jerry Springer Show, the upstairs neighbor's wife had stormed out, suitcases banging behind her. Then about half an hour later, the guy had shown up at Sloan's door. He was a mess. Seems his wife had found out he'd been cruising porn on the Internet.

(*"You know. Porn."*

"Porn?"

"Yeah. Dude on dude porn.)

Then the man had kissed him—he wasn't sure of the neighbor's name then, and he wasn't sure tonight. But he'd been hot in his unshaven, wife-beater, torn-jeans-and-baseball-cap-wearing way. The whole FF thought so. Sloan had jerked off thinking about him. So when the guy jumped forward and starting kissing him—

(a little sloppy in form, but it was a straight guy, so who the hell was complaining?)

—what was Sloan to do but invite him back to his bedroom?

It was against his better judgment. He didn't help men cheat. He'd had a boyfriend cheat on him once, and it had hurt like mad. It had taken him a year to get over it. And could he even consider a guy he'd dated for all of a month a boyfriend?

(In fact, it was meeting Asher and falling in love with him in three minutes that had done it, wasn't it?)

Sloan had told himself—his dick doing all his thinking for him (a dick that hadn't been touched by another man in six months at least, at the time)—that the reason it was okay was that the guy's wife had just left him. He couldn't help the guy cheat if his wife had left him, right?

Men really did let their little heads do the thinking, Sloan realized, especially when that little head was hard enough.

They'd had their clothes half-off, the front of neighbor-man's jeans bulging obscenely, and when Sloan dropped his pants—his own erection tenting out the front of his tighty-whities—the guy suddenly freaked out and ran.

Hadn't that been a blue-balling bitch?

After he'd gotten over the frustration of being run out on, Sloan was glad nothing had happened. He really wasn't that guy. The guilt would have been too much.

So when Max had jumped up and run off....

"Well, *I* need to talk. Do you have a few minutes?"

"Sure." Sloan stood aside and, funny, Max glanced around—like he was seeing if anyone was watching—before coming in.

"What's on your mind, Max?"

Max looked around the room before meeting Sloan's face. "Well, ah, first I want to apologize for running out tonight. It was pretty rude."

"It's okay," Sloan said automatically.

Max shuffled, rocked from one foot to the other. He was clearly uncomfortable.

"You want to sit down, Max?"

"Yeah. I do," Max said.

Sloan motioned to the couch.

"Some-something has happened."

"Go ahead."

"I…. Fuck. Spit it out!"

"Spit what oww—"

"I'm gay."

Sloan froze. His eyes widened.

Can't be.

"Seems everybody knew but me. My brother. My *son!*" He shook his head. "You knew, didn't you?"

"I—I…. Ah…." He wondered if *maybe*. Thought it would be hot *if*. But knew? No. Somehow he doubted even now. "Max. Um. Are you sure? Because if it's about tonight—"

Max face turned almost instantly red. Sloan had never seen a blush sweep up over anyone's face so quickly before. Like a character in a cartoon. "Yeah. It was partially about tonight." He looked down at the ground.

"Max, straight guys think they might be gay sometimes—"

"Sloan." He gave a half laugh. "I was *staring* at you."

"Maybe you're not a zero."

Max looked at him, his expression confused.

"A Kinsey zero."

"Oh." He laughed again. "*Definitely* not a zero."

"But that doesn't mean—"

"Maybe a five?" He slumped. "I can't believe I said that out loud."

Sloan didn't say anything. He was too surprised. He didn't know what to say.

"A lot has happened in the last few days, Sloan. A hell of a lot. Lauren heading out of town. Finding out Logan was gay. And the other day… I…."

Max's face went so red Sloan was alarmed. "Max. Are you okay—"

"I saw you in the shower at the gym. Um, naked."

"Oh!" Now Sloan felt a blush coming on "I didn't see you."

"No. I ran. Like I did tonight." He rubbed his forehead. "Guess I was trying to run away from myself."

"Yourself, Max?"

Max looked up. Nodded. "And when I was holding you the other night. God. I felt… I…."

"Yeah," Sloan said. "I know."

"Jeez. It took my own son coming out to me for me to finally see what other people knew already. That I'm gay. I've tried to pretend I'm straight. Or bisexual. But I knew. I knew. I just so didn't want it to be true. I've hated myself so much. And it's got to stop. I'm seeing I have all this internalized homophobia, and it's got to stop. It's okay for you to be gay. For my brother. But why not me?"

Sloan's heart went out to the man. "I understand that, Max. I tried to fight it too."

"But you *stopped* fighting it a long time ago!" Max said, and it looked like the man might start crying. "You were smart. You didn't get married."

"Well, it was sort of forced on me, Max. My fiancée walking in on me getting fucked." The blush hit. He couldn't believe he'd just said that. "I…. My fiancée left me, Max. You didn't have a Coop to seduce you. You got married. A lot of men do. They think it's the only way…." *And that's what happened to you, wasn't it?*

Max nodded as if he'd heard Sloan. "And now I don't know what to do."

"Max. You're not asking *me* what you should do, are you?"

Max looked at him. "I'm asking you if you can be my friend."

"Friend? Why, um. Well, of course I can."

"Because as much as I would like you to be more than that…. As much as I want you to take me to bed right now, I can't. I'm…."

"Married."

"I can't cheat on her, Sloan. I took vows. And it's not her fault that I lied to her. To myself."

Sloan let out a long sigh. "Good."

Saved by the man with a conscience. *Thank you, God, for saving me.*

Because if Max *had* asked Sloan to take him to bed, he thought he probably would have. Despite how he was feeling about himself and the sex with Leigh last night. Despite knowing that he wanted more than sex. Because what more could he have with this married man? All he could be to Max was sex. Or a thing on the side, which was only a step up. What he couldn't be was what he truly wanted. Sloan wanted forever. He didn't want to be some man's "mistress." And he didn't want to help anyone cheat!

"But I need to be gay," Max was saying. "I need to *see* what this is. Even if I can't have sex. I need to see a gay world. Be a part of it. Experience it. And I can't, really. You know? I can't let the whole town find out before Lauren does. She needs to know first."

"What—what are you asking me, Sloan?"

Max smiled, but his eyes showed…. Fear? Like a dog afraid he was going to be smacked?

"Be my gay friend? Tell me about things. Maybe take me to a few gay places. Not around here, but… I don't know. Maybe we could go to Iowa and all of us go to a gay bar. Or none of that. Just come over to my place and *be* gay. Anything. I don't know. Maybe have your friends come over and—"

"Oh, I'm not sure about that." That could be the last thing Max needed.

"Why?"

"They can be a bit… ah…."

"Much?"

Sloan started laughing. "Yeah. That."

"I got that the night when your chubby friend—"

"That would be Wyatt."

"—was waving over at me and calling me 'Mister Man.'"

"He actually called you that?"

Max nodded.

I'm going to kill you, Wyatt!

When Max didn't say anything else, Sloan looked up. Saw that scared puppy look. "I'm not sure what you want, Max."

"I just want to go out with you."

Out? "You mean like date me?"

Max's eyes went wide. "Ah. No. Ah. Not date. Well… I mean going places. Movies and stuff. Just…."

Were those tears forming again?

"I just need someone to be gay *with*. I need to… to try it on for size. See if it fits. Before I tell her. I just need a gay friend to be gay with."

Sloan didn't know what to say. Could he do this?

Something made Sloan's heart jump. It seemed to swell inside his chest.

Oh no. Don't you dare. Don't you dare start feeling something for this guy!

Or maybe that wasn't it.

Maybe not that. Couldn't you feel for someone without feeling *for* someone?

The look on Max's face was pure desperation.

Do it!

Oh, what if it were a mistake?

Do it!

"Sure, Max," he said, before he could change his mind. "Okay."

The relief shone from Max's face. He looked like a kid on Christmas morning.

"Thank you, Sloan. I know this is a lot to ask. I mean, the last thing you probably want to do is take on a student or something…."

"It's okay, Max. It'll be fun."

"Are you sure?"

"I'm sure," he said.

Sloan was sure he might just be making one of the biggest mistakes he'd ever made.

Chapter THIRTY-SEVEN

SO THAT'S what they did.

And it really was like dating.

Sloan would get so excited when he realized the time was rolling around again when he would be with Max. Max was…. Well. Wonderful!

He was smart and good. He was like a kid ready to take on the world. He asked millions of questions, and Sloan did all he could to answer them. Questions about being gay. About gay life. About Sloan's tastes. Most of the questions were only vaguely sexual or not sexual at all.

They went to movies. Science fiction and horror and action adventure and more than one chick flick. Two guys going out and seeing a movie and then talking about it over coffee after. It was fun.

Sometimes, though, Sloan was sure Max was pressing his knee against Sloan's.

Sometimes they would be sitting in the theater, and Max's hand would be on the arm of the chair—and he would let his fingers fall over the sides and barely touch Sloan's leg. Was it on purpose?

They went into the city several times, once to see the King Tut exhibit at Union Station—and oh, how amazing had that been? To see such stunning objects, made thousands of years ago! They would be standing, shoulder to shoulder, heads almost touching—

(so close they could have kissed, and Sloan wanted to kiss Max—as stupid a move as that would be)

—as they read the information about some stunning mask or statue. Sloan couldn't remember when he'd had such an amazing time.

Sloan knew Max wanted to go to a gay bar, but the man couldn't bring himself to do it.

"What if a student saw me there?"

"So what if they did? Straight people go to gay bars all the time."

"No," Max would say, shaking his head adamantly. "A rumor could start. I can see it getting to some friend of Lauren's and them telling her. What would I say?"

"Maybe we could go to a bar in St. Louis or in Iowa somewhere. Isn't that what you said? We could go with Dennis and Armel."

"Maybe," Max had said but changed the conversation every time.

Sloan liked the meals they had a lot. They became frequent customers of Café Namasté, and Max was surprised when he realized the owner—Earl Beebe—was gay. It became obvious that the man thought they were a couple, and interestingly enough, Max didn't correct him.

"How long have you two being seeing each other?" Earl asked them one afternoon.

"Just a few weeks," Max said.

"Ah." The handsome man had given them a huge smile. "New love. Isn't springtime love wonderful?"

But what surprised Sloan most was the time they spent in the garden.

As March slipped into April, the daffodils and hyacinths made way for creeping phlox—his mother had planted two types, one purplish and the other candy striped like tiny peppermints—and azaleas and rhododendrons—bushes with stunning bursts of pink pastel, red, white, purple, and fuchsia. There was the small-flowered but gorgeous dianthus, columbine in blue, purple, gold, and orange, and a virtual explosion of what Max called knockout roses. They didn't have much fragrance, but there were so many of the single- and double-layer petaled roses that they almost completely covered up the greenery.

They planted the bulbs that had come in the mail—the ones his mother had ordered. It was hard not to stare at Max's butt while he was on his hands and knees, bent to his task! Oh, it was so hard!

"I'm so happy that the yellows are doing well this year," Max said. "The reds and pinks and whites did great their first year, but the yellows, after two years, only really started to get going last year."

"How come you know so much about my mom's garden?" Sloan asked.

"I've been helping her for a couple of years now," Max answered.

A couple of years?

"We'd get on our knees out here every weekend and many an evening."

All that and I didn't even know.

"You were busy," Max said. "Your mom didn't mind. She understood. You had college, and then you needed to make a life for yourself."

Busy. Always busy. With work or my friends or falling in love with Asher.

And now I spend all my time with you.

"She wishes you had met someone…." Max had stopped then, their fingers working together as they planted annuals and spring bulbs. "You—you need to get out more without me. How else are you going to find Mr. Right if you don't get out there and meet men?"

Especially when I spend all my time with Mr. Wrongs. Men who won't or can't love me back.

Sloan sat up.

Back?

God. Am I falling in love again?

MAX COULDN'T remember ever being so happy. He didn't know when he'd felt so *alive*.

With each and every passing day, he knew it more and more.

He was gay.

"I'm gay," he would say every morning and evening when he looked at himself in the bathroom mirror.

Not bi. Or if he was bi, it was only by the slightest margin. What was it that Sloan had said that day?

"If I am, I'm not very bi. A Kinsey 5.5 or something. Maybe even .75."

I'm gay, he would think, and his heart would race at the acknowledgment.

And the more Max said it, the more he *thought* it, the freer he felt.

He tried not to think about Lauren. It was shitty and he knew it. But that would make him think about the fact that he was going to have to tell her. And then what?

He was happy, and thinking about Lauren and all the ramifications of Lauren made him nervous and anxious and *un*happy. So he didn't think about her.

When she called, he was careful to be light and happy—

(and gay)

—and ask her how she was doing and how the job was going and assure her that all was well in Terra's Gate.

Utmost, being with Sloan made him happy. Incredibly happy.

"Why it's almost like being in love," he would sing when no one was around, and then giggle like a schoolgirl.

Being with Sloan really was like dating.

Max would count the hours to when he would see Sloan again, and together they would find all kinds of things to do.

He liked all the things they did and discovered together. The Tut exhibit, finding new bulbs to buy in the *Harvest of Beauty* catalog, gay movies that Sloan would share. He especially liked one called *Shelter*. He so identified with the young man, Zach, who because of the pressures of family responsibilities had to suppress his homosexuality—and how he found shelter with a man named Shaun. How he came to terms with who he was. And oh, that first kiss! Oh, the first time they made love! Max's heart would race so! He bought his own copy and watched it over and over down in the basement. Sometimes when he couldn't sleep, he would put it in his laptop and fall asleep watching it.

The movie made Max think of Sloan, of course, and he wondered if he would ever have a chance to *be* with him. With any man. What would happen when he finally told Lauren?

"You—you need to get out more without me," he told Sloan one day while they were gardening.

(And he loved gardening with Sloan, getting their hands dirty, working up a sweat hauling in big bags of mulch and spreading it around the flower beds, getting to stare at Sloan's round little ass when he was on hands and knees before Max.)

"How else are you going to find Mr. Right if you don't get out there and meet men?"

It had nearly killed him to say those words, but it was true. Sloan was lonely, and he needed someone to love. How selfish would it be to take up all Sloan's time? He could tell Sloan was attracted to him. Sloan wanted to be sexual with him, he was sure of it. But he couldn't be that for Sloan. Max would not cheat!

It was the things in the dark that Max liked best. Going to movies, for one. He would let his knee fall over and rest against Sloan's, get some tiny bit of male contact—

(He would get an erection so hard that it brought new and vital meaning to the words "blue balls.")

—where no one could see them, even though they were in public. Sometimes he would put his hand on the armrest between their theater seats and let his fingers dangle off the edge to lightly touch Sloan's leg or thigh. It was spring, and that meant Sloan was wearing shorts and he could touch Sloan's skin—so smooth, and with a light coating of the softest hair.

It was the only male contact Max could really allow himself. And wasn't it probably too much?

And Sloan was so sweet and kind and intelligent.

In those first few days, he remembered Sloan working on a project at work and how excited he had been. The evening after he had spent an entire day at work gathering information and recommendations from co-workers, he had come home bursting with excitement, as well as fear that he wouldn't be able to do it. Max made a pot of vegetarian spaghetti, and they ate it and he helped Sloan organize everything into a presentation for his bosses. They'd stayed up until well after midnight working on it, and it was then that Max had been aware that their thighs were touching under the dining room table and how wonderful it felt.

Wonderful. And it was only legs touching.

What would it be like to run his hands up and down those muscular legs, kiss them, run a tongue up the inside of Sloan's thighs?

Max loved being with Sloan in public. He knew it was childish, but he would pretend that they were boyfriends. When they went to Café Namasté, he'd been surprised when the owner assumed they were a couple. It had made his heart race when the man asked how long they had been together, and before he even knew what he was doing, he'd lied and let the man think they were indeed a couple.

"New love. Isn't springtime love wonderful?"

Wonderful.

Max wanted to go to a gay bar, but he knew he couldn't. Not with Sloan, at least. It would have been one thing to go with Lauren or some of the female teachers who loved to go on Sunday evenings. No one would think anything of it if they saw him. But if he was with Sloan? Why, they would know.

Know what?

They would *think* they knew. They would think he was having an affair with a male student. And he would not have an affair. He couldn't.

One morning while meditating, he suddenly thought of Sloan—

(he did that a lot, but then he would smile and go back to breathing and plan to think about Sloan later—even if it was only moments later. After a while he would get back into his grove and lose half an hour or more in deep self.)

—and he began to wonder if Sloan might like to learn to meditate himself.

It couldn't hurt to ask.

So he did ask, and Sloan seemed interested, and the next morning they sat on the floor, legs crossed, facing each other. Max found the mat he'd bought for Lauren when he was hoping she would join him, but she had never even taken it out of the plastic. So it and the pill shaped pillow had never been touched. Why not let Sloan use it?

Of course, Max didn't meditate in the nude that morning. He had an idea that no matter how good his intentions, being naked with Sloan would be a really bad idea. They worked out together now but had decided to start showering at home. Max missed the steam room but again knew it would be a huge mistake to be naked with Sloan.

So they wore lose clothes, instead, and sat together, knees touching.

THE FIRST time Sloan joined Max for meditation, he was glad that Max started with the basics.

"It's always best to return to the breath," he told Sloan. "You want to empty your mind, and that isn't easy to do. I've been meditating for years, and I still suddenly think of something I need to get at the grocery store or about something I want to tell a student. Or what color we could paint the living room. Or if Logan needs new track shoes! So don't worry if your thoughts go all over the place. A teacher told me that our minds are like drunken monkeys, always swinging through the trees, branch to branch to branch, thought to thought. With time it will get easier, okay?"

"Okay," Sloan said. "If you say so."

And how was he going to do this? He was sitting on the floor in clothes that made him acutely aware of how little they both were wearing. Max's tank top was baggy and hung down in a way that totally revealed his hairy chest, and it was all Sloan could do not to reach out and touch it.

Is it soft? Coarse? What would it feel like to rest his own chest between those pecs?

And their knees were touching! His knees were against Max's, and those legs were bulging with muscles and covered in just enough hair to be sexy without making the man look like the beast from "Beauty and the Beast."

"Now, I was taught to count my breaths. One, in breath. Two, release breath. Three, in breath. Four, release breath. See what I mean? When you're counting, it is a little bit harder to think about other things."

"Okay," said Sloan, and he closed his eyes, took a breath. "One...."

"Wait a second," Max said.

Sloan opened his eyes and found himself gazing right into Max's beautiful blue orbs. They were so big and shining and.... Well, they were almost miraculous. Who knew eyes could be so beautiful?

"Sloan?"

"Y-yes?" God. Had Max been talking?

"My drunken monkey mind was able to ignore my counting and swing away to its heart's content—what was I going to have for lunch, did I grade those essays, should I call my old friend Cliff and see what he was doing—you know?"

Sloan nodded. He did know. He'd tried a little meditation the night before—he'd wanted to impress Max (like he always did) and get a head start—but it had been hopeless. He kept wondering what he should wear, if he should shower before he went to bed or when he got up, and a host of other things.

"So what I do is count in a way that takes a little bit more concentration. I count on the breaths, but instead of one, two, three, four, etcetera, I do something different. I count one, and then one, two. Then one, two, three. Then one, two, three, four.... See what I mean?"

"I *think* so."

"The idea is that if you are not only counting, but keeping count of the more complicated counting, you won't be able to think of anything else, and you will lose yourself in the nothing."

It did sound complicated. But as he looked at Max, Sloan knew he wanted to please him. He wanted to do this right. Make Max proud of him.

It worked for about four cycles. He had gotten to the four count when he thought about how nice Max smelled and wondered what kind of soap he used. *Something herbal. Probably natural, knowing him. I will have to remember to ask him later....* And he realized he wasn't counting.

"If you lose count, don't worry about it, just start over again."

How had he known?

The next time he made it to the sixth cycle before he began to wonder how Max would like the vegan dessert he had made for them both. He'd borrowed Max's cookbook that he had bought from Café Namasté because he wanted to make something Max would really like. He hoped it tasted good. Imagine chocolate desserts—or any dessert for that matter—made without refined sugar, flour, or any kind of dairy! The restaurant owner and chef made them without any of those ingredients because apparently, they were difficult to digest, were the source of a lot of diseases....

And then he knew he'd lost count again.

"Dammit!"

He opened his eyes to Max's smile. "It's okay. This is only your first time. It will get easier, I promise. And if you stick with it, you are going to see why I love it so much!"

Stick with it, huh? It would get easier? He didn't know about that, but he found that he wanted to love something Max loved so much.

So he tried again.

He didn't do very well that first day. They'd gone over the recommended time, but they had prepared for that. They'd picked a Saturday morning for Sloan's trial run so neither had any obligations.

The next time was only slightly better.

But the next day? He thought maybe something was happening.

Two weeks later, he was meditating in a way that made Max beam at him when they finished.

Anything to have the man look at him like that.

As it turned out, Sloan found he was looking forward to each morning with his friend. It wasn't just being with Max, either.

There really was something to meditation after all. It was bringing a peace he hadn't known in a long time.

And that was something he would always be grateful for.

Chapter THIRTY-EIGHT

MOST OF Max's questions were only vaguely sexual or not sexual at all.

Most.

Some, though, were very sexual.

"Doesn't it hurt? I mean doesn't it *really* hurt?"

"What?" Sloan asked. They'd been watching *Shelter* again. Max couldn't get enough of it. Sometimes he would pop the futon out while they watched it in Max's basement and almost cuddle with Sloan. Those were the nights Sloan would go home with his balls aching.

"Getting… well… when a man…."

"What, Max? In Logan's words, spit it out."

"Fucked!"

Sloan glanced over, and Max had thrown an arm over his face. He was probably blushing *again*.

Actually, it was charming.

"Are you asking me if it hurts to get fucked?"

It was hard to tell with the arm in the way, but it looked like Max nodded.

"Well, it *can*. Surely you looked this up online?" Sloan was almost blushing himself.

"All I find when I google is nasty porn."

"Hmmm…." *I think a lot of that porn is hot.* "Well, uh, sure. It *can* hurt. It can hurt pretty bad."

"Then why—"

"But if you're ready for it, if you're relaxed, if your top knows what he's doing, then no. It doesn't hurt. In fact—" Sloan gulped. "—it can be pretty awesome."

Max threw his second arm atop the other. "Lauren wanted to try it once. In college. She didn't like it at all. Started telling me to pull it out right away. We never tried it again."

"Well, I'm not sure why women would like it at all, but I can't speak for women. I mean, for one thing, they don't have a prostate. Getting your prostate massaged by a man's—" *Spit it out!* "—cock, when he fucks you, can be mind-boggling. He just has to know what he's doing. I mean, if he just jams it in there without relaxing you first. Maybe rimming…."

"Rimming…."

Please know what that is, Max.

"You mean, like, licking down there? The… the anus?"

"Yes. Oh. And I have to tell you, rimming has to be about the best thing on earth."

Max sat up. "Really?"

"God, yes. I like giving and receiving. I mean…. Wow."

Max looked away a minute, and then turned back. "It feels good?"

"Sure, Max. It feels amazing. Haven't you ever played with your asshole before?" Sloan grabbed the remote and paused the movie.

"I…. Not really."

"Damn, Max. You're missing out on something. Next time you… you know… masturbate, take one finger and sorta play around with your hole. You don't even have to stick it in. Take your time. Once you can get a finger in there, and use some lube or something, start looking for your prostate. You'll know it when you find it, believe me."

Max looked doubtful. "I don't know. I had a prostate exam once, and I thought it was going to kill me. I mean… I can't believe we're talking about this. He was careful sticking his finger in, but when he found my prostate, the way he pushed it…. God, Sloan. It was horrible."

"They don't really do it like that much anymore, do they? Don't they pretty much just do the blood test?"

"Well, this was a couple years ago." Max shrugged. "I was having a little problem, and the doctor just thought he should check it. My blood test was a little screwy. So he pressed real damned hard and then took a swab from the head of my penis, and damn, it hurt! I wouldn't wish that on an enemy."

"Well, I don't know of a cock that is going to jab that hard." Sloan raised a hand, and made a fist. He pointed at his top middle knuckle. "Let's say that's your prostate." He took his finger and rubbed across it. "And this is a penis. It sorta rubs it when the guy fucks you. Not slams into it. Believe me, it's nice."

"I don't know...."

"Seriously, Max. Just one finger. And take your time. You'll thank me later."

Max had turned back to the TV, so Sloan thought he must be done. He was glad. The dim light is what had made it possible to have the conversation. It was a bit embarrassing. Especially when he wanted Max to fuck him. There was no denying it any longer. He took the remote and turned the movie back on.

"A finger is a lot smaller than your cock," Max said. "I mean, I would think so."

"Ah. Yes. I'm not a porn star, but I'm bigger than a finger."

"I would think that would hurt."

Sloan glanced over again, but Max was staring dead ahead, straight at the screen.

"Do you think the two guys in this movie fuck?" Max asked.

"The actors or the characters?"

"The characters, Sloan!"

"I hope so. It would be a waste if they didn't. When they wake up that first morning, the way that Shaun is holding Zach? I hope he fucked him. I hope for Zach's sake he did. I hope Shaun showed him one of the wonders of the universe. I like to think it's why Zach is smiling in the next scene. He was thinking, 'God damn but if getting it up the rear doesn't feel *good*! Hey world. I *am* gay!'"

Max gave a nod. Didn't say anything. But even in the dark Sloan could see the wheels turning in Max's head.

"Max?"

Max only grunted.

"If you try the finger and like it? Be careful what you use next. Don't go ramming your wife's dildo up inside yourself. You could do some damage. Go to one of those sex shops. Buy a small toy. Small steps, okay?"

Max only grunted again.

Sloan turned back to the movie.

MAX LAY up that night after Sloan had left. He was horny, of course. He always was when Sloan left. Especially after their almost-cuddling nights. Max had gotten very close to Sloan tonight. They'd almost spooned, Sloan in front, Max behind. Sloan had been wearing a dark blue T-shirt (which looked so beautiful with his red hair) and some tight white shorts, and with his coloring, in the light of the TV, Max could almost imagine Sloan wasn't wearing any pants at all.

Tonight Max had rested his hand on Sloan's hip, gotten so close he could feel the heat of his friend. And all that talk of fucking? Oh, it had made him want Sloan all the more. To be inside him. Oh, what would that be like? To be inside a man? Inside his beloved friend?

And now he lay there, staring up at the ceiling, wondering something else.

What would it be like to have Sloan inside him?

He felt himself getting hard. *Hmmm*....

His body liked the idea.

Max closed his eyes, and of course, it was Sloan he thought about. Slowly, ever so slowly, he ran his hands over his body. He took his time. Made his erection wait, despite the fact it had been up and down half a dozen times tonight. He knew that once he did take it in hand, he wouldn't last. So this was the only way to prolong his pleasure.

Of course, there were always his balls, and he always loved playing with his balls.

(*"I like it when I sit down naked and my balls hit first, how the chair or the blanket feels on them."*)

The memory of Dennis's words made him laugh. Damn if Dennis wasn't right.

Balls were great.

And it was *great* to have a dick. He hoped women enjoyed their parts as much as he enjoyed his. Not that he ever really had before. He'd enjoyed them more the past weeks than he ever had. He'd even started watching himself masturbate in the mirror.

You used to do that.

Yeah. A thousand years ago.

You did it in high school.

But his father had put a crimp in that. For some reason his father's command to make kids had put a crimp in everything.

And dammit, why? Why had he let the old son of a bitch ruin his whole life?

So Max began to play with his balls. He was hairy, but miraculously, there was hardly any on his scrotum. His balls were still a bit low in their satiny sack, so he could still roll them around gently, and oh, it felt good, didn't it?

Was there anything finer?

Well....

Sloan said there was something else that felt pretty good.

(*"Seriously, Max. Just one finger. And take your time. You'll thank me later."*)

Slowly, Max let his fingers stray from his balls down lower... searching... searching.... *There. There it is. Just touch. Take your time.*

Hadn't Sloan said something about lube?

Max sat up, reached into the bedside table for the KY. Lauren needed it sometimes. He opened it, squeezed a little onto his fingers, rubbed it around between them. He wasn't going to use it cold like the damned doctor. An MD, and the man didn't think that cold lube was awful down there? Hadn't some doctor done the same thing to him? Wouldn't you get a clue?

Max reached down, found that place again. Let his fingers explore. *Interesting.... Hmmm....* He felt the tiny folds and wrinkles. Fascinating texture there. And... now they were smoothing out.

Should I?

Why not?

Leap!

He started to push inward with one finger. Just a little. *Not fast. Just a bit. In; back away. In; back away. Hmmmmm....*

Max grabbed his cock. God, he was hard.

He let the finger at his hole poke in a little farther. It was working. Just a bit at a time. Soon he was up to the first knuckle, and wow, it felt pretty… nice. In and out. In and out.

Max was surprised when he realized how much of his finger was in there. Second knuckle. Interesting. A little more? Yeah. It wasn't hurting. Not at all. It was….

OH!

Max yanked his finger out. He glanced down and… his eyes had adjusted to the dark just enough that he could see that he was leaking heavily. He usually didn't precum that much.

What the hell?

Wow.

That had felt…. What?

Go on. Try again.

So he tried again.

This time his finger slid in easily. His hole was well lubed and loose now.

He felt around and….

Oh!

That was….

He tried again.

Mmmmmm…. Oh… God…. Why…. Why, that feels good.

Max began a slow stroking of his cock with his other hand and….

Jesus!

Before he even realized it, he was having an orgasm!

His asshole clenched down hard on his finger, and his cock was shooting and shooting and—

Jesus!

Semen was jetting out over and onto his chest and belly and—

Whoa!

His cum splashed his cheek, right next to his lips.

Max collapsed onto the bed, not even aware that he had arched up on his shoulders and feet. Damn!

Had he ever had an orgasm so powerful?

He felt the semen on his cheek. There, next to his mouth.

Do it!

He let his tongue lash out before he could stop himself and touched his own semen and....

Not bad. Not gross at all. Salty and bitter and sweet all at once.

So if Sloan were to cum in his mouth, maybe it wouldn't be bad.

Cum in his mouth?

Where the hell are you going with this?

But of course, it was the hope that one day....

Max felt his lids getting heavy.

Tired.

So tired.

What an orgasm.

Yes. He would have to thank Sloan.

He would have to thank him a lot.

Chapter THIRTY-NINE

SO IT was the first Saturday of May, and that meant it was Porch Night. Tonight it was Asher's turn to host. Sloan had almost stayed home.

But it *was* the must-not-miss evening for the Fabulous Four, and at Max's urging, Sloan went.

At least the booze would be good. Among the occupations Asher could list on his resume was bartender—not unusual for an actor who hadn't made the big time yet. Like most actors.

The month before, when Wyatt had hosted, had been a very uncomfortable evening. First, Wyatt and Howard were fighting. The big galoot would come out and make crass comments about their pink drinks—Wyatt almost always made pink drinks, whether they were cosmopolitans or not—or what Wyatt had chosen to wear. Wyatt had foregone pink that night for a T-shirt with something that looked like the Mountain Dew logo, until you looked at it and saw it actually said "MOUNT AND DO ME." Sloan hadn't known what Howard's problem was—besides the fact the man was a douche bag—because the shirt was, to quote Wyatt, *hil*-arious.

Then Asher had shown up—late and half-drunk, and wasn't *that* a surprise? He had been pretty crazy too, talking about the sex party he was missing and would anyone be willing to give him a quick blow job? At which point he'd stared pointedly at Sloan.

The fucker.

Heedless of what was going on, Scott had been blathering on incessantly about another of his online romantic interests. That one was from Bangor, Maine, of all places. Six two, muscular, loved thin men, lonely, wanting to relocate, made six figures (or something like that. All of Scott's computer romances were similar stories), and Scott was in *love*. He *knew* he had found the *one*.

Of course, it had been no surprise to any of them that Mr. Right hadn't even sent Scott a picture.

"He's married," Scott said—defending his love interest before any of them could say anything. "But he's getting a divorce! He's *almost* ready to come out. He just doesn't want anyone to find out until he's ready and can set the legal wheels rolling. His wife could take him for everything!"

And Sloan, as much as he had wanted to say something, had no right to say a word. "Let he who is without sin cast the first stone," his mother used to say. That and "People who live in glass houses shouldn't throw rocks." Who was he, who was doing everything *but* fucking a straight married man, to say one word?

Scott had been so excited about the man he hadn't even heard—or had chosen not to—Asher's snide, even mean, comments. But they sure had surprised Sloan. Yes, he could get as frustrated, even annoyed, with Scott's online romances as any of them, but Sloan had never been cruel. And until that night, neither had Asher.

Sloan had finally decided he would get the hell out of there when Wyatt told Asher he should just go. "There are kegeling assholes aplenty just waiting for thy perfect golden rod, and we don't want to deprive anyone of a good rogering. Mayhap thou shouldst be on thy way?"

Asher had done just that. He'd left. It hadn't even been an hour since he'd first arrived.

So tonight? With Asher hosting? What the hell was that going to be like?

Sloan and Wyatt had driven into the city together—Wyatt rode with Sloan so they could arrive at the same time. It made Sloan a lot more comfortable. He had no idea what Asher might say to him if he arrived alone. Riding with Wyatt allowed him to have someone at his side. It would keep things casual.

To Sloan's relief, Asher was the epitome of politeness, a consummate host.

"Nice shirt," Asher told Wyatt, who looked back at him in total surprise. Wyatt was wearing a shirt in honor of the new Captain America movie, which had been released the night before: an image of the captain's shield, but with a pentacle in the middle instead of the standard star.

"I just had to have it," Wyatt said.

"It's perfect for you. Good call."

"Is he fucking with me?" Wyatt whispered to Sloan as they headed back to the balcony.

"Who knows?" was Sloan's only answer.

Asher's apartment, small though it might be, was lovely. The building was made of red brick and was over a hundred years old, but it couldn't be told from the inside. The apartments themselves had been remodeled, and the way Asher had decorated his made it look like something that could be photographed for a magazine—

(like Max's place)

—and when they walked in, they couldn't help but notice the mouthwatering smell. Had Asher had a dinner party before they got there? Why, it smelled like a big holiday ham. The balcony—Asher's version of a porch—was small, with brick going up to about waist height and the rest screened in against bugs and the weather. He'd been known to drag out a big space heater so they could sit there even in winter and watch the snow fall. The screen also gave privacy. With the lights off, it was hard to see in, and Asher had done many a trick out there—they knew because Asher bragged about it.

As you stepped onto the balcony, there was a patio-style love seat to the right, two chairs to the left, and a small ironwork table with a glass top in the middle of the room. When the propane heater was added, they got quite cozy together. And since this was Asher's place, there were candles, of course.

Usually, Sloan shared the love seat with Asher—

(and often Sloan would wonder if Asher might have been having sex right where he was sitting only a few hours before)

—but tonight, Wyatt made a beeline to one end—they'd talked about the arrangement on the drive in—and Sloan sat in one of the chairs.

Asher didn't say a word, and there was only the barest flicker in his eyes to betray he'd even noticed.

Of course. He's an actor. The only reason Sloan noticed was because he knew Asher so well.

The cocktails had lots of pineapple, as well as coconut, and went down so sweet and smooth Sloan wasn't sure if there was any alcohol in them. They were thick, and he was surprised to find out there was ice cream in them as well.

"I hope no one's on a diet," Asher said.

"Diets are for quitters," Wyatt said and then looked shocked when Asher laughed.

"I hope people want snacks," Asher said as a buzzer sounded through the apartment. "I'll bet that's Scott. I'll be right back."

"Is Asher okay?" Wyatt asked. "He's being nice…."

Once again, Sloan had no idea what was going on with Asher. He had come prepared for a drunk, but from what he could tell, the man was stone cold sober.

Scott came out on the balcony a few minutes later, a platter in hand, and looked down at the tiny table, its surface taken up by cocktails, candles, and a stack of small paper plates. "Okay," he said. "I don't know where to stick this, so grab a plate and dig in. Otherwise, it looks like someone will have to balance this on their head. I want them all gone, boys. Asher's got more coming." He lowered the platter to show some hors d'oeuvres that included ham—the wonderful scent they had smelled upon arriving—and chunks of pineapple atop some kind of pastry. The green leaves of the fruit had been set in the middle as decoration.

I'll bet Max would hate these, Sloan thought. *Except for the pineapple, I suppose, since it wasn't canned.* Max would approve of that, what with his worries about chemicals and bisphenol A. Wyatt grabbed several. There really weren't that many, what with the tropical centerpiece, so in short order, there weren't any left. Without even thinking about it, Sloan had made Asher a plate, which took the last of the snacks.

"Thanks," said Asher, who must have seen what Sloan had done, while joining them with a second platter and a stand-alone, high TV tray. He deftly set it up with one hand and snatched a tropical sarong from around his shoulders, draped it over the TV tray, and then placed the platter on top."

"Chinese dumplings," cried Wyatt.

"*Jiaozi*," Asher replied.

"Huh?" asked Wyatt.

"Gu-o-tie," Asher enunciated.

"Looks like Chinese dumplings," Wyatt said.

"Same thing. And the two little bowls are ginger sauce and sweet pepper jelly. Enjoy."

Ginger sauce. *Did he do that for me?* Sloan wondered. He was crazy about the stuff, would almost drink it, while Asher rarely used it.

"I have just one question, *bubula*," said Wyatt, with one hand on his hip, the other shaking a pointed finger.

"What's that, little *faygeleh dov-ber*?"

"Is that ham kosher?"

Asher laughed. "Wyatt, there's no such thing as kosher pork. Refill on your drinkie?"

"No. I mean, yes. No, I don't mind, and yes, more booze." He held out his glass and Asher filled it from a cocktail shaker that seemed to appear out of nowhere.

"How does he do that?" Wyatt asked.

Sloan shrugged. Asher was a magic bartender.

"Wyatt," Scott said. "We had this new client in today. A witch, believe it or not. She says she got fired because of her religion."

Wyatt nodded. "It happens a lot. Are you all taking the case?"

"I think so. Anyway, it got me to thinking. Isn't it about time for your big witchy-woo-woo thing?"

Wyatt's brows came together. "What witchy-*woo-woo* thing?"

"Your big annual foray into the woods. Witch-camp thing."

"It's not until July. And it's not a 'witch-camp' thing."

"Then what is it?"

"It's a men's festival. The Heartland Queer Men's Festival."

"I *hate* that word," snapped Scott.

"What word?" Wyatt asked sarcastically. "*Men*?"

"No. *Queer*. It's an ugly word. Gays shouldn't use it. It's derogatory."

"You just don't understand the word. Queer means nothing more than different. In our case it means different-spirited."

"*Witches*," said Scott. "A bunch of gay witches."

"Some are. But we get all types. Pagans. New Agers. We've even had a Christian or two. Straight men can be queer. And a few straight men show up every now and then."

"Hmpf," Scott muttered. "I've heard you talk all about it. Magic circles and lots of dancing naked around the bonfire."

"Maybe you should give it a try. Go with me this year."

"No way. None of that witchy-woo-woo for me. *Way* too weird. I am not running around naked for a week letting my dingle dangle."

"You don't have to be naked! It's not a nudist thing. *I* don't run around dangling my dingle. I wear a sarong. There are these two neat guys who sell them every year. Cheap."

"A sarong? No way I'd wear one of those! Might as well wear a skirt. What's wrong with real clothes?"

"Nothing. You can wear anything you want to wear. The nice thing about wearing a sarong is you're practically naked but you can cover your privates—and it gets hot in July. We've had festivals that were over a hundred degrees that whole time."

Scott laughed. "Forget it! No way, José."

"Suit yourself."

"And what about you, Sloan?" Scott asked.

"*I'm* not going to witch camp!" Sloan said.

"It's *not* witch camp!" Wyatt cried.

"I'm not talking about that. I'm talking about what's going on with you and straight guy."

"Oh yes," squealed Wyatt. "Mister *Man*!"

Sloan's heart started racing. "What about him?" he asked, praying that his voice didn't sound funny.

"We've seen you two all over town," Scott said.

"Yes! Dish!" Wyatt demanded.

Sloan's stomach dropped. *Seen by whom?* he wondered and then asked it out loud.

"*Every*body who's *any*body!" Wyatt said, his eyes filled with glee. "Is he letting you have any?"

God. Max was *not* going to be happy about this. "No, he hasn't 'given' me any. It's not like that. We're just friends." He looked over at Asher who was looking back with a totally unreadable expression.

"Just friends," said Wyatt. "*Suuuuure* you are!"

"That's all it is," Sloan insisted. "That's all I want it to be." Which was, of course, a bald-faced lie.

"Well I know *I'd* want more than that!" Wyatt grinned happily. "Why, I could spend hours just eatin' that ass!"

Sloan felt a flash of anger. "No, you won't!" he barked and immediately regretted it.

"Ah," said Scott. "I see how it is."

"Oh? And what do you see?" Sloan asked derisively—realizing too late he was only making it worse.

"You and your unobtainable men," Scott explained. "You've traded Asher in for a straight man!"

"Scott," Asher said. "Don't."

Scott gave Asher a glare. "Why not? It's true. Men drool over Sloan, and he doesn't give them the time of day. But let a man say he's *not* interested and—*Zing!*—Sloan's falling in love!"

"I'm not in love with Max," Sloan said and felt lead fill his belly. Because of course he was in love. Or falling there. He'd done it again, and the very thought made him want to cry.

Don't you fucking dare!

"Whatever," Scott said and threw a leg over the arm of his chair. His foot still almost touched the floor.

"Girl," said Wyatt. "You really are a long-leggedy thang, aren't you?"

Scott brought his foot around front and set it on the floor. "So what?"

"Stop it, Wyatt," Sloan whispered. They all knew how much Scott hated his body. For a minute, Sloan was worried that Wyatt would call Scott that hated nickname, Spider Woman.

"You don't have to whisper," Scott said. "I can hear you." He turned to Wyatt. "At least I'm not *fat*."

"I don't know what you're talking about." Wyatt crossed his arms over his belly. "I most *certainly* am *not fat*!"

"Of course not," Scott shot back. "I can see your six-pack from here, all six cans of it."

Crap, thought Sloan. *What the hell is going on with Scott?*

"Just because I don't starve myself doesn't mean I'm fat!"

"*Starve* yourself?" Scott snorted and pointed at Wyatt's stomach. "Since when have you *ever* starved yourself?"

"There is beauty in all kinds of bodies," snapped Wyatt. "I may not have a gym body, but at least I have a lover who *likes* my body! Where's *your* man, huh?

Scott's eyes flew wide, then grew angry. "Gym body?" He laughed. "You're the only person I know that goes to the gym as often as you do but never seems to really do anything. Except take lots of showers! You don't even have a bicep. Not one tiny bit of—"

"Listen, Spider Woman—"

Sloan sucked in a breath. Oh, this was bad.... *Say something! Anything!*

"—what about your pencil stick arms?"

"Enough!" Asher shouted. "We're supposed to be having fun tonight! We're supposed to be best friends. Be nice!"

They all three looked at Asher in stunned surprise.

"*You*, Asher Eisenberg," Wyatt said, "are asking *us* to be *nice*?"

"I am." He stood up. "I'm asking. We haven't seen much of each other—" He spared Sloan a lightning-fast glance. "—lately. Let's make the most of tonight. *Are* we the Fabulous Four, or not?"

Sloan was fairly stunned by Asher's words. His own thoughts had been running along a similar path lately, wondering if they all *were* still friends. But the last person he expected to voice such words was Asher. Why, Asher had believed it was stupid for their little quartet to have a name in the first place.

Sloan looked to his left and then his right and saw that Wyatt and Scott seemed to be just as surprised. And as he looked at his friends, all three of them, he wondered: *Are we? Are we the Fabulous Four? Are we fabulous at all?*

But then it came. Like water bubbling up from a spring. He *felt* it. But this wasn't cold. This? This was wonderfully warm. Such warmth!

It was love.

He saw Scott, and for all his idiosyncrasies and self-deprecation, who was it that had gotten Sloan through so much of the crap he had to deal with concerning his mother's death? Who made sure he ate, for God's sake? Showered? And for what in return? Nothing. Why, Scott had put himself in front of a knife for Sloan.

Sloan looked at Wyatt. Loud, crazy, queenie, and probably deeply self-delusional (especially when it came to Howard). But what would Sloan do without Wyatt? The little bear was always entertaining, always there with a joke, and had a heart the size of a Humvee. Wyatt had brought him food when Sloan didn't have the motivation to make ramen noodles.

And Asher! Oh, he was a jerk of the first order. Full of himself and always wanting—*needing*—to be the center of attention. But then he was an actor, after all. What actor *didn't* want attention? And Asher was a slut, don't forget that. How many times had Sloan driven into the city and the two of them had gone out to a bar to spend the evening together, and twenty minutes later, Asher was leaving with some him-bo? Sloan wanted to scream, "Couldn't you at least give me a couple of hours of your sacred time? You're going to get lucky tonight. You always do. Can't you wait just a little bit?"

But despite all of that, despite what had happened between them recently, despite the fact that the beautiful man had never been able to love Sloan, he had never been able to tell Asher to go away.

Sloan looked into Asher's blue-green eyes and saw… someone who was lost. Why else would he hang out with them? Asher didn't *need* them. He could have any friends he wanted. People stabbed each other in the back to simply be able to be around him. It wasn't money. He didn't have any. Not yet. And it was more than his godlike body and movie-star looks.

People *knew*.

People knew that Asher was going to be famous. They wanted to hang onto his coattails. One day he would be rich and famous, and he'd be nominated for and be accepting Tonys and Oscars, or whatever he was led to. Sloan had seen him act. Seen the magic that was Asher Eisenberg when he stepped out onto a stage. Seen his friend vanish and whatever character he was playing take his place. Jay Gatsby. Hamlet. Stanley Kowalski from *A Streetcar Named Desire*.

But Asher *did* need them. Sloan had no idea why, but he did. He was hanging out with *them* instead of the movers and shakers and hangers on. He needed *Sloan*, needed all of them. And goddammit, Sloan needed to be needed. Who didn't?

And who had reminded them that they were friends? Why, it was Asher.

"Yes," Sloan said. "We *are* friends. We *are* the Fabulous Four."

His friends, one by one, smiled—even if Scott's was only a flicker.

"Damn right," Asher said.

"We are," said Wyatt. "The *Fab*ulous Four!"

Scott nodded—and burst into tears.

Chapter FORTY

I WONDER if Sloan is okay?

Max let out a long sigh. He missed Sloan. One night apart and he missed Sloan.

I've fallen in love with him.

The thought came as a shock, but as he pondered it, let it shimmer through his mind, he realized it shouldn't have.

Oh no. This isn't good.

But God, it *felt* good, didn't it?

He couldn't explain why. But it *did* feel good. It felt good in a way that it had never felt with Lauren. But why? He and Sloan hadn't *done* anything. They hadn't even kissed. They hadn't held hands. Why did he feel this way? So wonderful! He felt like he was fourteen again.

Just *thinking* of the way he felt made him giddy.

Had he *ever* felt giddy with Lauren? Surely he had. Once? Once upon a time back in high school, at least? He remembered feeling weird and funny the first time he held hands with her in a movie theater. He couldn't remember what they had seen. Was it *Forrest Gump*? God, it couldn't have been *The Lion King*, could it?

He remembered sitting next to her, and…

… she had taken his hand, hadn't she?

And his stomach had filled with about a billion butterflies.

Then one day in school he had taken her hand for the first time where anyone could see, and all the guys had been so envious, and Lauren had been so happy she seemed to almost float.

And that was the first time he remembered thinking… *I'm normal. See. Just like everybody else. Normal!*

Except he wasn't "normal," was he? Not then, and not now. Although Sloan would surely argue that point, wouldn't he? Quote statistics and say when there were millions and millions of gay people, that qualified them as normal.

Max thought of Sloan and felt a rush sweep through him that made him feel....

Yes. Like a kid.

He wanted to laugh. He wanted to cry.

He could see Sloan's face—those warm brown eyes, like dark honey, his smile and the way his cheeks dimpled (especially the right one!), his red hair, which had to be constantly combed or it would stand up all crazy like a zany faux hawk.... He thought of those lips, and oh, what would it be like to kiss them? Max got shivers thinking about it.

Kiss a man.

Kiss Sloan!

He thought of how good it felt to hold Sloan that night, even though he'd been crying. How Sloan's body had molded with his own and...

... oh! Their bodies had still molded *so* closely, even though they were both men. Oh! Did that make any sense? How could that be? Weren't male and female bodies made to fit together? How had his body and Sloan's felt so right together? It made no sense. Being attracted to men made no sense.

Falling in love with a man made no sense!

None of it made *any* fucking sense!

(*"Max. Sometimes you gotta stop being the teacher. Some things just are. I don't know why. Sometimes things don't make sense."*)

"But they *have* to," Max cried.

Then, as if the idea had popped in from the ether, Max thought of something else. He almost gasped at the thought. Something the Buddha had taught.

The four imponderables.

There were four things the Buddha said that shouldn't even be pondered or wondered about because you could go out of your mind before they could ever be solved. One of them was wondering just how much we influence the world. It was something you couldn't know the answer to. Plus, it took away from the unselfish act of doing right in the first place. Wondering what meditation really does was another imponderable. Was he remembering this right? Wasn't thinking about karma one of them? And the nature of the universe? Where it came from? Was there a God?

Because we can't *know*. The Buddha taught that someone should not believe something just because they're told to, but should see if the teaching bears out through life's experiences. Imponderables were questions that will never have answers. Not in this life.

At first, that had nearly driven him mad, until a teacher, laughing, said, "See? See? It is true. Just wondering about the imponderables is driving you nuts!"

Max felt himself filled with wonder that day, at those words, as the full implications hit him.

And now today….

Could homosexuality be an imponderable?

Was it senseless to wonder why he was this way? Senseless to wonder why he had these feelings? Wonder why some men sexually desire other men.

Or fell *in love* with other men.

Was he wasting his time wondering such things?

Was it an imponderable?

Could he drive himself insane wondering such things?

(*"Max. Sometimes you gotta stop being the teacher. Some things just are. I don't know why. Sometimes things don't make sense."*)

"My God," he said.

It was as if a crack had opened before him and light had begun to pour through, illuminating him to the depth of his soul and bathing him in understanding.

He wanted to laugh.

He wanted to cry.

"My God! Some things just don't make sense!"

They should only be treasured.

That was when the phone rang.

Chapter FORTY-ONE

THEY GOT the story out of Scott after a shot of something strong. Sloan wasn't sure what Asher gave him.

It seemed that Mr. Bangor Maine had shown up, *finally*. He'd taken Scott to Jasper's—one of Kansas City's most romantic restaurants—for dinner.

("*It was so romantic! I was in heaven!*")

After that Scott had taken him home—

("*I wanted to wait, but the way he was looking at me! His eyes. His quirky little smile. He held my hand right there on the table. I couldn't help it. I couldn't wait!*")

—and a banging had commenced that was akin to a screen door in a tornado.

And then he left.

"He didn't even spend the night!"

After that, nothing.

"I e-mailed him, and nothing. I texted him. Nothing! I texted him a thousand times. Finally, he called and told me to leave him alone."

"Oh gods," whispered Wyatt.

Oh shit, thought Sloan.

"He went back to Bangor. He promised he would be here for four days, but he flew home to wifey the next day. He said there was no way he was going to leave her, ever."

"Oh, Scott," said Sloan. "I'm sorry." Scott had wanted this so badly.

"Are you? Are you really? All of you have been rolling your eyes behind my back, haven't you? Laughing? Telling each other that I was being an idiot *again*. I know it!"

"No, we weren't," Sloan said.

"He told me he was throwing his phone away. It was just a tracphone he bought from Walmart for twenty bucks. Walmart? My God! *Guys.* I let him *bareback* me."

It was Asher who got to Scott first. He pulled him to his feet— "Dammit, Scott. I could slap the shit out of you for that. But I'll hug you instead."—and into his arms.

Scott looked astonished.

Sloan and Wyatt got to their feet and joined them in a big, tight group hug.

"Scott," said Asher and then kissed him on top of the head. "I love you, man. I do. We all do."

"We do," Sloan said.

"That's right, SW," Wyatt replied.

Asher popped him on top of the head.

"Ooww!"

"We love you, Scott," Asher said again.

"Well, that's just *great*," Scott sobbed. "But I need a man to be *in* love with me."

"And you'll find him. I promise," Asher told him. "In the meantime, stop looking so hard. He'll come when he comes."

"Yeah," Wyatt said and then burst into song. "He'll be comin' aroun' the mountain when he *cuuuums*—"

Sloan chuckled and saw the corner of Scott's mouth twitch upward.

"That's easy for *you* to say, Asher. You're fucking gorgeous. Me? I'm *ugly*. I'm… I'm Spider Woman!" He let out another deep, echoing sob.

Sloan's heart wrenched. "Scott. You're not ugly."

"No," said Wyatt. "And who *is* as gorgeous as Asher? We all can't be Asher. You don't think I wish I had his abs now and then? That I wasn't so frippin' short?"

"And Scott," Asher said quietly. "Where's *my* husband? Do you see one? My looks and dick haven't snagged me one yet."

Maybe that's because you don't want *a husband,* Sloan thought and had to battle the bitterness that wanted to creep in. *You could have anyone you wanted.*

You could have me right now if you....

But that wasn't true, was it?

Sloan looked inside himself and to his amazement saw...

... that he *really* wasn't in love with Asher anymore.

He was finally free!

Or was he?

No. It was worse.

He was in love with a married man who was never going to be able to be what Sloan wanted him to be.

"Do you really think I'll find somebody?" Scott was asking.

"I do, Scott. I *really* do. Someone is going to be damned lucky to have you in his life."

"You're not just saying that?"

"No. But for God's sake, stop looking so damned hard. Desperate people attract desperate people. Or men who will only use them."

Scott nodded. "Like asshole married men from Bangor, Maine." He wiped his face on Asher's shirt. To his credit, Asher didn't say a word.

"Yeah," said Sloan. "Stop looking and just be you."

"The *nice* you," Wyatt qualified and got another pop on the head for his effort. "Owww!"

"Be yourself," Asher repeated. "That way the guy that finds you will love you for who you are and not who you're pretending to be."

Whoa, thought Sloan. *Is this really Asher?*

Yes. Yes it was. And *this* Asher is why Sloan had never told the man to kiss his ass and hit the road.

Dammit. I'm forgiving you, aren't I? Damn.

Chapter FORTY-TWO

"So I'll be home tomorrow, *chéri. C'est magnifique, n'est-ce pas?*"

"Yes," Max said into the phone. "It's wonderful." His voice—was that him speaking?—was mechanical. Something had stepped in and taken over for him. He was numb.

Lauren's voice sounded very far away. Of course, she *was* far away. She was in Paris, after all. But that wasn't it, was it? No. It *felt* like *he* was the one who was far away. Even the phone felt like it was at least a mile from his ear.

"I have had such an amazing trip. I wish I could say *how* amazing. Géraud took me to dinner last night, told me that I had been invaluable in reshaping the department. Can you believe it? *Géraud Després* said that *I* was invaluable! Can you imagine for one minute *Mr. Gowers* saying such a thing?"

Gowers was Lauren's boss at the Kansas City branch. And no, Max couldn't imagine such a thing. Lauren had often said—and Max had no reason to doubt her—that Gowers hated her. Found her a threat.

"That prick," said Lauren, "could learn a thing or two from Géraud about being a gentleman. Ah! He is nothing but *un misogyne.*"

Prick? Did she say prick?

"Anyway, I have a last few things to do before I take a quick nap. Oh, I don't want to leave! I can't wait to see you and Logan, of course. Two months away from my men. But, oh, Max! Oh! I love it here *so.*"

I know you do.

"I could live here! I think it would be so good for Logan, don't you? To live for a while, maybe a year, in France? Let him see other people, experience another world?"

"Maybe we can go this summer for a few weeks," Max suggested.

"A few weeks?" He could hear the disappointment in her voice. As if he had crushed her.

"Géraud says he could find you a teaching position here, Max. You could teach our employees to speak English for when they have business in the States."

"I'm not a language teacher, Lauren."

"Hey, Dad." Logan burst into the room. "Devin's here."

It took Max a moment to even understand what Logan had said. He was still a mile from the living room *and* the phone. Devin? Oh. Devin. Logan's boyfriend. The movies. They were going to see *Transcendence*. Logan wasn't sure it was going to be any good, but it had Johnny Depp in it, so he was happy. Max wasn't so much into Johnny Depp, but the movie also had Morgan Freeman, so it couldn't be a total loss. Besides, this wasn't about a movie anyway. This was about Logan and Devin going out in public, together, with Devin's parents knowing that they were boyfriends, and that was what Logan was so excited about.

"Would that be better?"

"I-I'm sorry, Lauren. What did you say?"

"Are you cutting out, dearest?"

"I must be," he lied and immediately regretted it. He wasn't a liar.

"I said that Géraud thinks he might be able to get you something at *la Sorbonne*. The university here in Paris. You could teach what you enjoy most."

"Since when have you started calling him Géraud?" he snapped. *Now why the hell did you do that?*

"Dearest, this is *France*. They are not like Americans. All is well, now, do not worry!"

"And your flight comes in at 7:20 p.m.?"

"*Oui*, it does. I cannot wait!"

"Ditto, baby."

The line went dead before he could say good-bye.

Tomorrow, Lauren would be home.

Why did he feel like the world was coming to an end?

Chapter FORTY-THREE

ASHER CAUGHT Sloan coming out of the bathroom. He was holding an empty platter. "May I talk to you a minute?" Asher asked him.

Sloan's stomach clenched. *No. I'm not quite ready*. But the look in those green eyes of Asher's made him nod anyway. "Sure," he said.

They stepped back into Asher's darkened bedroom, the only light a single candle on the dresser. Asher put the platter down and then put both of his strong hands on Sloan's shoulders. "I am so sorry."

Sloan looked up at him in surprise.

"I've been such a fuck. A real fuck. I don't know why you, why all of you, haven't told me to get the fuck out of your lives.... I'm so sorry for the way I've been. It's like I'm bipolar or something!"

Sloan shook his head. "It's okay, Asher. I've already forgiv—"

"No. Please. Hear me out. I'm sorry for the way I've treated you. Especially lately, but not just that. I'm sorry for being such an asshole at Wyatt's place last month. I'm sorry for making a fool of myself at your house before that, and for not calling you and begging you for forgiveness. A lot's been going on.... I thought... I thought I was going to get a part in a movie, and it didn't come through."

"What?" Sloan said, astonished. "When did this happen? My God, Asher—"

"It doesn't matter—"

"It *does* matter! I can't believe you didn't tell us!"

"I didn't want to say anything before because I didn't want to jinx it. And I didn't tell you after because I was so humiliated. I knew Wyatt and Scott would have a field day with it."

"No they wouldn't! Why would they?"

"Because the reason I didn't get the part was that they said I was too old!"

"Oh." *God. Asher? Too old?* "Yeah, I could see how you'd think they might give you hell for that."

"But," Asher said. "None of that matters. It's no excuse. I've treated you like shit. You're my *best* friend—"

"I am?" Sloan asked, startled.

"Christ, yes. I don't know what I would do without you! You're my constant. My due north. I... I.... If you only knew how many times I've thought, 'Now what would Sloan do in this situation?' You're my barometer. You're my guide."

"Damn, Asher." Sloan felt the sting of tears.

"But most of all, I'm sorry I couldn't love you the way you wanted me to. I've pretended I didn't know how you felt, but I knew. God. I knew."

Sloan's throat seized up. He couldn't believe what he was hearing. And.... He was shocked to realize how much he *needed* to hear it! "It— It's okay," he managed. "You can't feel what you don't feel."

"And I don't know *why* I don't. I love you! Sloan. *Fuck.* I love you more than the theatre!"

Sloan gasped. *What the hell?*

"But I'm not *in* love with you."

"Yeah." Sloan nodded. *Why?* he wanted to ask. *Why aren't you?*

"I wish I knew why," Asher said, and for a second, Sloan wondered if he'd asked it out loud after all. "But it's like there's this... block. A wall or something that keeps me from feeling."

"I know," Sloan said. "I kept thinking—"

"That if you waited long enough?"

Sloan nodded again. "But it never happened."

Asher shook his head. "Maybe I can't fall in love. If I could, it would be with you."

Wow. Wasn't life insane? But... but that was okay. Things were better now. "Asher. I understand. There was the longest time I couldn't cry over my mom's death. I know all about the wall. The one that keeps you from feeling. But finally, one night—"

(*The night you came over. The night you kissed me. The night Max held me.*)

"—finally one night I let go. The wall came down. It will happen for you too."

Asher sniffed. Were those tears in his eyes? "Do you think so?"

Sloan nodded. "I do." And he really did. "And I don't mean to hurt your ego, but, well… I think I've finally gotten over you. Lovewise, that is."

"It's because of *him*, isn't it?" Asher asked.

Sloan froze, and he had to will it away. He almost said, "Who?" But there were Asher's eyes again. He couldn't see their blue-green color in the light of the single candle, but he could see them looking into him, into his head. His thoughts.

"Please, Sloan. Get away from him."

"Why?" Sloan bit his lip—bit back more than just that.

"Because Scott's right. You're trading one man who *can't* love you for another. He's married, Sloan. He's straight! Maybe you could get some sex out of him. God knows I've fucked enough married men. Straight men. But you want more than that. You *need* more than that."

Sloan wanted to shout, "But he's not straight!" He didn't. How could he do that to Max? He also wanted to say, "And I'm pretty sure he loves me. And if I wait long enough…."

But hell. Shit. Damn.

Fuck.

Damn, Asher, but…. But he was right, wasn't he?

Max wanted him as his gay *friend*. And he'd already said he wouldn't cheat on his wife.

And did Sloan want him to?

Yes.

No.

Not really. Of course he didn't. And he wouldn't help a man cheat.

He remembered the co-worker who wanted to have an affair with him. Sloan wouldn't allow it. Moved his lunchtime so he wouldn't have to worry about even sitting next to him in the break room. What made Max any different?

Sloan sighed. It was a sigh that was soul deep.

I sat around waiting for Asher to love me. All I got was hurt. Now I'm waiting for Max to love me, aren't I? And he's not available. He's someone else's lover.

"There *is* a man who wants *you*, Sloan. Who will love you and love you the right way."

"Sure," Sloan said. But was there?

Well, it wasn't Asher.

And it wasn't going to be Max, was it?

So stop waiting, then, he told himself.

Three hundred and fifty million gay men in the world. There's going to be one who can love me.

"Sure," he said. He slipped into Asher's arms.

And finally he let go.

Sloan felt it. Felt it happen. *Felt* the letting go.

He let go of the way he'd thought of Asher for so long. And tried on the new way.

Hmmmmm....

If felt okay.

Chapter FORTY-FOUR

"WHAT'S WRONG?" Sloan asked. Max had been acting weird all afternoon, not his usual fun self.

Max had called early that morning and asked if he wanted to make a day of it. Since it was a Saturday, Sloan had thought, *why the hell not?* Besides, he had something to tell Max, and he had to go through with it, even though it was the last thing he wanted to do.

He was going to break up with Max—even if that was a ridiculous concept. They weren't a couple; they weren't dating, as much as it felt like it. Max *felt* like a boyfriend, when he was the furthest thing from.

Oh, if only Asher had known how off his advice had been. Don't trade me in for a straight man. How ironic. Because of course, Max wasn't straight. He was gay. But he was just as unavailable as Asher. The problem was there was something happening between him and Max. He was sure Max felt something for him. It wasn't wishful thinking like it had been with Asher.

No. It was worse. He had heard people talk about how tough it was to have long-distance lovers. This was like that. The problem was that distancewise, Max was right next door. He might has well have been orbiting Saturn, though. There was a gulf between them that couldn't be crossed.

So it was with a sad heart that Sloan knew what had to be done.

Max wanted to start the day off with a movie, and so off they'd gone. They'd gotten there just as the previews were starting, so Sloan had no opportunity to go forward with his decision. And he hadn't wanted to do it in the car. That seemed so… mean. Why not wait until they were sitting down and could really talk?

To Sloan's surprise, Max hadn't played his usual touchy-touchy in the theater. No sooner had the film begun than he had done something instead that had startled the shit out of Sloan. He had reached over, taken Sloan's hand, and then held it for most of the movie. Out in the open.

Nothing discrete and between the seats. No. It was right there, on top of the armrest. At one point Max had even pulled Sloan's hand over so it was resting on Max's thigh.

A shiver had passed through Sloan, and his breath had caught.

Of course, the big room was nearly deserted at that time of day. It wasn't like there was much chance they'd be caught by anyone of any consequence. But still.

There were times when Sloan could hardly pay attention to what was happening on the screen.

You're supposed to be ending it with this guy.

But it felt so good to have a man holding his hand. How long had it been?

But he's married! This can't mean *anything.*

I know, I know!

But it felt so good to have *Max* holding his hand.

I'll tell him at lunch.

Wouldn't it be okay to pretend, just a short while, that they were a couple?

Which was exactly what Sloan did. It was silly. Maybe it was immature. But he sat there in the dark and pretended that Max was his and he was Max's. That his wife had decided to stay in Paris and had given Max up, and now they were together. And that Max was proud and out and walked everywhere holding Sloan's hand. And that at night they spooned together, like they did sometimes in Max's basement, but instead it was in bed and they were naked and they held each other tightly and Max had just....

Sloan got an erection. It swelled up in his jeans, and he prayed Max couldn't see it. Boy, wouldn't that be embarrassing? But when he looked over at their interlocked hands, Sloan saw something that sent a wonderful little shock and tremor through his body. Max had an erection too. He was wearing shorts again today, and even though these were denim and not sweats or running shorts, the significant bulge was apparent.

So Sloan pretended other things, and his cock leaked in its confinement, and his shorts might very well show a wet spot when they got up to leave. But hey, he could always pull his shirt out and cover it up. Because as sticky as it felt, it also felt glorious.

This is only pretend!

Who cared? Because right now, pretend was all there was.

BUT WHEN they left the movie, Max did something else that shocked Sloan. He didn't let go of Sloan's hand. He held it as they walked out of the theater and into the lobby and out the back door to the parking lot.

"Max?" he asked, the only word he *could* ask.

Max looked at him with the most peculiar expression but squeezed his hand, and what was there to say after that?

They went to Café Namasté, and Max ordered one of their favorites, the vishuddha—the vegan lasagna. It wasn't really lasagna, not what would be recognized as lasagna. It was served cold, for one thing, and was made of layers of thin vegetables. There was no pasta at all. They'd tried it together one day and loved it.

"Lauren comes home tonight," Max said.

At first, Sloan wasn't sure what Max had said. It was very abrupt, without any preamble. The conversation hadn't been even vaguely going that way. They hadn't even addressed the handholding. They'd been talking about dogs, of all things, and how both of them had been thinking of adopting one and how Logan would be thrilled about—

Sloan stiffened, a bite of lentils and quinoa halfway to his mouth. He lowered his fork.

Lauren comes home tonight.

He was so shocked he could barely think.

Max took another bite of his vishuddha, and didn't look up. He took a drink of the water.

Hmmm… I still haven't asked why they serve their water at room temperature.

Now Max was looking at him, and his big blue eyes were swimming with emotion and what might be tears.

Sloan's mind started to work again. *Tonight? She's coming home tonight?* He opened his mouth, and miraculously, words started coming out. "I thought it was next week."

"I miscalculated," Max said.

"Miscalculated?" Sloan blurted with more force than he'd intended. "Didn't you have the date written on the calendar?"

"Yes," Max cried. "I did! She said two months. It's been seven weeks."

Sloan sat back, did the math in his head. "No. This *is* two months. *Today* is two months."

It can't be! She can't be coming back already. It can't be two months already. We have another week!

"What?"

Sloan put his fork down. Trembled. "It's been two months today." *That means she wasn't even really in Paris for two months, what with flight time and all.* He barely recognized his own voice. It was as if that someone that sometimes took over for him was doing its work.

You don't need to break things off with him now. The Universe has taken care of it for you. It's over.

Max placed his own fork down. "She called last night. I was so shocked I could barely talk."

You're shocked?

"I thought we had another week," Max said.

"We?" Sloan asked.

Max looked up, and those eyes were even wetter. If Max didn't use a napkin or something, he was going to be crying any minute. Sloan looked down at his own napkin, barely touched, and handed it to Max. His hand was shaking.

Done. It's all over.

Problem solved.

There is no fucking "we."

Max reached across the table and took Sloan's hand while he wiped his eyes with the other. Sloan looked down, saw their hands linked together, right there for anyone to see. He almost glanced around to see who might be looking and found he couldn't.

Earl Beebe, the café's owner, chose that moment to walk up to the table. "Is your food satisfactory today, lovebirds?"

They both looked up, and neither said a word. *Gotta say something. Anything.* "De-delicious as always," he said.

"Wonderful. Max? Yours?"

"Delicious as always, Earl."

Earl grinned. "You know, I'm going to bring you a piece of the hazelnut chocolate cream pie, on the house."

"T-that's okay," Sloan said. He realized he wasn't sure he was going to be able to finish his food, let alone a dessert.

"I insist!"

"Not sure I can eat it right now," Max said.

Was it for the same reason *he* couldn't eat, Sloan wondered.

"Then I will make it to-go. I want you boys to have a treat. I can just picture you gazing into each other's eyes—like you do all the time—but over candlelight." He winked. "Maybe in bed." He laughed merrily and sailed away.

We gaze into each other's eyes?

Max looked at him, then down at his plate. Sloan saw his Adam's apple bob, once, twice. Then he picked up his fork and took another bite of his vegan lasagna. The chewing stopped. Started again. Stopped. Sloan could actually see that it was hard for Max to swallow. He looked up. "Earl is going to think I don't like it."

Sloan nodded and began to force himself to eat. He wasn't hungry anymore. He didn't know what he was. Surprised, yes. And for some reason, angry.

Why didn't you tell me she was coming home this morning?

Why didn't you tell him that you wanted to end things this morning?

The answer to the second question was easy.

He didn't want to end things.

And now they were over.

SLOAN WASN'T too surprised when Max wanted to go home. He was pretty sure that Max had something else planned for the day, but his sudden admission that Lauren was coming home had changed everything.

This is for the best, Sloan tried to tell himself.

Max drove the extra feet to stop in front of Sloan's house instead of parking in his own driveway. It was just like Max. A gentleman always. But Sloan wasn't expecting Max to get out of the car. He followed Sloan to the door and then reached out and stopped him from putting his key in the lock.

"Sloan?"

He turned to face Max, who stepped in close. He took Sloan's hands in his own and stared deeply into his eyes.

Sloan forced himself to look away, to look around them instead to see if there was anyone about. This looked really funny. Anyone spying them would make the wrong assumption. "Max," he said. "Someone might see."

"I don't care," Max said.

"Max. *I* care. I don't want people talking about us."

"You don't think people are already talking?" Max asked.

(*"We've seen you two all over town."*)

Sloan shook his head. "No one is talking…."

"Of course they are. How could they not? It's a small town, Sloan."

Sloan took a step back, but Max didn't let go of his hands. "Who's talking about us?" he asked.

(*"Every*body *who's* any*body! Is he letting you have any?"*)

"Well, Earl for one," Max said, and then actually grinned.

Sloan tried to pull his hands away, but again, Max held on with a sure grip.

"And there have to be others. I know some of my students have been asking me who you are."

Sloan's eyes widened. "What?"

"I don't care," Max said. "I don't care what people think."

"Max! I care. I don't want people thinking I'm a home wrecker. The other fucking woman!"

"Fuck them. We know what's happening. And it's not as much as I want."

Sloan gaped at Max. Tried again to pull away, but Max was too strong. There was no way he was getting away unless Max wanted to let go. In fact, he chose that moment to pull Sloan into his arms. Their faces were inches apart. "Max!"

"Invite me in," Max said so softly that Sloan almost didn't hear the words, then stepped closer. Brushed his nose against Sloan's. Then Sloan's lips with his own.

A moan escaped Sloan before he knew it, and his knees went weak.

Get ahold of yourself!

Max's arms went around Sloan's waist and brought him up tight against his muscular torso.

"I'm going to kiss you now, Sloan."

No! And with surprising strength, Sloan pushed himself back and away. He quickly looked around him, up and down the street. A door slammed shut, but he didn't see anyone. God! Was it a neighbor who had seen them and run in the house to start the phone calls?

"I said I don't care who sees," Max said.

"Yes!" Sloan cried. "You *do* care, Max! I *know* you do. What about the Buddha? The Noble Eight-fold Path? How would *he* feel about this? What would he say? Which of the eight does this break? Right Action?"

Max stiffened. A pained expression filled his face.

"I don't know it like you do. But isn't the whole teaching about the ethical foundation of life? This isn't right, Max."

Max trembled. "Yes. You remembered."

"Of course I do," Sloan said, and then his vocal cords froze. He tried to say more and found he couldn't.

What are you doing? screamed a part of him. *This is everything you want!*

No it isn't, said another part of him. *You want someone who is yours and all yours. You don't want what Wyatt has. You don't want anything but a man who loves you and whom you can love. You want someone your mother would be proud of.*

"I was listening to you, Max. I was listening to everything you said."

Max reached for him and Sloan stepped away.

"Please, Sloan. Before it's too late. Take me to bed. Make love with me. *Fuck* me. I want you *inside* me. I've been doing what you said. Playing with those toys. I can do it. I can take you. *Fuck* me, Sloan. Before it's too late."

It was the hardest thing Sloan had ever done in his entire life.

But he wouldn't exchange a gay man who couldn't love him for another man who wasn't free to love him. He shook his head. "No, Max. I can't. I won't. I won't help you cheat. And you don't want me to. When you're thinking sensibly, you'll be glad I did this. You would hate me if I took you upstairs. Worse, you would hate yourself. I won't be the cause of that."

Max's big blue eyes were filling with tears again. This time he didn't try to wipe them. They began to spill down his face. "I don't care. I want you. One time. Before it's too late...."

Sloan shook his head. "It was too late before we ever started, Max." *God.*

Sloan saw it clearly right then. He saw he should never have let any of this happen. Not one movie. Not one meal. No letting Earl think they were husbands. Never pretending, even to himself, they were more than they were. If Max had needed gay friends, he knew he should have made sure there were other people around always. Wyatt. Scott. Hell, even Asher.

Max looked down, away, and back. He made no move to wipe away the tears. "I think I love you, Sloan."

Sloan closed his eyes, fought back his own tears. He shivered. *I love you, Max.* But he didn't say that out loud.

"You love me too," Max said. "I know you do. And fuck. I don't *think* I love you. I know it. I'll shout it from the top of the University Tower. I'll drive up the hill that looks out over this whole town and shout it out to everyone." He let out a sob. "I'm *in* love with you, Sloan."

Oh God. Oh God oh God oh God.... Yes. God. I am in love with you too, Max Turner. But he didn't say that either. "Go home, Max."

Max stepped closer again. "Please. Tell me you love me, Sloan. Do that much. Tell me you're in love with me."

Sloan swallowed hard and then said it despite knowing better. "Yes," he whispered. "I'm in love with you, Max." *And now I'm right back where I was before. In love. And it will take me a fucking year or two or three years to get over you. And it won't be worth it. The pain won't be worth how wonderful and wondrous the last weeks have been.*

With the pain, relief also spread across Max's features. "You do love me," he said.

Sloan nodded. He couldn't help himself. Hell. What part of the Eight-fold Path would lying break? "Yes, Max."

"Then take me...."

"No." He said it firmly. He said it with the solidity of concrete. Of granite. It bore no more argument. And he could see that Max saw that as well. A shudder passed through the man. And then his face…. It showed acceptance.

Thank you. Thank God. Because he knew right then had Max pressed it one more time, he would have surrendered.

Max stepped back. The tears still came, although they seemed to have slowed. He turned, took a step, then stopped and turned back. "One kiss? May I have that? Like your favor? May I go back to my life with one kiss?"

Sloan felt another tremor run through him. Knew it was a mistake. But he gave in for that one request. He stepped up to Max and kissed him.

It was a quick kiss. Almost—

(but not quite)

—chaste. He gave Max's lips just the slightest pressure, and even as Max's arms had started to come around him, he stepped back until he was leaning against the door.

Max stood, looked at him for what seemed forever. Then came the look of resolution.

And he turned and walked away.

Chapter FORTY-FIVE

THEY PARKED the car and went into the airport despite the fact that Max knew she would scold him for it. "Oh, Max!" he could hear her say. "I could have managed. You should have simply pulled up to the curb."

But he couldn't do that, and he had bought flowers on the way—

Guilt. Guilt guilt guilt.

—and given them to Logan to give to his mother. She would know where they truly came from.

Thank God Sloan had turned him down. If he felt like this now, what would he have felt like meeting his wife, fresh from being fucked for the first time in his life? He wouldn't have been able to live with himself.

But oh, the glory that it would have been. To hold Sloan, naked, flesh against flesh, skin rubbing skin. To see Sloan, really see him, naked and beautiful. To see his cock. He knew it would be as lovely as the rest of Sloan.

"Dad? Are you okay?" his son had asked him a half a dozen times on the drive here—

(or it felt that way)

—to greet mother and wife.

"I'm fine, Logan."

"Dad. You don't look fine. You look like shit."

He didn't even tell Logan not to use the word.

"I'm fine, son. I'm fine." And if he said it long enough, like the mantras he sometimes used when he meditated and his thoughts were so loud—so drunken-monkey—he needed the ancient words to drown them out. Mantras like: *Gate gate, pāragate, pārasaṃgate, bodhi svāhā.* Or of course the most sacred, *Om mani padme hum.*

Yes. Say it over and over and over again. Say 'I'm fine' until you believe it. I'm fine. I'm finefinefinefine.

"What are you going to tell her, Dad?"

Max fought the instinct to widen his eyes in surprise. Did Logan know?

"About Sloan."

Max gripped the steering wheel.

"What about him?" he asked, keeping his tone as calm and neutral as he could.

"About how you two are…." Logan's words drifted off.

"We're what?"

There was a long pause. "Come on, Dad. I'm not stupid. I know you two are…."

"What?" Max said, more sharply that he'd wanted.

"Well. Sleeping together, Dad!"

He spared a glance at his son. His boy's eyes were wide and full of concern.

"We aren't sleeping together, Sloan. I mean…." *God!* "I mean, Logan."

Logan rolled his eyes. "Dad."

"Logan. Listen to me. Look at me." Max looked away from the road just long enough to try and convey the truth with his eyes. "Sloan and I haven't had sex."

He looked at the road, saw the airport sign. Two miles. Looked back to Logan.

For a second he could see his son didn't believe him—

(which hurt)

—and then…. Thank God. He saw that maybe he did believe.

"Gosh. I was sure you were."

"I couldn't, Logan."

Oh, but not five hours ago he'd begged Sloan, hadn't he? And how would that be? Driving to meet his wife, maybe with Sloan still inside him?

I'm scum, that's what. Thank you, Sloan. Thank you for turning me down.

But oh, there was regret there as well, wasn't there?

"You're in love with him, though, Dad."

"Yes," he said and then was shocked at the admission.

"She'll know, Dad. She's like that. Psychic or something."

Dear God, she might. She was like that, wasn't she? He could only pray she didn't see it.

"What are you going to do, Dad?"

"I don't know."

"Shit, Dad."

This time he did say it. "Don't use that word, Logan."

His son just snorted.

Yeah. In this case it might have been a pretty stupid thing to say.

"Do you hate me, Son?"

Logan's head swiveled toward him. "Huh?"

"That I've fallen in love with someone besides your mother?" He clenched the wheel again, waiting for the anger.

"*Duh.* Of course not, Dad. You're *gay.* It was bound to happen sooner or later."

Max looked at his son in surprise. "You don't hate me?"

Logan shrugged. "You're my dad. I can't hate you."

Oh, but he'd come to hate his own father, hadn't he? For a lifetime of mental and emotional abuse. For forcing him to be straight—

He didn't do that. You did that. You let him do it. Dennis didn't let him. You didn't have to either.

"I mean, I'd say it's too bad you were *ever* with Mom, but jeez. I wouldn't be here, then. Too bad you two couldn't have been buddies. Gay guys have kids with their female friends all the time."

Max laughed. He couldn't help it. Wow. His son. Lately it felt like his boy was the adult and he the kid.

So there they were, waiting at the gate and the plane had arrived and the passengers were beginning to disembark. Slowly at first. A trickle. A lady in a wheelchair. A man who looked distressed and in a hurry—

Probably worried he's missed a connection. The flight was forty minutes late.

—and a woman with the largest head of hair Max had ever seen, obviously dyed. There was no red hair like that created by nature, outside the ass of a baboon. Then several people at once. Pause. More people. A family with several kids and a baby. No one. Then….

Maybe she'd missed the plane?

And then she was there, looking resplendent as always, even after hours and hours on a plane.

She was carrying a case on a strap over one arm (her computer bag?) and a huge garment bag over her opposite shoulder (*that's new*).

She was on a mission—of course she was: it was to get to baggage claim and to the curb as fast as possible—and then she looked up and saw them. Not a flicker, was there? She went immediately to the huge and dazzling smile he'd known for years. Then she was through the gate, and Logan rushed forward with the flowers, and she was saying, "Oh, Max, *chéri! Ce n'était pas nécessaire*. I could have made it on my own! Why didn't you just meet me at the curb?"

"I couldn't, darling," he replied and took the garment bag—

(and God, it was heavy)

—and hugged her and told her he loved her and that he had missed her.

"Well, there is no use being *fâchée*, is there?" she asked. "How can I complain about my men loving me?"

No. No reason to be upset at all. Why, the world was golden, wasn't it?

Then they went to baggage claim.

Lauren wouldn't have been able to handle things by herself. Besides her bag, she had also brought home a case of wine. Wasn't there a limit to how much you could bring back? What had the export tax been like?

They agreed to stop at a restaurant for dinner on the way home. None of them had eaten for hours, and so Max pulled off at one of the first exits.

They hadn't even ordered their food when Lauren asked it the first time. "Is everything all right, *mon cœur*?"

"Of course," he assured her and buried his face in the menu. It really was as if she could read his mind. Apparently, his answer satisfied her because she went right back to her story of the wonders of Paris and how she knew they would all love it there. That he and Logan wouldn't be able to help it. That they would fall in love just as she had.

When they got home, Max couldn't help but look next door. But Sloan wasn't home. His car wasn't even there. *Where is he?* Max wondered.

"Max? *Qu'est-ce qu'il y a?*" Lauren asked, and he realized to his embarrassment that he'd been standing there, staring at Sloan's house.

"There's nothing wrong," he assured her.

She looked at him doubtfully.

"I'm just tired."

To his considerable relief, Lauren told him she was tired as well. Exhausted. And she knew he had missed her, but would he mind terribly if they waited until tomorrow night for a proper "reunion."

He assured her that he could wait, and the relief from her request was immense. That made him sad. *I'm so sorry, Lauren. Something happened while you were gone. I'm not the same man.*

Or he was. He'd simply never been honest with her or even himself as to what man he was.

They had no sooner climbed into bed when he heard her gentle snores.

Max, on the other hand, took a lot longer to fall asleep.

Chapter FORTY-SIX

THE NEXT week was hell.

Chapter FORTY-SEVEN

MAX FOUND himself longing for just a glimpse of Sloan. Max knew when he left for work and would find excuses to be out on the front porch with his one cup of coffee—

(or sometimes second or third on a day that Sloan was apparently leaving later than usual)

—so that he could raise a hand, wave, and feel his heart catch up high in his throat.

The first time, and Lauren had already left for work, Max crossed over to Sloan's yard. "Good morning, baby."

Sloan had jumped as if he'd been goosed. He whirled around and simply stared. Finally he said, "Good morning, Max."

"How are you?" *Stupid question! Why did you ask him such a stupid question?*

"I… I'm fine, Max. A little late. Not going to be able to stop and get coffee on the way to work."

"I can get you some," Max said, pointing at his cup. "I've got a Keurig. It'll only take me a second."

"N-no. That's okay. I don't even have time for that. Have a nice day, Max." He turned and all but ran to his car, an old silver Oldsmobile Ninety-Eight that sometimes wouldn't start in the morning.

Don't start, thought Max. *Then I'll drive you to work and kiss you.* He could see it in his mind as clearly as if it were happening. And it wasn't a chaste kiss. Sloan would resist at first, and then their mouths would open and their tongues plunge—

The car started. Sloan put it into gear, paused. Gave a single honk of his horn.

Max startled. Of course. He was standing behind the car. He stepped to the side, and Sloan backed out.

"Sloan," Max called out as he finished backing into the street. Max jogged down to the end of the drive, coffee sloshing over the sides and hitting his hand. He barely registered the heat.

Sloan stared forward, and for a moment, Max thought he would just leave him standing there. Then he looked Max's way. His dark honey eyes were anything but warm. His shoulders slumped, and then the window slid down.

"Yes, Max? What do you want? I'm going to be late for work."

Max went to the car, leaned in to the window. "Do you want to jog this evening?" It had been one of the many things they had been doing in the last weeks—much like he and Lauren used to do. Sloan had been getting better every day, could run longer without needing to walk. And his legs! They were becoming a marvel. Sometimes it was all Max could do not to drop to his knees and run his hands up and down them. They must be like marble—

"Did you hear me, Max?"

"Huh? What?" Max hadn't heard. He'd been too deep in fantasy.

"I said I don't think that will be a very good idea."

"But why? You're coming along so well! You don't want to stop now."

"I'm going jogging with Asher."

"Asher?" he asked, shocked. "The guy who tried to—"

"Everything is worked out now, Max. I'm sorry. I have to go."

Don't go. Max's heart gave an aching lurch.

"Good-bye, Max," Sloan said, giving Max a meaningful nod. Max stood so that Sloan could leave.

Watching Sloan drive off had never hurt more.

"*TALOFA*, SLOAN," Peni said as Sloan sat down at his desk. The two of them had cubicles next to each other. They were hardly cubicles, though, with attached desks barely big enough for their computers.

"*Talofa*," Sloan said automatically and then, just as routinely, "*O a mai oe?*"

"*Manuia, fa'afetai. O a mai oe?*"

Sloan let out a long, shuddering sigh. *I feel like shit, that's how I am!*

"Sloan?" Peni asked. *"Are* you okay?"

He almost lied. He almost said, "Yeah! Everything's hunky dory." But he turned and looked into Peni's huge black eyes, filled with concern, and couldn't.

This was someone he *could* tell the truth.

"My boyfriend broke up with me," he said and bit down hard on his lower lip.

"Oh no!"

Then, echoing Peni's words from weeks ago. "Yeah. I'm gay. I know. There. I said it."

"God, Sloan. I didn't even know you were seeing anyone. You didn't say anything."

Oh, but he had, hadn't he? He'd been telling Peni all about Max.

"I mean, when the hell did you have time? You've been spending all your time with that straight guy. How long were you seeing this guy?"

"Two months. More or less." The time that Lauren was away. And now she's back. He felt the frigging tears want to come and fought them. God. He hadn't cried in months, and then since the night that he finally let it all go—

(in Max's arms!)

—and cried for his mother, all he'd done since was cry.

"God, Sloan. I'm sorry. It sucks. I know. I still haven't gotten over Bobby, and that was only a week."

Bobby.

Wouldn't it be funny if…?

"This Bobby of yours. I've been meaning to ask. Is he a big guy? Tall? Built like a football player with big, wide shoulders and dark hair and a hairy chest and—"

"Yes!" Peni cried. "Do-do you know him?"

Sloan gave a halfhearted laugh. "Aren't we a pair, Peni? You dated a lying son of a bitch who thinks with his cock and gets more action than Rihanna. And me? I was going out with a guy who wouldn't have sex with me because he was married."

Peni's big eyes grew even bigger.

"Fuck it," Sloan said. "I have five minutes to get some shit coffee in the break room and then the calls start."

"Maybe this would be a good day for lunch?" Peni asked. "With the way the manager worships you because of your new script, I bet we can swing an hour."

"Sure," said Sloan. "Anyplace you want. Anyplace but Café Namasté."

THE WEEK flowed like molasses in December in Alaska for both Max and Sloan. Each longing for the other, and neither able to do a thing about it.

Max had thought Sloan might be willing to be friends. But that didn't seem to be the way it was going to be. It was killing Max.

He wanted Sloan so badly. He still hadn't made love with his wife. She all but repelled him, and that made him feel worse. She was the same person. She was his wife. He loved her. He had made love to her a thousand times. A thousand thousand. And now he didn't even want her to spoon with him at night?

He was shit, he kept telling himself. Shit.

Because when she did ask him to hold her? All he could think of was Sloan.

And how his own body and Lauren's just didn't fit.

And Sloan? He just couldn't do it. First, he and Max had been boyfriends in all but sex. They had been far more than friends. Far more than the "gay" friends Max had asked if they could be. Sloan had begun to think that they could be more. That Max might realize he couldn't be a happy gay man and be ashamed of being gay at the same time.

Max had explained what the problem was. He didn't want to stand out. He didn't want to be one of the only gay couples on a romantic cruise. He didn't want to be the talk of the faculty at work. He didn't want—in his words—to "have to fucking order His & His towels from a gay web site."

But Max couldn't have what he wanted. He couldn't have both.

And Sloan needed a man who needed and wanted him, and who *could* be proud.

So, no. There would be no running. No more meditation. Not together.

But what about the mantra? Max was going to teach you mantras!

He would have to learn them on his own. He could. He had been continuing to meditate without Max. He'd even gotten Wyatt to join him. The first time it had been insane, but as his friend practiced on his own and then joined him in the evenings before a two-man porch night, he agreed there was something to it all.

Yes. There was. The meditating was keeping Sloan going. To his surprise he found he could still drop into that still and quiet place. It *was* the only thing keeping him going. Keeping him from falling so deep into depression that he might not crawl back out.

Chapter FORTY-EIGHT

EARLY ONE afternoon, a little over a week after Lauren had come back from Paris, they were sitting on the back deck and she was pouring Max a glass of wine from one of the bottles she had brought back with her. "It's a Châteauneuf-du-Pape. I just know you're going to love it."

Max raised an eyebrow. The cheapest Châteauneuf-du-Pape he could ever remember them buying was fifty dollars a bottle.

Lauren sighed. "I know what you're thinking. *Très cher.* Expensive. But no! Don't you worry. Géraud knew a man who got me *un prix magnifique*! You'll be shocked when you find out the little I paid."

But Max had already found out he didn't care. It had been a week of finding out things. One of them was that her trip had not been cheap. Yes, a lot of it had fallen under company expenses. But not all of it. Oh no!

Lauren's garment bag, for instance, had contained several designer dresses she had insisted on modeling for him. He'd sat on the bed, and she had come from the hall as if she were walking down a runway. It was the first time she had assured him that the price was not as bad as he might think. Designer dresses they were, yes. But yes, *Géraud* had gotten her miraculous prices. He knew the designer, and while the "genius" was not yet the toast of Paris, she knew he soon would be. And she? She would already be wearing his work when that happened. Wasn't that exciting? Besides. How could one go to Paris and leave without something designer?

Considering Max wore T-shirts until they fell apart, socks until the heels were gone, he didn't know how to answer.

It was at the first sip—which was indeed amazing, with a rich aroma of herbs and earthy in flavor—that Lauren said, "There is something I want to talk to you about, *chéri*."

"What?" he asked and took a large swallow of the wine.

She gave him a peculiar look and went on, "It is about my trip."

"Of course," he said and smiled. Had she spoken of anything but her trip? What else would she want to talk about?

"As you know, I was quite *le succès*. Géraud hated to let me go—"

"Hello, Lauren! Welcome home!"

They turned as one to see Sloan standing on the top of his back steps. Immediately, Max's heart began racing at the sight of him. "Hey, Sloan." Max's sullen mood was gone in a flash. He smiled, once more breathless from merely looking at him.

So close Sloan was, across the fence and in the next yard over. So close, but he might as well be miles away. Max could never have Sloan. And he was beginning to see that having him next door might not be enough. Just to see him now and again? It wasn't going to do. Especially when Sloan made it clear that they couldn't even run together. And Max had loved their runs. Had he missed running with Lauren? He thought he had. But even those runs with his wife didn't compare with jogging beside Sloan—a man, their muscles so alike, flexing, eating up the miles. The smell as they began to sweat, clean and exciting and masculine.

No. Because Max was truly gay. There was no bisexuality about it.

Oh, if only Sloan had let them make love. Then he would have at least that much.

Or would that have made things worse?

And it would have been wrong. It would have.

"*Bonjour*," Lauren said. "I didn't know you were still living here. Max didn't mention it."

"Still here." Sloan smiled. "How was Paris? I've been hoping for the chance to ask you."

"It was wonderful. You should go some time."

He shrugged. "Doubt it will be anytime soon on my budget," he said.

Lauren nodded. "*Oui*. You mother said you were a telemarketer or *quelque chose*?"

Max eyed her. The look on her face…. It was most… *un*Laurenlike.

"No. I'm a customer service rep. The calls come in to me. I don't disturb anyone at home. Don't think I could do that."

"Is there much of a *différence*?" she asked, her voice lacking the musical note it had held only moments before.

"Lauren," Max said, surprised at her tone.

"Oh yes," Sloan was saying. "A telemarketer is trying to *sell* something. I'm *taking* calls. And it's usually to help people."

"*Je vois*. Either way, it is why I think I am surprised you are still here. I figured you would sell the house."

"Well, the house *is* paid for," Sloan replied. "And Mom left me a bit of money. Enough to cover property taxes for at least a few years. And I don't know. I felt funny about the idea of selling the house. Mostly it's the garden, you know? Mom cared for it most of my growing-up years. She won awards. What if a new owner just decided to plow it under and put in sod?"

"That would be their choice, *n'est-ce pas?*" she asked. Her tone was almost cold now.

"Lauren," Max hissed. What had gotten into her?

She ignored him. "Would not selling the house give you enough money to live on for some time? You could buy a condo. The house there, it's quite a big place for one man, is it not?"

Max gaped at her.

"Yeah, I guess so," Sloan continued. "But every time I think of selling it, I look at the next phase of flowers she has coming in, and I just can't do it. It's the iris right now. I didn't remember she had planted so many colors. Did you know there are brown iris? I didn't. Silver and orange and so many more. And the peonies. I'll have to bring you some. They're gorgeous!"

"*Oh, c'est… gentil.*"

"Thank God for your husband." Sloan nodded in Max's direction. "He's been helping me out. I don't exactly have a black thumb, but it's not green either. If Max hadn't been showing me what to do, who knows what shape it would be in."

"*Ah, bon,*" Lauren said and shot Max a strange look. "Max didn't mention that either."

With a bang, Logan came out of the house, and Lauren's attention was diverted. "Hello, darling. Home already?" Their son had gone jogging with Devin. He hadn't told her whom he was with, though, and Max had decided that was Logan's business.

"Yup." He turned and noticed Sloan. "Hey, Sloan!" He grinned heartily. "How's it going?"

"I'm okay," Sloan answered.

Was he? Max searched his face, hoping to see the opposite.

What's wrong with you? You want him to hurt? Are you a complete asshole?

"I was just welcoming your mother home. I bet you're happy she's back, huh?"

"Sure," Logan said.

"Well, I have errands to run," said Sloan. "See you all later. And it's nice to see you again, Lauren."

"I'm sure," Lauren responded.

Sloan disappeared back into his house.

It was as if the sun had gone behind a cloud. "Jesus, Lauren. How could you be so rude?"

Lauren gave him a withering look and took a drink of her wine. She closed her eyes and let out a long sigh. When she opened them again, she was smiling. "Logan, you simply must try this. You will adore it."

"That's okay, Mom." He held up a Dr Pepper. "I got this."

Lauren shuddered. "*Ciel*! I do not understand. I offer gold and he wants aluminum foil."

"Relax, Mom. I like what I like." Logan sat down next to them at the glass-topped table.

"In France, a boy your age would be drinking wine."

"But, Mom. We're not *in* France."

"Which is exactly what I wanted to talk about. It is *heureux* that you are here. I should tell you together. Better than me doing this twice."

Max froze. What? He narrowed his eyes. God, what was she going to say? He'd known her long enough to suspect he wasn't going to like it. She was in business mode. She had the face that she most likely wore in boardrooms and when in front of employees worried that they were about to lose their jobs.

"As you know, things went well for me in Paris. And Géraud Després, my boss. He has offered me a full-time job."

It felt like a slap. A complete shock. And wasn't that stupid? Hadn't he known this was coming? Hadn't he known even before she left? Of course he had. And he'd chosen to pretend otherwise.

"I want to take it. Not only that, but I want for you both to come with me."

Logan's mouth fell open. It was as if the strings on the mouth of a marionette had been cut. His eyes bugged like a ventriloquist's dummy.

Max closed his own mouth, imagined that he must look the same as his son.

"What?" Logan exclaimed.

"Isn't it *incroyable*? Can you imagine? A new life for us all in Paris?"

"No!" It was Logan who had cried out, but it was as if he had sucked the words from Max and voiced them instead.

Lauren's smile vanished. "What do you mean, Logan?"

"I mean no. *Non*. Is that better? I mean I don't want to go! *Je ne veux pas aller*!"

"Logan, it will be a good thing. It will expand your life. And you know French so well. The language will be *aucun problème* for you."

Logan jumped to his feet. "I don't give a shit about that!"

"Logan," she said. "Do not talk that way to your mother!"

Max knew he should have been the one to say it. The trouble was he couldn't talk. Paris? Good God. She was actually thinking she could just bulldoze this through? Hadn't he made it clear to her? He had *no* interest in living in France. He didn't like the country, cared less for its people. He had never been able to figure out her love affair with the place. No. He liked it here. He *loved* Terra's Gate. He loved his job. He loved teaching.

He loved Sloan.

How would he be able to see Sloan if he lived in Paris? Even from afar?

"I'm not going!" Logan shouted.

"Logan. You'll do what your father and I agree is best. And I truly think this is best." She turned to Max and smiled. "Why, just my raise alone would mean you won't have to work at all if you don't wish to."

"Well, what if I don't think it's best?" Logan cried.

"Logan…," Lauren said.

"No! Don't you tell me I have to move to fuckin' France."

That was enough to pull Max from his silence. "Logan. There's no call for that."

Logan spun on him, looked at him incredulously. "Did you know about this?"

Max shook his head. "No, I just found—"

"Because I *know* you don't want to go any more than I do. Maybe *less* than me!"

"Logan…," Lauren said.

"Have you already told Mr. Géraud what's-his-face that you'll take it?"

"No. *Bien sûr que non*," Lauren said, her voice stiff. "I was waiting to talk to your father about it."

Logan shot his gaze back to Max. "Tell her no, Dad. Because. I'm. Not. Going. I'm not going to frigging France, and I'm not leaving Devin."

Lauren's brows narrowed. "Speaking of Devin," she said, voice as sharp as a knife. "I was hoping you had cooled to that boy by now. I've been meaning to talk to your father about *him* as well. I don't think he's a good influence on you. I don't want you seeing that boy anymore."

"Seeing? *Seeing?*" Logan laughed. "Mom! That 'boy' is my *petit ami*. And I will 'see' him all I want."

It was Lauren's turn to look shocked. Then she laughed uncomfortably. "He is not your boyfriend. You mean *copain*, do you not? A male *friend*?"

"No, Mom. I don't mean *copain*. I mean *petit ami*." He spun on Max again. "Tell her, Dad."

Lauren looked at him. "You knew about this?"

Max nodded. "Yes, Lauren. I knew."

"And you chose not to tell me?"

"I was waiting until we were all together," Max said through clenched teeth, then forced himself to relax.

"Surely he cannot mean it how it sounds. He and that boy are not *amants*. Not lovers? They're too young."

"They're not having sex, Lauren. If that's what you're asking."

She laughed. It was a high, unpleasant sound. "And you believe him?"

"Yes, I do."

"You naïve, naïve man."

"Hello!" barked Logan. "I'm *here*! Stop talking like I'm not. No, Mom. I'm not having sex with Devin. Because we're too young. But we *are* boyfriends."

Lauren shook her head. "I do not believe it. My son! You can't be homosexual!"

"I am, Mom. I'm gay. So get over it!"

"Logan," Max said. "Sit down."

"I don't want to sit down!"

"Sit down anyway. And don't make me say 'because I told you so.'"

Logan sat. He was obviously not happy about it.

Lauren turned to Max. Her eyes were aflame. "*Toi*," she growled. "This is *your* fault."

Max swallowed hard. "My fault?"

She stood. "Yes. *Ta faute*. *You* made him this way!"

For one instant the old guilt came back. Hard. But no. He was done with that. Done with the guilt!

"Did you think I didn't know?" Lauren cried. "Did you think I was stupid? Did you think I couldn't see? I will tell you what I saw! I saw you looking at men for years! I see the way you were looking at that little *pédé* who lives next door. You were drooling."

Max had to clamp his jaws shut to keep his mouth from falling open again. What? What had she said. "I—I...."

"You *what*, Max?"

"I wasn't drooling" was all he could say. He couldn't believe how stupid it sounded.

"You *were*. Just as he was drooling for you on the day I left. I knew it. *Je le savais*! I've heard it in your voice in our calls. You were growing more distant each time. *Tu couches avec lui*, are you not?"

"Mom!" Logan said with a gasp.

"Lauren, I'm not sleeping with Sloan!"

She looked at her son and gave him a grimace. "And you. *You* knew, didn't you? That your father is *baise* with that boy!"

Max stood up. "Enough," he cried. "Sit down. Please, Lauren."

She narrowed her eyes at him. She looked as if she might bite. He had never seen her this way. "You know Géraud Després wants me, *non*?"

she snarled. "As his *amant*? But I did not let him take me to his bed. Maybe I should have? Tit for tat?"

"Lauren. I haven't slept with Sloan. Not once. We haven't done anything."

She snorted. "*Je ne te crois pas!*"

"Lauren." He went down on one knee before her. "Lauren. Look at me."

Slowly, she did. He saw a million cmotions in her eyes, and only some of them had anything to do with anger.

"I haven't slept with Sloan."

She said nothing for a moment. Then: "But you want to. *Tu le veux beaucoup.*"

Yes, he thought but did not voice the answer. *I do want to sleep with him. With all my heart. With every molecule of my being.*

And she knew. He could see that she knew.

She stood up and strode past them and went into the house. When he went inside, their bedroom door was closed. He didn't check to see if it was locked. It might as well be.

My God. How did this happen?

Chapter FORTY-NINE

IT WAS too much. He wasn't going to be able to do this. He wanted to scream!

When Sloan had looked out that door and saw Max with his wife—her blonde hair looking like spun gold in the afternoon sunlight and she herself looking stunning in an obviously expensive blouse and those slacks with creases so sharp he could see them from his back door—why, it had nearly killed him.

He'd tried to be polite, but she had been her usual cold self. He had never understood her attitude around him. He remembered that even at the funeral she had been standoffish and cordial at best.

What had he done to her?

"What's wrong?" Scott asked when Sloan came back in the house.

"Everything," he said and sat down on the chair beside his friends. They were all three there.

"Wow," Wyatt said. "Everything includes quite a lot. You're bothered by the fee for using the locks in Panama? Are you upset by the unfair treatment of workers in India? I hear they have it pretty shitty over there."

Sloan tried to laugh, but couldn't quite pull it off. "I was getting your Diet Coke," Sloan said, and realizing he still had it, handed the can to Wyatt.

"What? No glass?"

"Rough it," Asher told him. "What were you saying, Sloan?"

"I heard voices. So I looked out the back door and there was… Max. And he was with his wife."

"Were they making out or something?" Wyatt asked sympathetically.

"No! They were not making out. But they could if they wanted to. It's their world. And God. She's fucking gorgeous."

No one said a word.

"Mind if I peek?" Wyatt said. "I promise it will just be a peek. I'll sneak a look out the kitchen window."

"Wyatt!" Asher said.

"Be my guest," Sloan said.

It took Wyatt a minute to come back. When he did he had a glass with some ice. He plopped down between Asher and Scott. "Wow. She *is* gorgeous."

"Tell me," Sloan said.

"And I mean *really* gorgeous. Like *movie*-star gorgeous. Like she should be doing ads for toothpaste commercials. She could be walking the runways at—"

"Enough!" cried Sloan. "Jeez!"

"You okay, Sloan?" Asher asked.

"No," Sloan said and gave a long shuddering sigh. "I am not okay. I am the farthest thing from okay." He stifled a sob, got in control. Squashed it down. No tears. Not today. "You were right, Asher. I've done it. I've gone and fallen in love."

"Oh, I hate that," Wyatt said.

"Hate what?" Scott asked. "Falling in love with a straight man or having to admit Asher was right?"

"Both," Wyatt said.

"He's not straight," Sloan said. It was out before he could stop it. He could only hope his gossipy friends could keep a secret. Not that it was necessarily a secret if what Max had said was true. What his friends said last night was true. That everybody in town knew.

He looked up to see all his friends staring at him. "What?"

"He's not straight?" they chorused. They couldn't have done it better that if they'd practiced.

Ah, well. Too late now. "No. He's gay. And he's as much in love with me as I am with him."

Scott's face folded in and became stone. "I knew it. I knew this was more than another of your stupid crushes."

Asher's face grew almost as expressionless. Only Wyatt seemed happy.

"But that's good news, right?" Wyatt said. "He can D-I-V-O-R-C-E the wife, and haul you off to Iowa and marry you. Or better yet. California! New York! You can get married and then go see *Kinky Boots* on Broadway!"

Sloan shook his head. "I don't think so, Wyatt. I think Max is M-A-R-R-I-E-D. I don't think he has any plans on getting a divorce. And I don't plan on being the other woman."

"But there are advantages to that," Wyatt said. "You get your own space. You don't have to worry about him snoring. He won't make you watch sports. He'll be on his best behavior because he wants to get laid. Hell! He wants to get *laid*! So what does he look like naked?"

"Damn," said Scott. "Don't you ever shut up?"

Wyatt looked wounded. "I just wanted to know if he's got a big one. You want to know too. Don't pretend you don't."

"That was before—"

"Before what?" snapped Wyatt.

"Before nothing," Scott said, and closed up again.

"You going to be okay, Sloan?" Asher asked.

Sloan nodded. "Someday." *Hopefully, it won't take three years, like it did with you.*

"Does this mean you're not going to tell me if he has a big one?" Wyatt said? "It *looks* like he's got a big one. I mean the way he fills out his shor—"

"I haven't seen him naked," Sloan said, cutting Wyatt off.

"Oh," Wyatt replied. "Bummer."

Chapter FIFTY

SLOAN SENT his friends home. He was grateful that they were all willing to be there for him but at last had determined that alone was what he needed to be.

He was trying to make up his mind whether to make something to eat or to order Pizza Hut again when he heard the knock at the front door.

And when he opened it, the last person he expected to see was Max's wife.

"*Bonsoir, voisin*! Good evening." She smiled and it was like she had a mouthful of the most perfect teeth he had ever seen. Could they be real? They were perfect. Not one flaw. The white of Greek marble.

She was wearing what surely must be an expensive outfit, similar to the one he'd seen her in earlier that day. Slacks. A blouse that looked as if it were made from a cloud, white and sheer but not enough to reveal the bra she had to be wearing. Yet somehow he knew, simply *knew*, that she'd worn what she was wearing to look casual.

I bet it costs more than anything I own.

She was holding a bottle of wine. "Do you mind if I come in?"

"No. No, of course not." Sloan stepped back. "Please. Forgive my manners. I just wasn't expecting anyone."

She nodded and walked in, back straight, posture beyond perfection. "I brought you something." She turned and tilted her head. "For watching after my husband while I was gone. And to make up for my rudeness earlier today."

"You weren't rude," he lied politely.

"I think you will like this. I know I would like a glass. Do you mind?"

What the hell? What was this about? "I—" No. No stuttering. He smiled a smile that he hoped could compete in some small way with hers. "That would be great. Do you want to sit while I open it?"

"*Non.* I will follow."

Sloan let her into the kitchen and she put the bottle on the counter. He found the CO_2 cork remover and took two glasses down, and thank God, they didn't have so much as a spot. He peeled the covering off the cork, then poked the needlelike point down into it. The press of a button and there was a hissing noise and the cork was free.

"We have one just like that," Lauren said. "Don't you love it? It even helps the wine to breathe."

Sloan nodded. "Yes. Max got it for me."

She smiled again. "Yes. I imagine you've drunk lots of wine together, *non?*"

Now what the hell was that supposed to mean? He tried the smile again and poured. He'd barely filled the first one a third of the way when she made a little noise and a glance showed her holding out her hand flat, palms down in the universal symbol of "enough."

Jeez, he thought.

Sloan poured the second glass to the same level and then held it out to her.

She took it, brought it to her face, closed her eyes, breathed in deeply. "Oh, *oui. Magnifique.*"

She opened her eyes and held her glass out. "To being neighbors?" she asked.

"Sure," he said. "To being neighbors." He almost took a drink but held it to his nose first, tried to make her see that he knew what he was doing, even if he didn't. He didn't know why, but he was having a very sudden rush of nerves. What was she doing here? Did Max know?

The wine smelled heavenly. He couldn't help but notice and looked at her in awe.

Her smile was back. But why did she look like a shark now?

He raised his glass and they drank. He was careful to make it only a sip.

It was amazing. There had been only one time he'd tasted anything like it. That had been with Max, of course. One night not long ago. One of the times that he was sure Max was about to kiss him—but didn't.

"My God," he said. "It's… it's like magic," he said.

"It certainly is," she replied. "It is Mazoyères-Chambertin, a red from *la Bourgogne*. I dare not tell you the price."

Sloan gulped air.

"May we sit?"

"Of course," he answered, not sure at all.

She reached out and took the bottle, turned, and walked back in that way of hers. Like she was royalty. Who did she think she was? She lived in Terra's Gate, not the Riviera. She was his next-door neighbor. She lived on a street of very affordable, middle-income houses. Why would she be giving him wine that she "dared not tell" him the price of?

He followed her, and she was already sitting on the couch, directly in the middle. He could sit next to her or in the chair opposite. And even though he felt he might—for some reason he couldn't explain—be stepping directly into a spider's web, he did sit next to her.

Lauren crossed her legs and relaxed back into the couch, looked around the room, narrowed her eyes at the painting above the fireplace. It was a print his mother had loved of a huge arrangement of flowers and fruit.

"So you have been keeping my husband company while I was gone, *non*? Or I guess I should say, he has been keeping *you* company?"

God. Sloan's stomach began to do somersaults. His nerves were jangling. What was going on? Did she suspect? God! Had Max told her he was gay?

"We've become friends."

She gave a little laugh. It sounded like the tinkling of glass. "Friends."

Sloan nodded.

Lauren took another sip of wine, then placed it on the table and poured herself a more substantial serving. She didn't offer Sloan any. "*Vous ne voulez pas dire amants?*"

"Excuse me? I don't...."

"I think you understand," she said. Her tone was completely calm. She could have been talking about anything. The weather. A recipe. "I asked you if you meant lovers instead of merely friends."

Sloan's mouth fell open. He hated it immediately, wished it hadn't happened. But she'd taken him completely by surprise. *Lovers?*

"No," he said. "No."

She laughed. It was a friendly laugh. An oh-come-on-now, we're-both-adults-here laugh. "Oh, Sloan. There is no need to deny. I am not blind. I've always known about my husband. Even when we were in high school. We would go swimming, and I would see the way he watched the other boys. The desire in his eyes."

Sloan didn't know what to say. His shock was so utter and complete he couldn't form words. She knew? She had always known? Christ! Did Max know? Did he even know she was here?

"He was on the wrestling team," she continued. "I am sure you know that already—"

"No," Sloan managed. He didn't know that.

"*Non*? I am surprised." She shrugged. "Anyway, I always saw that after a meet, when he had been caught in that tangle of male bodies and arms and legs, pinning each other down, sometimes crushing faces into the most intimate of places…. On those nights he would make love to me with an *amour* that he did not meet on other nights. I knew. The wrestling. That was his *taquinage*. I was his completion."

Sloan could only sit there. He found he couldn't even raise his wine to his mouth.

Lauren sighed. "I knew and I did not care. I knew that he didn't want that way of life. He wanted what *I* could give him and they could not. Marriage. A child. A place in society. Respectability…. *Encore de vin*, Sloan?"

It took him a second to realize she had asked him a question. Offered him more wine. He nodded, and she filled his glass nearly to the top. He took a proper swallow this time. Fuck sips.

The look on her face seemed to imply she approved.

"And we married, and we had a beautiful son. A boy. Someone to pass on Max's name. Perfect. We decided not to have a second child. One was enough for me. I think if men had to give birth, we would have gone extinct as a species millennia ago, don't you?"

All Sloan could manage was a shrug.

"Trust me. When he takes your ass? It doesn't come close to the pain of giving birth."

Sloan gasped.

"And things were perfect, Sloan. Everything. I might have wished to live in New York instead of this tiny town, but...." She shrugged. "He graduated at the top of his class. He could have taught anywhere. And while Wagner University is highly respected, he could have had so much more. But ah, that is okay. It was okay. I had my job, and it was taking me places. Taking me where I dreamed. And that dream is coming true. I have been offered a career in Paris. I plan on going. I plan on taking my family with me."

"Oh." Sloan said. Paris. Max was going to Paris. He suddenly wanted to cry.

No. That's perfect. If Max was gone, he could breathe. He would have a chance of getting over Max.

"But there is a problem."

"Problem?" The word came out high and sharp, as if he had swallowed helium.

"Yes. Max thinks he is in love with you. I saw it in his eyes. The fucking I can forgive."

Sloan gasped again. When she used that word! She couldn't make it any more ugly. He could scarcely believe she even knew the word.

"Men fuck. It is part of their nature. It proves to them that they are men. Spreading their seed, you see? Instinct, I've read. From millions of years." She laughed. "It is their weakness."

She took another drink of wine.

"That he fucked you? I can live with that. At least you cannot bring us some bastard child and ask for money."

"I don't want your money!" Sloan cried.

"That ends of course, now that I am back. And he can hardly continue your affair once we go to France, although there are plenty of *pédés* there. What do you think? Boys there who would be more than happy to spread their legs for a man like Max. But again, the problem we have is that he thinks he loves you. And I suppose I knew that might happen one day. Another good reason to take our leave abroad."

Then the words came. Perhaps Sloan's denial that he wanted any money had broken the seal on his lips. "Lauren! No! We aren't...." He couldn't say 'fucking.' "Lauren. You've gotten the wrong idea. Max and I haven't had sex."

She closed her eyes and waved his words away. "Sloan, *s'il vous plaît*. We are adults. There is no reason for denial. Max has already admitted it. He has begged for my forgiveness and wants to go to Paris as much as I."

Admitted it? But why would he do such a thing. Sloan felt a flash of anger. Was Max actually making him the bad guy? "No!" he all but shouted. "No. We aren't having sex. I don't know why he would tell you that. Max and I have *not* had sex!"

"Please, Sloan. I have already told you. Max has admit—"

"I don't fucking care what he said. We haven't had sex! We wanted to. But we didn't! He's married. We knew that going into it."

"It?" she said. "It? Is that the word you use for having an affair with my husband?"

"No! We didn't have an affair. We *didn't.*"

But oh, they had, hadn't they? Hadn't they had an affair in all the ways that truly mattered? He was in love with Max. And Max was in love with him. Surely Lauren could see it in her husband's eyes. *Her* husband's eyes.

"We haven't slept together" was all he could say. "We didn't, Lauren. He was faithful to you." Even though he wasn't. He was gay. He might be able to be faithful in physical deed. But surely he would fall in love one day.

Even Lauren knew that.

She was looking at him now. It was like she was trying to look directly into his mind. He could almost feel it, like fingers rummaging around in his brain.

"Lauren. I don't know why Max told you that. I don't know. I don't." The tears were threatening and he fought them with all his might. "But Max and I. We. Did. Not. Have. Sex."

For the longest time she didn't say anything. She continued to look deeply into his face. The fingers in his brain stopped, though. Thank God.

Then she took a long, deep breath and her high-raised shoulders seemed to… collapse. Her expression changed. Pain replaced the surety that had been there before. And when she spoke again, it was without the commanding tone she had used before.

If anything, she sounded like a little girl.

"You are not lying, are you?"

Sloan shook his adamantly. "No. No, I'm not."

"You haven't slept with my Max?"

Your Max. And why not say that? He was hers.

But why did it feel like Max was his?

"No. I haven't."

She looked away, peered down at her glass, then put it on the table. "You want to."

He gulped. And decided not to lie. "Yes."

"You are in love with him."

Sloan sighed. "Yes."

"And he is in love with you." She was speaking in statements. They were not questions. But to this last, he did not reply.

She turned and looked at Sloan.

"So what do we do now?" This time it was a question.

Sloan had no idea how to answer her.

Chapter FIFTY-ONE

"Maximilian?"

Max had just begun his meditation—sitting on his pillow, legs crossed before him, hands in lap, forefingers and thumbs touching—when Lauren called down the stairs. He looked up, took a deep breath. *Om mani padme hum.*

"Yes, Lauren?"

"May I come down?"

"Of course," he said and was glad that he hadn't meditated naked, as he normally did. Not that she hadn't seen him naked a million times before. But there was something different about it when it was in his special place, and he was in his sacred time. That and the disastrous conversation from earlier today—

(the screaming match was what it had been. When his world had come to an end.)

—that had finally sent him to try and find peace in meditation in the first place.

She came down the stairs, her feet quieter than normal, and he was surprised when he saw she was barefoot. Lauren practically wore her shoes to bed. She was never one to kick them off after a long day at work.

She stood in the doorway, leaning against the threshold, and her expression startled him. Whatever he was expecting—anger, determination, damnation—it wasn't there. Instead it was…. What? Sadness?

He held out his hand. "What's wrong, Lauren? Come here."

She trembled, then came to him, even sat down on the floor.

"Let me get you a—"

"I've done something terrible, Max. And I don't know if you'll be able to forgive me." He saw that her eyes were filling with tears, and for some reason, it made him want to cry as well.

"Lauren? What is it?"

"I—I…." She looked away.

"What," he asked, concerned, their horrible scene from the afternoon forgotten. This was his wife, after all. He loved her. "Tell me."

"I—I…." She turned to him. "I went to see your *amant*."

Max stiffened for an instant, willed himself to relax. *My lover?*

"Lauren. He's not my—"

"*Ssshhh*," she said. "He is. In heart, if not deed."

"Lauren…."

"Max. I did something terrible. I did not believe you. And I went there and tried to trick him into admitting you two had made love."

Max eyes widened. *Oh shit. Lauren. How could you?*

But of course she could. Anyone might have done the same. She had come home to find out he was involved with someone, even though he had never been sexual with Sloan. His heart clenched in pain. *Oh, Lauren.*

She must have misinterpreted his expression because she dropped her face into an upturned palm. "I'm so ashamed. Maximilian."

"No. No, I understand…." He reached and took her hand in one of his, cupped her cheek in the other.

Her huge blue eyes opened to him, and a tear spilled out and fell to the carpet.

"I went over there, Max, and told him that you had already admitted to taking him to your bed. And you should have seen him! I was so sure that he would fold. That he would tell me that you two had cheated. And instead! Why, he was so upset, and I saw that I was wrong. You *hadn't* cheated on me."

Max looked away. Hadn't he?

"And now here I am. And I have miles and years of apologies."

He looked back. "You? Lauren. *I'm* the one! I should have told you a long time ago…."

"Ah, Max. It is as I said. *Je savais*. I *knew*. In high school. I *knew*."

What? "W-what?" he managed.

"You were the perfect gentleman. *Trop parfait, mon chéri*. You never tried anything. Not once. When all my friends were either complaining endlessly about their boyfriends always trying for sex? Or maybe worse? Telling me how great the sex was? You never made a single move. At first I wondered if there was something *wrong* with me, that you didn't want me. I thought I would die when you took my hand that day in school. I thought I would float away. Suddenly…. Oh, my dearest. Suddenly, every girl wanted to be me! And I…? Well, I was *amoureuse.*"

Max remembered that day well. The day he had surrendered to the inevitable direction that he thought his life had taken. "Oh, Lauren."

"*Non*! I knew what was happening. That father of yours. Your fear of what people would say. Your anger at your brother."

"Anger?" *Anger? At Dennis?*

"Yes, *bien sûr*. He revealed he was homosexual, and then you felt you couldn't. That's what happened, isn't it? You thought you had to pass on your name. You talked of it so many times. I could tell why you were angry, and I didn't say a word. I *knew*."

Max sat there stunned. He had no idea what to say. He couldn't keep saying her name, and he had no idea what else to say. Lauren had completely astounded him.

"I knew and I was in love, and I thought that if we had sex…."

And they had, hadn't they? A lot of sex. Any of his friends would have been envious. Cliff, his best friend, almost hated him.

("*It's not fair! You don't even talk about sex. I thought maybe you'd tell me one day you were going to be a fucking priest. And now you're doing it on the chimney tops!*")

"And it was good sex, was it not, *chéri*?"

"Of course it was," he lied. Because how could he tell her the truth? Especially when he had been lying to himself? Then and for all their married life. He said it was good, or at least as good as it gets, and how was he to know that holding a man—

(Sloan!)

—one evening on a porch in the dark would move him more profoundly than any intimacy he had ever experienced?

She smiled. It was a sad smile, and in her eyes he saw she knew even now.

"I am the *traîtresse* of this piece, *chéri*."

"No, Lauren. You're no villain."

She gave him a gentle laugh, sighed, looked away, turned back. She nodded. "Yes. I think I am. Because if I had really loved you, I would have made you face the truth. I would have made you see what you were and stood by you when the shit hit the fan."

Max's eyes went wide, and he burst into laughter. *When the shit hit the fan?* "Oh, Lauren!"

"Yes, Maximilian. That is what I should have done. You would have found a lover, like your brother did. And I would have found another man. Perhaps for me a better man? *Non.* Not better. More suitable. A man who wants life big! Who wants life abroad! A man who wants the things I want."

Max's heart hurt. "We would never have had Logan, then."

"Yes. True." A pained expression came over her face. "Oh, Logan. I feel so much shame there as well. When I began to suspect he too was gay…. Oh, the things I said! How I was afraid of his relationship with Devin!" She shook her head. "I see now he was just *making* me acknowledge what I had tried for so long to ignore. That you are gay. I got so mad! It felt so unfair. But now? Now I see the truth. He is our *grand succès*! He proves that we were not a waste."

"Lauren. We weren't a waste. Don't ever think that. We were not a waste."

"What then, *chéri?*"

"You must never, ever think we were a waste. Promise me that."

"I will promise to try, all right?"

Max's heart ached all the more. *Oh, Lauren, I do love you.*

"And I love you, *mon amour.*"

They looked at each other for the longest time and then Max leaned forward and pulled her into his arms.

"*Mon amour,*" he replied.

"No," she whispered. "I think perhaps that honor belongs to someone else."

Chapter FIFTY-TWO

SHE TRIED to send him away, tried to send him to Sloan, but there was no way he was leaving her. After a while he took her to bed instead. They held each other until she fell asleep.

When her soft snores came and she rolled over, he slipped out of bed and out of the house.

After the second knock, Sloan opened the door. "Oh God. Max. I've done something horrible."

Max shook his head. "No. I am the villain of this piece. If I had only been myself. Manned up to who I was…." He stepped forward, reached for Sloan's hand, brought it to his mouth, and kissed it. "There would have been so many less hurts."

"Max?"

"I am in love with you, Sloan. And if you can wait just a little longer, I think I can be yours."

"Oh God, Max. I will wait as long as you need me to."

Chapter FIFTY-THREE

THE FOLLOWING days were painful for everyone. Max was flooded with guilt as he and Lauren began to make plans for their new lives. This woman had been his wife for one-and-a-half decades. He loved her. He knew he always would.

And he had hurt her so.

They didn't make love once. He couldn't. And thankfully, she didn't seem to want him to either. That made him feel worse in some ways.

I wasted her life. Where could she have been if I had just been courageous enough to come out? Now here she is at thirty-five having to start all over.

And then she shocked him again.

Lauren had opened another bottle of her wine, and they were sitting on the couch watching *Forrest Gump* on DVD.

The movie where we held hands the first time, Max thought. "Are you sure?" he'd asked when she suggested it.

"Very sure, *mon chéri.*"

Then halfway through: "I think Logan should live with you."

Logan gasped. Max's eyes went wide. He paused the movie. "Lauren?"

She let out a long breath. Turned to her son. "I would like it if you would spend the summer with me. Or at least a part of it. I know you probably have all kinds of things you want to do with Devin, but I think it is a fair exchange."

"Mom?" He looked as stunned as Max felt.

Lauren turned to Max, then back to their son, and then looked back and forth between them as she continued. "I think you need each other. You can help each other figure out your new lives. What better place for a young man becoming a gay man to be than with his gay father? *Et toi,*

Max. This can only help you. I think he may be a better teacher for you than you can be for him right now."

"But Lauren." Max shook his head. He could hardly believe what was happening. "I don't understand. Why are—"

"And won't it be best for me? I will be needing to find a place. I won't be living in a hotel. Logan, you still have school left, and you will be graduating. How foolish to try and do that in another country."

"But I just assumed—" Max began.

"I thought for sure—" Logan added.

Lauren cut them off with a smile. "Ah, *mes hommes*. Lights of my life."

He wasn't her man. She wasn't the light of his life.

I wasted her life! I wasted mine.

And that hurt so deeply. The waste. He was a horrible man.

"It is time for me to do the right thing for all of us. I lost sight, *vous voyez*? I forgot that this was a family and not just me."

"No you didn't. You—"

"I did, Maximilian." She took a drink of her wine. "I did. *J'ai oublié.* And *now* I will think of this family. I will do what is right."

And later, upstairs—

(Max was sleeping in the guest bedroom and that made him feel guilty because she was still here and all he could think of was that he wanted Sloan in his bed with him)

—Lauren said, "Oh, Max, my *chéri*. Can you ever forgive me? I feel in my selfishness I have wasted so many years of your life."

She had stunned him again. "Lauren! I was thinking the same thing. I'm the one who wasted yours—"

She shushed him. "Don't be *bête*. You are not to blame."

"But I am!"

"Then we are *coupable* together. And now? Now we put things aright."

Max pulled her into his arms and held her tight. "Oh, Lauren."

"I feel more guilt even now," she whispered.

"Lauren…?"

"That I am excited to see where my life is going now. I am sad. I am. But there are *tant de possibilités*. It is like we are both poised on the edge of a great adventure."

So many possibilities, Max thought. So many indeed.

"Will you sleep with me tonight, Max? Not sex. Just let us hold each other?"

"Of course," he said.

That is just what he did. And when Sloan came to his mind, he simply smiled and thought about how excited he was. Sad. But so excited to think of where his life was going now.

So many possibilities.

The adventure was about to begin.

Chapter FIFTY-FOUR

TWO WEEKS later she was gone. Sloan had watched from an upstairs window as they loaded the Scion. He knew he was taking the chicken's way out, but it seemed somehow wrong to wish her well, to tell her good-bye. Too much like, "You lost. He's mine now." Wasn't she in enough pain?

He had instead let the sheers drop back into place before the window, taken a step back, and said, "Mom. Is this right? Have I made the biggest mistake of my life?"

He wasn't expecting an answer, of course. He hadn't seen his mother's "ghost" since the night he'd cried in Max's arms. Not even when he wanted to. He found he couldn't even imagine any more what she would say. He hardly heard the echoes of her weird and funny advice anymore, and that he really missed.

"I think it's wonderful, Son."

He whirled around, and she was standing there, smiling.

"It's the best thing for everyone. For Max. For his family. But for you most of all."

He knew she wasn't really there. It was in his head. He knew it.

He didn't care.

"You think so?" he asked.

"I'm sure of it," she answered. Because that is what she would say.

"And I finally have my grandchild! You'll tell him about me, won't you?"

"Of course," he said.

She looked wonderful. Her hair was full and thick and bright red. Her eyes were warm and the color of dark honey. Her smile was radiant. She was wearing one of her dresses, nothing fancy, but oh, so her. Knee-length, covered in a pattern of flowers—of course. And not surprisingly, a pair of sensible shoes.

"He's a handsome boy, that Logan."

Sloan nodded.

"I think it's a good thing that Lauren decided to let him stay instead of taking him to Paris with her. Being in another country would do him good, but right now, a young gay boy needs to be with his gay father. His father needs him too."

Wow. Would she say such a thing?

Of course she would. She was saying it wasn't she?

But she's not here.

Isn't she?

"I'm in your heart, my boy. My baby boy. I always will be."

"Do you like him, Mom? Max?"

"Oh, baby. I adore him. And just look at the garden! Thank God he's been helping you."

Sloan laughed. "Yeah. I don't know what I would have done without him."

"I don't know what *I* would have done without him, there, at the end of the season? Before you moved in? The weeding. The raking. The mulching. Getting everything ready for winter. It was a hard winter too. Without everything he did, who knows what all might have been lost? But everything is glorious. One of the best springs ever."

Sloan's heart stirred and filled with love and light. "Yes. A spring I will never forget. Ever."

"The evening primrose is stunning there on the hill, by the driveway? A carpet of pink. I love it so. Something to be appreciated where it is because it just doesn't work all that well in a vase, you know? Oh! And I was so happy you brought in the forsythia. Same vase I always use. The long branches of golden yellow flowers! It's like sunshine right there in the middle of the dining room."

Sloan nodded. "Yes, it is."

She sighed. "Ah, well. Time to go. You need to be ready for when Max gets back."

"No!" he said, and felt his heart near break. "Don't go!"

"Ah, but dear. You said it. I'm not really here?"

And she was gone.

"No!" he cried.

Sssshhhhh…. I'm in your heart. And I always will be.

Chapter FIFTY-FIVE

MAX HAD never been so afraid in his life as when they stepped into Sloan's bedroom.

Sloan had the lights off except for a small bedside-table lamp, and he had placed a scarf over that so the bed was bathed in a gentle pool of warm orange light. "Is that okay?" Sloan asked. "I want to see you."

Max nodded. He wanted to say "I want to see you too," but couldn't. He hoped Sloan could see just how okay it was from his eyes. Then he smiled when he recognized the music that was playing. One of his favorites and something he'd given Sloan. The soundtrack to the movie *Little Buddha*. He was thrilled when Sloan had liked the movie.

Sloan took a step and now they were touching, but only the slightest bit, torso to torso. Sloan looked up at him with those amazing eyes, but of course he couldn't make out their warm-honey color in the light from the lamp. Somehow, though, they seemed even warmer.

Then why am I so fucking scared?

"Max?"

"Yes?" he somehow managed in a voice barely above a whisper.

"Do you want to wait?"

"God, no," he said in a tone that was more sob than anything else. "N-no. I've waited too long."

"Do you know that I—"

"I love you so much, Sloan. I've never felt like this. My—my heart. It's pounding!"

Sloan laid a hand on his chest, looked up at him with raised brows. Then—oh God—laid his head on his chest.

"Oh!" Sloan said. "I can hear it…."

He looked up then, and Max dipped his head and kissed him.

Sloan gave a small cry and kissed him back.

It was the kiss Max had waited for all his life.

The floor was gone, but he didn't fall. He was floating. He wanted to cry. He wanted to laugh.

Oh! oh oh oh oh! This is what it's supposed to feel like!

It was waves rolling on a beach. A waterfall crashing from a thousand feet high. It was drifting on clouds. Flowers bursting into bloom.

Their mouths opened to each other, and he felt the tiny touch of Sloan's tongue, and he opened his mouth all the more, touched Sloan's with his own, giving permission for entrance. Sloan moaned again.

Or was it him?

Their tongues did a dance, and again he thought, *Oh! This is how it's supposed to feel!*

He felt like a child.

He felt like a *man*.

And why, oh why, did he feel like crying?

Sloan's arms came up and around him, and Max's heart rushed, and he took Sloan into his own arms. Pulled him tight. Crushed his groin against his lover's—

(and weren't they lovers already? Of course they were!)

—and felt that Sloan was hard already, just as he was.

He shifted his hips so that his erection rubbed against Sloan's, and somehow, he didn't ejaculate in his pants. It was close.

Max had worn a nice shirt that day. And jeans. Real shoes. Not his usual shorts and T-shirt. He'd done it for Lauren. He'd wanted to look good for her.

He did it for Sloan.

He wanted to look good for Sloan.

God! Why do I want to cry? I'm so happy!

Sloan was unbuttoning his shirt.

Oh Jesus. What if he doesn't like the hair?

"Oh God," Sloan said. "Oh, Max. So… I mean. Oh, Max!" Sloan ran his fingers through the hair. "So soft and thick. So *man*!"

He liked it?

"Oh, Max. Your chest. So hairy…."

Too hairy? "You don't like—"

Sloan's eyes went wide. "Oh no! I love it! So sexy. It reminds me of Mr. Kelso."

Max's brow shot up. "Mr. Kelso? Who is that?"

Sloan covered his face. Gave a chuckle. "He was a teacher I had a crush on in grade school."

"And I remind you of him?"

"He was so manly, and he had a hairy chest just like you," Sloan explained.

"Wow. You were *always* gay, weren't you?"

Sloan bit his lip. "Yes. Born that way."

Wow. Wow, wow, wow.

"Please don't be disappointed in my…." Sloan ducked his head.

"What?" He pulled Sloan closer. "How could I be disappointed in you? What are you talking about?"

"Max. I don't have a single hair—"

Max laughed. He couldn't help it. He couldn't imagine being disappointed in anything about Sloan. "Oh…. Oh, Sloan." He opened Sloan's shirt, and button by button, Sloan's chest was revealed to him. "Oh," he said. Not one hair. Not one. "Oh, Sloan! So beautiful." He wanted to laugh. And he buried his face in that chest. Kissed. Licked. Found a sweet nipple and sucked it into his mouth. Sucked hard.

God! Too hard?

"Oh, Max! Yes!"

Max grinned even while he sucked all the harder. *Not too hard! Not too hard at all!*

And then they were kissing again, and the clothing somehow went away, and they were in bed and pants were gone and underwear was gone and oh, oh, oh! There was Sloan's cock. And it was the most beautiful thing Max had ever seen. So white and surrounded by a froth of bright new-penny-red curls. The head a beautiful pink purple, and he grasped it in his hand and it was *so* hard and his bush so soft…. And Sloan's balls. They hung in a smooth sack, and oh, not—one—single—hair on them, and he found he wanted them first. He bent and gently took them in his mouth, first one and then the other, and they felt so amazing in his mouth. The skin, like satin.

There was also the scent of Sloan.

Man.

Sweet and musky and clean and not too soapy and not too strong.

Perfect.

Oh, how they felt in his mouth! There was nothing like it. Nothing. There really was nothing at all like this. He couldn't describe it if he wanted to.

Max could feel the hardness of Sloan even at the base, the deep and very base. It pressed against his forehead and he looked up and saw a glistening, sparkling pearl form at its tip. He let Sloan slip from his mouth and moved up so that that luminous drop was close to his face, and when he breathed he found the scent was amazing.

He took Sloan's cock into his mouth.

"Max!"

It fit. Sloan's cock fit perfectly.

Max had never felt more alive.

The cock in his mouth—so living and warm and smooth and so…

Alive.

Cum for me, lover. I want to drink you.

"No!" Sloan shouted, and pushed Max away. "Not yet! I want you."

Then Sloan shifted them about so they were face to cock, cock to face and he was inside of Sloan's mouth and—

The world went away.

How could anything feel like this?

He was sure he could cum instantly and then—

Max did.

To his joy and shock—

(*too soon! oh no!*)

—he was exploding into Sloan's mouth, and the world went away.

He didn't think anything could be like this.

Did he pass out? Because now they were face to face, and Sloan was laughing gently and kissing him, and then he was kissing back, and he felt that stubble, oh so slight, the one he'd imagined, the one that told him he was definitely kissing a man.

He sucked Sloan after that. He sucked him until Sloan spilled into his mouth, and he drank the offering down like Châteauneuf-du-Pape or Mazoyères-Chambertin, and it was so sweet. Had he ever worried that he wouldn't like it? He needn't have. He would drink from Sloan forever.

Later, he supposed, when he thought back, they must have slept.

But he awoke with Sloan straddling him and slicking him up and then he was inside his lover and he was in love.

Chapter FIFTY-SIX

THEY AWOKE to a beautiful late spring morning.

They made love again.

This time Max insisted that Sloan take him. He had to know. He had to know if he could give himself to his lover as his lover had given himself to Max.

He could.

Chapter FIFTY-SEVEN

THEY DIDN'T rush to go anywhere.

Logan was with Devin, and Sloan secretly hoped they'd made love.

Then he remembered there was something he wanted to tell Max.

"Max?"

"Yes," his lover said.

Sloan smiled. He was so happy. He didn't know such happiness was possible.

"Something I wanted to tell you."

"Oh? All I need you to tell me is that you're in love with me."

Sloan laughed. "Oh yes. Tell me you're in love with me."

"I am in love with you, Sloan McKenna."

Sloan laughed again in complete joy.

"No! I want to tell you this." Max was kissing his chest. Licking his nipples, now burying his face in Sloan's armpit, nibbling, sucking…. "Stop!" he cried, giggling.

Max pulled back, his eyes full of lust. "But you smell so good! Have I told you how sexy you smell?"

Sloan snickered. He couldn't help it. "I like the way you smell too, Max."

"I want some more," Max growled and was back into his armpit.

Sloan pushed Max back. "Let me tell you!"

Max fell back onto the mattress. "What?"

Sloan smiled. "I was doing some research."

Max sighed. "On what?"

"The Dalai Lama."

Max looked at him. "Yes?"

"He's changed his mind."

"About what?" Max asked.

"Homosexuality."

Max shifted. A new interest was in his eyes. "What?"

"He admitted he was acting out of old-school thinking. And that maybe he was wrong. He said he thinks nuns and monks should be celibate. That taking vows of chastity was a part of their life. But now that he is more educated, he said that mutually agreeable homosexual relations can be of mutual benefit."

"Mutual benefit, huh? His Holiness said that?"

Sloan nodded. "And enjoyable and harmless." He didn't say that was for non-Buddhists. And was Max actually a Buddhist?

"Well, it's certainly enjoyable," Max said and threw back his head and laughed. Then he looked at Sloan. "I don't care what his Holiness says," Max replied. "Because the Buddha said it all. He said to find out yourself. Find out what is wrong and right for your own self."

"He did?"

"He did," Max replied. "And I know that this is right. And that's all I need to know."

And that was all Sloan needed to know as well.

B.G. THOMAS lives in Kansas City with his husband of more than a decade and their fabulous little dog. He is lucky enough to have a lovely daughter as well as many extraordinary friends. He has a great passion for life.

B.G. loves romance, comedies, fantasy, science fiction and even horror—as far as he is concerned, as long as the stories are character driven and entertaining, it doesn't matter the genre. He has gone to literature conventions his entire adult life where he's been lucky enough to meet many of his favorite writers. He has made up stories since he was child; it is where he finds his joy.

In the nineties, he wrote for gay magazines but stopped because the editors wanted all sex without plot. "The sex is never as important as the characters," he says. "Who cares what they are doing if we don't care about them?" Excited about the growing male/male romance market, he began writing again. Gay men are what he knows best, after all—since he grew out of being a "practicing" homosexual long ago. He submitted a story and was thrilled when it was accepted in four days.

"Leap, and the net will appear" is his personal philosophy and his message to all. "It is never too late," he states. "Pursue your dreams. They will come true!"

Visit his website and blog at http://bthomaswriter.wordpress.com/ or contact him directly at bgthomaswriter@aol.com.

Also from B.G. THOMAS

http://www.dreamspinnerpress.com

Also from B.G. THOMAS

http://www.dreamspinnerpress.com

Also from B.G. Thomas

http://www.dreamspinnerpress.com

Also from DREAMSPINNER PRESS

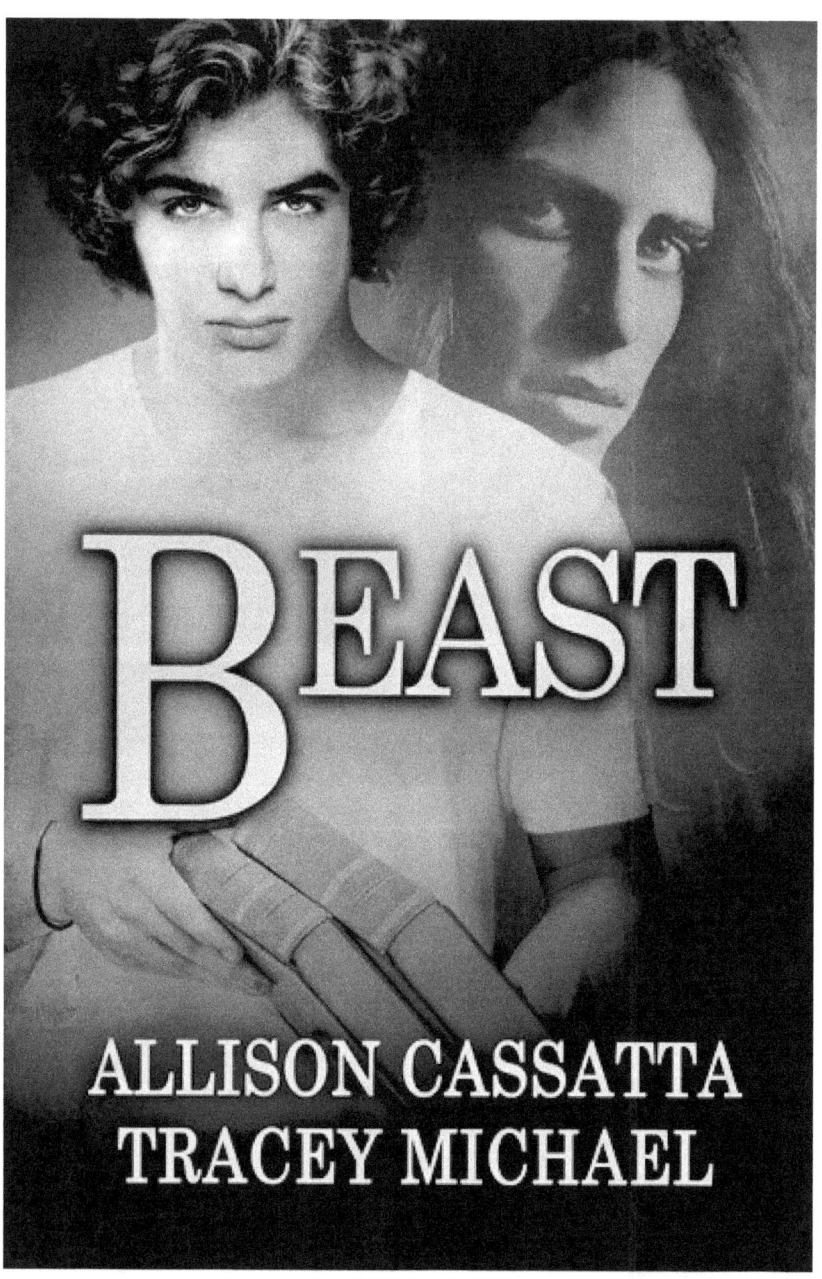

ALLISON CASSATTA
TRACEY MICHAEL

http://www.dreamspinnerpress.com

FINAL
ADMISSION
SUE BROWN

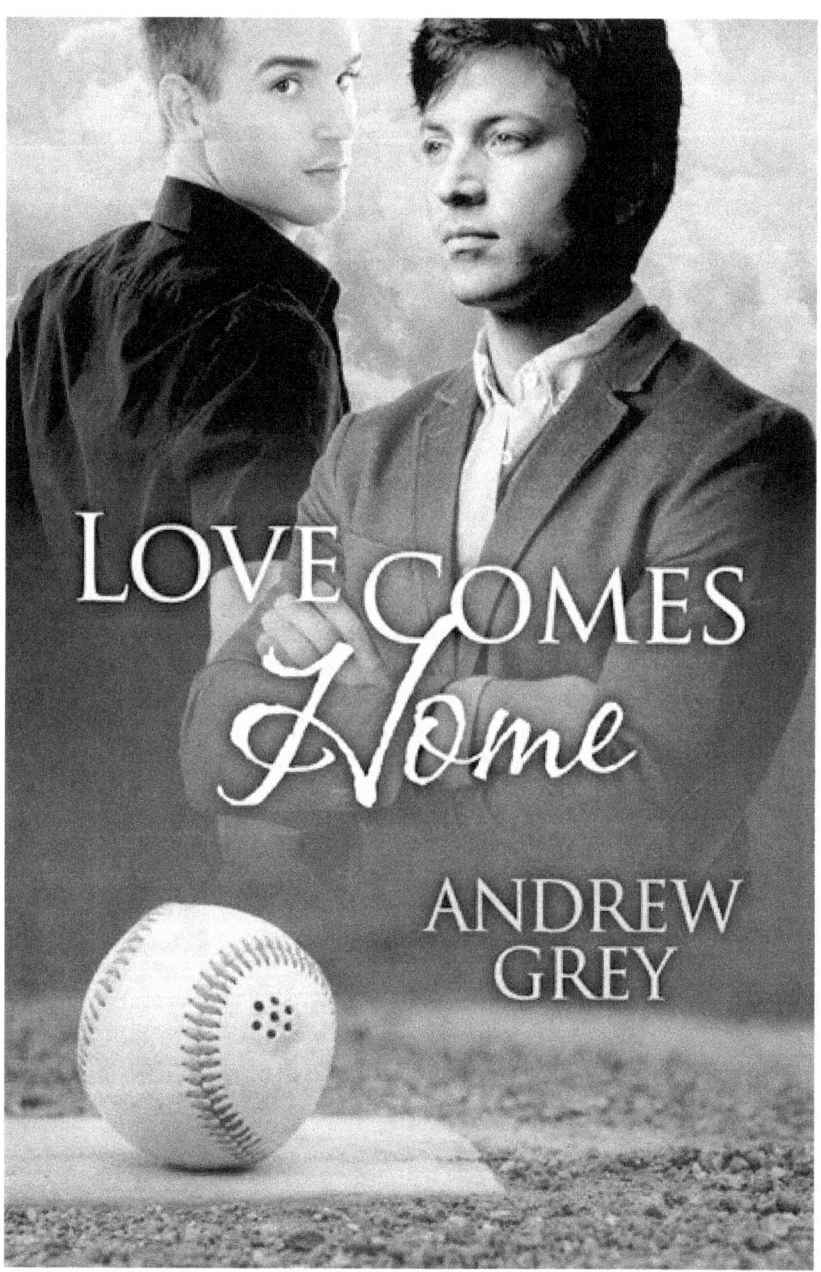

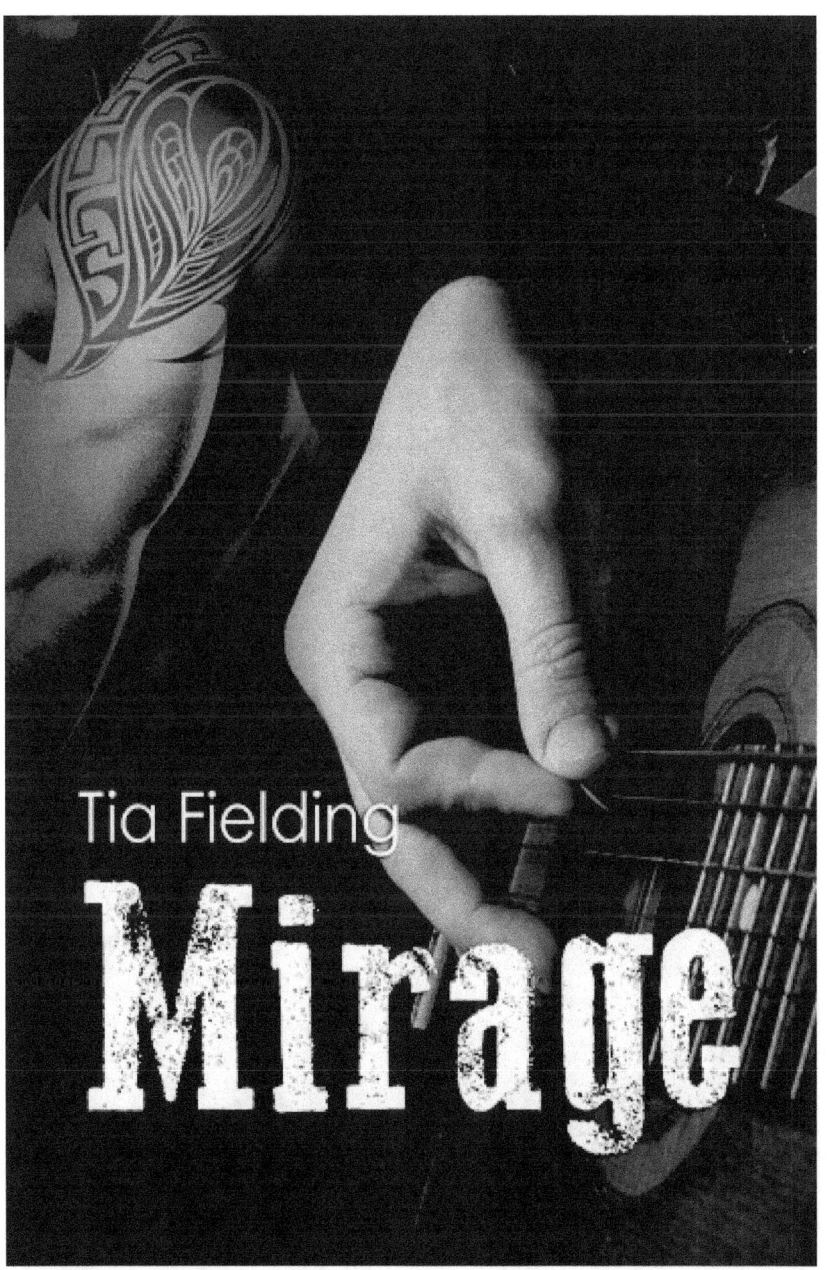

Tia Fielding

Mirage

NOT JUST FRIENDS

JAY NORTHCOTE

For more of the
best M/M romance,
visit

Dreamspinner Press

www.dreamspinnerpress.com